To Diane
I hope you love
my book. Thanks for the
Support. Renee Rose 7/13

Egyptian Labels

RAVEN ROSE

Library of Congress Control Number: 2013900403
ISBN: Hardcover   978-1-4797-7618-4
               Softcover   978-1-4797-7617-7
               Ebook   978-1-4797-7619-1

Lips and Rose image Copyright © 2012 Bg Knight.
Used under license from Shutterstock.com.

Brooklyn Bridge photo Copyright © 2012 Joshua Hiviv.
Used under license from Shutterstock.com.

This book was printed in the United States of America.

Rev. date: 2/19/2013

To order additional copies of this book, contact:
Xlibris Corporation
1-888-795-4274
www.Xlibris.com
Orders@Xlibris.com
125360

In loving memory of my grandmothers
Dionisia and Maude
For my husband Schmitty, being so
willing to read it over and over and over again
Also my brat pack
Enrique, Lucy, Lala, Lorenzo and my grand daughter Njivaharisoa
for being the unique souls they are.

Table of Contents

Chapter 1

Not to be mistaken for being whorish, let's say a tad exploratory, nevertheless, Egypt was talented and quite confused about her next move. Everyone was beginning to sense her indecisiveness. While watching television and glancing through her book, she gazed at her sleeping mate, Baron, and she sensed there was something missing in her life. She reached over and placed a kiss upon his brow, and he awakened with a smirk on his face. He reached over and began to caress her. His manly ways always could overwhelm her. She was fighting the temptation. She felt herself weaken.

As Baron laid his moist, yet gentle tongue around her inner thigh, he grasped her buttocks firmly in the palms of his hands. He began to wander around her navel. And as he laid his head on her stomach, there began a yearning inside of her. Baron too sensed there was no need for him to continue. There was a satisfaction in their bodies just lying on top of one another.

He gazed into her eyes for a long while, and then his lips became familiar with hers. He began to nibble at her neck and then slowly worked his way to her inner thighs. As he became more intimate with her areas, Egypt continued to squirm, making a fruitless attempt to regain herself and deny her emotions. He knew she was fighting a no-win situation, but she couldn't control her desires. It was important to her to express her troubles to him.

She then grasped his head and slowly directed it to her face and softly whispered, "Now, Baron, tell me, Baron, please I need to know, why do you still desire me?"

Women have a tendency to ask the most important questions at the most intimate moments and expect an answer. Well, knowing Baron, of course, he would have the answer without hesitation.

"Egypt, you know more than anything that it's your vibrancy and intellect. You're classy and sexy, and most of all *you're mine!*" replied Baron with a seductive smile on his face.

Egypt went to speak, but Baron held her by her hair and began to kiss her passionately. She went to push him away, but he grabbed her hand and held it back next to her shoulder. He held Egypt tightly to him. Baron bit her lovingly on the side of her neck and kissed her shoulder.

She reached over and then began to get aggressive. Thus licking him slowly from his lips to his legs. Egypt didn't miss an area. Baron gasped for air, and then she sat on Baron's chest, looked him straight into the eyes and said, "Since I'm yours, I'm going to take you and make you mine!" Then Baron's face was surprised; this was a side of Egypt that he had never seen in their year or so of involvement. It was exciting; he was overwhelmed, and he no longer could handle the sensational emotions. Baron gave in to Egypt. She then smiled and kissed Baron on the forehead and with a grin on her face, said, "Surprise!"

As day breaks, it finds Egypt pondering through her discovery. It hit her like a ton of bricks. Egypt no longer could handle the absence. The something missing was not only attention but the spontaneity, the magic, and the curiosity. They seemed to have just vanished. No longer is Baron the game to hunt, he's the gotten—now comfortable with being caught and so sure that she would always be there.

Deep inside she thought, *Soon absent I will be.* Suddenly she blurts out loud, "Don't ever get too comfortable with me, like I can't walk away or be caught again. I'll be the dust in the wind or that shooting star passing by your eye."

Baron was in the bathroom and wasn't quite sure of what was going on. He was too much in a hurry to even ask what it was she said. He had a business meeting with one of the most prestigious producers on either coast.

Gabriel Stout was a man that had no time to waste. His wealth was all self-made and mostly from swindling the little guy. Baron was quite his equal; he too had much backing behind him. His father was well-known throughout the underworld. His father at present wishes that Baron would pick up in the family business which they built from little to nothing to owning more real estate and people than any other organization or, for that matter, organized family. This was never Baron's interest, he was always aware of the family doings; it just never caught his attention.

Mr. Stout would not be impressed at all, so Baron knew he would be all on his own, never knowing that Stout had already been intercepted by his father.

Baron was very nervous and excited; he had never even heard what Egypt said. With all of this on his mind, he told Egypt to make sure that she was on time. This was too important of a meeting for her to be late. Baron looked at her and grinned and reminded her that she was his public relations and was in charge of all the arrangements for this evening.

"Oh, just a reminder, butter, let's not forget the seating arrangements we decided on last week," said Baron. Butter was the pet name he had given her. "Remember I don't want certain people next to each other. Don't forget to call, butter, and I didn't hear what you were saying, but I can figure out what it was about. Last night, right? It was one of our better encounters. You're an outstanding gem that glitters through the evening sky. Speaking of sky, butter, don't forget the patio and the pool cleaners. Love ya!" Baron said while running toward the door. He didn't realize she was standing by the door holding his attaché case. He grabbed it and kissed her and ran into his black Pantera, leaving Egypt in a whirlwind. She threw the paper she was holding in her other hand at him while he drove off.

She yelled, "I'm not some household convenience with an on and off switch. As far as last night savor the moment!"

With all of that she returned into the house and began to readjust herself before the tears fell. She ran and sat on the couch and started to throw the pillows at the door. Egypt tried to get herself together, and when she looked up, there stood Athelia.

Athelia asked, "Is everything all right, Ms. Egypt?"

Egypt told her, "There is a lot wrong and only one way to fix it." She knew things definitely needed to be rearranged, and she was the one to do it. She got up and picked up her mess and walked around the house as though she was lost for a while wondering if she could handle the discomfort and confusion that lies with this relationship. What has become of her place? Outside she is the important business partner, but in the home, she felt as though her importance relied on her performance in bed. Egypt knew that Baron loved her deeply, but there are moments like these which leave a question: What does he love the most?

She is very aware that she loves Baron Gianelli. He has every intention of marrying her. Baron had made several dates for their wedding, but Egypt was always saying she needed time. Now she has finally come to terms with why she so desperately needed more time to think. She doesn't want to be taken for granted.

At this point Baron was so wrapped up into Egyptian Labels that he had forgotten that there was even an Egypt. That's how she also felt. There were so many different thoughts running through her mind she just couldn't think without crying again.

Egypt looked into the mirror and asked herself what she should do. She gazed into her mirror and reached out and touched the image, and she shook her head. She didn't know exactly what to do about this. She knew that something most definitely had to be done.

She felt half-and-half, like she was in control of herself but lost control of the relationship. Not that she ever wanted to rule Baron. Just that at one time the direction of their lives was running together, now it's as though they only meet in the office or in the bedroom. This was an awkward feeling for her.

There was so much going on and still so much left for her to do before this evening. For this celebration there were extra people to help with the duties. Athelia was heading up the stairs when Egypt asked her to gather her things and pack them. Egypt went and made several phone calls to various people. She dreaded to make that one last call to nothing more than a two-legged pinstripe suited dog. He always would make it obvious his desires for her. There were many times he made verbal advances when Baron wasn't around. That was his son; even more so she couldn't understand Baron's mother Margaret, knowing the kind of man he was. And seeing what he would do in his marriage bewildered Egypt. She was glad that her Baron was so much the opposite of that cad.

There was something a bit mysterious about Nunzio. Something like a piece of him was missing. Nunzio had this air about him. People seemed to act strange around him, as if he were a king. She knew that he had money, but it was more than that. It was like life, like he had control of it.

She thought back to a time they all went to a restaurant. The kind where no one gets in without a reservation. He walked in and people began fussing over him, and they were seated at the best table and everything came to the table swiftly. She began telling herself he wasn't in real estate alone; it had to be a lot more than that.

Egypt went to her room and saw that Athelia had packed her and Baron's clothing and began to have a fit. She told her, "I didn't say anything in reference to Mr. Gianelli at all." Athelia realized that once again she was doing her usual, leaving Mr. Gianelli but never going anywhere. Egypt was always packing and unpacking. Athelia put a smirk on her face. Egypt noticed and asked, "What was that for?" But she was too busy to be bothered.

Egypt sat at the end of her bed and looked at the picture of her and Baron. Wondering if it was fear or respect or did he even notice that his father was making advances. It wasn't her imagination because a friend of hers mentioned it a while ago.

Egypt blurted out, "I'd rather burn in the realms of hell before I would consider sleeping with his father!" She then told Athelia, "Put this in my bag also. Oh yes, and don't forget to pack my pictures and anything that has mine and Baron's face on it. No, no, on second thought, just pack that one, leave the rest out on the bed. I have an idea. I don't want anyone else helping you do this. Get my shoes, make-up, and hair accessories and pack it also."

Athelia had never seen Egypt act this way. She seemed for real about leaving. She asked Egypt, "Ms. Acardi, do you think two suitcases will be enough? There is a trunk that belongs to Mr. Gianelli, should I go and get that?"

"No, I don't think so. Well, I'll have to get Dale to bring up a few boxes by way of the back door. Do not, I repeat. Do not let him know what you are doing," she stated emphatically. "I'll be back with an address where I will want all of these things sent to. Never in my life have I ever been so set about you keeping your mouth shut," said Egypt.

"I don't quite understand what it is that you're doing."

"Well, Athelia, it's not for you to understand, not even for me. It's something that it's time for me to do. Not to question just to do. Then deal with whatever happens from that point on," replied Egypt.

Egypt picked up the telephone to make that last call. A sigh of relief came over her. When she was told that Mr. and Mrs. Nunzio Gianelli had not returned from Italy, she was hoping that Nunzio would stay so he wouldn't be able to attend this evening's event. This celebration would mean so much to Baron. This is their dent into the production world. Once the papers were signed, everything they strived for revolved around these papers. She not only helped Baron, but most of all, she created the entire idea. Baron never denied any of the credit to Egypt. It was his shrewd business mind and determination which carried it to its success. After this was done, she knew much lay ahead for Egyptian Labels Inc. and them careerwise.

Egypt wished she could have done this on her own, but she knew that no one would listen to her. Mostly because she was both female and Puerto Rican. All ears had turned deaf to her. Yet once repeated by a man it was accepted, not easily, but it was. She knew it wasn't important to meet all of those people in reference to the company. Including seeing Mr. Stout and looking feminine and businesslike and yet have a touch of sexiness in her. Just to prove you can be very sexy and even more intelligent and have a business mind. Something that men just haven't acquired as of yet.

Well, it was getting closer to that time, and she was getting a bit hyper. Everything had to be just right. She didn't have to worry too much about the house and garden, just about getting to the meeting in one piece and not walk into the conference room and trip and fall flat on her face.

As she sat in between boxes and suitcases, she just smiled and gathered the papers she needed for the meeting. Egypt looked into her mirror wondering if this was the same girl that she was a year ago. As she reached the building, she recognized that this was the first place Baron had ever taken her. Riding up in the elevator, she noticed that she couldn't help but hurt inside and wasn't quite sure for what reason. She knew she was happy for what she and Baron built together, but by the same token, she was undoubtedly shaken up inside.

As she stepped into the office, the secretary took her trench coat and escorted her to the room where everyone was waiting. She stood outside looking through the glass walls with butterflies in her stomach. As she glared over the table, there he was, debonair as always. Her heart began to pound as he walked out of the room towards her and placed a kiss on her cheek. She gazed into his eyes and told him in a soft whisper, "This is not the place or the time for that, Baron."

Baron looked deep into her eyes and replied, "Just looking at you made me remember last night," and held her tightly.

"Baron, you make me feel that's all you see when you look at me, sex. Forget it, let me get into the conference room. Or is there someone else you're waiting on?" asked Egypt.

"No. We just finished discussing some other things and decided to stop a moment for coffee. I stepped out to see you before you walked into the meeting. Are you ready?" asked Baron.

"Well, considering I won't be on my back, I hope I don't fall backward. In that case if I do, I guess I wouldn't be nervous at all. I seem to have that down pat, right, darling?" said Egypt as she walked into the room.

Mr. Stout stood up, and everyone followed suit. He spoke of the merger of this new company with his major production company. He explained that by making Egyptian Labels a subsidiary of his major corporation, it will benefit and prosper; and it wouldn't lose its identity or its chain of thought.

The idea behind the company was a good one and helpful in finding up-and-coming stars, from there, the main branch, Micdele will buy out the remainder of their contract. The agreement is to make Egyptian Labels look like it has top of the line connections, when in fact the two companies are affiliated.

Mr. Stout looked over at Baron and announced, "Since there is no one I would trust more than Mr. Gianelli to head the company and Micdele has a prestigious name on its own, I prefer that Egyptian Labels carry its own weight and keep its original name. For the moment I think it would be in the best interest of the company if Egyptian Labels just handled music for now and begin in the fall on videos."

Everyone applauded him. Mr. Stout gathered everyone's attention and directed his next comment to Egypt.

"Never, my dear, have I ever met a woman with so much insight into the desires of others than you. You are aware of the needs of people which is a gift, and I am so glad to have the opportunity to ask you to also take part in the growth of what I am aware now, which was your idea. Baron had mentioned many times you were the one with the concept and perception. With that I hope you will take into consideration to work for us as vice president of productions. I know it has come as a shock for you, Ms. Acardi. I would be a lucky man to have you on my staff."

Baron was so surprised. Egypt had not yet closed her mouth as she was looking at Mr. Stout as though as he had gone stark raving mad. Everyone at the meeting awaited Egypt's decision like if they knew what was going on in her mind. With a smile on her face, Egypt opened her mouth, and they all began to congratulate her.

Egypt looked him in the eyes and said, "No." All at once everyone stopped talking and just glared at her. A few voices spoke out, "Is she crazy or what?" She then sat back into a seat. Baron stood up and went over to her and grabbed her by her arm and started heading her to the door. She pulled Baron's arm off of her and looked at him as if he lost his scruples.

"Don't even look at me that way. What the hell has gotten into you? No! No, you definitely didn't hear what he said, did you? Why, what's wrong? Isn't this what you worked so hard for? Everything you ever wanted was to create a company and watch it prosper," said Baron in a whisper. He didn't want everyone in the room to hear what they were discussing.

Egypt couldn't quite gather her thoughts fast enough before Mr. Stout asked her what was wrong with the offer. He wanted to know if there was something more she had wanted that might have been overlooked. Egypt stressed, "It's nothing of that sort." She was making plans that would keep her from giving this as much attention as it would truly require.

Baron looked over at her as happy as any one person could be. He, and many others, were under the impression that Egypt was pregnant and that she was announcing it in a roundabout way. But it wasn't.

Egypt looked at them and quickly told them, "Get that look off your faces." She cleared her voice and said, "What I'm trying to say is that

I'd love to fit this position, and I'm sure I'd do a fine job. I trust your judgment, Mr. Stout. I am sorry to say though I cannot at this present moment."

Mr. Stout looked over and stated, "Ms. Acardi, it will not only be a disappointment to me but to many other people as well who were looking forward to working with you. But the office will be waiting for you whenever you decide to come and join. I'm in hopes Mr. Gianelli will be able to convince you to come and work with us."

As Egypt stood up to leave and let them continue with the meeting, Baron stepped up making mention he'll return in a few minutes. They walked out of the office; then, Baron grabbed Egypt and asked her, "Why?" He knew that this was not Egypt's behavior, and she had been acting very strange lately. She told Baron that she would be able to explain it much later. That tonight during the celebration he would understand why.

Then she reached over and grabbed his chin and kissed his cheek. Then kissed him with all the desire which she had never done before in public. Baron became aroused and wanted her right at that present moment. Egypt stressed to him, "Stop being foolish and go in and tend to the business at hand. There will be time for lovemaking later." She wanted to make sure that this would be one of the most exciting evenings ever.

Baron informed Egypt that after the party would begin the true excitement and began to grin. Egypt just shook her head and walked out to the reception area. As she rode the elevator, she continued to think that she was nothing more than a sexual sight to him. The more she thought on it the angrier she became. Inside was a fire that had built up over a period of time that she wanted to release in the worst way.

But by her moving in such a hesitant way, it will only prove to backfire if not thought out in a calm state. Egypt moved with the quickness through the building. Everyone realized her peculiar behavior, especially Baron. Baron had followed her out of the building. He watched her run toward the car.

"Egypt, where the hell is the fire!" shouted Baron. She nearly jumped out her skin. She didn't know what to say to him. She turned around and looked at him angrily. "Well, where are you going in such a hurry, or who are you going to meet? Don't just stand there looking at me crazy, I'm serious. You've been acting too out of the ordinary. Are you going to answer me or just stand there?" asked Baron.

"If you want an answer, why don't you answer it yourself? You seem to already think you have the answer. Since when do you question my moves? You never acted like this before. Why the sudden change?" asked Egypt.

"No, that's my question. Why the change in you? I never had just cause to think anything wrong. Now you're behaving like there is reason for me to question you. You're too jumpy, and you're never jumpy. If anyone knows you, it's me, darling, so let's stop the shit here," said Baron.

"Damn you, Baron, you scare me out of my wits. If you wanted to kill me, just shove me out a window. Don't use surprise tactics. I'm not used to so many important things going on at the same time. I want this evening to be just right. I turned down something that means so much to me, and I hope I did the right thing. Baron, please, there is too much going on for you to be thinking about fitting me in a secret rendezvous, especially today," said Egypt.

Baron replied, "I realize you're under a great deal of pressure, and I won't lean so hard on you." He smiled and placed his hands on her face and winked and gave her a kiss.

Egypt leaned toward his hand and kissed it while it was on her face. She looked deep into his eyes and said, "Don't ever forget that I truly love you and that there is no one else who could ever take the place of you, Baron. No matter what happens to us I love you."

He didn't know what was going on, but he knew that something was up. "Listen to me, Egypt, there are times where I move so fast and our company keeps me on the go. Don't think that I don't love you because I do. There is another woman in my life, but her name is Egyptian Labels. Which is still you. I want this for you more so than for me. Butter, for the record, I love you more than you would ever understand."

She smiled because it had been sometime since she heard those words from him. She couldn't help but feel that it was initiated by her statement. Little did she understand that Baron did adore her and wants so much to marry her.

As Egypt left to head home, she suddenly remembered she hadn't made the arrangements for Baron's mystery gift.

Chapter 2

The evening was all set. Everything and everyone was in place and gathering for their duties and waiting for the guests to arrive. Baron walked the house with the pride of a king looking over his kingdom and awaiting his queen. There was live music on the patio surrounding the pool, and as the music began, Baron gazed at the water in the pool and drifted into the past. He could never forget how he met Egypt.

She was walking down Sixth Avenue at Eighth street in Greenwich Village. She was magnificent. Quite different from all the women he had dealt with before. As she ran across the light, which was in his favor, he sped up and slammed his brakes creating a loud screech. Egypt was stuck in her spot as she stood there as pale as a ghost. As Baron recalled, Egypt was outstanding.

He jumped out of his car and went over to ask if everything was all right. Egypt yet could not get it together to speak to him. He walked her to the sidewalk and opened his car door and sat her down.

Baron asked "Where were you heading?"

Egypt muttered, "745 Fifth Avenue. I have to sign some papers dealing with the release of my first album."

"By the way, what's your name, lovely lady? That's if you can speak now, can you speak?" he said as he laughed lightly.

Egypt looked unamused and said with a very thick, heavy accent, "Jou ming do I speake deEnglish? Why jou tink because me es Puerto Rican, I es a stupido? I tink jou tink I es de toilette senorita. Well, let me tell jou something. No need jou assists, no."

Baron jumped in and replied, "I had no intentions of insulting you at all, senorita. I only wanted to help you and make you laugh. You were so frightened."

"Let's get it on the record. I'm not a backward person as so many of you think. I'm just as intelligent as a white woman, so I don't need your sympathy or your ride. Please stop the car at the next corner, thank you very much. Not that I really needed a ride in your fancy expensive sports car," Egypt said with the most up-tempo attitude.

"First of all, I am so confused about what has happened, and I'm not going to let you out of my car until you at least let me know your name. Nothing else but your name and—what are you doing!"

"What am I doing over here, you mean? I forgot. I guess I'm somewhat out of my territory. I'm a singer, darling, and my name is Egypt Acardi, better known as just Egypt. Just in case you need any other criteria, I'm a graduate of Columbia University, and I have a BS. I attended for five years, and yes, now I have become a singer. Any gripes with that, tall and handsome man?" said Egypt. "Not really, except, Senorita Acardi—"

Egypt jumped in to say, "You can kill the senorita bullshit, thank you." Baron was most impressed with her attitude and the pride she had in being a woman and in her stand at being a Hispanic. This itself set a tingle in his stomach. Someone with spice and strong—not wimpish. A very excitable, charming, ravishing, and all in all a sexy lady. Baron gathered himself, pulled over, and got out of the car, opened the door and reached for her hand. He kissed her hand and asked, "If at your earliest convenience may I be granted the pleasure of your company and intelligent conversation at Marque for dinner? Your presence will set the night off for a most momentous evening. I would be most honored and delighted to finally have a night out with a lovely and very sensual woman to enjoy an intellectual conversation."

Egypt looked at this man like he had just lost his mind.

"At this present moment I'm involved with a gentleman whom I'm about to see upstairs," she lied.

In fact, she had no one in her life. For every man had seemed to only want her as an arm piece. She wanted to be more than that. She worked so hard to get where she was, and she wasn't about to be seen as an object for just mere pleasure and appearance.

She was taken in by his eyes. They were very much like hers, hazel, except his hair color was jet-black with much body to it, and he was very neat and tall. His eyes were set back, and his cheekbones were high. He appeared to be Italian. She had been very wrong before, but she didn't dare ask.

Baron was not disappointed. He knew that there would be some challenge to her. But how was he going to do this? First he said to himself, "I haven't yet told her my name."

They began to speak at the same time. Egypt tried to ask his name while he made the same attempt to tell her his name. They both began to laugh. Baron felt that was a blessing in disguise.

"My name is Baron Gianelli," he was about to say until he remembered that his family is rather well-known. He figured that she would not approve.

He quickly changed his mind to state, "Baron Gianelli would love to escort you as well as your boyfriend out one night."

Egypt was stuck and knew deep down she wanted to do so, but how could she after she said she was seeing someone?

"No, I'll be too busy, but thank you for the attempt to kill me first then offer nourishment." As they both continued to giggle, she went into the building wondering what caused her to act so outlandish. She realized that he appeared to be a very nice person and that she needed to set aside all of her inhibitions and relax.

Baron recalled that day as though it was yesterday. As he stood there gazing into the water, several people tapped him on his shoulder. "Oh yes, I'm sorry my mind is wandering."

"It should, man. You have come a long way and did it all on your own with no help from the family."

Baron looked as though something was missing but he spoke. "Thanks, Sherm, it wasn't all done by me. I had a lot help from Egypt. This was her idea. This is our baby together."

Sherm looked quite impressed by Baron's honesty to his lady. He asked with a grin, "Speaking of baby, when are you two finishing it off?"

"I can't speak for her, but as soon as possible for me. I never thought I would ever find someone like her."

"This party is great, and the turnout is more than I expected you would get, Baron. I've seen some people here that I haven't seen in ages. They're forever telling me they're too busy to meet with me," Sherm said all excited.

Baron noted this and told him, "This is not a party for business. It's a party for entertainment that's why everyone is enjoying themselves." He then stressed the point by saying, "We are good friends, right? And you know that has never prevented me from grabbing you by your neck and helping you fly out of windows before, right?"

They both began to laugh. It was a personal joke between them. Baron grabbed him by the back of the neck, squeezed it, and patted him on his back, sending him into the middle of a crowd of sexy ladies. This, Baron knew, would keep Sherm very occupied.

Several guests had stopped to speak with him in reference to his next move. He continued to state that this was not an evening in work, just pure pleasure. As he looked over by the pool, he saw someone waving toward him. It was his father. He knew that Egypt would be very thrilled (which was the understatement of the world). Yet he was hoping the two of them would get along.

"Hello, Nunzio. Where is Mother?"

"She's over there. Don't worry about her. Where is the woman of the hour?" he said with a wild grin on his face.

Baron was much annoyed with that and said, "Don't even start, okay? This is not the time or place, and I have had enough of your overzealous comments about her. You always make her feel inadequate. First of all I tried to ignore it, but I felt as though I should let you know what you were up to. I have much trust in her and for that fact my Egypt has morals. More than I can say for you, Dad. I will not allow you to humiliate her or me this evening, so keep your comments to a small roar. I realize she is desirable, but, Father. She is going to be my wife and your daughter-in-law. This ain't *Cat on a Hot Tin Roof*, Big Daddy."

With this Baron stepped away from his father because his temper was rising, and he had that sudden urge to remove his father's neck from the rest of his body. Then he spotted Mr. Stout.

Mr. Stout was dressed to a tee and looking as important as the head of a family. Mr. Stout walked over to Nunzio and led him to a secluded area. "Well, what else do you have in store for the young lady, Nunzio, because the little lady isn't biting the bait, and it appears that your son doesn't have much hold over her either."

Nunzio looked at his glass, glared at Gabriel, and broke the glass in his bare hands. He said to Mr. Stout, "There hasn't been a woman or man yet I have not been able to control. And Ms. Egypt will not be able to walk away from me that easy."

Gabriel asked, "So what am I supposed to do if this Puerto Rican can't smell the bait without the Sazon on it?" Mr. Gianelli looked at him and in a very powerful voice said, "Let's get two things straight. That so-called Puerto Rican is the lady my son intends to marry, and since she will become the next Gianelli, we will hold on to our remarks or we will be forced to eat what we say. You may not like it, but get this through you head. She will be baring the grandchildren of Nunzio Gianelli. Have I made myself clear? Regardless what I may or may not want, that will let me know if she is worthy of the name that has come from Italy."

While this conversation was going on, Baron was walking closer to them. A young lady with the most ravishing eyes approached him. "Deep sexy brown," she said to him. Baron looked a little bewildered. "What the hell is this woman talking about?" "Deep sexy brown," she repeated. "That's what they call it. My eyes, darling. That's the first thing men say to me. 'Your eyes are beautiful,' and I always have to reply with that. So should I call you the Baron or Baron, or should I be very formal and say Mr. Baron Nicholas Gianelli?" Baron looked deep into her eyes and began to smile. He grabbed her and spun her around. "Angela, you little bitch! You disappear and just pop up like that?"

"Come on, Baron. Do you think Father didn't have his damn goons wherever I ran? So I got tired of trying to outrun him and decided to come home and give Father a chance to run me into the ground. I'm surprised they didn't tell you that was why they made the trip to Venice in the first place.

"Dear Mr. Nosy Nunzio found out about Franco DeLucco. As usual he did what he felt was important. Daddy created so much tension in him that one day Franco and I were arguing about Daddy, and he smacked me."

"He what! Where the hell is that bastard, I'll murder him! Where the hell does he get off hitting you?" Baron was outraged by this and stood aside from his sister and looked closely at her and said again, "Angela, I would die for you—"

Angela cut in to tell him, "Look, baby, there is nothing to worry about. Like I was saying, Father knew what family Franco came from and was ready to put a contract on him, but I pleaded with Father to leave him alone, and I would return home with him and Mother. So here I am, back in Shit City covered wall-to-wall with shit men. Now I hope you have some live ones here. I saw that Sherm and I can't believe you still speak with the moron. Speaking of morons, here he comes, and like the dust—I am in the wind. See ya, love."

Baron laughed out loud and blew a kiss to his sister. That was Baron's favorite sister out of all his siblings. Baron's oldest brother, Antonio Mario Gianelli, was an architect who never married and is still seeing the same girl since high school. He has cheated on her since then, but she is a simple, soft spoken girl who would fly to the ends of the earth for Tony.

Then came Nunzio Francesco Gianelli III who is married to a lovely lady. Nunzio doesn't like her because she has no desire to bear any children. He would like to have the Nunzio IV running around. Baron disliked thinking about his oldest sister, the firstborn. She couldn't handle her father too well and killed herself when she was only seventeen. This brought back very harsh memories of how his father never took the time to understand her or any of them that didn't fit into what he thought they should be.

Ann-Margeret was so alive. Wild in her own way and very outspoken. Angelica (her given name) reminds him of Ann-Margeret when she was younger. There was Elisabetta, the image of their mother. She too isn't married because Father controls her every move. She began to stand up a bit to him since she met Egypt. Egypt had just began to slip a little bit of spine into her.

Then came Baron. He was quite the opposite of them all and was thankful for that. Angelica and Greenwich Village walked hand in hand. Their father hated that with a passion. That was his baby. She wasn't a baby anymore. She had grown up to be the loveliest of them all.

Angela slipped away from Sherman to get by Baron again. "Say, love, we have to do some talking. It may not be too important right now, but I think we should speak. Then again you are the only person that I know I have to really talk to." Baron grabbed his sister by the hand and walked her to the swing he had near a small pond in the yard.

"So tell me, little one, what is on your mind?" Baron said as he smiled at her while sipping his drink.

"Baron, I'm pregnant!" she blurted out in tears. Baron didn't know what to do, except to hold her closely to him and explain that everything will be all right.

Margherita walked over to them and reached out her hand to her daughter and said, "I was hoping you would come to me first, but I should have known you would tell Baron first since you told him of your menstruation before me. Don't worry, baby. I may have been quiet in front of all you children while you were growing up, but I had much say in what went on in the household. Don't worry about your father, Angela, just you leave it to me. Answer me—do you feel that Franco loves you?"

"Momma, how did you know that I was pregnant?" said Angela.

"I could see it in your face that there was something troubling you while you were in Italy, yet I recognized it from when I was pregnant with Tony. Now answer my question."

"Mother, I know that he loves me. I told him I will be back soon. If I'm not back within the next week, he will be here. Momma, I'm his wife!" she said in tears, "and I didn't even tell him, but I told his mother."

"Angela, rest assured he knows now, and if this man loves you, he will be here. If not tonight he will be here in the morning, so I know we have to work fast on your father." Baron turned to his mother and said, "Now what is it you think you can do, Mother, you stayed in your place so long?"

Margaret replied with, "Think hard, darling. When you were small, who was right there next to your father with the paperwork? I know him, and he has always needed me except he never wanted you children to ever feel he was any less of a man."

Suddenly there was a change in music. Baron and Egypt thought that would be a good way of knowing that dinner was to be served. They all began to walk to the dinner table when a gentleman dressed in white walked over to Baron and asked if he was Baron Gianelli because he had something for him.

Baron saw this magnificent album dressed in silver. The front of the cover was engraved and designed with leaves which surrounded a picture of Baron and Egypt's first time out.

He opened the album, a step-by-step journal of their lives together. Baron was truly touched. He was about to look up to see where Egypt was hiding when the last page caught his attention. It was a handwritten letter:

> *My Dearest Baron,*
>
> *I want you to realize there is no one else in my life except you. I am so glad we did this together, and there is no place I would rather be. But as I helped you to achieve your goal, so must I find out what it is for me to achieve. I leave you with this: No matter how hard it may be and no matter how fruitless it may be, remember your ideas are your stepping stones to a much brighter life. I do love you, but in my heart, I feel you have grown out of love for me and so I shall make it easy on you. I am in the wind . . .*

Baron slammed the book down, and before he knew it, the guests were surrounding him and the help was seating them. How was he to explain this to the people who were awaiting him? He lifted up his head and proceeded to the table in which there was no place setting for her at all.

As Baron gathered his emotions, he glanced over to Athelia and looked at her curiously wondering if by some chance Egypt could have left some sort of clue to why she did this. It had to be more to it than what she wrote in her letter.

There was so much conversation going on until Baron stood next to his seat, and there came a silence. Everyone's eyes were on him, and his throat got thick. He looked over to his right side where his most important person in the world sat. Egypt always would tell Baron, "When you look over your right side, I will be there for you. Remember the most important person sits at your right."

He smiled because Egypt had done the seating arrangements and there sat his heart: his mother. His mother looked at her son and knew something was wrong. She reached over to him, placed her hand into his, and said, "This is all yours now. Work well."

Baron felt a warmth come over him. "I can feel she is gone, but she loves you and she will return someday. And if not, son, there is no pride when it comes to love. Go after her, but allow her the time to do what it is that she feels she has to." Baron whispered to her, "Mother, you knew all along that she planned this?"

"No, Baron, but I saw the lovely album on top of the dresser. I opened it and read it, and I'm glad I did so now I can be there for you. You have all these people here, so let's go on and do what it is she wants, which is the very best for you. Recall, son, that this is her baby, so treat it as well as you would treat her. Never deny this any attention."

As the guests awaited to hear what was going on, there was small talk until Baron cleared his throat to announce, "There have been a few new things to happen to all of us, but first we will tackle one thing at a time. I can see it in everyone's eyes: Where is Egypt at a time like this? She has gone on a very important trip. A trip she is going on for both of us. But she sends her regards to everyone."

Margaret looked at her son with pride; he had handled that very well. The servants began serving the dinner, and people started asking many questions of Baron. As he stood up, he announced, "At my father's table there was always one main rule and so it will be at mine. We eat, we drink, we don't discuss business, enjoy."

As dinner had come to an end, Angela grabbed Baron, pulling him underneath a tree out in the yard. She wrapped her arms around him embracing him and said, "Bro, you know that I'm here for ya! I'll never understand why she left you, but I won't say anything against her. Mother told me so much about her, so I could only guess she really loved you. I just can't figure it to happen to you. Baby, you have always had the worst luck with women like I with men until Franco. I miss you much, I need you, I do," and broke down in tears.

"Baron, I hate Father. I do so much, why? If I didn't know better I would think he had something to do with Egypt leaving."

A certain look came across Baron's face when Angela said that to him. Baron walked away from her. She made an attempt to hold him as he pulled away. She knew that it was time for him to handle this on his own. As he looked up into the sky, the deep misty midnight could not hide the pain and anguish which was cutting through him. The not knowing was the most painful. When did this all happen? Why he couldn't see it coming annoyed him. As it began to eat him away inside, he never thought he would ever feel this way again—so angry at himself for allowing it to happen. He and many men like him feel it is a weakness to show certain emotions. Little do they realize that they are more of a man when each emotion is handled with the utmost attention and care.

When you think about it, most relationships which are good or can be good fall because someone is trying to maintain a certain image. Now where has that image left Baron?

He listens to the music fading away in the background, and the lights go off. The emptiness becomes stronger as the night rolls in. The feeling that she will not be there hits a lot harder. For some reason, nights are meant for two, and when you bring it in alone, when there was always someone there to comfort you, it's hard. So hard that even the strongest of men feel it. They may keep it to themselves, but they too feel it. They may keep it to themselves, but they feel the anguish and the hurt as well.

Out of nowhere Baron felt moisture for a moment. He thought there was dew in the air, but there wasn't. He found himself wiping a tear from his eye. Baron said with a tearful voice, "Egypt, why?"

At the same time there was a tearful woman broken and scared, hoping that her decision won't be something that she regrets forever. Baron was her life and her friend. Egypt recalled how long it took for her and Baron to get together. They were so much alike and yet so different in many ways. Between her pride and his macho ways, she wondered how they ever came from just being friends working together to lovers.

So much alike yet so different, but the attraction was there. She remembered the inadequacy of when they first slept together. It was so funny.

They just had finished some business, and they had gone out to eat. Baron said, "Well, I could've picked someone worse I guess."

Meanwhile, Egypt remembered looking at him like he lost his mind. As she stared into her coffee, it all came to her. They were just sitting there.

"I know that you had better explain that shit real quick or I'm gonna be in yours before you take your next breath if you're lucky enough," she said with a wild tone.

"Think hard. What's happening right about now? Look at everyone, they're watching. As soon as you lift your head, they'll turn theirs." Baron smiled as she did, and she saw that it was true. They both began to laugh.

"So, Baron, you have heard the same about us. I guess we forgot to do it, but whoever it is doing it for us must be having a ball." She began to laugh.

Baron looked at her in a very strong masculine way and said, "I would rather it be me."

Egypt's face fell to the ground. She never expected something like that to come from her friend, her working partner. This was someone she argued with and whom she could speak to about other relationships. Someone she learned to respect and trust. All this was too much for her to handle since she felt that this was not a joke like so many times before. Baron looked so serious, and his eyes just cut right through. She excused herself and swiftly got out of there and into her car. She remembered arriving home to a message from Baron on her answering machine.

He apologized for making her feel out of place. Egypt was angry with herself because that wasn't why she left. She had to leave or else Baron would have known that she too felt a certain urge—a yearning for him too. She picked up the phone to call him, but she couldn't. Egypt took a deep breath to make sure she was still breathing. When she noticed she was acting like a child, she began to undress in her living room, throwing her clothing randomly throughout the apartment. She walked into her shower and drenched herself under the water, hoping to erase the feeling of stupidity. When she stepped out of the shower and reached for her towel, it wasn't where she placed it. She looked down, and it wasn't on the floor.

Egypt looked over to the toilet, and there was Baron sitting there with the towel in his hand. "Is this by chance what you're looking for? I don't think someone as beautiful as you should hide yourself in a towel," he said.

Egypt snatched the towel and ran into her bedroom slamming the door. "I'm sorry. I came to apologize in person but there was no answer at the door, and I became worried. Your car was there, and I knew that you had to be in here. So I remembered you saying in one of our conversations where you kept your extra key and I let myself in. When I walked in, I saw your clothes thrown everywhere, and of course curiosity settled in. I heard the water, and you know the rest," he said talking through the door.

Egypt opened the door looking wet and angry in her robe, half-opened, revealing that she was not yet wearing anything. Baron looked at her with hungry eyes. Egypt mashed him in the face and replied, "Wouldn't you have felt foolish if I would have stepped out of the shower with someone else, now wouldn't you? You're so lucky that I just didn't knock the hell out of you. What the hell makes you or gives you the right—what the hell are you doing?"

Baron was walking away from her saying, "Something like this needs background music."

"Forget the damn background and don't walk away from me when I'm angry, that's a big mistake. Listen, where was I? Oh, yeah. What gives you the right to just come into my bathroom and just sit there?"

Egypt's attitude and voice changed and became real sweet. "Baron, love, how long were you in there?"

"Long enough to know more than you would have ever told me."

As he began to laugh, he said, "You shouldn't talk to yourself out loud now, should you? I'm a—how you say—interesting in a—what was that phrase?"

Egypt became beet red. She didn't know whether to be angry or embarrassed by what just happened. Now the game was over; they both knew what each other was thinking. As the soft jazz music played in the background and there were no lights on except what was coming through the windows, it set a mood which no words can describe. Baron reached over to Egypt and looked straight into her eyes and directed her slowly by opening and closing his hands.

Softly he said, "Come here to me, come."

Baron's lips were moist and speaking without moving. Egypt was taken. She couldn't speak. She found her legs moving without her thinking. She gazed into Baron's eyes as though she was frightened of what is to come. This was a friend, a love. A man she could never see herself with. Yet she too knew that she felt something.

As their lips embraced, the fear within her vanished and pain began. A sharp pain. A pain of pleasure she had never felt before. Her legs gave way, and he—on time—placed his arms under her and lifted her up in a swift, gentle movement. She collapsed like a frightened child in his arms. Baron walked into the bedroom and placed Egypt on the bed. She looked overwhelmed. Baron said, "Please don't say a word."

Egypt closed her eyes and wrapped her arms around his neck and hugged him a long time. He too held on to her. When they looked at each other, they both passionately kissed and devoured one another. He kissed her like this was what he had wanted for so long, which in fact it was. Egypt had never imagined something like this would, or could, happen.

As Baron slowly and succulently nibbled on her neck, the feelings became more erotic. She sighed out loud and asked Baron to continue. This is what he had been waiting for. He became wild with her body like it was a feast beyond feasts.

As Egypt watched Baron undress, she removed her robe. His eyes glimpsed over at her, and he released a passionate sigh for he too waited for this moment.

Baron grasped Egypt's breast ever so gently as though she were a china doll. He molded her body in his hands and caressed her. Egypt placed her hands on Baron's shoulders and laid him down. She then gently kissed him and placed her legs over him and sat on his lap. Baron braced himself. Egypt looked down at him and smiled and said, "Surprise!" A warm sensation came over her.

Egypt awakened from her daydreams to realize she had spilled her warm coffee on herself. "Damn, what's wrong with me? It's over. I can't go back now, not yet. I've got to make sure that it was meant to be." Egypt screamed, "Baron, Baron, why? as she wept into her hands. Egypt wasn't quite sure now if this was the right thing to do. She loved him so, and she knew he loved her too.

"Where do I go from here? Tell me where, Baron?" She looked out of her window into the night and softly cried, "Baron, why?"

Chapter 3

Several months have passed by and Egypt was seeing a gentleman by the name of Demetri Coolidge Anchor. Egypt found that wild and the name fit the man. He was a producer and promised to help her in every way that he could. So far he hadn't done anything, except sleep with her. She had given everything she could and had received nothing. She refused to admit that she had made a big mistake dealing with this man. Never before was she treated like secondhand news. Egypt felt like she had reached the bottom of the pit and was choking on the cherry seed. Worst of all she was unable to climb out of this predicament. Not that she really tried.

Many an evening she would sit and recall the past, only to break down into tears. She wanted to get to a point where the past no longer existed and the pain would end. But she was only fooling herself.

Late one evening in October she was walking home and her legs collapsed underneath her. A strange man ran over to help and called an ambulance. When the ambulance arrived, Egypt was very feverish and in much abdominal pain.

"What could be wrong with me?" she wondered. They had the gynecologist examine her. The doctor asked if she was sexually active. She informed the doctor that she was only sleeping with one man and knew that she couldn't be pregnant. But the doctors insisted on running the test. Egypt was very upset and looked her doctor straight in the eyes and said, "Why don't you go and feel up some other bitch because you don't give me a thrill." The doctor was quite angered by that remark and left Egypt right there.

After several hours had passed by, they looked at her chart and shook their heads. One doctor entered and asked several questions again. She was very upset because she had already provided the female doctor with all the answers. Then it dawned on her. They kept asking the same questions just differently worded. She began to panic. What was it? She was hoping that it was not the HIV II virus. She began to yell. She wanted some answers and wanted them now. The first doctor came in and asked her to settle down—that there were a few more tests left and they need the results in order to be able to make sure they are not misdiagnosing her. She told Egypt not to panic—that everything will be over briefly.

She began feeling like a pincushion. Shortly, thereafter, two physicians came into the room with papers. One looked so serious, and the other seemed to be very nonchalant. They proceeded to ask the name of her sex partner.

She told them honestly, "There is no one else but the man I'm presently seeing." She gave them his name and asked, "What's wrong with me?" They informed her, "Don't be alarmed, this can be treated. It's only a simple yeast infection that appears to look like other things. The only difference is that it is passed as if it was a venereal disease. But there's also something else wrong with you."

She looked puzzled. The female doctor explained, "Trichomoniasis has been resting there for a long period of time and has created a urinary tract infection which can be treated outside the hospital with antibiotics." She was relieved that that was all it was, but she was angry because the only way she thought she could have caught it was through Demetri. But the doctor informed her that sometimes crying and getting upset throws off hormone levels and creates these infections also as well as many other different reasons too numerous to name. But Egypt knew she was going to use this as a tool against Demetri. She felt now that she has the key to escape her own prison she placed herself into.

There was a certain anger that was racing through her body. When she thought about it clearly, she knew it was because of her being upset about everything going on around her. Every time she picked up the paper, Egyptian Labels was doing something new and moving up the ladder. Worse of all, moving without her. She had to keep reminding herself that it was her decision to go and no one else's. But this character had to go and quickly.

Since Demetri wasn't expecting her, she figured, "Why not just stop by?" She had the key but never used it. Demetri knew that it was just something he gave her to keep peace and faith—which it didn't do.

When she reached his home, she noticed that he was up. She knocked on the door, but there was no answer. She used her key, went in and upstairs to the bedroom. She knew one thing, he was in the shower. To Egypt's surprise there he was, but through the steam, she saw that he wasn't alone. Egypt's heart began to pound. She started to run out of the room, but something held her there. She watched him caress and fondle this other woman. Egypt felt herself getting sick inside, but she stayed. Demetri stepped out of the shower, and Egypt swiftly threw his towel at him. Staring at Egypt, all he could do was just open his mouth. For him, there was no way out of this. No way at all.

She held back all the tears and started to laugh. This sent a chill down Demetri's spine. The woman in the shower heard the laughter and asked, "What's going on?" and Egypt answered with, "Nothing is going on, just ending." She then turned away and told Demetri, "I would scream, cry, and get truly dramatic, but what the hell. Thanks, you made this so easy. Now, good-bye."

Egypt placed his keys on the table on the way out. He came from behind her and grabbed her by the arm. She pulled back telling him, "Now don't make a scene, just let go and leave me alone. Can't you understand it doesn't really bother me? Remember? Fish, sea, ocean, etc. So many men, all those sayings. Now let it be."

Demetri let go of her and announced, "You never did care, did you? All that I did for you, you were using me." Egypt began a hysterical laugh. "Using? You want to start, right? So let me finish. You're nothing more than a cheap copy of a screw magazine. What you called lovemaking was nothing more than a refresher course in play-tap. Caring, I guess, this is a true way to show caring. Silly little me, why, I should have known that. Your attention span and intelligence run neck and neck. It began in the middle of your pants and ended there. Well, that's if you could find any means to locate the middle of your pants, considering there isn't a marker there, just a little piece of string. Yes, I was fool enough to stay, but you, yes you showed me the true meaning of disgust. It begins with you and wraps all around you and ends with you. Next time you need a woman in your life you can handle, just go under your bed and blow up Daphne. I guess she can thrill you, you sick soul. Now that I have read you, rewritten you, and placed your ass on the shelf, get some other ass to dust you off."

Demetri was so angry, he reached out for Egypt, but the other woman began to laugh. Demetri turned to her and said, "Since you find this so funny, bitch, you and Queen Bitch can get the hell out!"

He grabbed the other woman who was putting on her shoes to throw her out, but she just laughed and told Egypt, "Look, babe, don't let me break up your little thing here."

Egypt replied with, "Little? You got that right." The two of them laughed. The other woman looked over to Demetri and, put out her hand, and said, "I did a few extras, so where's the rest of my money?" Egypt blurted out in laughter. "You had to pay for it? Couldn't hold out, huh?"

Demetri threw them both out. The two just walked down the block talking, and Egypt asked, "How did you get started in this line of work?" The woman said to her, "Don't worry, baby, you'll never end up here." Egypt took a deep breath and said, "Who knows? Look, I'm Egypt, so what's your signature?"

"They call me Fay."

"So what is your name if you don't mind my asking?" said Egypt.

"No, baby, I don't mind. It's Fatima Aguilar," she said with much pride.

"Well, Ms. Aguilar, you're one spunky honey. You're pretty as well as exotic. I don't want to insult you, but what are you? Where are you from?" Egypt asked with much curiosity.

"I am . . . ," Fatima stopped and looked at Egypt strangely. "I am Hawaiian and Seminole Indian."

"Wow! What a combo. That explains your earthy appearance. Fatima, you're beautiful and carry yourself with class. You sound smart, so why?"

Fay looked a bit touched. She hesitated to answer and said, "Look, it's not why it's I have no choice. I came here with little to no money at all. I'm from Nevada where my family, and I lived on a reservation. My family did what they could so I could go to college, but the money didn't last. I attend New York University, and if they found out, I would truly be screwed. I don't want to do this, but I'm going to finish my education one way or another. Before you ask let me tell you.

My major is United States Law, and hopefully I'll be a corporate attorney. Don't even look at me strange because I know that it doesn't fit me that I'm walking the streets and want to do that, but—"

Before Fatima could finish, Egypt and she had walked across to Greenwich Village where Egypt lived. She invited Fay upstairs. When Fay walked into Egypt's apartment, her mouth stood open. The apartment was a flat with three bedrooms and looked as though it came out of a magazine page.

One room was so Native American that it hit a place in Fay's heart. There was a little papyrus on the wall, a bear skin rug on the floor, and a rack where Egypt was in the process of making a woven rug the old-fashioned way.

Fatima stood by the rug and touched it. A tear fell, and she could no longer stand the pain anymore. Egypt grabbed her and wiped her eyes and held her close. Fay pulled away and tried to gather her emotions. It had been a long time since she had been home. Many of the things reminded her of home. Especially the rug.

Fatima took a deep breath, looked around, and apologized to Egypt.

Egypt just smiled, nodded her head, and shrugged her shoulders as if it was okay. Fay looked over Egypt's shoulders and noticed the most magnificent mural of Egypt and a man.

She walked over to the mural and stood under it and said, "Egypt, this is beautiful. Who is he?"

Egypt looked around to see she was looking at Baron. Egypt replied, "Fatima, he is and always will be my heart. He is my ex-fiancé, and I left him."

Fatima looked angry. "Yeah, all the men are the same. They all fuck up one way or another. They don't know when they have a good thing."

Egypt cut her off to announce, "No, you're wrong. He was far from that. He gave me everything. Come, look here."

She then took Fatima into the next room, a bedroom. It had nothing in it but things related to Egyptian Labels, with her and Baron's name all over. Fatima looked quite confused.

"If these things are true, why are you here and not there enjoying the money and luxuries that go along with it? Shit, if I made a business this successful, I would be right there with it to make sure everything was going well and no one was stealing or destroying it."

Egypt answered, "First of all, Baron has my share of the profits automatically deposited in my account which I had when we were together. He always wanted a company like that, but he just couldn't get it together. Well, I had the right ideas, and he had the know-how. We put it together, and we made it. But the key is we did it together and that is great and all. You see, if it wasn't for Baron, I wouldn't have made it, even if it was my idea.

"He went out and pushed it. No one wanted to take a chance with a Puerto Rican, especially a Puerto Rican woman. I was taken as a joke, and he took over and did it. Fatima, he always said to everyone that it was my baby, but to me, it became his. I want to do something all on my own without help. Something I could go out and make work. Something that is all mine!"

"Egypt, this is yours. This is you. This man loves you or else he wouldn't keep it going and running the way he knew you would want it to be. You're so lucky and can't even see it. It's so damn strange that some people go through hell with a man to stay with them and others get a man who will climb every mountain and swim every ocean just to end up leaving him.

"Look, babe, you better take a look at what it is that you want and realize each day you stay away the heart can mend and someone else can get in. Is that what you want, or you really don't care? You had better think quick. They say if you're slow, you blow, and I ain't talk'n' about a horn either."

All Egypt could do was just stand there with her mouth open and look at Fatima like she was right. Deep down, Egypt knew that there was no true reason why she couldn't stay there and try to figure out a way of getting these emotions together. She was hoping that Baron would have looked for her; then, she remembered that Baron was always the kind of man who wouldn't get in the way of anything she deemed important. That was one of her reasons for loving him so. She was confused now more than ever since her decision.

Egypt walked over to the telephone and picked it up to begin dialing. She heard him answer the phone and called out Baron's name. She hung up on him. All Fatima could do was walk into the other room and shake her head.

Egypt walked behind her saying, "You made it sound so easy, but in fact it's not. I have to go back when it's the right time, and until then I have to stand on my own. Once you realize there is love, you know that it will be waiting."

Fatima looked at her with an evil smirk on her face. "Are you very sure of that? From what I've seen he is one hell of a man. But who am I to speak love? It comes around like a breeze in one port and then right out the other. Well, let me go. I just met you and probably outstayed my welcome. And besides, I have classes to study for. I walk to school but only on certain days. I'll see ya!"

"No, don't go! Are you sure you're okay by yourself? If you want you can hang around here. Since I left home I've been kind of lonely, and anyway, I like your honesty. It's up to you," Egypt said with a desperate tone. Fatima looked at her with a gleam in her eyes as if to say yes, but she knew that both their ways and lifestyles would clash. She thought it best to tell Egypt. "No, but if I could, you would make a very interesting roommate, that I could state. But you best figure out what it is you're going to do and quick."

Egypt and Fatima walked to the door, and she left as quickly as she entered Egypt's life. Egypt sat back and looked up through the skylight and began to gaze into the stars. What a beautiful night. So much has happened to her in one evening. From hospital to ex-boyfriend to intelligent prostitute, to alone again.

Egypt was thinking that this was becoming a habit, being alone. She remembered that she hung up on Baron. His voice, just a simple "hello," rang through her like a chill. What was it that he was doing before she called? She couldn't help but wonder if there was anyone in his life as of yet. He must have someone because she had a lover even though she loved him more than anything else. As she rolled over in her bed, an article in the paper caught her attention: EGYPTIAN LABELS HITS TOP TEN OVER ONGOING PRODUCTION COMPANIES.

Egypt picked up the paper and started to throw it across the room when she noticed there stood Baron looking as radiant as ever. She held the paper to her bosom tightly and drifted off.

When Egypt awakened, the emptiness was driving her into a whirlwind . All the things were just getting all caught up, and there seemed to be no way of getting out of it.

She got dressed into a pair of old denim blue jeans and grabbed her old leather jacket and a few things she put into her bag and hit the subway.

As she rode, she placed her dark glasses on to cover the tears filling in her eyes. As the people got on and off pushing and arguing, she looked on how things have changed. She stepped off and changed trains and got off a few stops later.

As she walked up the stairs, there were things on her mind she had momentarily forgotten. But she thought of her loneliness and continued to walk.

As she walked, she passed a park and began to cut through; the people were staring at her. Several guys walked up to her and tried to speak to her. She took off her glasses and talked to them in Spanish, "I'm not going for it, so you better back off."

They called her several unkind words in Spanish, and when Egypt turned around, a voice yelled out, "Manteca!"

She stopped in her tracks and thought for a moment. But she kept walking. "So, Manteca, you can't speak anymore? What happened, you forgot your language? Or you're not Spanish anymore, traded it in for white?

"No, I know. You decided to go out slumming. So how's the sights?" he said in a bitter voice.

"Stop it, Louie, damn it! Leave Manteca—I mean Egypt—alone!" said a familiar voice.

"Gimme a hug, Mommy. You look so good. Yo, girl, the good life sure agrees with you. So, girlfriend, what brings you around? We see Sharla now and then, but you, you've been gone it seems like for a long time," said Evelyn.

"Hey, Evelyn! Whatever happened to you? Look what's going on. We were so close. You finished high school, right? Did you finish business school? Come on, talk!" But before she could speak, there was a cry close by. When Egypt looked, it was Evelyn's sister walking over with a stroller and a little toddler. "Evelyn, I waited for you in the house. I can't watch them no more, and you know, Mommy. She's screaming she had hers and so on. So I dressed them. She said if you're gonna hang out in the street, keep them out there with you.

"Oh shit! It's you, Egypt! Yeah, girl, I heard about your company. Rumors say you living the white grenga life. So hook me up. I sing in a couple of Spanish clubs," said Carmen.

"Look, pain in the ass leave Egypt alone. Why should she hook you up if she ain't on no record herself? Baby, the girl can sing her ass off. Since we all used to hang out, she would sing and dance all over. But Egypt ain't like the way the rest of us were. She still hung out and hung with school.

"Yo, Carmen, man she bust out them first and second letters all the time. I used to keep that good ole F-lag. But go do what you were goin' to," replied Evelyn.

"These your kids? They're so cute. When did you get married? No one told me. Why didn't you tell Momita? She would've given you my number," said Egypt.

"Maybe because I never got married," said Evelyn.

"Oh, I'm sorry if I said something wrong. So who's their [Egypt quickly thought twice about the question she was going to ask]—what's their names?"

"Manuel is my first, he's fifteen months old, and Juan is gonna be five months. I might as well tell you I'm two months pregnant now. I hope it's a girl this time.

"I know you want to ask me who's the father. Manuel is one of Danny's sons, but Juan and this one are Louie's kids. We're always on and off. I knew sooner or later you'd know."

As Egypt stood there in shock, all she could say was, "Louie's kids?"

Evelyn looked her in the face to answer with, "Are you mad or—"

Egypt cut her off and gave her a hug. Egypt said, "What? Why would I be mad at you? Stop. That's all water under the bridge. What was between us was over before it even started. Plus he never really cared for me. Remember how he used to act? One minute he was jealous, and when we finally got together, he wanted his freedom too. I wasn't going for it. He wanted me and what was that bitch's name? Damn, oh yeah, Renee. That's when I left. He wanted me, and I still recall the choices were up to me. To stay or go. I knew he'd be hurt if I left, but he said he would understand. He knew I deserved what I needed, but he just couldn't handle it then. He claimed he'd be my good, good friend no matter what. Please!

"That pile of shit statement will never leave my mind. I guess he attacked me when I stepped off. I never regretted walking because I couldn't stand seeing him and that bitch walk through the streets. So, baby, I'd never be angry with you. Anyway, he didn't love me."

"So you think, Manteca. He went bad ever since you left. When Louie heard that you were Egyptian Labels, things got bad. Anyway, a lot of us know he loves you. It hurts to say, but he has called me and a few others Egypt while screwing," said Evelyn.

"You've got to be kidding. That man never even tried to find me. Even though, I know I wouldn't have come back anyway. If that's true, and he did that to you, why are you with him?" asked Egypt.

"I was lonely and scared of being alone with Manuel. I saw that he was hurting too. I hoped we could mend each other, and Louie ain't all bad, man. He does work, and sometimes when he's got the money, he gives me a couple of bucks. I get odd jobs, and anyway I live with Mommy. I pay her no mind. She always complains whether it's good or bad. So who listens? But I don't want to talk about my life. What's the hell up with you?" asked Evelyn. "Look, instead of shaking the baby up and down, why don't you be a real mother for a change and stop talking to Ms. High Class. Yo! I said go in the house and fix me something to eat cause I'm hungry," said Louie as he shoved her out the way."

"Okay, Manteca, I gotta go. See ya soon?" said Evelyn in a low tone.

"I thought you two weren't married or even lived together. So, Louie, don't handle her like that. She has the baby in her arms," Egypt said angrily.

"Look, Ms. High Class, I can handle my life any way I damn well feel like it, and you can kiss my ass!" he spat.

Egypt tried to hold her temper, but she blurted out, "Fuck!"

"Yeah, baby, we used to do it so well. You weren't like these other bitches. The top of the line. Is that why you're back? Tired of that lame piece of white meat? Wanna have some good Latino stuff? Good life may be good, but that good old stuff always calls 'em back," said Louie as he began to laugh out loud. Evelyn just stood there in shock, grabbed the kids, and ran away. Egypt looked at him in disgust. He leaned over to hold and kiss Egypt. Out of nowhere she smacked the hell of him and pulled out a pocket knife.

"Remember I'm from here too. I used it before on you. This time I won't make a mistake and just leave a scar. This time I'm gonna leave a memory. Comprende?" Egypt was hot under the collar.

Louie backed off. He said, "It's okay, baby, you probably couldn't deal with it no more. High life probably made you boring anyway."

When Egypt composed herself, she noticed someone in her mother's window. When they noticed her, they closed the curtains. That's strange.

She thought at this time her father should be at work, and the rest of her family could be hanging out, but she knew Momita had to be home.

When she rang the bell, there was no answer. When no one came out, she thought the bell didn't work. She knocked on the door but still no one came down. She stood there for a while and kept knocking. Mrs. Martinez walked out of her apartment, and Egypt asked her if she had seen her mother.

"I just hung up with her only a moment ago. I heard the buzzer ring while we were on the phone," said Mrs. Martinez. Egypt told her that was her ringing the bell from downstairs, and no one buzzed her in. She wondered what was going on. She was missing home—well, her family at least. Before she could leave the building, she saw Jose and Gina. She smiled and ran over to them. They all embraced and laughed because they were all so happy. They talked for some time in the hallway. Then Egypt's brother asked, "What did Mommy say when she saw you?"

Egypt explained, "No one answered the door."

That's got to be a bit strange because I know she's there. I just seen her in the window," said Gina.

"What in the hell is going on? I just talked with Mrs. Martinez. She said she heard the bell in the background when she was on the phone with Mommy. Is something wrong?" said Egypt.

"Stop it, sis. I bet she was in the bathroom or something and couldn't get to the door," said Jose.

"It's funny, Jose, but I thought I saw her in the window, and I'm positive she saw me. I know she knows what I look like," said Egypt.

"Just come on upstairs with us and let's see what going on. Why are you carrying a big bag? Egypt, are you coming back home? What happened to that hunk of a man you're living with?" asked Gina.

"I left him, Gina, and got my old place in Greenwich Village again. Things were changing," said Egypt.

"Yo, sis, did that Italian scum hit you 'cause I'll go over there with my troop, and we'll take care of him. Nobody'd ever know," said Jose.

"That's okay, Jose, he never touched me. It's too much to explain. Nothing to do with women or money or any kind of abuse," said Egypt. She looked at Gina and started to laugh. While Gina searched her pockets for something, Egypt said, "So, Gina, you'll never change, lost keys again? Try your pants pocket."

"Forget it, I have mine. Man, you'll always be ass backward," replied Jose as they went in the house.

"Momita, come here!" yelled Gina. "Sit down and take a load off. Oh yeah, Egypt, Noel and Dionisia moved out. First Poppy and her had it out. He was up early one morning and saw Dionisia take a pill out of a container and place it back in her dresser. He just walked right over to the drawer and took the pills out. Then he started screaming at her and questioning her. She tried to explain to him that she's not a child no more and stuff. Guess who's here? Jose, go see if she's still sleeping. Where was I? Oh yeah. She told Poppy that if she wanted to have sex, she was gonna do it regardless. I think he shouldn't have screamed at her like that 'cause she never disrespected the house. I knew what she wanted to say that I did, but she didn't. They don't know. Then he reached back and slapped the shit out of her."

"Poppy hit Dionisia? Her pride and joy? Mommy must have hit the roof, didn't she?" said Egypt. She took off her jacket and put up her feet.

"Yeah, you know Momita. Yo, Egypt, didn't you learn anything out there with those rich people? Get your shoes off the table. Damn, I do the cleaning around here now that all of you ran out. Jose just dusts the air and sweeps his shoes," said Gina. "Yeah right. Don't listen, sis. You know Locita? She's losing it again. I still have to take her for her shock therapy," said Jose as he walked toward the kitchen and slapped Gina on the head.

"Get off me, you dumb spic," replied Gina.

"Remember, that's Mr. Dumb Spic to you," answered Jose. "Oh well, disregard the nutcase. Anyway, she turned away from Poppie, and then Momita jumped in and told Poppie off. He said she got those Pota habits from Momita, and out of nowhere, Dionisia came out and punched the shit out of Poppie and said, 'don't you ever call my mother that!' and she went for him. We jumped in and pulled her off and out the house. She punched Jose trying to get at Poppie. You should have seen his face. I laughed for days, she really messed Jose up."

"She came back later that night with Dennis. He looked right through Poppie and dared him to make a move, but nothing came out of his mouth, just the eyes told it all. She gathered all of her stuff while Dennis waited in the living room. Poppie got up and walked to her room, and then Dennis jumped up and told Poppy to please leave his wife alone. Poppie likely died. That morning they had eloped. She was going to get married, but she wanted him to be stationed somewhere she could be with him. Right now he pays the rent, and she lives by herself till they make arrangements to live on base. He's in the air force. He's in California, and she's supposed to go there in two months," said Gina.

"You think her ears can rest, motormouth? And I noticed you didn't tell her about you. All my sisters have abandoned the Puerto Rican men and drifted off to other color schemes," Jose said, acting like he was stabbed in his heart and he fell to the floor.

Gina and Egypt began to laugh and jumped on him and hit him, and they all began laughing. Egypt looked up and saw her mother standing there. She looked cold as ice. *There is so much pain in her eyes, or is it anger?* thought Egypt. The other two stopped cold and looked confused. As everyone stood up, Egypt went to hold her mother, and she stepped in another direction. Jose stood next to Egypt.

"What brings you into my home?" asked her mother.

"Why are you acting like this, Momita? You haven't seen her in a long while. Be happy," said Gina.

"Oh, are those your bags?" asked her mother.

"Si, Momita. Are you going to just stand there with that look on your face, or can you say what's on your mind?" replied Egypt.

"So you having problems out there and you just pick up your bags and come running home? No phone call to see if we even live here or if we're alive? We weren't good enough to remember when all the money was flowing. What happened, Manteca? He took it all from you and sent you to the street? You didn't have a good enough background for him, or was he tired of getting it for free and went out after a nice white girl and threw away the trash? So you came here with your problems and I got enough of my own?" she said, turned her back on Egypt, and walked away.

"Momita, how could you say that shit to me?" asked Egypt.

Her mother just looked at her with pain in her eyes. "Do you even know the things that your familia—excuse me—my familia has been going through? While you're running around with your top-of-the-line friends, do you think we are flying on that same old magic carpet? No, Manteca, this familia is water to you, and yes, you now are, Manteca, lying above us. You may be there, but you came from here," replied her mother.

Egypt grabbed her head and started to cry. Her brother held Egypt close to him and asked, "Momita, what the hell is wrong with you? What kind of shit are you on? Remember you told her to make and enjoy it. What now, you're going to condemn her for enjoying it? Yes, that's right walk out! See, when someone wants to talk to you, you always walk out. You only want to hear what you want to hear. Stay here, Egypt, I'm calling Noel."

"Don't bother, he's on his way. I told him what Momita did already. He wasn't too far from here in his car," said Gina.

"Don't worry we're going to get this straight. Did you call Dionisia? Stop smiling. Damn, Gina, you run and tell everything to Noel and Dioni. I know she's not coming, or is she?" asked Jose.

"You remember she won't come, but she wants to know what

happens anyway. So I promised her I would always keep her in touch with things," said Gina.

"Jose, why didn't you call?" said Egypt. Jose just looked down at his feet. "Manteca, I guess I felt that maybe you wouldn't want them to know where you came from," he sighed.

The doorbell rang, and Jose rose to open the door. Standing there was an older version of Egypt. She and her brother favored each other. He was a sharply dressed handsome Hispanic man. Standing tall and classy, he reached out for his girl and spun her around. They exchanged a few pleasantries and began to catch up on each other's lives.

"Noel, why don't you clean up your act? You know it's dangerous what you're doing. You know, you are a very talented man, and you could draw anything at a glance. But for you to be out there in the street and working a simpleton job, you can get caught and go to prison," lectured Egypt.

But Noel just laughed and said, "Don't worry, I'm still thinking about going to school to be a commercial artist." Egypt knew better than that; he was always going back to school.

Their mother began making a lot of noise in the kitchen and yelled, "Is that my son?" Noel went into the kitchen to calm her down. They hollered for a minute, and she walked out and looked Egypt straight in the eyes.

"Well, say it! I heard you anyway when you were talking to Noel. So, Momita, tell me what I did so wrong? Something I know you wouldn't have done if the opportunity came along for you. This is too much for me to handle, you know. All I wanted was to spend some time with my mother, father, and everyone. But why are you doing this to me? Momita, would you do this to any of the rest of us if they didn't make it the way I did? Is that why you're acting like this, because I made it and you kept Poppy from making it? You know that's why I went for it and that Poppy wanted me to keep going and not to stop. You think it's all fun and games? You're wrong there. It was very hard work, and as far as doing it on my back, forget it. It may kill you to have noticed I was talented, but you were so damn busy. Forget it, I don't want to fight. I didn't come here to fight. I came home to be with my familia. I don't know why you're treating me like this. I wanted to come home, that's all. I'm your daughter!" yelled Egypt.

"Yes, you're my daughter. I expect my daughter to call her familia now and then, to put a stamp on a card to say 'I'm okay.' You want to run back home for whatever the reason is. But do you stop to wonder if the familia may lay up and wonder how the daughter is doing? Or if the daughter wanted to be known as 'their daughter'? You expect me to be your mother all the time, right, mi hija? Well, let me tell you, I want a full-time daughter, not a part-time one. If you can't be my daughter all the time, I don't need or want a part-time child. So in that case I don't need a child none of the time. A full-time daughter or a no-time daughter," her mother said. She headed back into the kitchen. Noel went in after her. He was so angry with what she had said.

"I don't believe she said that to me," said Egypt with tears in her eyes.

Noel stepped out of the kitchen and walked over to Egypt. He looked at her and shrugged his shoulders. All she could do was wipe her tears. She walked over to Jose and Gina and kissed them.

"Well, Egypt, I think it's best that you leave for now. Give Momita some time to think about what she said. I don't think she means what she said. You know Momita, she's easily excited. Those your bags?" he said pointing at her black shoulder bag. "Well, if you need a place to stay, you're welcome to stay with me. My car is downstairs. Come on, let's go," Noel said, picking up her bag. "If Poppy comes home and sees this, he and Momita will be at it. Bad enough when he comes home then finds out."

They all walked out and went downstairs. Everyone was so quiet and confused. It seemed no one wanted to talk first. Egypt was torn and mad all at the same time. She wanted to be home, and in some ways she was glad this had happened. She didn't feel comfortable with her old friends, like she was years ago. She had outgrown them. Not that she was better than them, she just wanted more than a man and children. She wanted to be on top.

"Okay, let's melt the ice. I'm fine. It's gonna take a lot more than this to bring me to rock bottom. Remember, I'm from the old school, and I can take a lot more than that. I've seen more than you, Gina, so stop acting silly. It's okay. Come on, I'm still at my old place in Manhattan. You've been there, right? You know I'm not going anywhere else," said Egypt.

"Are you coming with me or what? Speak, Egypt," asked Noel. "No, I'm okay. I have a place. I just wanted to spend some time with everyone, besides I have to go back anyway. Thanks, and I love you. Take care out there, big bro, okay?" said Egypt.

Noel left, and the three of them walked toward the park. Egypt walked over to the benches and sat down. She looked up and around. She watched some people play handball, and she smiled. She got up and went to sit on one of the swings for a moment. Gina asked Jose to go see if she was all right. When he walked over, she stuck her tongue at him, and they laughed. He grabbed her off the swing and mashed her in the face. She chased him around the park as they laughed. Then the both of them chased after Gina. When the caught up to her, she was laughing with tears in her eyes.

"Egypt, are you ever coming back?" asked Gina.

"I'm not sure. Momita sure was angry, and I couldn't deal with another confrontation like that one. Hey, I just remembered that li'l bro said something about you and a guy?" asked Egypt.

"Between you, Dionisia, and her, I don't think there's been a race you lost." Jose laughed.

"I thought you were—," started Egypt.

"I was going out with Gary's cousin, but his family is too damn nosey. We always had someone in our business, and I'm like you, sis. That doesn't work for me.

"Go away, Jose, I wanna talk to Egypt without your face in the middle of it. Go find a corner and keep yourself busy," remarked Gina.

"Well, see ya, sis, and I'll try to stop by," said Jose.

"I've been talking to Dionisia's brother-in-law, Steve. He's in the Marines and older than me. I write him a lot now. He used to come to the house before Dioni, and Dennis got married. He would try to talk to me, and then when he went into the Marines, he wrote me a letter. I guess that's how it started. Then after a while, he wrote me and said he had a leave and wanted to meet with me. I said okay but never expected to act so strange around him. He opened doors for me, bought me things, but the whole time he never reached out and acted like he wanted to screw me. I mean, you know, I felt a little bit rejected, so I made a move on him."

"So what happened? Just don't stop there," asked Egypt.

"He kissed me back and asked me to take it slow because the military marriages and relationships can't stand the distance, and he didn't want to mislead me or anything. Right then and there I felt so stupid, and I didn't know what to say. I had Noel's house keys and knew he'd be away for a while, so I took him to the flat. Well, you have to see that place. It was set up for a sex king but not in bad taste though. When we walked in, he asked me was it my place and I told him the truth. We sat and watched TV for a while, and I made something to eat.

"We had been going out for like nine days, and he did nothing. I just couldn't understand why he hadn't tried to at least touch me. You know, I was kinda hoping that he wasn't still a virgin.

"He had the prettiest green eyes. He told me that my eyes were pretty too, and I broke out giggling. He asked me what was wrong, and I told him that's what was running through my mind. He told me that he found hazel eyes to be mysterious and interesting. My goodness, Egypt, I assumed he would say sexy, not interesting," said Gina.

"Can't you see he's respecting you like a young woman ought to be respected? I would feel proud to have a man like that. You know that's not the way it is here," said Egypt.

"Better than that, I think I'm falling in love with him, and he doesn't want to hurt me. Nothing happened that night. We kept talking and writing each other. Next thing you know, I'm not going out as much, and I find myself acting different and waiting faithfully to hear from him. He came back three months later for like a week. We had a great time, and again nothing. So that was it. I got mad and started seeing Dave. When what the hell happens? I get pregnant by Dave, and then Steve shows up. What a time to get leave! He had been writing, but I stopped answering because I felt funny about the way he was treating me. I didn't tell him. Instead I ran away again. Dave left me and I had an abortion then I called Steve's mother's house, and she told me that he was on forty-eight hours leave before he had to go out to sea, and he wouldn't return until his mission was over.

"She gave me his address, and we started to write again. The last time I saw him was about a week ago. Egypt, he took me for a ride to the mountains upstate, and it was so beautiful. He had flowers and a gift for me. It was the most beautiful gold chain I've ever seen. We made love I guess because I never thought sex could make you feel like that. The lights and the room were perfect. I'm afraid I'm not sure if this is real or just a classy way of making me feel special then dropping me later," said Gina.

"Gina, no one can answer that, but just take it slow. You have to realize he's in the Marines and that will always come first. What do you think he wants from you?" asked Egypt.

"Don't laugh, but he really said he's falling in love with me. He wants me to go to college, and he even sends me brochures from different schools. I mailed him something [she smiled], and I just hope he likes it. I bought him a jacket. I thought about him and said to myself with that body, he would look good in leather," said Gina.

"No, not you! My baby bought something for somebody without expecting something in return? Growing up, huh?" replied Egypt.

"I've been used a lot while you were gone, and I thought I would never be cared for," said Gina.

"So you feel like he cares? Just be careful, and don't get pregnant by him. His people will say you're doing it to get out of where you're at, like he's your meal ticket, and if that's what you want, don't do it. I hope everything works out for you, and to me, he sounds like he cares. Who's to say? Just don't bank so much on sex. Enjoy the man and his attention.

"Well, what else is going on? Gina, does Noel know what you're doing?" asked Egypt.

"Yes and no. Yes, to the fact I go there and no to what I do there. I'm careful because I know Noel would try to kill a guy if he saw me doing something with them. Even when he used to see Dave kiss me, he would push him up against the building. I'm so blown away about the way Steve is concerned about me. What do I do if he wants me to—"

Jose yelled out the window, "Gina! It's lover boy on the phone. What? Tell him to call back?" He laughed.

"Don't be funny. I'm coming, tell him to hold on. Look," she said to Egypt, "I'm sorry I gotta go. Love ya, Egypt." She kissed Egypt and ran to the apartment.

Egypt headed toward the subway to go back home. She turned and looked at the apartment and saw her mother in the window. Egypt just stared and then turned her back and walked away.

It was still early by the time she returned home, so she jumped in the shower to try to relieve some of the tension. When she stepped out with a towel around her, she saw the newspaper she had last read. "Egyptian Labels," she read and felt proud but sad. This was her and what she gave up to achieve this. Now she has chosen to back up to try regain the things she so desperately wanted. But did she really want to let go of Baron?

It was nearly 6:00 p.m., and she was getting ready to leave again but didn't know where it was she wanted to go. She just needed the air.

Meanwhile, Angela was talking with Baron about Egypt. She felt that it must have been Egypt to have called and hung up on him last night. But he was too sure that if it was her that she would have spoken to him and not hung up.

Baron felt as though Egypt had found someone else and was starting anew, just as though he thought he should begin anew too. But there was something holding him to her; A hope that she wouldn't return and be married.

The phone rang again, and Baron jumped. He looked at it in hopes that it would be her. His sister picked up the phone. It wasn't for him. It was a friend of Angela's telling her that Franco had been injured.

She fell to the floor with the phone still in her hand; and Baron lifted her up, took the telephone, and got the rest of the information. He went and got a glass of wine for her.

"Sip slowly, Angela, take it easy. We'll find out what happened. First things first, you're pregnant, so take it easy. Franco isn't dead, okay, and he'll be fine. I'm not letting you go if I don't think you can handle it. So get yourself in order and calm down. Angela, listen to me!" Baron said raising his voice at her.

Angela was breathing very fast, and she began to experience bad pains in her lower back. She didn't want to show Baron that she was in pain, so she got up and walked over to the window and said, "Are you going to take me, or am I going by myself?"

Baron looked at his sister knowing that she was in pain. But he knew that if he didn't go with her, she would go by herself. All he could do was get her coat and place it on her shoulders.

They left for Cornell Medical Center, which they weren't far from. They hailed a cab and headed for the hospital.

When they arrived, Baron was worried about Angela because she was barely able to walk upright. He grabbed on to her arm and helped her in. She held herself very well without any expression of pain on her face. The only thing on her mind was if Franco was going to be okay.

As they waited to hear from his surgeon in the emergency waiting room about the outcome, she started cramping up. Angela got up and started to walk away from Baron when she no longer could hide what was happening to her.

Angela began to cry out loud, "Baron, help me! I'm afraid something bad is happening to me. Baron, please help me make it stop!"

She took a few more steps, and her water broke. Angela screamed, and Baron ran to her and lifted her up like a little baby. He ran to the nurses' station, and they placed her onto a stretcher. Baron was all twisted around. He couldn't figure out what the hell was going wrong with everything around him. All he knew was that his father had better not been behind any of the shit that was transpiring tonight. He knew that his father didn't like Franco or his family, but Franco was Angela's husband and father to his grandchild. But for some reason his father's name was on the tip of his tongue. Baron wondered and quickly shook it out of his head whether his father had anything to do with Egypt's decision to leave. *No*, thought Baron. He knew that his father was crooked, but he wouldn't stoop that low.

A nurse walked over to Baron and asked if he was any relation to a Franco Delucco. Baron stood stock still with no expression at all. His face paled, and his tongue went dry. When he attempted to speak, a muffled sound came from his mouth.

The nurse looked down toward the ground and began to speak softly. Baron felt like something was caught in his throat.

"Mr. Delucco is now in ICU. He can have one visitor only for ten minutes. He's still very weak, but he is a fighter. Would you like to see him now?" asked the nurse. "Will he make it?" Baron asked with a slight quiver in his voice.

"There is no telling at this point. He underwent extensive surgery, and now the healing is up to him. Seeing all that he has gone through and knowing that he can speak slightly means he is a fighter." She added, "There is nothing else the doctors can do for him."

Baron walked down a long and narrow hall which was cold and uncomfortable. He felt as though he was on a long journey—destination unknown. When he reached the end of the hall, there was nothing but some hospital equipment and unemotional people.

When Baron glanced into the room, he saw Franco lying there with tubes and monitors all around him. Franco opened his eyes and with much pain on his face tried to speak. Baron reached over and told him not to try to speak or move. He told Franco, "Finally, I will have the last word." Franco smiled with ease. He looked around and signaled to Baron to come closer.

"Franco, what's wrong? Try and stay still gumba," said Baron. Franco muttered, "Where's Angela?"

Baron was lost for words, but he knew he had to tell Franco. He looked worried and sensed that there was something wrong. Baron took a deep breath and blurted out everything. Franco tried to sit up, but Baron reached over and laid him back down, reassuring him that everything was going to be all right and that she was in good hands. Baron knew Angela was going to lose the baby since her water broke, and she wasn't far enough along so that the baby she carried was still underdeveloped.

Baron looked over at Franco, smiled, and told him, "Keep the faith, man." He couldn't understand how this happened to him. Franco didn't have any enemies in the states, but he felt that his father was behind this. He knew that Nunzio didn't know about Angela's pregnancy or of their marriage because she chose to keep that hidden from him until the right time came. He had an idea that this would not have happened if Nunzio would have known that his baby girl was pregnant and Franco's wife; he would not have ordered this hit.

A soft mutter came from Franco, "You're nothing like Nunzio. You have been by my side since the beginning, but I can't help but feel the Don had something to do with this. When I have my first son, he will bear your name." With that Baron could not help but smile and hurt inside. He knew it would be no time soon for that. Franco continued to speak until his voice began to fade. A tear came to Baron's eye, and there wasn't too much more he could take for now. He never had his life thrown apart like this.

As he watched Franco sleep, he wiped his forehead and placed his hand in Franco's and patted it. All he wanted to hear is that his sister will be all right.

When he left the room, he walked over to the nurses' desk and asked questions regarding Angela. He took the stairs to her room. When he went up there, he made a call to his office and informed them that he would be in and to send flowers to both Angela and Franco. The secretary gave Baron all his messages then stated, "There is a woman who has made several calls by the name of Fatima in reference to—"

Baron cut her off to say, "I don't know any Fatima. Just tell her if she calls back that I will get in touch with her later." The secretary tried to tell him, but he hung up on her.

When he approached Angela's room, she was crying, and he couldn't take another step. Angela said, "I know you're there, bro, I need you." Baron stepped in and saw his baby sister looking torn apart which filled him with unbearable pain.

He walked over to her and held her in his arms, and she just broke into massive tears. All he could do was hold her tight and explain to her that she had to be strong for Franco.

"Angelica Delucco, you have a husband downstairs who needs you, and you must be strong so he can heal quickly. Do you hear me, Angela? I was down there with him, and he's still very weak and this will only serve to make him fall if he doesn't have support from you. Baby girl, I know this is painful, but listen, you still have Franco, and there will come another time when it will be right for you. So hold on, girl, I love you so much, Angela. Please, stop crying," said Baron.

Angela took a deep breath only to say, "Don't tell me it wasn't Father, Baron. I know this was his doing, and when Franco's father finds out, that will only mean that all hell will break loose. When I get my hands on Father, he'll wish that Mother never had me. I'm so tired of overlooking the shit he has done to me. Baron, this is it. If this didn't happen to Franco, this wouldn't have happened to me. So it's about time the Gianelli clan took action against the Don and show him what Gianelli really means."

"Angela, please stay calm," replied Baron. There was nothing that Angela wanted to hear. She just closed her eyes. Baron told her he'd be back later to see her and Franco. He had to check on some unfinished business. All that was running through his mind was: was it their father or not?

As Baron went down the steps, he saw two men walking up to the floor Franco was on, and they didn't look as though they would be visitors.

One man was carrying a small bag, and the other was looking down the steps at periodic intervals. Baron leaned to the side to make sure they wouldn't be able to see him. He walked several steps behind them and when they got to the area where Franco's room was. Baron knew there would be no one from this area that would have known that Franco was in the hospital, except the people who hit him in the first place. Franco had no family or friends here in the states, or so he thought. One guy went into the room while the other one stood outside the door. Baron realized that there was something wrong and yelled to the man, "What's going on?"

The man looked at him and realized that he was the Don's son. The man tried to open the door to warn the other man who was putting an air bubble into Franco's IV tube, but Baron cut him off and clipped him. When the man who was inside saw his friend get hit, he ran over to help the one in trouble. They all began fighting, and one man pulled out a gun and shot at Baron.

One of them said to the other, "What, are you crazy? Don't you know who he is?" They somehow managed to smash Baron on the back of his head with the butt of the gun and then ran. One of them shot at the security officers as they came upon them. The other one yelled out, "Cool out with the shooting, man. There's oxygen in here. Do you want to blow us all up?"

When the police arrived, Baron was getting his head wrapped. They were trying to get some answers from him. But the doctor attending him insisted that they leave Mr. Gianelli alone. With all of that commotion, he knew that his father was involved. He had that gut feeling.

Baron told his doctor, "Look, I have to get out of here. Could you make sure my sister, Angelica Delucco, doesn't find out about it?"

But as in any other place, hospital gossip travels, and it reached Angela's floor already and she was making her way downstairs to see about her husband and brother. By the time she got down, Baron had already left. He was on his way over to Nunzio's office, and he was hot.

When Baron reached the office, he was greeted by his father's personal right-hand man, John. He was shocked to see Baron bloodied and his head bandaged.

"What the hell happened to you, Baron? Who did this to you? When the don sees this, all hell is going to break loose. Talk to me, who did this?" Baron didn't say a word. He just went straight to his father's office and pushed the door open. When Nunzio turned and saw Baron, he held out his arms and smiled until he noticed that Baron was hurt. At that note, Baron punched Nunzio so hard that he fell straight on his back and began bleeding from the mouth.

Nunzio's men went to step in, but he told them to stay out of it. He smiled, and much to Baron's surprise he backhanded Baron so hard his face looked as though it was wiped off.

"Now is that the way we greet our father?" replied Nunzio. Baron went to strike his father a second blow, when one of Nunzio's goons reached out and grabbed his arm.

"You fucking murderer!" Baron screamed. "You killed your own grandchild. When are you going to learn that everything can't be the way you want it? Damn, you let her live her own life," said Baron.

"Calm down, get your senses straight. What the hell are you talking about? Okay, one thing first. You come in here, hit me, and then you're screaming 'I'm a murderer.' Baron, since your prize piece left you, you've begun to lose it," replied Nunzio.

"Leave Egypt out of this because if I find out that you had anything to do with that, I'll be your worst enemy. Damn you, your daughter had been married to Franco for a while now, and Mother and I knew. But who can tell you anything for fear you would have done something stupid. Angelica was pregnant, Father," said Baron.

"Angelica, my baby?" said a shocked Nunzio.

"Yes, your baby. She was pregnant, and when she heard that her husband, Franco—Father, do you get it? Franco Delucco is her husband, your son-in-law. When she heard he was shot, she got all upset, Father, and I was there, Father, to watch her lose your grandchild."

"Shut up, get out, Baron! Just get the hell out!" Nunzio shouted in a roar.

"What, Father, too much for the don to handle? He fucked up and killed his grandchild. Oh, I know that you won't admit it. You can lie to all of us, but you're the one who's gonna have to live with it. You, the Don, killed his grandchild that you so much wanted."

With that, Baron gathered himself, walked out his father's office, and slammed the door behind him. Nunzio told everyone to leave his office, walked over to his bar, and fixed himself a drink. He sat down, drank the whole glass in one shot, placed his hand on his forehead, and closed his eyes.

Later, he informed his secretary to send flowers to his daughter at the hospital and to her home also. Mr. Gianelli turned his chair to the window and glared out over the city.

Meanwhile, Baron went to his mother's house and told her of the entire ordeal. She was quite upset and went straight to the hospital to see Angela. By the time she arrived, Angela and Franco had talked over everything. Franco was furious at Nunzio. He knew that their families didn't get along, but since their marriage, his family had forgotten everything that took place years before. He couldn't understand why they never could tell Nunzio of their union. "Now that your grandchild is dead," he told Marguerite, "when I get well enough, me and my wife are going back to Sicily, but you had better say good-bye to her first. You know I've been a fair man with Angela always, but now I'm forbidding her to return to the states. If anyone chooses to see her, they will have to come to Sicily."

Franco was holding Angela's hand, and she let go in surprise. He looked at her and said, "If you choose not to go, you can stay, but I'm not staying before what took so long to burn stirs up again."

"Franco, I love my mother, but to say I can no longer come home to see them, that's too much. Mother has nothing to do with what has happened," said Angela.

"Angelica, what makes you think I can live near the man who tried to have me killed and not retaliate? I want to kill that man. I don't care that he's your father. He doesn't care about your feelings. Doesn't he realize you love me! Or must I swallow my pride always? No, I am a Delucco. My name holds much power! Must I remind you, Angela? It was I who kept them from killing your father in Sicily. Why? For you, because I love you. I let you leave to come home to explain our marriage. Then my mother told me of your pregnancy, and I came after you. Why? That was my child, Angela, my child. Do you understand this? Don't expect the Deluccos to take this lightly. My father will want blood for blood. The decision is yours—to stay or leave with me when I'm well enough to travel. I will not speak on this again," said Franco with pain and anger in his voice.

"Franco, I will return with you to Italy as soon as I help Baron find Egypt," said Angela.

Franco agreed that they both will help Baron. Little did they realize much trouble will lie ahead of them.

Nunzio had already placed many deterrents in Egypt's way to keep her chasing her dream. He wasn't going to make it easy for them to get together again. Nunzio wanted Egypt and knew if he put some trouble in their way, there would be no turning back for them.

When Baron finally got himself together, he took care of all his messages except for one. He continued to look at the name of Fatima on the page. He called his office, and the secretary told him that she was trying to tell him that this young lady called about Egypt. Baron yelled at her, but she reminded him, "At the time, you didn't want this message, remember?" He recalled the conversation, and she added, "She didn't leave a number where she could be reached. She just made an appointment to see you, and she said if you didn't show up you wouldn't get in touch with her no time soon."

Baron replied, "Where and when is this appointment?" She answered, "Well, sir, you only have twenty-five minutes to reach there. You have to meet her at the corner of Astor Place and Broadway. She said she'd be wearing a green jacket and a very short green skirt with black bike shorts underneath, and she'd be carrying a black attaché case. Not to worry, she knows what you look like."

Baron hung up the phone and hailed a taxicab. He was so confused and upset that he forgot that he was parked straight up the street. When he jumped into the cab and told the cabbie where to go, he noticed that he had passed his car. Baron yelled at the cabbie to pull over, threw a twenty at him, and ran back to his car. He jumped in and headed straight for his destination.

By the time he arrived, he was several minutes late. He stepped out of his car and looked around, and she was nowhere in sight. As he was ready to step back into his car, a young lady of the evening approached him. "If your girl doesn't show up, I could give you a good time." He just looked at her and got into his car. As he was preparing to pull off, he saw a woman that fit the description his secretary gave him. He jumped out of his car only to run through traffic and nearly get hit, running through crowds, pushing and shoving people out of his way. When he looked again, she was heading down the subway stairs. He followed her down and leapt over the turnstiles to see the train pulling away. He walked back through the doors and saw the token booth clerk asking, "What's your problem?"

Baron walked back to his car and opened the door to get in, but someone's arm prevented his doing so. It was her.

"How did you do that?" asked Baron.

"Do what?" she asked with a smile on her face.

"Now, tell me, how much you want for the information, and I'll give it to you," replied Baron.

"Well, I don't think you have as much as I would want. Forget it, Mr. Gianelli, but what you do have is connections, and this is what I want from you," said Fatima as she handed him an envelope. "Read it and reply within three weeks. You can reach me by just calling 555-9099. An answering machine will give me your message and then I'll get in touch with you. Don't worry, I brought you proof that I know where she is." Then she gave him a picture of him and Egypt together. She had taken it while in Egypt's apartment.

Before Baron could ask her anymore questions, she stepped away and disappeared in the crowd and was gone.

Now the ball was in his court. He wasn't quite sure what he should do. Egypt left him; the game is hers. He wasn't positive if he showed up she would want him anyway. She made the rules, and he always broke them. He wasn't able to come to terms with this one. When they were together, she was happy, or so he thought. But when they were among other people, she didn't show the same emotions.

When he returned home, all he could do was go to his bed and lie down. When he took a deep breath, he smelled a sweet aroma. He turned his head to see Tash, a beautiful brown-skinned woman with jet-black hair and deep brown eyes. She was a beautiful black woman.

She gave Baron a drink and sat next to him on his bed. "How in the hell did you get in here, Tash? I thought you would have been married by now, or did everything I warned you about blow up in your face as I said it would?" said Baron.

She placed her drink down and reached over to Baron stroking his face and hair. "Didn't you miss me, baby, just a little? Think about all the good times we shared together." She attempted to seduce him, but he was on to her. Tash leaned toward him and kissed him passionately. He grabbed her by her hair creating pain for her. He lay on top of her kissing her until she hurt. She placed her long nails onto his back and scratched him slowly. This sent a chill up his spine. He ripped off her negligee to get at her breasts. He devoured them, and Tash began to speak sexually to him. He grabbed her and threw her onto the floor.

"What the hell is up with you? Is this the way you and your 'dream love' Egypt made love?" she asked.

Baron looked down at her to say, "Tash, what made you think I would ever touch you again? I can forgive almost anything a woman could do to me except what you did. Tash, you said you got rid of our child after saying we would have it. Then you turn my life around and throw nothing but disorder into it. Do you think I could forget that you said you were pregnant to take me away from Egypt? When I refused to stop seeing Egypt you, said you'll have the child and never let me see it. Then when you saw that nothing you could say or do to me would make me leave her, damn you, you took revenge by saying you had an abortion and asking me how the death of my child feels. Get the fuck away from me, Tash. A little news for you, darling. Not that I was cold or gave a damn, but I later found out that you were never pregnant in the first place. That's why you were so eager to sleep with me then. Hoping you could get pregnant. This is not the time to play games with me. I don't believe in hitting a woman, but I sure as hell want to knock the shit out of you! I'm in no mood for your games. Why are you here anyway?"

"Baron, you could never realize that I loved you. You gave me what no one else ever did. A chance. And I left you and didn't expect you to find someone else. So when I came back only to find out that you did, I didn't want to lose you. I know it sounds strange that I left you and became upset because you were with someone else. Baron, I didn't want to lose you. Do you understand that's why I did that?" said Tash.

Tash broke down into tears. She reached out to Baron for comfort, but he turned away. He looked at her and started to walk away from her.

"Why are you walking away from me, Baron? Can't you see that I'm sorry? I didn't mean to hurt you so," she replied.

"Oh yeah, for the record, Tash, does my father have a larger one, or was it his experience which kept you returning to his bed? Oh, fair warning, don't deny it. Better than that—come with me."

He walked over to his desk and unlocked one of the drawers. "Here is something you might want to see." He handed her a large manila envelope, which she opened. She glanced at its contents and began to cry.

"Why are you crying, dear?" he said sarcastically. "Did he catch your bad side? From what I gathered by these and more at different locations, you were enjoying yourself. You were no different than the others in my life. Father got to them one way or another, except for Egypt. Look, put on your clothes and leave me alone."

All Tash could do was gather her clothes and go into the bathroom to dress. Tash was so thrown apart she could only get herself together to go. When she was ready to leave, she walked over to Baron and went to say something, but tears just came to her eyes.

"Baron, be happy," she said and left. "Baron, you idiot!" he yelled at himself. He was upset because he felt bad about what he had said even though he knew he wanted nothing to do with her. He was so confused and hurting.

He walked over to the mantel and placed the picture that Fatima gave him on it. He finally opened the letter that she handed him at their meeting. He read what was inside. It stated that she wanted to be named one of their corporate attorneys for Egyptian Labels.

He knew he had no control over that. That would have to be in the hands of Mr. Stout himself. He knew Mr. Stout was not fond of female attorneys. This task sounded simple but was very difficult in deed. He had no idea of how he was going to do that. He still wasn't sure if he should look for Egypt or should he just wait for her return. He remembered what his mother said—to give her time, but he so wanted to see her. Throughout all of the things that happened in the course of one day, he needed to just rest and try to think of other things.

The phone began ringing, and Baron wasn't going to answer it, and when he finally did, a familiar voice said, "Baron?" He answered, "Yes?" But there was no answer.

He replied, "Egypt, is that you? Speak to me!" He heard the phone go dead and then slammed it down on the receiver. Again it rang. He lifted the phone quickly and said, "Egypt?"

"No, darling, it's just your mother. I'm calling to see how you're feeling. I heard what happened, and I'm so sorry. Your father said he had nothing to do with Angela losing her baby."

"Mother, do you really believe him? And forget it, Mom, I'm too tired to go through it again, I just want to go to sleep. Mom, look at the time. Why are you up so late?" asked Baron.

"I've been trying to call all evening to let you know that Franco said that Angela would no longer be able to come back here again, not even to visit. But they're staying long enough to help you find Egypt."

Baron stayed quiet for a moment and said, "Mother, don't expect me to tell them to stay because I know that Nunzio—"

"Your father, Baron, your father," replied his mother.

"Your husband, Mother, I knew he had something to do with it, and I won't rest with that. You know he almost got me killed today in the hospital?" Baron said angrily.

"Your father loves you dearly. He wouldn't have anyone hurt you or your sister," she said.

"I never said he didn't love us. It's just that his ways of ruling our lives end up hurting us and putting our lives in danger. Like tonight he thought getting rid of Franco would solve the problem. No, Mother, it doesn't work like that. It just became a bigger one. Now through this he has lost his daughter and grandchild. Is it going to end, or is he going to kill all of us that don't follow his rules? Or have you forgotten Elaine, Mother . . .

"I'm tired, and I don't want to talk anymore. Mother, I love you, but he is your husband by choice. He is only my father by force. I had no ruling in that matter. Good night, Mother," he said and hung up the phone, finished his drink, and threw the glass against the wall.

Chapter 4

Egypt gets all her mail at her neighborhood pizzeria. Considering Jack, the regular mailman who can't see too well, and even though he messes up a lot of the mail, the people on his route don't seem to mind too much. They all know he'll be retiring in a month or so.

Egypt ran down the stairs and found her mail in the mailbox correctly. She was certainly surprised. There was a tap on her shoulder, and she turned around and smiled. There standing before her was Gary.

"You disappeared on me for a few days. I haven't heard from you, and I got worried. I even left messages on your answering machine. Why didn't you call me back?"

"Can you ever understand me? I'm like the wind."

"Yeah, Egypt, and you're the night. But I never disappear. How many years have we known each other? A long time, right? You don't see me disappearing in your hour of need," he said.

She grabbed him and hugged him tightly. Gary was a masculine, well-built man, about six feet tall, and has rugged good looks. His hair was black, and he had the most scrumptious green eyes you ever saw on a brown-skinned black man. His eyes are dreamy; they beckon one and make a woman's knees weak, and the only vocabulary you have for his is "yes, yes, yes . . ."

Gary felt for Egypt, but he kept it well hidden. So long as they were friends he was happy with that. He was from her old neighborhood, but nothing came of their relationship, except just warm, close friendship.

Gary's family wasn't too fond back then about a black man being with a Puerto Rican girl. They would always tease him about Egypt and her brothers and would tell Gary not to let them get too close to their car.

"Do you remember the jokes about your brothers and the cars back in the days?" asked Gary.

"Yeah, Gary, I remember. Let them spics close enough to your car and all that's left is the key in your hand," replied Egypt. They both laughed.

They left the pizzeria and walked down the avenue to the bank. Gary walked in to use the automatic teller machine, came out, and moved his eyebrows.

"So is it off to a motel or lunch? Wait! Don't say anything I'm getting a psychic picture." He moved his hands to his head. "Oh yeah, soft lights and wine—very good. Oh, mirrors all around. Oh, and I see you standing there looking radiant. Then you walk toward me and begin to undo your hair and take off your shirt. Oh, and you're thinking—you—oh, Egypt! Those thoughts are too much for my delicate ears. Okay, it's off to the motel!" said Gary and he laughed.

Egypt reached out and punched Gary in the chest and laughed. She grabbed his arm and in a sexy voice said, "I guess we're off to have some hot, juicy, tender, raw, succulent beef. So which way to the steak house I'm starving, it sounds good to me."

Gary's face fell. "You got me that time. I was all ready and dreaming, lady. You're too much for me. So how about going to Tony Roma's at the corner? Their food is workin'."

As the two of them walked over there, Egypt bought a copy of the Enquirer but didn't really glance at it. They were so busy laughing and giggling like they were back in school.

When they got to the restaurant, Gary asked the waiter for a nice spot so they could look out the window.

Egypt ordered their food and were served within minutes. Gary kept staring at her until she finally spoke.

"Gary, is there something wrong? Is my food hanging off my teeth or something?" asked Egypt.

"No, I just want my question answered."

"What? What?" she asked impatiently.

"So anyway, what brings you back here?" asked Gary.

"What? Is there something wrong with me moving back over here? You forgot I was only subleasing the place. I felt like living in it again," she said.

"Okay, but what about Mr. Perfect himself? Is there something wrong in paradise?" asked Gary.

"Nothing is wrong. Why does there always have to be something wrong just because I want to spend a little time by myself? I can't understand why I can't just up and walk away from everything I had and just start over again. Because I had everything anyone would have killed for and just left it, nothing has to be wrong."

"Listen to what you just said, stupid, and for just one minute be me or just be real and answer that question for me. Okay, Egypt, you're not talking to a wall here. Somewhere in the depths of my head lies a brain. And upon occasion I tend to use it, from time to time that is," he said sarcastically. "If you don't want to talk about it just say so. Don't insult my intelligence. I've known you too long. At such a young age you've accomplished so much—a company to help people reach their dreams, and you just up and walk away and that's that? You don't have to be Einstein to figure it out, so just tell me it's none of my business and I'll drop the whole conversation until you want to talk about it. So what are you gonna do? So what are you going to do?" asked Gary.

"Okay, I'll tell you. First, I want it to stay between us. It's truly hard on me, but you're a real close friend. Well, Gary, it's like this: Mind your own fucking business, just from one friend to another," replied Egypt with a grin.

"Well, I guess I asked for that one, huh, didn't I? You're still a smart ass now, aren't you? So I think you're not going to tell me the truth, so I'll put you under the lights and make you sweat it out. I'll force the truth out of you on way or another. We have our ways, Fraulein. Ha-ha-ha," he said menacingly.

"So what am I going to have to do to get the answer to my question? Okay, I didn't wanna know why you came back anyway. I truly don't care. If you wanna keep it to yourself, I'll respect your decision. Who am I to sit here and try to make you talk about something you're obviously not ready to deal with? Even though it's best to reveal our frustrations in order to cope with our lives, and if you don't care to help yourself handle your problems, what can I do?" He felt as if he was talking to himself.

"Well, say something. Just don't sit there and keep eating, you're hiding behind your food—look at yourself. Twenty days down the line you'll gain weight, okay maybe thirteen ounces or a pound possibly. It doesn't affect me if you just ignore me. So?" said Gary dying to know her reason. "So are you through? For someone who really doesn't give a shit, your mouth continued to talk for ten or fifteen minutes."

"Well?" asked Gary.

Egypt continued eating and acting as natural as she could. She wanted to tell him, but it just wasn't the time. She felt it best to keep this to herself, with so much she had been through with Demetri and seeing him like that with Fatima and all.

She thought about Fatima and what became of her. "Well," she figured, "since I don't know how to get in touch with her, if she needs me, she'll call."

As she picked up the paper she bought, the headline caught her attention. It read:

WHERE HAS THE "BARON'S" LOVE GONE?

She wished that those junk magazines would just let it lay, but she knew better. She knew that she couldn't really walk the streets much, that's why she enjoyed her job with Dr. Kamekano. She had returned there sometime after her breakup with Baron. She had something special with her boss. She worked well at her job and was very important to him.

Gary was still running his mouth trying to pick up one of the waitresses. He got up and told Egypt he had to make a phone call and that he would be back momentarily. She stood up, and when he walked away, he said, "You are a perfect gentle lady," and laughed.

When he got to the phones, he called one of the junk publications managing editors and told her that he had seen Baron's missing partner. He gave her the location. When he returned to the table, she was ready to go. Gary was trying to make excuses not to leave, so he ordered some drinks in order to make a toast. When they received drinks, he spotted photographers and sat closer to Egypt to make it look as if their lunch was more than what it was. But as they began to toast she noticed someone looking really hard in the window. She glanced out and saw a man with a camera whom she noticed to be familiar to her. When the thought hit her, she grabbed the paper and covered herself, but the flashes started to go off.

How in the hell did they find me? she thought to herself. "Gary, help get me out of here. All I need is to start some sort of scandal for the company, and I don't want Baron to think I was out manhunting, and I sure don't even want him to think I'm out seeing someone. Especially since I haven't read or heard of him out with anyone either. All these stupid junk papers portray him as the 'lonely, lost, brokenhearted man left high and dry.'" She knew that was somewhat true. *But,* she thought, *that's the only way I could leave him. Just 1, 2, 3 out.*

Gary helped her out of the restaurant, and she was lucky enough that the photographer caught only a few bad shots of her. She could only wonder what they were going to write about her and Gary. She could bet it would be a good one since she had hid from them all too well.

Gary was disappointed that they didn't get caught. He was definitely up to something. He just wasn't letting Egypt in on it. He hoped to gain something out of this. Not money, just something he wanted from her, and he's been wanting it for a long time.

When they had returned to her apartment, Gary acted so surprised to see those photographers showing up. "Well, in some ways," he thought, "I wasn't expecting a photo session."

"Gary, I hate things like that. I've been trying to avoid situations like that. More shit just keeps happening to me. I must have been a real bitch in another life, and I'm paying for it now. I can imagine what the tabloids are going to say tomorrow morning. Baron, damn he'll get a hold of the news, and it won't look good for Egyptian Labels, you know, with me not being there and all, it'll look terrible. I put too much of me in that business just to start letting these shit magazines destroy the good standings of my company. I'll figure something out, Gary. And you know, I wonder who tipped them off anyway. Well, one thing at a time. I'll call my girl at the company, and she'll put her ear to the ground and find out what I need to know. At least I have a few people in there that will keep an eye out for me. Right, Gary? Gary? Gary? Call on, Gary, come in, Gary. Where the hell are you? What, have I been talking to space again?" asked Egypt.

"I'm sorry, babe, I've been trying to figure out who noticed us there. I didn't notice anything funny. Maybe someone spotted us from outside. See, we shouldn't have sat by the window and anyway you very seldom sit next to one," said Gary.

While Gary was trying to figure out a way of getting her back into the public's eye again so Baron would think she was happy without him, he thought, *I've got to be careful because Egypt will turn so quickly and completely and hate my guts forever more than she would rebel.* He knew that she would see blood, so he had to try to put things in the right place.

Egypt, on the other hand, wasn't thinking about anything more than just her and Gary being good friends. Whatever could have been never happened, and that was behind them now anyway. She had to get together with her career. Between the office work and maybe going back to do what she did best was going to be a tough choice. She knew her talents varied. Between medicine that she didn't finish and her singing that she didn't finish either, she just thought about how she wanted to be left alone.

Some really strong realistic thoughts began eating at her, so she asked Gary to leave. He went to kiss her good-bye, but she turned her head quickly and ended up on her cheek. She asked him what he was doing for dinner tomorrow, and he smiled and said invitingly, "I'll supply the drinks and the desert, you know what I mean?" Egypt laughed, and they agreed on the time and he left. She had to get a lot of things ready for tomorrow. She noticed that everything from her past was all in front of her face now. *Somehow,* she thought, *if you don't clean out your closet, sooner or later, the piled-up junk will land in your lap.*

She had to get it through her head that Chai was very much in love with her, and she at one time loved him. But what she had with Baron, no one could ever compare it. She felt like she could scream and break a few things, "But what will that solve? Just a mess on the floor and a worse headache than the one I have hanging over my head now." She started to put the apartment in order and give her brother a call.

When she phoned the house, Egypt's father answered the phone, and they spoke for a while until she heard her mother's voice in the background. It hurt her so much but she was bullheaded, and when it came to her pride, it was too much for her to swallow. She told her father, "There is so much pain in my heart. I don't want you to worry too much you know I'll heal like I always do. I just need some time to let things settle down."

"I'm glad to hear that. You know, since that confrontation there has been no peace in this house? Me and your mother aren't really talking to each other. But Jose is doing well."

Egypt had talked Jose into going back to college. She was so glad of that, and she reminded her father, "Poppy, don't forget not to tell Momita that I'm paying for Jose's tuition and books. If he thinks he could be a good doctor, I should at least support him. He may or may not do it, but he deserves every chance. It's better than being on a corner, and besides he passed high school, maybe not all that well, but with hard work, anyone who wants to can become anything they want."

Her father laughed. "My words exactly. Egypt, your mother really does love you. It's just that it hurts to feel like your child is ashamed of you. She'll leave it behind her if you just give it some time. Lord knows best, and he says to forgive."

Those words touched her, and tears began to well in her eyes. She quickly asked, "How's Dionisia?"

"She moved out of New York sometime ago." He knew he had told her before, but he realized she was grasping for straws because she was crying. Softly he told her, "Dioni and her husband will raise their children the right way."

Jose walked in, and her father handed him the phone. He spoke of Gina and her doings, and while they were on the phone, their mother kept asking, "Jose, who's that you're talking to?" And he would reply, "No one you would know, okay?"

Egypt told him of the things going on with her and Chai. He remembered Chai and expressed how much he likes him. He asked, "What did Poppy say about that?"

"Well, he's happy for me, and besides, he trusts Chai. Jose, how come you stopped going to his office?"

"Because of the way you left him—the way you just flat left him hanging." She couldn't argue with that.

"Egypt, I have to go study. This is nothing like high school, and I don't want to waste your money and the tuition and expenses are so high. You know, some of the professors remembered you, and I have your old chemistry teacher?" They both laughed.

"Jose, I have to go too and get things ready for tomorrow and buy some stuff for mine and Gary's dinner." He laughed and said, "You better watch out. Gary may be on the move." She laughed and told herself, "That's absurd, not Gary . . ."

The next morning when she reached the office, there was something different she noticed. For some reason she didn't want to go inside. She was getting bored because the job wasn't really what she wanted to do with her life. She didn't have anyone, and most of all she was always missing Baron. She had to do something really soon about this, but the question really was what was she going to do about Chai? She noticed that for the past few weeks they had started to begin to get close, and she wasn't sure where this was leading.

"Yes, Egypt, we were watching you for sometime wondering if you were going to come in or remain out there. So get ready. Today we work on overload. We're booked solid through the evening, so when it's time for you to take lunch, let me know so we can go together," said Dr. Kamekano.

"That's okay, Doctor. I really don't mind staying in for lunch if it's going to be busy. It's best that we stay in, don't you think? Remember, if I'm not mistaken, that Mr. Ditmic is under close observation. And remember at anytime he'll need surgery. Did his family sign the papers for the operation? Well, there are so many reasons not to go out," said Egypt.

"So why don't you tell me the most important reason?"

"What?" asked Egypt confused. She knew why she really didn't want to go out with him. *He couldn't possibly know,* she thought.

"Why don't you know, Egypt?" He seemed to be knowing her thoughts. "You've given everyone but the most important one of them all. Well, just say you don't want to go, Egypt. You shouldn't make any excuses. We've been around each other too long to even consider playing games. So what's it going to be, lunch or not?" asked Dr. Kamekano.

The phones began ringing, and the secretary called Egypt. It was a patient that wanted to speak to her. She moved her eyebrows up as if in surprise and walked to answer the call. Chai smiled.

The day passed quickly, and when Egypt looked up to see the time, Dr. Kamekano was staring at her. He reached out his arm to her. What could she do but accept his invitation and smile.

"Shall we go?" he asked. He took her hand and wrapped it around his, and they left the office. Egypt was wondering, *Why the interest?*

They went to a very posh and expensive restaurant located on Park Avenue. When they stepped in, she felt a cold chill run down her spine; it was the way Dr. Kamekano was handling her as though there was some interest on his part. He never acted like this before with her.

He noticed that she appeared uncomfortable, so he slowed down a bit to throw her off. But she kept her guards up and kept a look out for every move. She thought, *It's tempting. He has such a beautiful oriental body, and he is intelligent and I once loved him dearly.*

"Egypt, what's on your mind? You're watching my every move. You're not enjoying this, are you? But looking at you sets the afternoon off."

Lunch passed without incident, and when they were done eating, they went back to the office to finish with the rest of the patients. Dr. Kamekano left and asked Egypt to lock up with Dr. Lee, an elderly physician. When they were done, they locked up, and she hailed a cab to her loft in the village.

When she arrived home, there wasn't much to do except put the meat she bought earlier into the oven. She jumped into the shower and was out in a flash. As she dressed, the bell rang, and she ran to the door half-dressed.

She got to the door, and Gary stood there with a bag in his hand and his mouth open. She pulled him in and slammed the door and went to finish dressing.

"Well, do you always greet people at the door that way? If you do, then I'll come over more often. So let's try it again. I'll leave and you answer," he said with a grin.

"Would you come in, fool? You're too much," she replied.

As he walked around the loft in amazement with the different cultures that decorated it, he stepped back, and the stairs leading up to her bed caught his attention. He so wanted to sample the taste of her. As chances would have it though, in her eyes he's just an old friend from her school days. He was once interesting to her like a new doll to a child that never got broken in because something better came along.

Egypt, he remembered, was fickle with everything. He noticed that she changed a few things around. He reached out for a strangely shaped bit of glass. As he put one in the light, it sparkled like a prism. It was fascinating to him.

While he was captivated by the glass, Egypt put on some soft music which made the loft more inviting. Before he could put the glass down, she took it from him. She held it as if it were a newborn baby. Gently, she placed it down. Gary wondered why the possessiveness of the trinket.

Suddenly, the atmosphere of the loft changed. She became subdued and even with the music; there was a silence in the air he couldn't fathom. She walked over to a chair which was oddly shaped with one long leg. She turned on the lamp next to it on the table, and as it lit the wall behind, there displayed on the wall was a brilliant and most striking painting. It was the plans for the front of the Egyptian Labels Building. She had it done so she could always have her dream next to her.

"It looks like the company building, doesn't it? Well, I described it to the architect with Baron, and he designed it just the way I wanted. I was in tears when we first started. Things went well, but after a while, there were so many limits; and because we were large in size but not in pocket, with much thought and deliberation, we knew we would have to merge with another company or go under. The problem for Baron and I was to find a company that would just be a silent partner and allow us to run the company as we had been and, most of all, not change the name," said Egypt.

"You know, to have so much and walk away from it, you're either crazy or there's some sort of problem at home. Which is it? Can I guess?" he asked.

"No, I'd rather go and—do you smell that?" She sniffed. "That's my dinner! Oh, damn it, I hope I didn't burn the rice and beans. I remembered how much you liked it. You always begged for it at my mothers. I haven't made that in such a long time. Matter of fact, I really haven't cooked like this since E-Labels started moving fast. I didn't have the time so Baron had housekeepers and cooks anyway, so I went with the flow. I would cook once in a while," she said from the kitchen.

"Oh god, are you trying to poison me?"

"Oh, it's okay, stupid, we're safe. I just have to add a little ah . . ."

When she looked around her, Gary was leaning over her shoulder. He was so close she felt everything that made him different from her. He smelled the aroma of the food, and he slowly sniffed her neck. This sent chills down her spine. It had been sometime for her. *This is an old friend, that's all,* she told herself, *and this is only an innocent dinner date between two very old and dear friends.*

So why am I getting aroused by his touch? she continued asking herself. Gary was striking in every way. His hair very suave, and his clothing very Greenwich Village with a pinch of GQ. She stepped to the side because she was losing it. She so hoped it wasn't going to be one of those evenings. Chase and run. *No,* she thought. *He's not doing it intentionally. Maybe it's just desires getting the best of an innocent suggestion.*

She placed the food in the platters and went into the dining area.

Gary stood next to the refrigerator watching her. When she gazed over at him, he smiled. She said to herself, *Oh no, not one of those evenings, I'm not in the mood for it. What can I do to change things?*

When she served the food, Gary went to open the wine and pour it into the glasses on the table. Egypt knew she had to move quickly, but no ideas came to her. He walked up behind her and called her name softly. She turned so fast because the voice sounded so close into his arms. In the same movement, she pushed him away. She became on edge; she didn't want to hurt his feelings by coming right out and turning him away, so she had to do something and fast.

She grabbed her back and leaned forward. Gary grabbed her and asked, "Are you all right?"

"Yes, I'm okay, just womanly pains."

"Oh. Do you want any Midols?" he asked hoping she said no.

"Don't worry. I already took one, and it should be working soon."

"Do you want a glass of wine then?"

"No, because since I took the medicine, it wouldn't be wise to mix alcohol with it. You never can tell what'll happen."

"Yeah, you're right," said Gary, and they sat down to eat. She smiled in relief that the chase was detoured for now.

When dinner was through, they went into the sitting room to watch television. Gary turned on the TV, and Egypt went to sit down. She sat on his jacket which was hanging over the couch and jumped up and said, "Damn! That scared the hell out of me."

She placed the jacket onto another chair, and they began talking about the good old days of the Bronx. She said to him, "There are times that I'd rather leave behind me though." Gary suddenly jumped up, startling her, grabbed her hand, and suggested, "Let's go for a walk in the moonlit night."

"That would be a perfect topper for a good evening," she replied.

She put on her jacket, and they went walking down Sixth Avenue. They looked in the closed shop windows, and when they reached McDonald's, there were some artists on the corner sketching people. Gary asked Egypt, "Would you like one of them to sketch you?" She said, "Yeah, that would be fun."

She sat there for fifteen minutes letting the artist draw her face. When he finished, there was a crowd of people around her. Someone asked her if she would be interested in modeling. She replied, "No thanks." When the artist was through, she got up, and Gary paid for the drawing and handed it to her. She said, "No, you keep it."

"I think it would be best if you kept it because you could hang it up and have a memory of our evening together."

They continued to walk down the path of the village, and they ran upon a basketball game in a small park. As Egypt watched the game, Gary placed his arm over her hip. As he moved his hand down to her rear end, she quickly moved it off.

"Don't even try it," she said.

"Sorry, it was worth a try. I wouldn't be a man if I didn't make a move on it. Anyway, I just wanted to see what your reaction would be. I wouldn't have done anything more."

"Yeah right, and I'm deaf, dumb, and blind and slightly off set."

"Okay, okay, I was wrong, man, trust me. I respect you, and that was a really dumb move on my part. Come on, you wanna head to my place?" She made a strange face. "So what's the problem with that, and why did you make those faces at me?" he asked.

On their way back to her place, she stopped by one of the women selling flowers to buy one to give to Chai in the morning. She explained to him that they had been going through some changes. But one thing she failed to notice was the change in Gary's expression as she talked about Chai and their relationship. She continued to talk of her job and what it was like working with him. And most of all she wasn't sure how she felt for Chai, but she knew that she was still in love with Baron. Gary was so upset that he didn't hear what she was saying. All he knew was that she and Chai were talking again. Somewhere in the conversation he had to come to terms with the fact that Chai and Egypt were together and that they were nothing but friends. He took a deep breath and kept talking to her as if they weren't ever interested in each other years ago. Most of all, he still held a torch for her.

Egypt noticed that somewhere in the conversation he was lost. She started laughing because he just stood there looking like "what did you say?" She pointed at her apartment, and he looked surprised that they arrived so fast. When she opened the door, he attempted to go in, but Egypt stopped him. She gave him a kiss on his forehead and closed the door.

She couldn't understand what she had that every man she met had to make it their personal duty to go after her. She jumped into the shower and heard the phone ring. By the time she got to it, it had stopped. She hoped it wasn't Chai. She remembered that she was supposed to call him, but with the dinner and the walk she took she forgot.

When she was preparing for bed, her doorbell rang. She answered it thinking it was Gary coming back to get his jacket that he left after they ate.

She said through the door, "I was wondering how long it would take you to realize you left your jacket here, Gary. Come on in the door is open."

"Can I still come in even though I'm not Gary?" asked Chai.

"Oh, I thought you were my friend Gary since he just left a while ago. Come on in, Dr. Kamekano," she said. "Thanks," he replied, "I would even enjoy it more if you would please call me Chai again."

"Okay, Chai. Why did you come by this evening?"

"Well, I'm not going to try and lie to you, Egypt. I did miss you, and it's been several years since I've seen you, and when my eyes gazed upon you, it enhanced everything I had been waiting for in our reunion. All of those emotions I had to put behind me. In that one glance, my heart was in rapture. It was like the feelings had never gone, just waiting for that right moment. We went places and enjoyed each other's company, and I would like to do so again, Egypt. When I think back then, everything was fine. A few months before you disappeared, we went to Tokyo and ventured to Hong Kong.

"I remembered our first evening in Japan. You were so amazed at seeing cars on the wrong side of the street. You gleamed like a child at Christmas."

"I remember, Chai. We sure went places. You showed me the Far East in its pristine state. The gardens were beautiful and unique. Nothing I could have imagined in a lifetime. Your family and friends were so attentive. I recall very well a small basement restaurant. Do you remember the name? Yes, you do. Remember it was decorated in grays and whites. Wasn't it Hirmatasu or something?"

"Close but no cigar it was Hiramastu. Yeah, you were in shock to have authentic French food in Japan. That was an experience."

"I'll never forget the times we spend together. So, kind sir, what's on your mind? I can tell by your expression that there's something weighing heavy on your shoulder."

"It's been a while for me as far as finding a young woman who's intelligent and beautiful and having the caring touch as you have."

He then opened a bottle of wine and asked her for some glasses. Egypt couldn't deny she was still attracted to Chai; she wasn't quite over him yet. It wasn't so simple to just walk away from him like she did Demetri; she had been involved with Chai for a very long time once.

"Egypt, at one time you could call me Chai, and now it seems like it's hard for you. I never made advances on you in a hard way. I always treated you like a lady at all times. I have much respect for you, and I wouldn't want to make you feel like you were being used. If my being here upsets you, I'll go. Just tell me," he said as he put down his glass.

"No, Chai, you don't upset me. I don't mind. So, Chai, you look great as usual. Did you know that you're so handsome?" she said.

Chai looked straight into her eyes and kissed her very gently as though he was afraid she would turn away. Much to his surprise Egypt was very receptive. He slowly removed the glass of wine from her hand and placed it on the table. He started kissing her neck, and she sighed softly.

Chai had such a gentle touch about him that she found irresistible. He unbuttoned her pajama blouse and kissed down her stomach. She gasped for air. He picked her up and took her into the bedroom.

"Before we go any further, do you want me to make love to you?" he asked.

Saying nothing, she nodded her head as they walked up to her bed. He laid her back gently on the bed, leaned over her, and cupped her breasts in his hands and began to feast on her womanly charms. She grabbed hold and became very familiar with him.

As they rolled around in the bed, electricity flowed through their bodies. Excitement, lust, and passion they both felt. Chai stopped to look down at Egypt and then kissed her passionately on her lips, and she kissed him back hard.

Chai led her up off the bed and to the bathroom where he drew a bubble bath. Before they got in, he brought back wine in glasses for them to drink. After they bathed each other, he began making love to her among the bubbles. She was so dazed by him, and she found she couldn't resist his touch. She smeared bubbles on him and laughed.

He looked at her and smiled. "I hope this doesn't have to end."

"Please, let's just enjoy the moment now and worry about everything else later," she whispered.

As he got out of the tub, she handed him the towel and walked out. When he left the bathroom, Egypt was nowhere in sight. Then he heard her voice coming from over his head. He looked up toward her bed, and there she lay in a beautiful negligee. He stared openmouthed at her and walked up the stairs to her. She could see all the definition of every muscle of his body. Chai was a very well-built man. She mentioned, "Clothes do you no justice. How did you get such a gorgeous body? Do you lift weights or something?"

He said, "I've practiced martial arts since I was a child and that's how I've acquired this 'gorgeous physique' as you keep calling it."

"You know, you remind me of Bruce Lee. Is there any relation?" she asked. He just laughed at her. He remembered her asking him that years ago. He just wanted to take her in a way that he had never taken any woman, in a way Egypt had never been taken. Just so he would always have this experience with her in his memories.

Chai slipped the negligee off her shoulders and nuzzled up to her breasts. He carefully laid her on her stomach and began kissing and massaging her back and buttocks. Chai embarked on Egypt like no man has ever done. She grasped the sheets on the bed and was pulling them off. A surge of pain entered her body from head to foot. Sensing this, Chai caressed certain areas of her body in order to relax her as he continued to indulge on Egypt's forbidden fruit. He moved gently within her, relaxing her as he did so. This was an area unfamiliar to her, yet he made it pleasurable. As she moaned in both pain and sensuality, she reached her peak of enjoyment, and he followed soon behind. As they clasped each other in a pool of sweat, he held Egypt close to him and whispered, "I'm not letting you go that easy this time, Egypt."

She couldn't reply; she was so worn out that all she could do was curl up and go to sleep. He covered her in the sheet, kissed her tenderly on the forehead, and quietly dressed. He wrote her a note and left it on the bathroom mirror, expressing his love and enjoyment of last night.

Several months had gone by, and Egypt and Dr. Kamekano have continued seeing each other on a regular basis. He was the first man, since Baron, that she felt this comfortable with. She knew that there would be no one who could take his place; she just wished that Baron would have looked at her as more than just sexual pleasure. Thinking of him, she cried in front of a patient. The patient handed her a tissue. Egypt smiled and thanked her.

She walked over to the phone to call Baron just to hear his voice. As she dialed, Chai walked up behind her and asked, "Have you gotten the results of Mrs. Anderson back yet?" She slammed the phone down, startled.

"What's wrong, Egypt?" he asked.

"Nothing, darling, nothing. You startled me. I was only going to make dinner reservations for us tonight," she lied. "Good idea. We're going to be very late here tonight, and hopefully Mr. Ditmic won't go into cardiac arrest because I would hate to go to the hospital for surgery as tired as I am now."

"If it's going to be too much for you, I'll make the reservation for another time. It's okay, you know I understand. I'll lock up for you tonight with Dr. Lee. Go home and get some rest. You look worn out," she said and kissed him on the neck.

He smiled, kissed her good-bye, and told her he'll call her later. The rest of the afternoon passed by uneventful, and she and Dr. Lee locked up the office. When Egypt got home, there was a woman waiting at her door, but her back was turned to Egypt. She didn't recognize the woman until she turned around.

"Fatima, what brings you out of the wood work? I haven't seen you in ages. Come on upstairs so we can catch up on each other." Egypt led the way up to her apartment.

"Did you pass the bar?" she asked.

"Yeah, I did, and it'll be a matter of time before I start working with a very reputable firm. Egypt, rumor has it that you're seeing your old flame, Chai, again. Is that true?"

"Yes, it's true. How did you know?"

"Well, I always keep my ear to the ground, and I find out things. Don't you think you're leading Chai on? I mean, you know that you'll eventually go back to Baron, so why do you even see Chai when you still feel the way you do about Baron?"

"What makes you think that I'm leading him on, and why would you bring up Baron? Chai makes me happy. Maybe I don't love him like I do Baron, and I know there will be no one like him. But I'm not going to keep hurting people. Fatima, I do want to go back, but look at all the things that have happened since. I thought I left to find myself, but I've found nothing but unhappiness until Chai came along. But even so, I'm still not doing what I want to do in life. I miss the excitement of lights and people and the music. I can't be running back and forth like that." Fatima gave her a strange look. "Stop looking at me like that," replied Egypt.

Fatima took a moment before she spoke. "Egypt, who am I to say anything about using people and denying emotions? I think you need to get yourself in order and go after what you really want and what gives you happiness. You know how I hate to see you like this. I know we haven't known each other that long, but I'm still a friend. Maybe it's none of my business to get into it with you, and I didn't come here to lecture you, okay?" She changed the subject. "I have some good news. Are you ready? Get this: I finally met someone, and he knows about my past and everything. He seems really nice too."

"So does he have a name, or do I have to guess?"

"Well, he is a bit of a square on the outside, but on the inside, behind closed doors, he gets loose, honey. His name is Chang Lee. He's Chinese and knows the martial arts and everything, and plus he's a science major. He's got an important family in Chinatown."

"He sounds like a really nice guy to me. So when do I get to meet him?"

"I know, why don't we go down there tonight?"

"Are you crazy?" said Egypt. "You should know how dangerous it gets down there at night. You're going mad, girl. So tell me more about the new love of your life, like does he have future intentions with you or what?"

"You're a nut, Egypt. I think it's too early for all that because we've only been together for a short time. What? Are you planning my wedding already? Come to think of it, I wouldn't mind marrying him. He gives me so much respect and treats me the way I should be treated," she said and spun around onto the couch.

"I was wondering when you would sit yourself down," said Egypt. "Do you think I will make a pretty bride? Or do I make a better hooker slash student?" she said in a painful voice.

"Fatima, why would you say that? Remember you had to go to college and that's all you could do to get you through your last semester, so stop torturing yourself."

"It hurts, Egypt, you don't understand. It hurts. He may know what I've done, but somewhere along the way, he'll throw it up in my face. You know the old saying, 'What you do in the dark comes out in the light,'" said Fatima.

"I understand. I have a lot of skeletons in my closet and even more now. I could never tell Chai that I still love Baron. I know it'll only hurt him, and I already did that to him once before. I don't want to make that a habit plus Chai has been the only one really helping me in sorting out my life. I also hurt the way you do inside, wondering if the past is going to slap me in the face. I don't think I could ever return to Baron as much as I've been with other men. I couldn't even let him know. I'd rather him remember me the way I was when I left him than now. I work hard to make ends meet plus he deposits my weekly check in my old account from Egyptian Labels. Baron still looks out for me, but by now, there must be someone in his life. You know he's good-looking, and he could have any girl he wants. And before me anyway there were others. They left him and hurt him too, but at least I explained my leaving him and didn't lie or take anything from him or had another man. I left to regain my identity, which I realize now that I never lost when I was with Baron. I used to be an important woman in a world that I so much wanted to be a part of. Well, that's enough thinking of depressing thoughts."

The phone rang, and when Egypt answered, it was Chai asking if she would come over. She explained, "Chai, I have company, and you know it would be rude to leave, especially since I haven't seen this particular friend in ages."

In the background Fatima was saying, "I'm about to leave anyway," prompting Egypt to go. She told Chai, "Okay, I'll be there soon," and hung up. When Egypt arrived at Chai's apartment, he was wearing an oriental robe. She entered and marveled at the splendor of the place and took off her shoes. He sat on the floor and reached out his hand to hers. "Egypt," he said, "I want you to meet my family." He pointed to an open door to her left, and she entered a bedroom. On the bed was the finest silk kimono she ever laid eyes on. She put it on and stepped out wearing it.

He stood up and smiled at her. He took her by the hand and led her through a hallway. She felt nervous and held his hand tightly. She tried to look in his face since he was ahead of her. She was out of his view. It was like he was pulling her along, and she never realized how strong he was until then. When they reached the end of the small corridor, a couple stood in the back room as if they were awaiting her arrival.

"Egypt, this is my father and my mother." Chai's father stepped forward to look at her, and their eyes met. She saw his mother bow slightly, so she gathered that she should do the same and bowed to his father. He returned her bow, and then his mother stepped forward and bowed to her and she returned her bow.

"My parents will only be here for a short while, and I wanted them to meet you and to be witness when I ask you to be my wife and bear my children."

Surprised, Egypt looked him in the eye and said, "Chai, I need some time to think it through." "Is there love in your heart for me?" he asked.

She knew that the only man she truly loved was Baron, but she didn't want to hurt Chai again, especially in front of his parents. She replied, "Yes, there is love in my heart for you, Chai, but I cannot honor you with a vow of marriage." She knew of Japanese customs from Chai and that tradition plays a large part of their lives. He smiled at her. He was pleased to see that she took an interest in his family customs.

As his father led the way to the table, he held her hand and smiled at her and motioned for her to sit on the floor. Chai's mother went into the kitchen and brought out cups and a vaselike jar. She poured out for everyone some strange liquid Egypt never had before. They all began to converse in Japanese, and Egypt thought to herself, *What have I gotten myself into now?*

Chai and his parents stood up, and when Egypt saw this, she rushed to get to her feet. Since she wasn't accustomed to the clothing Chai had given her to wear, she somewhat lost her balance.

Chai's father reached his arm to catch her before she fell and helped her to sit back down. Chai's father mentioned, "It's nice to see someone so interested in our native dress, I haven't seen people wear such things in a very long time. In Japan everything is so Americanized, and a lot of the traditional costumes aren't worn except for a special occasion."

Egypt replied, "Really? I would have thought that something as lovely as this robe, the women would be wearing a lot more often."

He continued, "The last time I wore an entire costume like this was when I married Chai's mother. The one thing that has never changed in Japan is the laws of marriage and family. It's a serious thing in Japan, nothing like in America where one day married and the next day it's dissolved. Marriage is still respected as it was before. Maybe not as harsh, but it is not easy to enter into marriage and then divorce."

When he finished his statements, Egypt felt a lump in her throat. Chai was smiling from ear to ear. He never thought that the day would come that he and Egypt would get back together. He thought he lost her forever.

He would be really surprised if he knew that Egypt was shitting bricks because she was not in love with Chai—not the way he should be loved. Egypt was caught in a corner she didn't know how to get out of. She knew she had to do some quick thinking or else.

Chai's mother was watching every move that Egypt was making. It was as if his mother was actually reading her body language. Egypt felt like she was sitting in the dock with the prosecutor staring at her trying to break the truth out of her. It was like they knew that she didn't love him enough to become his wife. A soft tender voice interrupted her thoughts and called, "Egypt?"

The lump in her throat fell to her feet. *Oh my god, she's gonna call me out,* she thought. She took a deep breath and listened. Much to her relief, his mother said, "Egypt, you have much beauty and grace. I can see why Chai was so taken with you." Egypt replied, "Thank you. You are a beautiful woman too, and I see the resemblance of you in Chai."

Chai's mother continued, "Chai told us of your intentions of becoming a physician's assistant but ended up furthering your interest in music instead. What happened with it?" she asked. She knew about the way things went for her and Chai's relationship. She didn't mention it for fear of upsetting her son.

Chai Kamekano respected his family even though he didn't allow anyone to inhibit him or become too involved in his personal affairs. He was every bit a mature man that Egypt could hope for, except for Baron.

After everyone had gotten to know each other a little better, Chai's father said, "Egypt, I'm sorry we have to leave you, but we haven't gotten used to the time difference and we should rest." They rose and bowed to each other and walked out to their room at the back of the apartment.

Chai and Egypt walked into the front room. He removed his outfit and reached out for Egypt, and she walked to him slowly. He removed her hairpin which held her hair up, and he laid her on the couch. He kissed her, and she pushed him away and asked him to stop. She was in fear that his parents would walk in suddenly and see them. He reassured her that they were in for the night.

"They know I'm not much for the traditions of the old ways, and we used to see each other before. They know we have a special relationship considering they noticed all the marks and scratches you left on my back. They asked me about it."

Egypt turned away from him. "Egypt, don't turn away from me," said Chai.

"Don't turn away from you, Dr. Kamekano? Why didn't you tell me?" she asked.

"Why are you calling me Dr. Kamekano? Egypt, if there's something wrong, tell me. And don't say you're scared or something. I'm feeling like something strange is going on, like there's a serious problem, and don't tell me it's because of the drink, that's not making me feel like this. Egypt, look at me!"

"Chai, please," she said desperately, "I'm so . . . I'm so . . . ," she said and fell into Chai's arms sobbing. "Chai, I need time. I do," she replied pleadingly.

He held her tight to his chest, and she looked at him and they kissed. He saw in fact that she did need some time to think things through. He went to call a taxi for her. "By the way, that outfit is yours to keep. You look beautiful in it, and if you want to go, Egypt, then you can go. I'll never hold you back. Listen, if you don't love me, Egypt, just tell me." He held her with such desperation as if to say, "Please say you do."

"I think it's best for me to be alone now. Oh, I don't know what I want," she said. She reached her hand out to Chai, and he placed it on his face. She kissed him; and he kissed her back passionately, grabbed her, and took her to his bedroom. Egypt was consumed with something different, but she surrendered all the same. Chai wanted so much for Egypt to be his; she wanted so much to tell him that this was not what she needed. She couldn't seem to do this because she hurt him terribly before. Four months after their split is when she met Baron.

Egypt dressed quickly because it was late, and she had to get home. She watched Chai sleeping so peaceful and thought, *This time I could leave a note on the pillow for him.* She hurried to leave while he was still asleep. Just before she could walk out the door, a soft voice spoke.

"Such a late hour is not the time for a pretty lady to be out unescorted. Why don't you wake Chai up so he can take you home? If we were not here, you would stay. We know you and Chai have been together. He talked of you so much a time ago. Egypt, may I speak with you for a moment?" she asked. "Come sit here."

Egypt walked over to the couch and sat down with the kimono across her lap and listened to Mrs. Kamekano. "Egypt, I know Chai loves you dearly, but in my heart, I feel that you don't love him the way he loves you." Egypt sat there feeling as if this woman could see right through her. She thought it best not to say anything just to listen. All she could do was wipe the tears off her face and tell her, "It's late and I should go. I have to open the office for Chai since he's got surgery in the morning." His mother walked her to the door, and Egypt left.

On the way home she couldn't help but cry like a baby. She wanted to go home so badly. Home back to Baron, and she knew she couldn't. When she got back to her loft, she checked her messages, and there was one from Gary. *He sounds like he needs to talk. Let me call this guy to see what's on his mind*, she thought. She rang him and he didn't answer, so she left her own message.

In the morning as she dressed, she noticed she had knots in her stomach. When she left, Gary was waiting for her on the doorstoop. "Where were you last night?" he asked.

"I went over to Chai's. I met his parents. They seemed like nice people. It was okay I guess. Anyway, where the hell were you last night? I called and got no answer. What's up?"

"Oh, it was nothing important." He felt this was not the time to tell Egypt how he really felt about her. "Hey, I'll walk you part way, all right?"

"Great, let's go." They walked for a couple of blocks, and when they got to the corner, Gary said, "Hey, babe, don't worry. Just relax and everything will be okay, and I'll be by in a couple of days to check on you. See ya!"

She turned the corner and headed for the office. She had her usual day at work—sick patients and the usual pain in the ass know-it-all ones too. As she got the office together and ready to close and she was returning the medications back to the cabinets, Chai walked up behind her and touched her. He had taken her by surprise, and without thinking, she took him by the arm and flipped him over her shoulder onto the floor. It was one of the many moves he taught her for self-defense.

"Egypt, I see you still remember the moves I taught you. Boy, you're good, I can say that. At least I can feel good that you're somewhat safe from attacks," Chai said and smiled. "Maybe I should start watching my back with you. Are you taking classes behind my back?" They both laughed.

"You shouldn't startle me like that. Anyway I wish I was as good as you are. I bet those secrets in the room you keep locked is that you're a ninja," she said.

"Oh, a ninja could never be known, just only to another ninja, dear lady. Now may I have the honor of taking you out tonight?" he asked.

"No, not tonight I'd like to be alone."

As she kissed him gently on his lips, he grabbed her by the arm as she stepped away. He asked her, "What was it that my mother said to you last night? Since then she's been acting very strange, even for her. Tell me, I know she talked to you but what about I don't know. She told me she talked with you before you left."

"Chai, your mother wants the best for you, and she only wanted to make sure that I loved you enough and wasn't going to hurt you again."

She walked out the office, and Chai looked after her. He felt something strange. Like if their relationship was going to end. "If that is true, I better put my guards up to spare me the pain."

When Egypt got home, she called Chai and said, "Chai, I'll be home for a few days because I need time to think out the things happening around me. Can you spare me away from the office?"

"Yes, I can spare you for a few days, that's all. Is that it?"

"Yeah. I'll see you later. Chai—," she started.

"Yes?"

"Nothing. I better go, okay?" she said and hung up. After she hung up, the phone rang. She just looked at it and refused to answer it. After it stopped, it started again, and she picked it up, angry, because she wanted to be left alone. She shouted, "Leave me alone!" into the receiver and slammed it down hard. She started throwing things around the room, anything she got her hands on. She turned on the stereo and raised the volume very high. She opened a bottle of Puerto Rican rum, poured a large drink for herself, and gulped it down in one swallow. Feeling the warm liquid in her stomach and the effects flow to her head, she began dancing wildly around the loft in total abandon. The doorbell rang. She drifted to the door and yelled, "Go away!" A voice screamed back through the door, "Let me in, Egypt!"

She stopped dancing long enough to realize it was Gary's voice through the door. She opened the door, grabbed him in, and kissed him hard on his mouth. He pulled her off of him and tried to help her to her bed. As he started undressing her, she spoke. "Gary, stop, I'm okay now really. I know what I'm doing, and I know what I'm feeling. Did I ever tell you I never stopped liking you since high school? And at this present moment I feel real attracted to you and I wouldn't mind." Then Egypt grabbed Gary by his neck and began unbuttoning his shirt and kissed him on the neck. She kissed his neck down his chest and to his stomach.

Gary wasn't sure of his feelings right then, but she was arousing him in ways he never dreamed she would. He held her off and tried to tell her, "Stop, Egypt, you've been drinking, and this is really not the way you feel." She stopped for the moment, long enough to calm down, and offer him a drink. Gary took several long gulps straight out the bottle and was somewhat satisfied. A soft and romantic ballad began playing on the stereo. She poured herself a drink, and they drank a toast together. "To sad times," they said together and clanked their glasses together.

As they listened to the soothing music, Gary began messaging Egypt's shoulders. He began to gently sniff her neck and kissed her shoulders. He whispered, "Egypt, you smell so good, and your skin feels so smooth." She turned to him and kissed him passionately on his lips and begun to nibble his neck, chest, and slowly made her way down his stomach and got intimate with him.

The phone rang, and she jumped up and held her head. It was killing her. When she answered, it was Chai saying he'd be right over. As she looked around, she saw she was naked, and there lying next to her was Gary naked also and looking out of it. She tried to tell Chai not to come over but to no avail. She hung up and shook Gary.

"Gary, you have to get dressed. Please get up. Do you hear me, man? Don't even try it. Get that head off that pillow! Gary, if you don't, I'll—"

She took the glass of remaining rum off the stand and poured it on his face, and he gave a yell. "Would you get up and out? Chai is on his way over please," she begged Gary.

"Okay, Egypt, I'm up. What in the hell did you say?" he asked.

"I said Chai is on his way over. And Gary if you haven't noticed, you're not dressed. I'm going to get in the shower, and you pull off the sheets, get on a pot of hot water, and pour that small bottle of black liquid in it, the one on the kitchen table. Thanks, I'll see ya, okay? Oh, and, Gary, I don't want you to think that this changes our friendship. I really do love you, and I'm sorry but too much is going on right now," she said.

"Egypt, we're friends and what was was and what is now is. If you would keep that in mind, you could solve some of those dilemmas you seem to keep running into." He turned to walk into the kitchen to put on the water and the strange black mixture into pot. He dressed quietly and left.

She thought she heard him say something but shook it off. When she got out the shower, she began to mop the floors and generally clean up. The bell rang, and she yelled, "Come in!" Chai walked in and seemed surprised to see her with a towel around her head and a robe on and scrubbing the floor. He laughed out loud.

"What's so funny?" she asked. "It's just you look so different, and I've never seen you that way. I'm just looking at you through the eyes of a husband," replied Chai. She knew she had to tell him but now wasn't the time. She made up some excuse for him to leave and told him, "Chai, I'm going to visit an old friend in the morning, and I need to get some sleep because it's a very long ride." "Okay. I'm sorry I bothered you though. Have a nice visit with your friend, all right? And I'll see you in a couple of days," he said and he left.

This is getting a little out of hand, she thought. "My life is in total chaos. I'm doing everything I don't believe in. From lying to downright denying happiness to myself. When is the shit going to end?" she screamed.

She noticed to herself, "I have slept with guys from one end of the globe to the other just trying to run from who I truly love." She decided it was time to stand up for herself now and go where she knew she belonged. "First things first," she said. "I have to tell Chai."

That was the hard part because she cared for him. She too, in a way, had begun to even fall back in love with him. She called him up and invited him to a late dinner.

"Egypt, isn't it late? I thought you had to get up early tomorrow."

"So I want to see you and tell you something. Besides, I'm famished, and I haven't eaten since lunch. Will you meet me?"

"Okay. I miss you already. Where do you want to meet?"

"Meet me at the Canal Street Station. I'll be wearing my black skirt, the suede one, and my royal blue silk blouse."

"Good. In one hour, Egypt?"

"Yes, and don't forget."

He took her to a part of Chinatown she's never been before. She thought it was beautiful. The restaurant he took her to was simple, unaffected, but the food was great. She felt like she was in the Orient.

She couldn't tell him what she wanted to at that point because he wasn't listening. The only thing she got across was, "Chai, I don't think we ought to sleep together for a while. I need physical and emotional space to think correctly. Too much is happening all at once." She was thinking, *It's not been that long that I was with Baron, and I still love him too.* Actually, it's been five months, and things were still moving too fast for her.

Chapter 5

Fatima was growing impatient waiting to hear from Baron. When she got a message on her service, it was from him. "Fatima, I talked to Mr. Stout, and I finally got him to take it into consideration. You'll have to present yourself to Mr. Stout and that would be the final touch. Don't forget to dress to impress."

Fatima called Egypt early the next morning to tell her the good news. "I did it! I did it!" she yelled elated and flew all around her apartment.

"Did what?" Egypt asked.

"I got the job, you idiot! I actually did it!"

"What job?"

"The job I told you about a few weeks ago. You know, the one with the big company."

"So when do you start?"

"Soon I hope." She thought to herself, *It paid off.* At least she hoped so. Fatima hoped that Baron wouldn't go and shoot his mouth off to Egypt about their little deal. *One thing that Egypt does not like is betrayal,* she thought. Egypt was a woman of her word, and if she found herself up against a wall, she wouldn't change her colors. And she certainly wouldn't forget that it was her company, and even though she was absent, the company was in her name and whatever she says goes. Mr. Stout had his hands tied and that's the way it would stay.

Fatima made all the arrangements for Baron to see Egypt but not until she had the position for sure. She wasn't that stupid. Baron wasn't a slouch either. If she tried to dip on him, he would string her up but good. Fay knew she would have to deliver Egypt into Baron's hands.

"Egypt, I better go 'cause I'm late, okay. I'll call you later?"

"Bet, Fay. Catch ya later," Egypt said and hung up. Fay dressed and headed for the office where Baron stood in the lobby waiting for her. Fatima was indeed dressed to impress. She had her hair up, little to no makeup, and dressed so conservatively that Baron didn't recognize her. When Baron looked at the young lady who answered to the name of Fatima Aguilar, he had to look twice. Fay just didn't look the same. When she approached him, he had a surprised look on his face.

"What a difference. I would have never known you. I hope your presentation is as good as you look, and I think you'll be a shoe-in. Word to the wise—don't bat an eye at him or crack a smile. He feels that women try to use their charms instead of their brains to get a grip in the business world. He prides himself on thinking on top and not from down below," Baron said.

"This'll be a piece of cake. Observe me, and please use the three Ls."

"What's the three Ls?"

"Baron, it's simply *look . . . listen . . . and learn . . .* Isn't that so simple? Now try it. I'll have this job without a doubt, and you'll get the information on Egypt. I'm a woman of my word, Baron, so let's get this started," said Fatima.

They got in the elevator and rode to the eighth floor. They walked into the offices, and they both could see that Mr. Stout wasn't that interested in interviewing Fatima. Mr. Stout looked into her eyes and noticed he knew something was familiar. He couldn't quite place her, but he knew that he would remember it. He motioned for her to sit down, and she felt the tension in the room. As she presented herself, Mr. Stout remembered where he saw Fatima. He said to her, "I remember now. It was at a seminar quite a few months ago. I remember I was a speaker there, and I also remember you had a lot of questions and some very valid statements."

Fatima nodded and said, "Yes. That's where you saw me." She felt relieved that he was unable to remember that they had a recent encounter in lower Manhattan during a convention for one of his subsidiaries, Laurdele Productions.

"I must admit that I was quite impressed by your intelligence and decisiveness."

"Thank you. Frankly I'm surprised you remember me."

"Why shouldn't I? Not often do you get a package deal: beauty and intelligence wrapped up in one. But something else about you is very familiar. Don't worry, I'll figure it out. I always do. Faces never evade me for long."

"Well, I'm sure I look like a lot of other people. Are you married by the way, if you don't mind me asking?"

"No, I don't mind you asking. The more we talk, the quicker I'll figure out where else I've seen you. Ah, well, marriage, yes I am, and she's quite happy."

"And what about you? Aren't you happy?"

"I didn't say I wasn't. But every marriage could use a little spice. Spice. Spice. I've seen you—have you ever—been to—no. It couldn't have been you." He thought to himself, *Could it be?*

"Well, Mr. Stout, I hate to cut the conversation short, I have a lot of things to take care of. It was a real pleasure, and maybe we can finish this some other time."

"Perhaps lunch, if you have the time?"

"If I have the time," she said nervously.

Baron was shocked at Mr. Stout's and Fatima's conversation considering that no more than ten minutes ago he was going to just introduce himself and explain to her that the company wouldn't be looking for anyone at this present moment. For a man who wasn't interested, he held an hour of conversation with her. Before Baron knew it, she was on her way into Egyptian Labels.

As Baron escorted her to a cab, he could only shake his head and congratulate her on winning her battle. He reminded her, "You know that maybe you've won the battle, but there is still a war on. By the way, where is the information that I asked for?" Fatima handed him a postcard which had Egypt's whereabouts and other information written on it. He looked at it and stared at Fatima.

"Baron, why are you staring at me like that? It's like you're piercing me with your eyes, and it's giving me the idea that there's something wrong. Is there?"

"Yeah, I want to make sure that this is in fact the correct information. Remember I can have that position taken away just as quick as you got it. I need a number," he said.

Fatima went through her bag and pulled out a piece of paper with Egypt's handwriting that she had been carrying around with her. Baron looked at it and told her to come with him. They walked across a busy street to a pay phone.

"Now stay right here. I'm going to call this number to see if in fact it's Egypt."

"Wait a minute. Don't you feel it's too early? She's still at work and won't be home till late," Fatima stressed.

Baron dialed the number anyway. The phone rang several times, and when he was about to hang up, a message came on. It was Egypt's voice. After he heard the message, he hung up. He turned to Fatima and looked her up and down and shook his head. Fatima smiled and turned away to hail a cab.

"Wait a minute. Don't you feel like you just turned your best friend in? I know that you must be good friends with her, or you wouldn't have her number on you. She keeps herself really quiet and doesn't like to go out much. She'd rather stay home, I know."

Fatima replied laughingly, "Shows how much you know her, darling, because she doesn't just stay in. She goes out, and trust me, she has a social life." With that, she got into the cab and pulled off.

She left Baron standing there wondering, "What has she been up to? I should give her a call." He remembered what his mother said about giving her some space and take it easy with her but not to let her get away. Baron had everything he wanted in his hand but didn't know what to do with it. He placed the card inside his jacket pocket and went back to the building.

As Baron looked up, he saw the hieroglyphics on the front of the building. It was a saying of Egypt's in which only few people knew just what it said. It showed simple pictures that only ones knowledgeable in the language would know. It looked like a man and woman walking up stairs and a funny shape which to the trained eye meant stars. There were a few other markings as well.

What it stated basically was a couple walking up stairs to a gateway for the heavens where they drink together. He remembered that Egypt said Egyptian Labels was the way for up-and-coming people who have talent and no money can feel equal to the rest of the world where they get treated no different from anyone else. He remembered her saying, "Here they are together. Young men and women equal." Just then he realized that he needed her.

When he went up in the elevator, Mr. Stout got in and began talking to him in reference to Ms. Aguilar. Mr. Stout said, "I'm very impressed with her capabilities, and I think she is a very lovely lady. I know she will be an asset to this company."

Baron wasn't paying much attention since he had so much on his mind. All he was thinking about was Egypt and how he could approach her and not get hurt in the process. He wondered if she even wanted to get back with him at all and if she already had someone else. He recalled what Fatima had said about her going out and not staying at home anymore. That threw him for a loop, and he couldn't concentrate anymore. He felt it would be best if he just went home to relax for the rest of the day.

By the time he returned home, there was a message on his machine from his brother Anthony. Baron was surprised to hear from him, so he knew it must be important.

Instead of calling him, Baron went over to Anthony's office. When he arrived, Anthony was preparing for a meeting. They shook hands and walked into an inner office where Elisabetta and Nunzio Jr. were already seated.

"What the hell is going on?" asked Baron.

"Have a seat, Baron and I'll fill you in," said Anthony. "Angela already knows what's going on even though she is still in the hospital. I'm going to call her and put us on the speaker so she could hear us all at the same time." He dialed Angela's number and was connected to her. "Hello, Angela, how are you, honey?"

"I'm doing okay. So what's up?"

"Well, some of you know why we're here today. There is something that this family has to straighten out and that's Father. I was just given notice that the word out on the street is that another family, unknown as of yet, that's planning a hit on Father. Now we all know that he's been making many mistakes toward the wrong people."

Baron wasn't interested in what Anthony had been saying. His mind was elsewhere. Angela stated, "What goes around comes around. Okay, Baron, I say it's up to you to get Father to back down and change his mind."

Baron was startled out of his wanderings to say, "Let someone else do it." They all looked at him strangely, and Baron thought that they must all be crazy.

"Why don't you ask the person who's the most informed? None of us was ever interested in Father's business, except maybe Nunzio here." Nunzio Jr. would have been the most capable, but he enjoyed life itself too much, and their father never put too much trust in him.

"If not Nunzio, then why not Francesco? He worked with Father closely, and he is his favorite nephew." Francesco seemed to favor Nunzio Sr. tremendously like he was Nunzio's double.

Elisabetta spoke up. "I still think it should be Baron to deal with Father. You are the youngest son, and I think you would be best able to approach Father."

Angela added, "Why don't you suggest to Father that he retire and move to Florida with Mother?"

"He'll never go for that," said Anthony. "He might if Baron talks him into it," Elisabetta stated.

"I don't think Father will listen to me now since I just tried to wipe his face off with my fist. I don't know, maybe I should just wait for the right moment," said Baron.

"What will become of all the things that Father built? Maybe we should let Mother in on this. She might have something to add, and she could probably put all this into prospective," said Angela.

Nunzio Jr. and Anthony laughed. They both said, "Mother?" Anthony said, "Angela, you know you're still young and wild. I don't think you realize the importance of this choice."

"What do you mean? I know full well what I'm talking about."
Angela slammed down the phone.

"Don't you think this should be taken care of right away? Like tonight, maybe, Baron?" Elisabetta said.

"Yeah, maybe tonight," Baron said and rose from his chair. "I'll tell you all what happened later. I better get going."

While Nunzio was in his car, he received a phone call from someone who he thought was somehow familiar. The voice informed him, "Your time is up, Nunzio." He grabbed the door handle, opened it, and ran. There was a great explosion, and the car was engulfed in flames. Nunzio screamed in pain as the lower half of his body caught on fire. There was pain in his voice as he yelled, "Help!"

He fell to the ground and looked back to the car. He saw flames and smoke rising out of the damaged wreck and realized that the others in the car didn't survive. Throughout the street, the alarms and engines sounded in a furious race to come to the rescue. Nunzio glanced again at the car and thought, "If I hadn't answered that phone, I could have been burned to a crisp like them."

Somehow, he noticed, Joe had tried to escape the inferno, but the fire surrounded him and swallowed him whole as he was too late to evade them. As Joe tried to run, the fire only seemed to increase, and he finally dropped. All Nunzio could think about was the pain and the sounds of the engines, and he tried to hold in all that he could.

By the time the paramedics arrived, Nunzio succumbed to the pain, and he fainted. The medics began taking his vital signs, and others flocked over to the wreckage to see if they could save anyone else. They carried Nunzio to the ambulance, and one of the medics told a detective, "There's no one else alive here. Those others in the car are burnt toast, and the one on the street is burned to a crisp. If I were you, I'd call the coroner. There is nothing else we can do."

The coroner's meat wagon arrived to pick up the remaining corpses. When the scene was cleared, all that was left were a few spectators and an offensive stench of cooked flesh.

While driving to his father's house, he passed by ambulances and police cars coming from an emergency. This motorcade unsettled his nerves, and he decided to check out from where they came.

As he pulled up to the catastrophe, he noticed firemen putting out a fiery car and saw that it was his father's by chance of the license plate. He exited his car and approached a detective. He asked, "What happened here?"

"There seems to have been an explosion. There was one man known to have survived, but he's burned pretty badly. They just took him to the hospital. The rest of the occupants of the car are known to be dead. It looks like one of them tried to escape, but by that time, he had already caught on fire and collapsed in the middle of the street. The medics told me that the one man they saved was burned pretty much over 30 percent of his body, mostly his legs."

"Thanks, Detective," said Baron. He got in his car and phoned Nunzio Jr. about the explosion. Nunzio Jr. then called everyone and told them each to come to the hospital.

By time Baron reached the hospital, nurses informed him that they contacted Mrs. Gianelli and she was on her way. All Baron knew was that there was going to be a war on the streets of New York and that he definitely didn't want to be involved. He had no choice because no matter what, Nunzio was still his father. There was the fact of pride and honor to be thought about.

His mother and Elisabetta arrived within a few minutes after Baron. They received the news as soon as the authorities realized who the victim was. Baron tried to hold back his anger, but when he no longer could do that, he hit the wall with his fist.

Elisabetta walked over to Baron and said, "Baron, it's not over yet. The battle may have been won, but they definitely won't win the war."

Baron looked surprised at her because he thought she was the quietest of all his brothers and sisters. Francesco showed up, and Baron spotted him.

"Francesco, oh, I mean Francis, did you get the news from Anthony yet?" asked Baron.

"I only talked to Nunzio, and he called to tell me what happened to the Don," replied Francis.

Baron took him aside and gave his cousin the particulars of the meeting that took place earlier. Francis looked very surprised because he thought that it would be left up to Tony or Nunzio Jr. "Yeah, I agree that maybe you should be the one to talk to him. I remember Nunzio saying that only one of his children had his spunk and drive, and that was you."

He added, "Nunzio knew that you wouldn't become a part of his empire he built. But he did respect you."

He confided to Francis, "I'm going to work with you closely on this, and I want this to remain between us. I have too much to lose, and I can't afford that. Egyptian Labels is too important to me and so is Egypt."

"I know," Francis agreed and walked over to his aunt and held her in his arms.

Baron was torn between his belief of honor and loyalty to his family and his love for Egypt. He hadn't forgotten about the information Fatima had given him. It was too much for him to deal with at one time.

The doctors gave them some good news. He said, "Mr. Gianelli is in stable condition right now, but we will have to monitor him for the next couple of days or so until he is out of danger. Maybe then we can move him into a private room from the ICU." Baron took aside the doctor and asked, "What else is there that you're not telling me, Doctor?"

"Mr. Gianelli, there isn't much more we can do for him right now except make him as comfortable as possible and stabilize his condition so we can tend to the more serious of his injuries. He was burned over 30 percent of his body with the most damage to his legs and back. There is the possibility of infection, and if it spreads, he may never walk again and also he could be rendered impotent. We can't be sure until the skin grafting is completed and we run more tests. The best thing for all of you would be to go home and get some rest," said Dr. Komachi.

"Thank you, Doctor. I know you're doing the best you can at this moment," replied Baron. As he left the hospital and drove home, he realized that there was a void in his life and it was beginning to interfere with his thoughts. It would have to soon be confronted.

He walked through the entire house trying to gather his thoughts. He lay across his bed and looked into the skylight out on to the stars. He pictured Egypt's face and how much he missed her touch. He lifted up the telephone only to hang it up. He got up and went into the shower.

Egypt was in her apartment watching television with Chai. They were lying in the bed, and Chai was kissing her on the back of her neck when the news flash came over the TV. She straightened up and raised the volume on the set. There was Baron pushing the cameramen out of the way of his mother trying to leave the hospital.

Egypt picked up the phone to call Baron, but Chai grabbed it and asked, "What are you getting ready to start? And why the sudden change and who are you calling?"

Chai rose and began to pull on his clothes. "I'll leave because for the last couple of days you've been very distant with me, and I'll give you the space again. But, Egypt, don't reach out to me unless that's what you want. I have feelings too, and I may have all the honor and self-respect in the world but it doesn't mean I don't hurt. It just means that I carry it well, that's what's called pride. But I don't have that much pride. I can tell you that I do in fact love you and want to marry you. It now depends on if you feel the same way."

"Chai, please don't be angry with me. There isn't anything wrong. I, well I—what I'm trying to say is . . ."

Chai walked over to her quickly and kissed her passionately. She began to remove Chai's shirt since she wanted to make love to him right then and there. He grabbed her by the hands and stopped her attempts.

"No. I want you to know that I love you, and I want you to want me because you love me," he said as he kissed her hand.

Egypt told him, "There's much more that I feel for you. It's not just physical here." But Chai stepped back and looked her straight in her face. "Please express yourself to me the feelings you have within." Egypt just looked at him and smiled. Chai walked away.

"No, Chai, listen. I do love you," she said.

"Well, if you do, tell my why."

"You know why. You know how I feel. You're loving and understanding. You're everything I could want right now."

"Yes, for right now, but what about later? What about you? What do I do for you? You're just describing qualities that your neighbor could have. Darling, when I'm with you, we don't even have to touch and I feel close to you. Egypt, your smile creates a rhythm in my core . . . but all you can give me is 'you love me' because I'm understanding? Your doctor can do that too. Do you know how I feel? Oh, Egypt, darling, do you feel for me at all? Why are you with me, or is this just a pause for you?"

He walked closer to her to say in a painful voice, "All through what I have said you didn't protest, not even budge at all. So maybe I'm filling the void in my life. It just so happens that my physical capabilities come in handy for your personal pleasures, so you hold on. I do love you now and always. I'm not going to go through that ride without protection. Do you think that just because I'm a man you can't hurt me? *If you prick me, do I not bleed? If I do not eat, will I not hunger? If I am tired, do I not sleep? If my heart is hurt through grief, will I not cry? If I am pierced by an arrow in my heart, will I not die?*"

Egypt tried to stifle a laugh. "Okay, maybe I stepped a little in the poetic pool, but you do hear what I'm saying to you. I had to ask you because I need to know, but I can see you still haven't an answer for me," he replied. "I can't help but love you."

Egypt sat down and looked at the floor, but there wasn't much she could say behind all of that. Chai reached out and pulled her to her feet. He held her by both her arms and kissed her. He began to nibble her shoulder, and a deep sigh came from her. All the passion within her became aroused. She held him tight and uttered the words, "I love you," and stopped.

She looked him in the face, and tears filled her eyes. All Chai could do was remind her, "This seems to be the only time when you can say those words to me." And he left the apartment.

Egypt cried, and she felt very out of place. She realized that she made Chai feel the way Baron made her feel. She never thought that all men were the same. She stopped to remember that Chai Kamkano was not just any man. She had him on an emotional roller coaster. She had asked him for space physically and emotionally and called him as soon as she needed a little comfort. The problem was as soon as she saw Baron, she turned off like a wet flame to anyone else.

She picked up the phone to dial Baron's number. She was lonely physically, but she knew she couldn't call him because she was afraid of the consequences if she talked with him. She would want to go to him since she was still weakened by him.

She put down the receiver because she thought she heard the bell ring. She put on her robe to answer the door, and there to her surprise stood Baron. She tried to close the door on him, but he held it open and asked, "Please, Egypt, can I come in? If you don't want me to, I'll go."

"How the hell did you find me? Leave me please. I'm not the same person who left you. I enjoy my freedom, and I'm happy. So what do you want, and why are you here? Well, answer me!"

"You look so beautiful, Egypt. How have you been?" he asked.

"You haven't heard a damn word I've been saying, have you? Answer me, why are you here?" she asked.

"My father, Egypt, my father. I know that you never cared too much for him, but I can't believe this is happening. So much has been going on since you left, well, since you've been away. I have a feeling that he's going to die. The thought of him dying never crossed my mind," he said softly.

Egypt reached over and caressed what she thought was Baron as she stood there in front of the door. The scene vanished, and she realized she was daydreaming and that Baron was far from her. She felt even worse than before. She began to wonder if she was starting to fall apart.

"No, not me. I can handle my decision to stay away from the man I love truly." She placed her heart in front of her this time and said, "I think I'll go and see Baron because he is in need of his friends right now." *Especially people who cared for him.*

She dressed and headed over to his house. When she arrived, she thought she saw through the window that Baron was kissing some woman. Egypt's curiosity, mostly anger, made her get as close as she could without setting off any of the alarms on the windows. She searched her purse and found she still had the keys to the alarm system. When she looked closer, she saw that the people kissing were his brother and some girl she knew not to be his steady.

She looked relieved that it wasn't Baron. She walked into the garden and saw that the light in the bedroom was on and suddenly went out. Egypt thought she had no right to just step in and out of his life. Just as she had people in her life, she could only wonder that he too must have some sort of companionship. She remembered her sex life was very busy, and she could only think that it was the same for him. Little did she know he had other things on his mind, mostly her. Egypt turned tail and got out of there before she got caught.

On the way home, she passed Gary, and they went back to her place. She told him what she'd done, and he laughed. She got upset at him and threw some pillows which were behind her at him. Then she laughed.

"What the hell have I done with my life, Gary? Save me please." She laughed.

"Save you? Egypt, how can I save you? Save you from what? The only thing you seem to need saving from is yourself. So what should I do?" he asked.

"That doesn't sound as though you're joking. Are you kidding, you can't really believe that, can you?" questioned Egypt.

"Stop and think about everything you've done to yourself. While you're at it, think about what you've done to the people's lives you touched. Think hard. Can you actually say that everything has fallen in some sort of order, or has everything lately been in an uproar? Just try and do what's right for you and that will help. Most of all, slow down, girl, your beauty is escaping you," he said.

Egypt reached out to Gary and fell apart at the seams. She looked as though she was a child who had lost her favorite doll. He could only hold her and say nothing; he had said enough to her already. He hoped that she heard him clearly.

Egypt pulled away abruptly and wiped her tears and told Gary, "You're absolutely correct," and placed a kiss on his cheek. She walked to the door and asked him to leave because she needed time alone to do a lot of serious thinking.

He walked over to the door, closed it, and approached her; but she stepped away. She told him, "Go, Gary, and don't push it, okay? You say one thing, and now you're going to tempt me into what you warned me of?" She looked at him as if to say "leave." She smiled and opened the door for him.

"I hope this means you've made up your mind about who you want to be with," he said.

"Trust me, Gary, when I decide, it'll be the right choice, but first I have to choose me. So there," she teased. "And good-bye for now," she said and shut the door.

Egypt ran to the phone and picked it up only to hear Fatima with a lot of background noise. She couldn't hear her clearly. All she heard was something about Baron. She kept asking, "What about Baron?" but she still couldn't make it out.

She was very upset at this point. Fatima couldn't help but wonder what the hell did she call her for. All she could do was slam down the phone in frustration. Egypt thought, *If it isn't one thing it's another—anything to throw you off.*

She picked up the phone to call Chai, but she couldn't. Not after he said that she would keep hurting him. She knew that's not what she wanted to do right now. She wanted something, but what it was, she just couldn't place it. One thing that she did know is that she wanted a man. One that would be easy to be with and understand how strong she really is and one that would know that she doesn't want to be looked at as a mere woman but his equal. And in the same token, she wants to be treated as feminine and raise children.

She was so confused that she made a drink and sat in the place where the portrait she had made for her and Baron was. She glanced at the empty space over and over again and noticed that it was gone. She knew that Chai wouldn't have touched it.

What she remembered was that she had seen Gary admire it, but that was a while ago. She cleared her head. She thought, *Gary is many things, but he definitely doesn't feel threatened by Baron's presence. Not too many people know where I am except . . .*

She repeated to herself, "Except I can't, for the life of me, figure out who could have taken it."

She thought it just could be misplaced. Only if she knew that her friend had betrayed her trust. Fatima also knew that she could have bitten off more than she could chew this time because Egypt is no one to take lightly. For more than one reason, the topic of Baron was built on trust, and Egypt really believed in Fatima's friendship.

She had very few female friends since she had this thing about trusting anyone—male or female. Egypt had learned at a very young age that trust can only be built on one's self and not others because very few people betray themselves.

Egypt decided that it was best to just call it a night and make peace with herself. In the morning she would try to track down Fatima. She lifted up the telephone and called Chai. When she heard his voice, it comforted her. She told him, "I called just to say good night and I want to tell you that you're a good man and I believe that I have every intention of getting my head on straight. That's all." And she hung up.

The evening was still young, and at the token spot, there lay Fatima trying to get her life into some sort of order. She knew that Egypt figured that it was her who told Baron and that she would search high and low looking for her. There would be no hiding, not at this point. She would be too hot.

She gathered her attire for the evening and ran out to party as she does so well. This time she wouldn't be looked at as a prostitute even if she does go to bed with someone. She laughed at herself because she hoped that she would get a chance to tell someone her "price" since it's been so long that she's slept with a man and not gotten paid.

She thought about her boyfriend Chang Lee who she did have feelings for, but she just wanted to be seen with him to move up the social ladder as quickly as possible. She didn't want to lose him in the event of her plans; she just had to take it slowly and make sure he never finds out. One thing she didn't plan on and that was him showing up there at this affair.

Fatima was very late for the party, and she was hoping that Baron wouldn't be there because he would only make her feel even more uncomfortable.

When she arrived, she began to mingle with the guests and started to do what she did best—fish for information. Anything that could help her move up. She had a knack for using her beauty to get where she wanted to go, and tonight she would make no exceptions.

As she began to make her way through the crowd, she caught a glance of Mr. Stout. She walked over toward him, and he seemed pleased that she had come. He showed her around to the many people there, and he introduced her to a Mr. Lee who was representing his father's company while he was out of the country on business.

"Mr. Lee, this is one of our associates, Ms. Aguilar. Ms. Aguilar, Mr. Lee."

"Chang, what are you doing here?" said Fatima.

"Well, I guess that you two must know each other. Then I'll leave you alone."

As he walked away, Mr. Stout kept looking over his shoulder to hear what they were saying. "You never told me you were coming here. Chang, you never even told me that your father's company had anything to do with my boss. Chang, stop looking at me like that and say something. How long have you been here? Chang Lee say something or else!"

"Or else what? I guess, Fatima, you're really wondering how long have I been here watching your every move. Long enough, Fatima, long enough. All I can say is continue with your behavior. There's no need for you to act any different because I'm here. If I meant anything to you, you wouldn't have acted that way in the beginning. So carry on. Please don't let me put a damper on things," he said angrily.

"Chang, don't be angry. Look, I didn't even know you'd be here, but realize I work for these people and I have to be friendly to their clients." Chang cut her off to reply, "Clients belong to the company, but you looked as though you wanted them to be your clients. It didn't look as if you were a woman in love with a man at home, some place other than here. Tell me who you would have chosen if I didn't throw a damper on it by being here?" he asked.

"You ignorant bastard." The next thing she knew Chang had stepped away from her, and she reached out to pull him back. He took her hand off of him.

"Don't touch me, Fatima, just continue to enjoy yourself and act as though we just met, and remember I will deny I know you because the woman I was going out with had respect for our relationship. You, on the other hand, are not the woman I thought you were. I didn't make the mistake. You made it. Never think the man is easy just because he appears to be quiet. Have a good evening, Ms. Aguilar. It's been very interesting," he said as he walked away from her.

Fatima felt her stomach hit the floor. He hurt her more than if he could have beaten her up for ten rounds. She never thought anything like this could happen to her. She looked around to see if anyone had seen them talking. She became upset when she saw Chang enjoying himself in conversation with a few important men. She knew that Chang wouldn't throw himself at any female. He had too much self-respect for that. She felt so dirty, and she hadn't been with anyone, but she would have if she hadn't run into him here. A gentleman that she was giving light hints to came over to her and asked her to his hotel room. When she looked around, her eyes locked on Chang's. He looked and nodded his head and eyed her as though he told her, "Don't stop because I'm here."

The man grabbed her arm and led her out of the party. She walked around confused and hoped that Chang would have stopped her, but he didn't. Fatima returned to the room to see that Chang hadn't moved at all and seemed not to care. This hurt her very deeply. She wasn't used to rejection; any man she had wanted had always wanted her. She knew she was beautiful, and all men had desired her.

Chang looked at her and gave her his back. He was not impressed that she didn't go. This upset her so much that she left and caught a cab.

When Chang arrived home, he saw her sitting there. This angered him and so he asked her to leave. "I won't go," she told him. "I have to speak with you, if only for a little while."

He looked at her and let her into his place. On the foyer wall hung a beautiful picture of them. He showed her the portrait and slammed it on the floor. He asked her to speak quickly and leave. Fatima was a little lost for words.

"You said you had something you wanted to tell me. So speak, or should I place money on the table or would you like it placed in your bra? I wonder if you're wearing one," he said.

"You sure know how to hit low. I never thought you could be so cold. I really think there is nothing I can say to you, is there? Chang, you really don't understand. Would you stop walking away from me? I'm talking to you," said Fatima.

Chang walked into his bedroom, and Fatima followed behind him. She stood there talking while he undressed and then he walked over to her and asked, "Are you finished?" He began to kiss her. He had made love to her before but not like this. It was more like if he just was using her as his personal pleasure. He showed no emotion at all toward her, and she noticed that it was more like a performance and not pleasure.

She stopped him and asked, "What's going on?"

He looked straight in her face and said, "Aren't you used to this? What do you expect? Emotion, love, and concern? Are you kidding? There's no way that I'll allow myself to have anything to do with you again, so if this isn't good enough for you then leave," he said.

"I don't believe that you're really saying this to me and meaning it. Chang, you're just hurt. I bet—"

Chang cut her off to say, "I don't think you're hearing me right." He grabbed her by her face and told her, "I couldn't hold my head up even if we walked together down a dark alley among strangers. Don't you get it? You are dirt to me. Trash. You are what the Japanese call *busu*. You are hideous," he replied.

Fatima grabbed her clothes and only got on a few things before she ran out of his apartment and into the night. She was hysterically crying and lost, soulwise. As she walked home, she realized she never felt so lost and hurt by anyone. For the first time in her life, her games were played on her, and the pain was too much.

When she arrived at her apartment, all she wanted to do was take a shower and sleep and try to forget what happened to her. She was a strong woman, and she wasn't going to let this destroy her or her future. But she felt so hurt. As much as she tried to talk herself out of the fact of being hurt, she knew that it just wasn't going to work. All she could do was try to forget him.

Chang had no choice except to hurt her to make her realize that hearts can be broken and no medicine can ever take the pain away or mend it. She took people as though they were a toy and everything would be just okay in the morning. He felt that she had to realize that people had feelings and that she too can be hurt. He figured he would be just the one to show her. She acted as though just because she was beautiful, it was okay to do what she pleased, and she didn't realize that if you cut somebody, they will bleed. He did care for her, but he had too much pride and wasn't going to allow her to think that he was a "transformer" to be molded at will. No, there was no way he would even dream of playing that role.

Fatima cleaned the makeup off her face and took the towel off of her head and began to brush her hair. She slammed the brush on the counter and started to cry. As soon as she did, she got herself together again. As she looked into the mirror, she threw the towel at it. She was so disappointed in what she was looking at. She betrayed her only true friend and hurt her love. Chang and Egypt were the best things that ever happened to her life in a long time. But knowing Fatima, she wouldn't stay down for long.

She had this air about her that she couldn't accept failure, and whatever she wanted she would get. That came from never having anything and that as soon as she could, she vowed that she would never lose it.

With all that attitude, she could understand why there was that hurt feeling inside her. She knew Egypt was going to tear her apart. She would have to set up a good rapport with Baron so that he wouldn't tell Egypt where he got his information from. She got up from her dressing table to go sit in her living room which was richly furnished.

Within a short period of time, this victory with Egyptian Labels has changed her. Yet she still felt that she must keep her true self hidden from Egypt. She had been seeing Chang for a while before she told Egypt, and now she was lost. She needed her friend to talk to, but she didn't know whether Baron had spoken with her yet. She just couldn't go and ask her friend to stand by her side after she had turned on her like she Judas. She felt low about that. No matter what, she had to try to get back with Chang. She didn't know how she was going to go about it except that she had to give it a try.

As time plays its toll on people, the mind can weigh heavy on the conscience. Fatima couldn't help but think of all the men she had dealt with in such a short period of time, and worst of all, the fact that she has finally made it depended on the fact that an old John remembered her and hired her. There was so much invested in this decision and so much at stake. She felt pressure from every angle, and at this point, all she could think about was crawling under a rock. She got tired from all this reminiscing, and since she had a very big day ahead of her the next day, she decided to try to get some sleep.

She curled up in her bed and threw the satin sheets over her head. As she lay there, she began to toss and turn as she attempted to sleep. She held her pillow tight and kissed and hugged it as if it were Chang. She fell fast asleep with the pillow in her arms as if it were him.

She slept that whole morning and most of the night and woke up once because she had a nightmare about Chang. It threw her for a loop, and she got out of the bed to take a shower. She thought it would calm her nerves. It did just that, and she drifted back off to sleep.

When morning broke, there was going to be a full day in front of her. When she realized she slept through a whole day, she thought, *Damn, this business with Chang and Egypt must have gotten deeply to me. I never slept that long before. I gotta make sure I keep my head on straight today.*

She began to ponder in her mind just how she would deal with Mr. Stout. She was almost positive that he would remember her. She hoped that she could work her way around this or even have Baron get her through this.

Then she realized where she made her big mistake. She should never have given him all of the information on Egypt right away and now too soon in the game she played her trump card. But if she put her mind to it, she would be able to come up with something. It would only take her a matter of time and not too much of it either.

The receptionist was busy dealing with an up-and-coming rap group and trying to handle the phones and awaiting Fatima's help. She was totally lost at her desk. Many people were walking in and out of the office, and it looked like complete chaos. The strangest outfits and hairstyles that anyone could imagine, she saw.

"Hello, Egyptian Labels, can I help you?" uttered the receptionist.

"Serinah, I'll be in really late, so please reschedule all of my morning appointments for tomorrow and I'll keep all my later ones. You know, Serinah, this means we must inform Mr. Gianelli of the new changes. Also get in touch with his secretary and make sure that the pressing for Harlem Knights is on time. The albums are to be shipped and on the market by the end of the month, and due to a few missed memos, we have fallen behind. But we won't go into that again, so make absolutely sure that everything is done today in an orderly fashion," said Mr. Chesterfield.

"Yes, Mr. Chesterfield, I hear you loud and clear. Good day, sir," replied Serinah and hung up.

"Man, word up if that man keeps this shit up I'm gonna jap him, man. He knows that damn memo was put right in his uppity hands. That's okay. He keeps walking with his nose up, the damn birds won't get a chance to shit in it because I'm gonna relocate the jammy. All right, people, chill out. This is an office, and I'm the only one here," she said to the clients waiting. "Some of you have appointments for this morning, and I'll have to reschedule you for tomorrow morning. So give me a little time and I'll be with you. Thank you," said Serinah.

Mr. Gianelli's secretary was standing there and laughing inside. She admired Serinah for taking this job and sticking with it. She showed promise for the company because she is the only person to last, working closely with Mr. Chesterfield.

Baron's secretary walked over to Serinah and asked if she needed help handling the crowd. Serinah was so angry with Mr. Chesterfield that she couldn't help but carry that ire over to everyone.

Serinah calmed down, and she and the secretary cleared the crowd. While they were both laughing about the nerdy way of Mr. Chesterfield, Mrs. Jackson stood there listening, unbeknownst to them.

Mrs. Jackson was a very lovely middle-aged and tall black woman who was a stickler for office decorum. When they saw her, they stopped right in their tracks. Serinah started to look busy at her desk, and Heather, Baron's secretary, placed a few strands of her blonde hair in her mouth and scurried to her office.

Heather is a fun-going twenty-seven-year-old, and Serinah is nineteen and very talented and has a way of making people feel at ease. She is a very outlandish, abrupt young lady. She is a very classy model-type until she opens her mouth and the street pours out.

Mrs. Jackson said with a deep and orderly manner, "Young woman, I am aware of your age, but there is a time for socializing and a time to conduct ourselves in a business fashion. These things may be too new to you but something that I suggest should become habit-forming. Your position here may appear to you as unimportant, but on the contrary, you hold the door to this company. The majority of the calls come through you and then funneled out. You must remain on top of things or they will form a chain of reactions I don't think you could crawl out of to save your soul. So if you begin to sink, call for back up. Do I make myself clear?"

She walked out of the office and down the corridor to her office. Mrs. Jackson was the head of marketing. When it came to pulling money together and locating finance, she was queen. There wasn't anything damn near she couldn't do.

Baron's secretary received a call from the office of Carlos Montana. Heather informed them that Mr. Gianelli was in a very important meeting and would be obtainable shortly. She knew that he hadn't even come in as of yet.

Chapter 6

Angela was well enough to make it her business to find out what's going on with her brother. Baron had earlier told her to stop worrying about him and to take care of her husband.

As she prowled around Baron's desk, she saw a slip of paper with Egypt's name on it, but before she could read it, Baron stepped in and snatched it from underneath her. She was very confused about her brother's behavior.

She walked away from him only to quickly turn around and ask, "Where did you get the address, and when are you going to call her?"

Baron advised her, "Stay quiet about this whole ordeal, Angelica, because I have no intentions of finding her." He made sure that she wouldn't go searching for it by putting it into his pocket. She laughed at him and told him, "Don't worry because I'm not going to attack you and take it from you. It's safe from me today."

They both began to laugh. Baron asked, "How is Father doing?" The smile left her face, and a totally different expression was sitting there. "Tell me the truth damn it."

"Well, Baron, it doesn't look too good for him. The worst is yet to come. When Father finds out about his condition, he is going to be a nutcase or even worse— he'll make Mother's life a living hellhole."

"Angelica, give Father more credit than that."

"What? The man who put the *W* in the word *whore*, not freak out when he finds out that his stallion will never rear up for all the fillies? You know, Baron, this will be the first time in Mother's marriage that she'll know that he isn't having an affair. It was like a second job to him, and you know that Mother wouldn't dare think of divorce. So the Don himself for many years has had his cake and ate it. He wouldn't be eating no more," she said as she chuckled. "Angelica, you're such a bitch," said Baron.

She said with a ghoulish grin, "So with any luck, you think he'll kill himself?"

"What the hell is your problem? What makes you think that he would consider doing anything like that? Damn, can't you give in a little? Why don't you give him some credit like I said before?" Baron thought for a moment. "I see what you mean. We are talking about Father, aren't we? I hope within the next few days things will be a little different," he said and changed the subject. "Anyway, how is Franco doing? Is everything okay with him?" he asked. "Oh, he's coming along fine. Thanks for asking about him."

"Did he take it hard about the baby?" he asked quietly.

"Of course, now that he's convinced it was Father who was responsible for my miscarriage and that he did it on purpose. Franco was going on and on about this and that, that it was just too much for me to take in all at once, so I decided to leave him there going off at the mouth."

She looked at Baron and said, "My father has done many things, but as far as his children are concerned, he does have a heart and Baron," she said as she began to cry, "Baron, did Father really have the hit put on Franco? Please, I have to know, and for some reason, my gut feeling tells me you're holding the key to my question. Now it's time for you to stop covering everybody's dirt. So what? Yeah, come on and fix your lips up to speak, Baron. I know that you—"

Baron walked out of the room. "Come here! Stop, Baron, don't treat me like a child. I have every right to—"

Her eyes narrowed with thought. "So it was Father that put the hit out on Franco! Father can't leave me alone, can he? I should go up to his hospital room and unplug him and watch him die!" she spat.

Baron looked at her and slapped her hard. She stood there stunned for a while. She removed her hand from her face and said, "That doesn't change how I feel toward Father. (If he thought that hitting her would install instant respect or make her feel bad, he had another thing coming.)

She turned to leave but instead said, "Nothing is going to bring my baby back. I still love you, bro, but I just don't understand why you still respect him no matter what that fuck does. He doesn't deserve no respect from me when he is the reason for your child being dead," she said and walked out abruptly.

Baron went to the door to call her back, but she was just too hurt and took off in her 5.0. Baron didn't feel too good inside at all. Too much was happening at once, and he decided that he had more important things to do than worry about anything or anyone else. He got into his own car and left without calling the office to let them know he wouldn't be coming in. He started on the parkway when he realized there was some unfinished business he had to take care of before doing anything else.

Baron called Francis on his car phone to let him know he was on the way over. They spoke briefly exchanging a few pleasantries, and Baron hung up. When he arrived, they greeted each other warmly as if getting together in a suite at the Helmsley was an everyday affair.

Baron looked throughout the rooms and asked Francis, "Who's that in your shower?"

Francis called out a name, and the loveliest black woman entered standing in nothing but a towel, dripping wet. Baron's mouth dropped to the floor in amazement because much to his surprise he had never seen Francis with anyone before. Especially someone black.

"Baron, it's okay. This is Karessa. Karessa, this is my cousin Baron. Get used to looking at her. I'm about to tell the family we're getting married as soon as possible. So what do you think? Isn't she lovely? And she's very intelligent too," said Francis.

Baron reached over and took Karessa's hand in his and kissed it. He smiled to say, "I would hug you, but you're in a towel. I wouldn't want my cousin to think I'm anything like my brother." To Francis he said, "Congratulations, Francis. You've caught a very fine lady."

"Well, you don't know me yet, but I will leave you two alone and get myself dressed and I'll see you shortly. It was a pleasure meeting you, Mr. Gianelli. Why don't you stay and make yourself comfortable. Fix yourself a drink," said Karessa as she walked out of the room to finish dressing.

"The Helmsley Palace suits you well, Francis. Karessa is a real beautiful woman. How is the rest of your family taking it? Well, not that what anyone ever says to you matters. First of all, we can't talk here. So let's go and Karessa—Karessa. That name sounds familiar. Francis, is she—no. Are you marrying *the* Karessa of Karessa Fragrances? Are you joking me? Where did you meet her?" asked Baron.

"I was standing here wondering just when you would put things together. You're getting slow, Baron, this I see. I've been seeing her for some time now, and it's been hard to keep it away from everyone, especially your father. You know how he was about Egypt. Imagine Karessa. But anyway, I think I did a good job." Baron walked over to the bar and made himself a drink and sat down opposite Francis.

"What about your mother? What did she have to say?" asked Baron.

"My mother thinks Karessa is a lovely woman. I don't think she's giving her real opinion though. She's too afraid it would push me to Karessa. What she doesn't realize is that this time I'm really in love."

"Francis, you really look like a man in love too. I don't think I've ever seen you like this before. She must be treating you right and taking good care of you for you to be so genuinely happy about all this," said Baron.

"You know Father was no problem at all because he was the one telling me to watch out for Nunzio because if he got wind of this, he would try and bed her in a minute. The Don is an amazing man. My uncle has won himself a reputation that precedes him," said Francis as he laughed. "Remember Uncle trying to get a hold of Egypt. He wasn't going to stop until he had her or destroyed your relationship with her," continued Francis.

"I hadn't realized that everyone was aware of his desire for her. Many times I wanted to punch the hell out of him, and there were many times I told him off, but he continued until one day Egypt smacked the hell out of him in a crowd of people. You know that didn't make him stop. It seemed to excite Father even more. Come to think about it, my sister was right. I guess he would kill himself," said Baron.

"Who would kill themselves?" asked Francis.

"Francis, I have to take care of something. You just made me realize a lot of things in a short period of time about my father and his way of thinking. I'll meet you tonight for dinner, so bring Karessa, and this way we all can talk and get to know each other. I just have to get in touch with Angelica," said Baron.

"Angela, how is she doing? Bring her with you because it's been a long time since I've seen her. And her husband, is he okay? Baron, you know I didn't want anything to do with what happened to Franco. I washed my hands of that situation because of my love and respect for Angela. She's my girl. I can remember when we were kids that anywhere I went, there she was tagging along right behind me. Bring her, I miss the baby. I always called her baby," said Francis.

"Don't worry, she'll be with me this evening. She hasn't changed. She's still on top of things. She figured it was Father. I just don't have the heart to confirm it for her. Frankly, I can't figure him out. Sometimes I just can't," replied Baron.

Baron left the hotel and headed out on a journey. He located Angela, and he didn't know what to say to her. He said, "I love you, Angelica. I'm sorry for what I said earlier."

She replied, "You know I could never hate you, you're my big bro." She reached out to him and hugged him. "I'm the baby, remember, we have no sense. We always forgive. Look, Baron, I may love you, but if you ever lay a hand on me again, I'll kill you." She laughed, and he held her tightly.

"Angelica, I made plans to go out to dinner with you, Francis, and his future wife," said Baron.

"There's no way I could sit at a table with him. Are you losing your mind totally, Baron?" she yelled.

"Listen, he didn't have anything to do with it. He just told me he was left out of that. Father must have known that Francis would have told you. You're too close to him for him to do anything like that, and he's hurting inside about it. He didn't think Nunzio would actually do it. Yeah, Angelica, Father did it because he just wanted to do what he thought was right for you. According to him you're still a child. Remember he really went out to Italy to get you before Franco's family could put a hit on you. That's why he hit Franco's father. He couldn't understand why nothing happened to you there. So before anything happened, he and Mother went to get you. Father didn't know that everything slowed down because you were married and pregnant. If he knew, he wouldn't have done that. I went into his office, and we had it out. Angelica, I never hit Father in my life, but I couldn't handle what he'd done to us. I felt he had to realize I wasn't going for it anymore. I guess I was a little late. In my case I should have made him respect my personal life. But you can't hold Francis responsible for what our father did," said Baron.

As he kissed her he said, "I'll be back later to pick you up. Don't forget to look stunning as always because Francis' lady is gorgeous." With that he left her and was on to another destination.

There was so much running through his mind from beginning to end, and he was going to try to fix as much as he possibly could. He called his office, and the secretary was quite upset because he missed meetings and was behind on some work. It wasn't like him not to call or come in without notice. He told her, "Tell everyone something and get rid of whatever it is that I have planned for this evening because I'm spending it with my family. Call my mother and tell her to be ready to go out tonight and Angelica is going too. Make sure there is a car to pick her up." He thanked his secretary and added, "If anything major happens, call me at my house because that's where I'll be." And he left.

As he drove home, he saw a familiar sight which he couldn't ignore. He passed by it and looked around. Baron parked his car and walked around the neighborhood. He saw a lady feeding pigeons and sat nearby and watched.

While watching the lady feed the birds, he glanced over and saw there was a woman who looked like she was someone he had known. He rose to walk over by her, but by the time he approached she was inside the door. He stood there for a moment then started to walk away when the number on the door looked familiar. He looked around and the name of the street he recognized. It seemed strange to him and he felt like he was in the Twilight Zone. Baron walked to the door and stood there staring and contemplating what he should do.

Egypt was scurrying around her apartment in a towel trying to locate her bathrobe. She just finished her hair and was ready to spend the rest of the afternoon or what was left of it on herself. She might go shopping and take herself out to dinner. A day for her and her alone. To find or relocate herself.

As she began to give up looking for her bathrobe, she found it anyway and then the bell rang. She wondered who it could be because she thought she told everyone not to bother her, so Chai gave her a few days off. She wasn't going to answer the door, but she couldn't stave off her curiosity of not knowing who it was. She grabbed her robe and raced like a little girl to the door and opened it without asking who it was, which she never does. She lost her breath and couldn't move for a moment. She looked and said nothing. A voice so soft and tender spoke.

"It's been a long time, and I just wanted to see you and say hello and that I understand why," said Baron.

Egypt stood there looking surprised as a child who would have really seen Santa. She stepped back from the door and looked behind her.

"I understand if there is someone here I don't want to come in. Like I just said I only came to see how you were doing and to say hello. Take care, and I wouldn't dream of stopping by again without you knowing," he said. He reached over and kissed her hand and walked on down the steps.

"Baron, wait, come in. I'm just shocked because I never thought in my wildest dreams to see you on the other side of my door," she said as she took a deep breath. She smiled and said, "Come in and sit down."

He entered, and she showed him to a chair opposite her. "I heard about Nunzio and I was going to call you, but I didn't feel right. I know you wouldn't have hung up on me, but it just didn't feel right. Anyway, how have you been, Baron? Can I offer you something to drink? Wait a minute and let me put something on," she said.

"No, you don't have to. I shouldn't stay long. You look lovely in that. That's just how I remember you. Beautiful and graceful," said Baron.

"Why don't you stop, you know I look terrible. By the way how's the business getting on? Mr. Stout must be shocked that I've stayed away so long."

"You're right on that one. He was so sure about it that your office is still sitting there waiting on you. Have you been receiving your salary on time in your account?"

"Please, I haven't been really living off that. Oh, because you found me home, you must be thinking that I stay in. Well, I do have another job, and I keep myself busy. How about you?" She got up and went into the kitchen and brought out the drinks and handed him his.

She walked in front of him to the couch and lay on it in a very sexy manner. "Come, tell me how life has been treating you lately. A handsome man like you must be very busy now," she said.

"If you're asking in a roundabout way if I'm seeing anyone, no, because I'm too caught up with family matters, and now that Angelica is back, so much has happened and I really don't want to get into it. I know you've enjoyed your newfound freedom," he said with a broad smile.

"Why, what makes you say that? Have you been following me? By the way, the shock has worn off, so how the hell did you find out where I've been if you haven't had me followed? You know I would have never thought you would do something like that to me. My life is mine, and so long as I never took anything from you, you had no right to get someone to find my whereabouts. How could you Baron? I really—"

Baron cut her off and sat next to her and covered her mouth with his hand. He said, "Egypt, would you be quiet for a moment and stop running your mouth. Just give me a chance. I didn't have you followed. Someone came to me and brought it to my attention." He removed his hand from her mouth. "I wouldn't have searched you out. You left, and I had to wait for a while to allow you to get whatever it was straightened out in your life. Until then I was waiting for you. But don't get me wrong I wasn't going to sit back and wait much longer for you. I'm in love with you, but that doesn't mean I'm an ass. Let's get that straight. Furthermore I understand a lot of it was my fault as far as my lack of attention and behavior toward you. I know I took you for granted and allowed my father to mistreat you and that was the worst of all the wrongs that any man could do to his woman. Especially if he loves her. Egypt, I'm not here to ask you to come back, just to understand that I'm sorry for everything and that I do still love you very much. There is nothing more that I would want but to have you with me again, but more than that I want you to know that I see what the real problems were. There were a few on your side also, but I hurt your pride and I should have seen that. I fell in love with you because of that. You are a very proud woman, and, Egypt, I am sorry."

Egypt was lost for words momentarily. She couldn't help but have tears in her eyes for he moved her heart. There was so much she wanted to say, but so many things have happened between then and now that she just couldn't tell him that she wanted him back. And then there was Chai, and she couldn't just walk out on him like that again. Everything Gary had said she saw too clearly now. About lives and how they are so delicate. She couldn't help but cry loudly into her hands. Baron held her close to his chest, and Egypt looked up into his eyes. He wiped the tears from her face and held on to him tightly. Baron lifted up her chin and kissed her tenderly on her lips. Egypt wasn't understanding. Baron never stopped with just a simple kiss.

She held her head down again and thought that he might have known about her and Chai. Maybe the person who gave him the information told him everything. She just stood up and walked away from him. Baron stood up and approached her to give her comfort. "Baron, please tell me who it was," she asked.

"It was a young lady named Fatima," he replied.

Right then and there she was sure that if Fatima told Baron where she was that she told him everything else. But Egypt couldn't figure out why she would do this to her. She thought they were friends and anyway she never did anything to Fatima. It didn't fit. Everything that people do she believed they did it for a reason. So why?

"She wanted something, right, Baron? What was it, you or money?"

"Simple, Egypt. Your friend just wanted a job at Egyptian Labels as one of its attorneys. She's good, and I can say that much for her. She came from nowhere and paid for her education by herself and struggled. I guess she saw an easy ticket in and couldn't let it pass. Plus I just had to at least see you, and it was like if it was placed right in my hand."

"That little puta . She didn't work all that hard to finish school. Did she tell you how she did it?" she asked.

"No, not really. She just spoke to Mr. Stout, and he made the final decision. I just had to get her in to see him and give a good recommendation and that was that." He continued, "Why, do you know something that I should?" he asked as if he didn't already know.

She was about to tell Baron, but she felt that she would take care of Fatima in her own way. It wouldn't solve anything by telling him. Not right now. So she thought it would be best to wait a little longer before letting Fatima know she found out everything. She thought that's what Fatima was trying to say over the telephone when they had that bad connection. "It's nothing, Baron. Can I get you another drink?" she said as she took his empty glass away and began to fix another. "What made you come by today anyway?"

She handed him his glass, and he drank more than half of it and placed it on the table. As she sat down next to him, he looked at her hair and placed his hands in her locks.

"It still feels beautiful, and please don't take this the wrong way, except I can't leave until I tell you this. I had a lot of time to think about it and more time than I would want to admit." He held her by her shoulders and lifted her up. "I love you," he said.

He kissed her, and she held on to him as they lay down on the couch. Baron began to nestle her earlobes and kissed her neck. Egypt started to kiss Baron hungrily on his mouth. When he stood up, he lifted her off the sofa to her feet. Her robe had fallen to the floor and he placed his hand behind her hair and kissed her as he picked her up off the floor and into his arms. He carried Egypt to the bottom of the stairs of her loft bed and set her down.

"May I take you up to the boudoir and make love to you?" he asked.

The next thing he knew Egypt headed up the stairs and waited for her prince. When he got up the stairs, he was wearing nothing but what his mother brought him into the world with. He looked at her with passion in his eyes, and she was filled with desire. She had dreamt of this chance again and never thought it would come true.

As Baron had never done before, he approached Egypt like he wasn't sure what to do. She sensed that there was something wrong. She asked, and all he could do was sit up and stop.

"Egypt, I can't. I don't want you to think this is all that I want from you. Isn't this where we or, should I say, where I went wrong? All you said before is I just needed you in bed, and I don't want you to think that. So I can't," he said.

He got up and took the sheet with him down the stairs and began to get dressed. When she came down the stairs, he handed the robe to her. She just pushed her hair into some sort of order and told him, "Don't go."

He said to her, "I think it's best for the both of us if I go." For once in her life she so much wanted to be used in a sexual way by him. All she could do was sit there and watch the man she truly loved walk out the door.

Egypt began to feel really sick, and her stomach was tightening in knots. The phone rang, and it was Baron. He said, "Egypt, would you come to dinner with me tonight? I promise there's no pressure." Egypt agreed and hung up.

A few minutes later, the phone rang again. It was Chang Lee. He wanted to speak with her about Fatima. He told her everything that had happened between the two of them. She asked, "Where did you get my number?"

"It was in Fatima's book. She's gone, and I don't have any idea where she went. I thought maybe she told you where she might have gone."

"Well, Chang, I don't think Fatima will be coming near me for a while, considering what she done to me."

Chang asked, "What happened between you two?"

Egypt said, "She betrayed my trust in her. I'm not really angry with her, just disappointed. Anyway, she couldn't be far. Just don't stay in her apartment waiting for her. Why don't you just go home and relax and she'll show up sooner or later."

"Okay, Egypt. Wait, here's my number, just in case you do hear from her. I guess I will go home and wait for her there."

Egypt told him that only because she couldn't be too sure if Fatima would bring another man to her place. She didn't want Chang to get hurt by seeing Fatima in full action.

There was not too much left for Egypt to do as she got dressed to head out shopping. She couldn't help but to continue to think about Baron's behavior in bed earlier. She wondered if it was true if Fatima told him of her men. She was very disturbed about it, but this wasn't going to upset her day.

She went from store to store shopping then she got a brilliant idea. She ran to a pay phone and called Sharla. She knew she was in town for a while. There's nothing more that models like than shopping, especially in New York City, mainly Greenwich Village.

Sharla had a flair for looking different. There was nothing that would stop them. Egypt met Sharla at the Vogue building near Thirty-fourth Street. By the time Egypt got there, she saw a young lady that appeared to be Sharla, but she was so surprised to see her with long beautiful hair. It hadn't been that long since they had seen each other. Egypt hugged her and asked, "Who made the tiny braids in your hair so long?" She saw this look on a female singer, and all she left out was the earring in the nose hooked to the ear.

"When did you get the earring?" asked Egypt. Sharla just laughed and said, "It's a black-Hispanic thing." The two of them headed out on their mission of charge it!

When they reached the stores, Banana Republic was their first stop. After they went safari shopping, Sharla asked Egypt, "Why are you so happy? It's been a long time since we've been shopping together." Egypt replied, "I know. Ain't it a shame?" And they giggled like a couple of schoolgirls.

Egypt pointed to an artist on the sidewalk toward Sixth Avenue. She told Sharla, "Come on. Let's both sit and let him sketch us. That way we could do a double portrait. This way, we could never forget this day." Sharla asked her again, "Why are you so happy?" But again Egypt just said to her, "Smile and I'll be right back."

The artist, an oriental, started to draw her picture, and all Sharla could do was smile. Sharla was a stunning young woman. Hispanic looking in appearance really, with light colored eyes, almost hazel, and dimples on each cheek. She was much better-looking than Egypt. She had the height Egypt lacked, but Egypt made up for it with her smile and sexy and sensual aura.

When Egypt returned, there was Sharla with a crowd of people round her. Several men and women recognized her from her appearances in all the fashion magazines, and they stopped to look. Egypt was finishing an ice cream sandwich and carrying more bags. She had gone to the novelty shop up the block. She stood next to Sharla and told her where she had gone. Sharla asked, "What did you get?" All Egypt said was, "Some lotion with flavor and a few more exciting things to enhance the evening." Sharla told her, "It's been sometime since I've gone in that kind of store. You make me want to buy something in there too."

The man had finished with Sharla and did a very good job. He began on Egypt, and Sharla went to the same novelty shop and gathered the items she wanted. By the time Sharla returned, he was finished. They both wanted the sketch, but Sharla gave it up to Egypt. The man told Sharla, "I would love for you to come to my studio sometime so I could get better lighting and do a more detailed portrait of you."

Sharla was flattered by this but told him, "I'm leaving soon for California to do a show. But give me your number, and I'll call you when I can." Egypt asked the artist if he would do a sketch of someone for her. She gave him a deposit, and the man mentioned, "Hey, I know this person in the photograph. It's the doctor that my mother goes to for her heart."

"Yeah, he's a heart specialist. A friend of mine."

Egypt and Sharla left. Sharla was confused about her actions. It had been so long since Egypt acted like that.

"Okay, I waited long enough for you to answer me, and I just about had it, lady. No, spill your guts. It's killing me not knowing, and you've had more than enough time to hold it to yourself. Now it's time to say it all. Well, talk," said Sharla.

"Well, all I can tell ya, darlin', is that I'm confused about who I really love. I decided to channel the confusion into positive energy. So I act happy and really I am very happy because I found out that Baron's still in love with me and making an effort to change his attitude when it comes to me. Yet I feel something for Chai too. Damn, there are so many feelings I'm going through that I'm just not sure I'm going to stay as happy as I am now."

"So, lady, once again you've managed to baffle me with your outrageous situations that seem only to find you.

"Do you remember when we were around nineteen and you loved Victor? And his brother Manny liked you and told Victor he was your man? Boy, it took you some time to convince him that his brother meant nothing to you. And you even pulled me in on it. That was so funny—the things we got into. We had true fun," said Sharla. "Do you remember when you thought you were pregnant by that guy—what the hell was his name?" asked Egypt.

"Oh, you're talking about Greg," answered Sharla.

"Greg, yeah that's right. Whatever happened to him? I haven't seen him in such a long time it isn't funny. Whatever became of that damn man? I remember that you had him wrapped around your little finger. Did he ever get married? He would have made an ideal husband."

"Hold on. He and I started dating again around a month or so ago. Can you believe that? Don't fall to the ground. We met again at a show, that fine hunk of a man has changed. He's a lawyer now. Close your eyes, honey, or they're gonna fall out your head. Worst of all I'm thinking about getting serious with him. He already told me that he wants to go out with only me. I think that'll be a change of pace—to just go out with only one guy," said Sharla.

"I'm so shocked I can't say a word. You get the prize for the surprise. So let's celebrate the happy occasions. Let's go back to my place then hit Madison Avenue for some shoes. Okay, my silly friend?" asked Egypt.

They both dropped off their things at Egypt's place. When they arrived, there was a message on her machine from Fatima, and before she could hear what she said, she cut if off for the next message. It was from Chai, and he told her he was leaving to go for a few days to Chicago. She smiled and told Sharla, "This is my chance to eat that cake and save the rest till later," and began to snicker.

When they stepped out the door, Egypt remembered there was something she had to do. She ran back into the apartment to hear her mother's voice leaving a message on the answering machine. By the time she reached the phone, her mother had hung up. Egypt played back the message, and much to her surprise, all she said was to make sure she would call tomorrow at ten o'clock in the morning. She thought nothing of it.

She stepped back out the door, and Sharla was already gearing up to shop again. They caught the bus this time and headed uptown where all the "classy bitches" shopped according to Sharla. She enjoyed shopping up there only because the women seemed so upset to see a black woman able to afford what they can and sometimes more. Sharla loved when the sales people would recognize her and give her special treatment. Egypt would get a big kick out of watching her friend acting silly. They two got along so well. They were about the only two from the old neighborhood, besides a few of the fellas, who did well for themselves.

When they arrived at the store, customers glanced at them as though they didn't belong there. This was one of Sharla's favorite stores when it came to designer names. She had modeled for most of them anyway. Two of the women in the store began to whisper to each other, and they continued to stare at them.

"Well, should I start, or should you? If they look at us again, I'm gonna step in her chest," said Sharla as she took off her sunglasses.

"Excuse me, Ms. Rivera, can I help you? Would you or your friend care for a drink from the bar?" asked the store manager.

"No, that's fine, unless she cares for something. Yes, this is Egypt, the founder of Egyptian Labels," said Sharla.

"My pleasure. I have heard much about you. Not too long ago your name was all over the papers. If there is anything that I can assist you with, please ask for me, and I'll be more than glad to help," replied the manager.

"That won't be necessary. I already saw what I wanted, and I'll have one of the workers help me. It seems those ladies are having a hard time with or handling something," said Sharla.

Egypt and Sharla gathered the things they wanted to purchase and hurried out the store. When they got to the door, they both began to laugh. One of the ladies seemed to have a small heart attack when she heard who they both were. Sharla grabbed Egypt by the arm and dragged her down the block to show her a poster.

There stood a picture of Sharla in a bathing suit if that's what you would call it.

Egypt told Sharla, "I think the string you're wearing is a bit too thick. You couldn't see enough." Sharla laughed. They both stood there and agreed that no matter what changes they seem to go through, they both haven't really changed much inside and for that they were happy. Egypt told Sharla, "You know, I had a lot of fun today. Like I haven't had in a long time. We have to do this again sometime and soon. This day was such a delight." They headed back to Egypt's place.

Sharla left Egypt, and she got ready for her evening with Baron. She figured it would be a night of intimacy. She put on her sexiest and most low-cut dress. An emerald green affair. The color fit her well. By the time she was ready, there was a knock at her door. She asked, "Who is it?"

A gentleman replied, "I'm here to pick up a Ms. Arcardi."

Egypt opened the door to see standing there a man in a chauffeur's uniform to escort her to an awaiting limo. She really was excited about this romantic evening. She so hoped to bring Baron back to her apartment.

She had everything ready for when she brought him there. As she rode to the restaurant, she thought of how it would be a quiet little table, hopefully with a candle and smooth music playing. She figured some jazz would be to her fancy.

When Egypt arrived at the restaurant, she gave her name to the maitre d', and he walked her toward a table of people. She was a bit shocked, especially to see Margherita sitting there. She took a good look to see two men stand up. As she approached the table, she saw it was Baron. She smiled. Egypt went over and kissed his mother on the cheek. Baron introduced everybody at the table. Karessa and Egypt had seen each other before but weren't quite sure where it was. Angela and Egypt got along great since they both enjoyed many of the same things.

The evening went very well. Francis and Karessa told everyone the date of their wedding and asked Baron to be the best man. While talking of their doings, Karessa remembered where she had met Egypt. They had both been at the same university for a short time when Karessa left to finish somewhere else. They both spoke of people they knew in common.

After dinner came to an end and everyone went home, Margherita took Egypt aside to tell her, "I know how much my son loves you. I miss you very much, especially in my time of sorrow, and I would like you to keep in touch with me."

Egypt knew this would be hard because of Chai, but she told her she would. Baron kept the conversation limited. *All he did was keep a respectful appearance in front of everyone,* thought Egypt. First thing she thought was that they were going to spend the entire evening together. Little did she know that it wasn't going to happen because Baron wasn't to take Egypt the way that she thought he would. They got into his car, and he drove her home. He walked her to her door. As she opened the door to let him in, he kissed her and said, "I have to go."

Egypt was speechless, she just stood there. Baron walked off into the night and got into his car. He had to head to his office. He mentioned it to her while driving her home, but she didn't really think he was going. He did say he had to go and finish a few things. Egypt had decided to step out herself.

She walked down the block to make sure that he had in fact left the area. As she ran down the street, she saw Gary coming toward her. She slid to the side of the building. As he passed by her, she felt her heart beating a mile a minute. When it was clear, she got into a cab and went off into the night. Once again, the night-rose was gone and in full bloom. When Egypt gets set into something, it's extremely hard to turn her from it.

Chapter 7

As Baron walked through the house, there was a sense of being complete as when Egypt was home. He jumped straight into the shower. He wanted to make love to Egypt. All he thought about was the look on her face, if only she knew that he was suffering also. Baron started to sing and make noises trying to take his mind off of the guilt feelings that were hurting inside. When he got out of the shower, he felt like going to the corner bar for a drink. As he walked around with his towel wrapped around him, he felt suddenly tired and he went back into his bedroom.

He turned the radio to soft jazz. Baron lay on top of his sheets and just began to drift away with the music. All of a sudden he felt something soft on his lips, and there standing over him was Egypt.

"I see you never changed the locks."

They continued to kiss, and he heard her say something through a mutter about the mountain coming to him since he never returned to the mountain. Baron knew that this time he could not turn away from her.

He began to make love to Egypt as though it was to last forever. He played with her hair and caressed her soft smooth skin with his lips. As he nibbled on her breasts, she sighed with ecstasy as she held on to Baron as though she were afraid he would leave. They rolled from one end of the bed to the other. Egypt lay on top of Baron, and as she looked down at him, her hair covered her beautiful tender breasts which were in full bloom. He grabbed hold of them and began to suckle them so gentle as not to bruise them.

She held his hair and began to feast on him also. As she devoured every inch of him, he filled the room with sounds of pleasure.

Egypt then kissed the beads of sweat on him. Baron placed his head into her bosom, and she stroke his wet hair. He stood up with her around his waist and slowly lowered her down. She held on tightly; she was afraid she was falling. He had no intention of letting her go; he continued to make passionate love to her. Egypt was startled by this. It was exciting and vibrant—something that was totally new to her. He placed her on the bed, and all she could do was smile. When Baron sat up, he reached for his drink and sipped from it and told her that the night had just begun for them. She could only keep on smiling because she knew that the night had just awakened a new dimension for her. She wasn't about to argue or ask questions.

While they were all tangled into one another, the phone rang. Baron had not stopped, but Egypt reached for the phone and handed it to him. She covered it up and said, "It could be important, maybe it's something about your family." Baron wasn't really in the mood for this. He took the phone with a bad tone in his voice. It was Jessie. He told Baron that they were having megaproblems with one of the groups they were trying to sign up and that they didn't want to sign a long-term contract with Egyptian Labels.

"Don't do anything till I get there. They're too hot to let them go short. I expect them to go platinum in no time at all. Just call Johnson. I want figures on paper and a contract redrawn but saying the same thing. I'll work around their lawyer. I'll worry about that, you just get the things I'm going to need. Get in touch with Heather and have her make all my plane and hotel arrangements. I'll be there, just hold your ass, okay." As Baron hung up, he looked so confused.

Baron opened his mouth. Egypt put her hand over his mouth and said, "Go ahead." She appeared a little disappointed in this, but she understood.

Baron began to wonder what he was going to do about his cousin Francis. There was a lot of unfinished business dealing with his father. Egyptian Labels took a back seat too many times. He got up and started getting ready to leave. Egypt covered herself with the sheet and sat up. She was dwelling on what he had said to Jessie and asked, "So what's going on with Egyptian Labels, Baron? Are they pulling in a lot of profit since merging with Stout? What kinds of overhead are we dealing with?"

"A large part of the money goes to child-care activities and the Foster Children's Foundation. Don't worry. There has been a big change since you left me." Egypt looked at him with a dirty expression and remembered quickly that in fact she did leave and she said nothing to his statement.

"The offices have hired many new employees and the inside of the building changed. Stout put in his own touches to an extent but not too much. I'm going to jump into the shower. Want to join me?" She shook her head no and he went in.

She put on her clothes and slipped out just as she slipped in on him. He came out talking to her and saw a note that read "See you when you return."

When she arrived home, she went straight to sleep. By the time she awakened, she had forgotten to call her mother. She went into the shower and heard the phone ring and ran right back out. Her mother called, and she told her, "I'm sorry, Ma, I forgot to call you, but I just had the most wonderful night of my life."

Egypt noticed that her mother was silent. She stopped talking for a while and then asked her mother, "Why are you, out of all people, so quiet?" Egypt stood there with her mouth open, and the tears started to run down her face. All she could say was, "How long was he sick?"

She fell to her knees and cried. "My father, why God? Why him?" She was so surprised but no one else was. They had known he was very ill, but Egypt had stayed away so long and hadn't kept in touch. She wanted to know why no one told her that he was so sick. As she sat on the floor, her mother told her, "I called out of respect for the fact that you are his daughter. Since you had no concern to visit us to see if things were fine, then there is no reason for you to stop your life to see a dead man." She said good-bye and hung up.

Egypt couldn't do anything but cry; she was so hurt. This hurt more because she knew that her mother was right. She hadn't made any time for them in so long. She hadn't even noticed how much time had gone by. She was so into herself, which wasn't like her at all.

Once again Gary came into mind. It had seemed as though his words were going to leave a dent in her mind and haunt her till the end of time. By the time she had gotten herself in some sort of order, she called Chai and told him what had happened. He too felt the pain of her father passing on.

Her father and Chai had known each other for sometime. When they had begun to date, her father had wanted them to marry. It was Chai who had saved his life on several occasions. Egypt told him, "I'm not even wanted at home."

He said, "Regardless of how they all feel, you have to go home because you owe that much to your father." She agreed. He reminded her that it wasn't too long ago that he told her that her father was sick again. Egypt told him, "I thought it was like the other times. I couldn't ever think that he would ever leave me. I had become someone only because it was his belief in me which kept me going."

"Egypt, don't worry, everything will be all right. I'll go with you if you need support. I love you, and you know I couldn't stay away at a time like this."After Egypt hung up with him, she called Marguerite and told her everything that had happened with her family so that Baron would know why she disappeared for a while.

Sharla called Egypt so she could hear her cheerful voice, and much to her surprise, Egypt was as down as an ant hole. Sharla also knew Mr. Acardi and came from the same neighborhood as they, except that Sharla's mother moved back to Puerto Rico right after her husband was senselessly killed in a robbery. When that happened, she vowed to get out and become something good. Just as Egypt had done also. The difference was that Egypt became too wrapped up in her own affairs that when she got with Baron she forgot about her family. She knew she was wrong for that, but there wasn't anything she could do about it.

Sharla came by the apartment to comfort Egypt. Gary had heard the news and came by also. He and Sharla hadn't seen each other in a while, and they talked amongst themselves while Egypt found out what she could on her own. There wasn't much money to bury him, so Egypt arranged everything without her mother's knowing. She wanted to at least help, so they wouldn't be set back by this. They didn't have any insurance, so it was going to be very hard for her family. She went to get some air and asked them to just watch the apartment and take whatever messages came in.

As Egypt walked through Washington Square, she felt so lonely and empty. She went to the arches and leaned next to them and began to remember everything that her father had always told her. He always asked her, "Is that what you want?" She would say, "Yeah, that's what I want." He would reply with, "Then don't stop till it's yours. If you can't get the exact, then get better. Never settle for second best."

Only she and her father were close, and everyone else was close to their mother. The tears just flowed as she stood there quietly. She wiped them away just only for more to fall down. She was the apple of her father's eye and knew it. She had done what the rest of them hadn't done. Get an education and use it. The only one coming close to success was her brother Jose who is still attending Columbia University for medicine. Her other brother and sisters were heading down the road to nowhere. But her mother would always nurse them back to help and cuddle them. She never understood her mother. She always thought her mother was jealous of Egypt and her father's relationship. Her father didn't take too kind to Gina and Noel's street ways. But her mother would do leaps and bounds and bend backward for those two. It was like their house was divided into two sides. It was like war in their household.

Sharla and Gary were hoping that Egypt was handling things well. When Egypt walked in the door, Sharla gave her a hug and told her, "I understand what's happening to you, and you know I'm going to the wake and funeral and I'll be there for you."

Gary said he would too. He said, "That's all I seem to be doing lately with so many people dying from over there and all." Egypt walked over to her picture of her family and just closed her eyes.

The wake was scheduled for tomorrow evening and the funeral to follow the next day. She realized that that's why her mother's voice was on her answering machine yesterday morning. She wished that she would have caught that call because by her forgetting to call back made matters worse.

When she finally got herself under control, she had to help the best way she could. Egypt, Gary, and Sharla went out for the day. By the time night had come, Chai had stopped by with some food and wine to comfort her; he didn't want her to be alone at a time like this, so he stayed there with her and slept on the couch.

In the morning Egypt got herself up and just looked at herself in the mirror, and Chai came up from behind. He held her tightly and kissed her as to show her he was there for her through this. Egypt turned and looked him in his eyes.

"I have you and many friends, but I have lost my family. What can I do? They don't really want me there tonight. I feel like my mother is going to be upset when she sees that I've taken over the expenses of the entire thing. Who's going to help my mother and brother? What am I going to do?" she asked.

"You will walk in there with your head up with respect and love in your heart and accept whatever comes at you as though it didn't hurt and then continue on as you have been doing. I believe that death is to remind us that we are only borrowing life for a while. Unlike a library book, we just don't know when we must give it up. So we'll do this together if you want, but you're not alone. You're making yourself feel that way. I'm not saying not to feel bad. You're wrong in the fact of not keeping in touch, but that doesn't mean you didn't care. That's wrong on their behalf to make that assumption that your heart had grown cold. You're going to go and be the woman I've loved and respected," he replied.

"That's so easy for you to say. Don't think it's going to be so easy to do. You're right, I am strong, and I'm not going to let this knock me. I love my mother, but there is no time like the present to show her that I am a woman. And if I have done a wrong, I can stand and accept what happens. Chai, what am I, crazy? She's going to eat me alive and make me feel and look like dirt in front of everyone," said Egypt.

"Will it be the first time? No, so go, do what you have to, and it will soon be over. Stop worrying about yourself, and remember she is hurting too right now, and her anger is from the pain of knowing she is alone now and her life has taken a big turn," said Chai.

As he left her, she decided to just sit in quiet somber and think of yesterday, the present, and what she had to accomplish before she reached a certain age. When she looked at the time, she only had a little while to get herself together. Egypt dreaded every minute of putting on the black clothes. That was her favorite color, but this was not for pleasure or looking good. This was for the real meaning of black—to show mourning. Egypt knew that her mother was going to be wearing black for the first year or so. She so wanted to call her mother and speak with her about what had been going on in her life. She knew that this wasn't the time or was it going to be the right place for such a conversation.

Baron had called to tell Egypt he wouldn't be back until that evening, and he would go with her to the funeral. He also said that he ordered a limo to take her to the wake. She told him, "That won't be necessary, Baron. You don't have to go with me tomorrow. You don't know my family, and I would like them to know you under better circumstances." He reminded her, "I met them sometime ago, and they seemed to like me."

"You don't understand. They, especially my mother, were very disappointed in my behavior lately. That I was always around them, and then all of a sudden, I meet up with someone and I find my way to the top. They think I'm ashamed of them and of where I come from. I know where I came from, and I know what it was like to be without many things. I remember school and the street—the street that caught almost all of my friends and didn't catch me. I remember everything and that's why I want to help people with natural talent to grow without the pain I and many others had to endure. Baron, it hurts to think that they really believe that I could feel that way," she said.

"Egypt, I am going with you. I can't let you face that alone tomorrow. I'll be closing the deal in around two hours, and I'll be going home," he said.

When Egypt heard the doorbell ring, she realized it was time to go. She got herself ready and walked to the limo behind dark sunglasses. As the driver drove up to the funeral home, she felt her throat get tight and dry and her knees weaken beneath her. As she stepped out and walked close to the door, she turned away. She knew that she had to go in there except her heart began to pound in her chest with pain. When she finally opened the door and walked in, people greeted her with condolences on her father's passing.

As she got closer to her father's viewing room, she was given a card which read, "Jose Carlos Arcardi: His birth and his death." To see that in black-and-white seemed to make it all the more real.

When she looked in the room, she had to turn away and walk out. Her mother had seen her and stood up to follow her, but before she approached, Sharla and Gary grabbed her hands and walked her in the room and halfway down the aisle and let her go the rest of the way herself. Egypt nodded her head as if to say hello to her family. She couldn't speak because she was holding back the tears. When her mother saw Egypt nearing the casket, she came up to her as if to remove her, but Jose stopped her. He grabbed his mother away from Egypt and whispered to her, "I don't want you going near Egypt."

Carmen looked at Jose angrily and said, "Don't jank me, Jose, I'm jou mudder." "This is not the place to show whatever it is you have bottled up inside."

"Here I don't want her!"

"She is father's daughter, and by the way she is also yours. Egypt has every right to come and say good-bye."

"She had no right to chrow her money into dis. She jus choing off her denero. It would have been fine da way it was going to be. Jou know she don't care. She just here to slap me in de face to cho people the things she could do."

Jose Jr. stared cold into his mother's eyes and began to speak to her like he was the man and she was the child.

"There is one thing I learned from Egypt and that is that "forgiving is an art and anger is common." She has been paying for my education and helping Gina with her problems, and many of the bills are paid by her. Things in the house are from her. Just Father didn't want us to say anything because no matter what, Egypt could never do anything right in your eyes. You could accept all the problems Noel brought into the house. Matter of fact any one of us could bring problems and you were there but not for Egypt, and this has been going on since we were small. Worst of all, Mama, we all saw it, and it hurt her to know we all knew it to be true. Why cause problems now?"

"Jose, she didn't know what was going on in our lives, and did she call to check? No, she was too busy. She no cared, dinero doesn't take da place of amor."

"She and Father kept in touch. There was a short period of time when we all lost contact which was around the time father took ill. But father made us all promise not to tell. When Dioni called Father, he made sure he told her not to tell Egypt. She and Egypt called one another. She never lost us, Madre, just you. That's because you pushed her out. So you need to drop that attitude now."

This was the first time Jose had taken charge of a situation such as this one with care. He avoided any confrontation with her, but he had had enough. "So love your loser son Noel, but I demand that you show some respect toward your daughter. She has done something with herself, and you should at least be happy for her." Jose got up and went over to Egypt, and they held each other tightly.

When he looked at her, he could see that she had been crying. He told her, "Look, Carmen is under control now, so don't worry." Egypt got a hold of herself and tried to hide her pain. They stared at their father in the casket, and Egypt felt her knees buckle underneath her. Jose steadied her, and she touched his hand and placed her scapular from her first communion on him.

Dioni went up and stood in front of Egypt and held out her arms, and they embraced. With a tearful voice, Dioni whispered in Egypt's ear, "Gina and Dave are married now. Father, Jose, and I went to the wedding. She and I are both pregnant." Egypt hugged her again and said, "I'm happy for the both of you. Take care of yourselves."

Egypt sensed that her mother wasn't too excited about her being there. So before anything would make this night a shamble, she walked to the back of the room and sat in the last pew.

As she sat there alone and lost, the emptiness was eating away at her, and she realized that someday it will be her—a thought that had never dawned on her before. There is no time for games and losing time. It was here for us to make the best of it. She saw her brother Jose standing up front and about to speak. He looked back at Egypt and winked.

"I choose to speak first about my father because I knew that no one would mention the most important thing about him which was his morals and his belief in the family as a unit. Father and I would argue and say mean things to one another, but before walking away, he would always say, 'through my love I fight with you.' I never understood what that meant until my sister Egypt told me. It was through his love that he worked two jobs, and it was through his love for me that he continued to believe in me. That he would always set good examples and go to church from time to time and he worked hard, and many times he would get up in the morning with the strength to go on and that would make me do the same. He never told me that we, his children, could ever make him hate them. But he wanted the best for us, so we wouldn't raise our children ducking bullets. He will not always be here for me to touch again, but no one can ever take him from my heart. Many people think that a spouse's life takes a dramatic turn. True, but the children's life will never be the same, especially when the figure of that individual was so strong and proud that no one or nothing can ever take its place.

So I turn to you, Father, and say you are at peace, and if there is to be a place for those like you, then you are in the kingdom of peace. Until we meet again, Father, until we meet again," Jose said, kissed his father, and walked straight out of the funeral home and wept.

There wasn't a dry eye after he had finished. When Egypt looked over at her mother, she realized that somehow there had to be peace, but she wasn't quite sure how it was going to come about. Somehow it will come, but for now it will be left alone. Egypt left to talk to Jose, and the priest was about to say the final words. But he spotted her leaving and called her to the front. She walked up to him and glanced at her mother. When Carmen stood up, Egypt stopped.

"I couldn't add anything that my brother has already said. Other than that I also love my father dearly," said Egypt with pride.

She then turned around and walked out of the room and found Jose. She went up to him and put her hands on his shoulders. He grabbed her hands and turned to her crying. She held him tightly to her bosom as if he were her child. They were both feeling lost. Their father seemed to be there with them even if only to give them inner strength.

They looked at each other and smiled as they embraced again. It seemed that they knew that the only way things would work is if they stuck it out together. Egypt knew it would be hard with her life and getting back with the company and trying to be there for Jose. But she knew more now than ever he would need her. So he had to get a grip on her life and take control. Baron had mentioned that her family was his family now and always. She wondered if that was true or not. She shook her head and wondered if she and Baron had discussed anything about their relationship. She felt that she wasn't going to assume anything, and she wasn't sure after this what she wanted out of life. The only thing she was sure of was that she still loved Baron.

Jose walked her to the limo and smiled at her. When she stepped in the car, she said softly, "This is not the end, just a new chapter in your life, Jose. Remember that time is like a library book. I was told that sooner or later you have to give it back. The moment we took our first breath the only true destiny we have is death. So with this borrowed time on life, we must make the best of it and achieve the sky and enjoy it. So, little man, you are now the *man*. I love you," she said with tears rolling down her cheeks.

As the limo pulled off, she felt that she had made a mistake by being with Baron so soon. When the car pulled in front of her apartment, she told the driver, "When you return to Mr. Gianelli, inform him that I won't be needing his services tomorrow." She went in and got in her bed and fell asleep.

The next morning, after Egypt pulled herself together, there was Chai at the door to take her to the church. She looked as stunning as a woman could look for such an occasion. She wore a beautiful black dress and hat with point d'sprit. This made her look extremely enchanting. She told Chai, "You know, my father always loved me to look my best, so for him, I will make sure that I look as good as I possibly can, within reason and with respect to what the day means and all." She went on to say, "Chai, you look wonderful too. I'm really happy you came."

"You're a good friend, and your father had wanted us to marry," he said hoping to score a few points in his favor. When they arrived at the church, she looked at her mother and saw the toll it had taken on her. She looked weak and tired and a little on the distraught side. Her mother just looked at her and so did a few members of the family as though they really didn't want her there. But due to the fact she paid for it and Jose had jumped down everyone's throat, all they could do was look and stare.

They were all quiet and kept their distance. Carmen walked over to Dr. Kamekano and thanked him for coming and spoke with him for a while. She said nothing to Egypt and acted as though she were a stranger to her eyes. This hurt Egypt, but she was going to keep the faith. Her aunts came over to talk with her, and this gave her some comfort. A couple of them asked her, "When will you ever marry and whatever happened to that Italian man you was with?" Egypt didn't say too much. It made her feel good that there were some people who welcomed her.

Chai walked over to Egypt, and everyone stopped talking about her personal life and asked her, "Who is the handsome man?" Egypt introduced her family to Chai and told them that he was one of her father's physicians sometime ago.

Soon after the formalities were over, the mass began. The immediate family was asked to sit in front. Everyone sat in the first pew, except Egypt. She sat in the back of the church since her mother didn't really want her there. She told Chai that she needed to be left alone while she was in the church, so she made him sit up front with the friends.

When the service was over, Chai walked to the back and held Egypt's hand. They got into the limo, and the driver started to close the door, but Jose jumped in there with them. He smiled and told her, "Stick in there, kid, you're gonna knock them out." She smiled because her father used to tell her that. She kissed him, and they rode together.

They reached the cemetery, and they all got out in somber silence. They stood by the burial site, and the final words were offered by the priest. It was quick and swift. Egypt and her brothers and sisters were waiting for their mother to fall apart since she held her cool for so long. Egypt's mother looked over at her while everyone was putting their rose on his casket. Egypt made sure she was different. She placed her father's favorite flowers on him—beautiful yellow and red tulips.

Egypt refused to go to the gathering customary after funerals. Instead, she gave Jose her new address and told him to visit and to call whenever. She and Chai went to his place, and she lay down and fell asleep for several hours.

When she had awakened, she was wearing her negligee, and Chai was on the floor reading a book. She sat up with a smile and thought to herself that she was one of the luckiest women in the world; she had two men who really loved her and treated her like gold. The problem was that real soon she was going to have to choose between one of them before she lost both. When she realized that it was getting late and that soon Baron would be looking for her, she tried to figure out a way of leaving without stirring up his curiosity. She walked around as if she were a lost pup. She finally told him, "Chai, I really need some time alone, okay?" And she left.

When she arrived home, she sat quietly in her apartment, lit only by candlelight. When she heard from Baron, he was on his way over. She told him, it wouldn't be necessary to comfort her at this time. She sat there and thought about how she left Chai so she could be with another man. She crept into her bed and knew the game was over. Not only will tomorrow bring a new day, it was going to bring a new beginning for her. *The change is about to happen now*, she thought.

Before she went to bed she placed a long-distance call to a man she had met sometime ago. There was no time to waste, and she had to get in the mood fast. When she was done making arrangements, she had a flight waiting for her to leave within the week.

She called Sharla next and asked her to stay in her loft while she went away on a trip. She explained that this was something she should have done a long time ago. In the next couple of days Egypt ran around making all the last minute arrangements she had to make. She was tired at one point, but the excitement of her future made the adrenaline rush through her and feel spaced-out. As the end of the week drew near, she was ready for anything. When the time came for her to leave, she flew out of her apartment and caught a cab straight to the airport without so much as a good-bye to anyone.

She slept on the flight almost all of the way. When she arrived, she felt a sense of relief. Nothing like new faces and a totally different way of life.

There was a gentleman standing there with a sign which had her name on it. She got into the loveliest of stretch Mercedes-Benz limousines. She had never stepped foot inside of one before. She was thrilled at all the attention she was getting so far. It was going to be a long ride to her final destination.

Egypt enjoyed the view of the countryside. She had never seen anything like this in her life and just relaxed and took it all in. As they entered into a gate, she didn't see the house and wondered where the hell they had it hidden. Much to her surprise, there stood before her the most enchanting home. She thought this is what he called a simple dwelling. It looked on the order of a minicastle if she wasn't mistaken. The gentleman helped her out of the limo and gathered the few bags she had brought with her.

She was thinking what kind of people live here. It can't be Carlos Montana. He sure doesn't act as if he owned something like this.

When she walked into the house, a woman showed her the way to a patio in back. There waiting for her was the most divine man she had ever come across. All she could think of was how good he could be. He walked over to her and kissed her upon her head as though she were too delicate to touch. They began talking of life and what she had wanted to do with hers. She had explained that her father passed away, and this helped her to decide to stop wasting time on things of no importance. Carlos told her, "You can begin tomorrow morning, and it's going to be business all the way."

Carlos had his secretary show her the grounds and make her feel at home. She told him, "I would just like to go to bed and try to get rid of this jet lag so that in the morning I can perform at my best." He showed her to her room, and she showered and went to sleep.

While she slept, all of the arrangements were being finished, and all the papers were being drawn up for her to sign before the shock of her father's death wore off since nothing he said ever made her come before. It would be one hell of a surprise to them in the states when all of this hits ground.

When Egypt awakened, it was four-thirty in the morning. She was still a bit tired. She arrived at the recording studio, and the first priority was to make a demo. She chose her music and began to sell her voice. Everybody stood back in amazement since not too many people can say they have ever heard her sing. Just a chosen few of which Carlos was one.

Years ago he had asked Egypt to work with him. He was pleased that she showed up now. He believed it had a lot more to do with just her father's death. By the time she had finished rehearsals, she felt as though she were a kite in the sky. She hadn't remembered feeling like that in a long time. She said to herself that there was no way she was going to let this opportunity slip by her again.

A few months had gone by and she worked harder than ever to show Carlos that she had what it took to be a success. It took more than just talent to make it out there. It took finesse, style, and more than anything else, a positive attitude; she knew she needed work in that department.

Carlos didn't want to get her hopes up, but he had a gut feeling about her that let him believe that he wouldn't have too much to worry about.

A possible tour was being thought out very carefully by him and other promoters. He had the job of booking a tour for the hottest male group in the business. They were expected to bring in a large capital, and the fact that she would open for them was going to do a lot for her future career. He knew that they had to work her to the core to be ready in time. She had to capture the people out there in a certain way or else she would be through and thrown away like a used gum wrapper.

"Egypt babe, come on get up. You're expected at the studio in an hour. Hey, sleeping beauty, arise and join us common folk," bellowed Carlos. He knocked on her door. When there was no answer, he opened the door and walked in. As he glanced into the mirror he saw Egypt sprawled out across the bed. She was only covered from hips to knees. Carlos couldn't move; it was like his feet were nailed to the floor. He saw her breasts were exposed, so he turned his head away from the mirror and stared at her. An urge went through him to reach out and touch her. He never saw her in that way. To him, she was just a lovely and very talented woman.

Egypt began to stir, and he didn't want her to awaken with him in the room. Her eyes opened, and she thought she saw a swift movement, but she just took it as though her eyes were playing morning tricks on her.

Carlos knocked again on the door and once again called out her name. She replied, "I'll be there in a moment, and I'm sorry I overslept."

When Carlos had slipped out of her room and had knocked again, he didn't noticed that someone had seen what he had done. He waited for her downstairs. When she came, she looked like a little girl running late to go out with Daddy. She ran down the stairs pulling herself together and dropping things and tripping. Carlos laughed and told her, "Your new wave attire is going to make an impression on the people at the studio." She didn't realize that her shirt was on inside out and her jean pockets were hanging out.

He continued to laugh as she looked at him as if he lost his mind. When she glanced at her shirt, she snickered and blurted out a loud chuckle.

Before they knew it, the end of the week had caught up to them. Egypt felt it was time to go out on her own and run rampant through the countryside. So she gathered a basket and headed for the country for a picnic. She asked Carlos if he would join her and he said his motto about "mixing business with pleasure."

"I just asked you out for lunch. Just to eat chicken and cheese and drink wine. I never mentioned that I was the feast. You need to lighten up a bit. Two adults who work together can also enjoy a meal and conversation without rolling in the grass. Unless you live a soap opera life," she said.

Carlos looked at her as if he wanted to change his mind and go. He walked toward her, kissed her hand, and replied, "Mon Cher, I shall have to beg your apology and sit this one out. Very good point, maybe when I can fit the time in my busy days. I am not as lucky as you. My time is kept tied up with more important things than going to a picnic."

"Well, monsieur, pardon moi that I take you from your busy schedule to have you waste time on such a demeaning thing as a mere picnic," she said as she walked off.

When Egypt found where she wanted to set up, she dropped everything and began to spin around like a child; she never felt so free. After she took out the food and ate a bit, she lay down and watched the birds in flight. A tear came from her eye, and she sat down and yelled, "Where ever I go, no matter how far, it seems you're always with me. Damn you, Baron!"

"Do you always talk out loud to no one?" said Carlos surprising her. "I've been working you too hard I see. So what an interesting place you've chosen to lie. The pond is only a few yards to your right," he said.

"I'm surprised you could tear yourself away from work. Why did you come and join me?"

"Nothing better to do. Besides everyone's face was hanging on the ground, and they needed a well-deserved break from things. No one else asked me, so I thought that the invitation could still be filled. Unless the person you were talking to doesn't want me here, I'll go," he said and laughed.

He stood up and started to walk away. She just kept eating as if she really didn't care. "Well, aren't you going to stop me and ask me to stay? I thought you wanted me here."

"If you want to stay then stay. If not then go about your merry way."

He asked her to take a walk over to the pond with him, and she went. As they walked, they talked about how the work was coming along and about how much more was left to do. She felt as if she were still at the studio. Carlos seemed to know only work and nothing else. He told her that tomorrow everyone will just pull the day's and the next day's load.

Then she gathered all the things and went back to the house. When she arrived, Carlos Montana was already at his desk, busy as usual.

One of the maids came to her and took the picnic things and told her that Mr. Montana instructed her to draw her bath and to take out her clothes for the evening. They were eating formal tonight. So off she went and did so.

When she came down, there stood some of the most handsome men she had ever seen in a long time all grouped together. The women walking around and mingling were all stunning. She felt out of place; she heard different languages, and she heard Carlos talking in his native tongue to a man whom she thought could stop a stampede of bulls. When Egypt went into the room, heads began to turn.

Many people heard of her, but this was their first time seeing her. Rumors had it that she was Carlos's secret lover held captive because her beauty would enchant any man; therefore, he kept her locked away for himself. He never mentioned that this was the night she was to be introduced to all the big socialites. Inside between the butterflies, she was burnt. Why didn't she know about this, she wondered.

The evening was a big success. When everyone retired for the night, Egypt placed a call to the states to talk with Baron to explain why she went off again. There was no answer, so she just lay down and cried herself into a deep sleep.

That morning she was off to work bright and early. It was like every day Carlos's schedule was filled with nothing but pushing for perfection. Egypt wondered if this man had ever loved a woman for long in his life. He must be hard to please. Always looking for the best of everything and if not giving, then pushing until he got what he wanted or breaks. He left early that day which was unlike him, but he left someone else in charge until that day's rehearsals were over.

When she went in the house, she saw Carlos speaking to a woman. She stood a little to the side where her face couldn't be seen. She heard Carlos telling this woman, "If there is something going on, it's none of your business." She slapped him, and he returned one right across her face backhanded.

She began to cry, and he exclaimed, "I want you to leave. None of this would've happened if I hadn't caught you with some man." Egypt couldn't make out the rest of the statement. Eureka held him close to her, but Carlos pushed her away and on to the floor.

"Time after time I told you not to push me too far. Just leave!"

She yelled, "You're involved with that cheap American bitch, aren't you?" Egypt realized that it was her she was talking about. Carlos told her again that this was just business, but she didn't want to hear it. She said, "I'm going to confront the cheap PR."

That was it for Egypt. She headed upstairs and pulled off all of her clothes and came down the stairs in the sexiest negligee. She walked straight into the room and made a drink for herself and Carlos. Egypt gave Carlos his drink and asked, "Am I interrupting something? I was wondering what was taking you so long." The young lady looked Carlos in the eyes and looked at Egypt like she wanted to rip her face off her head. Egypt got up and leaned on him to ask, "Is there a problem? If you two are busy, then I'll wait upstairs and leave you two alone." As she walked out the room, she told him, "Don't be too long."

Egypt was laughing inside and walked around the corner of the hall but didn't go up the stairs. She stood there listening again. The young lady was truly burnt by Egypt's entrance and exit. Egypt was holding in her laughter as they kept arguing until he finally told her to leave again. Eureka stormed out of the room, and with that, Egypt busted out into a roar of laughter.

Egypt walked in the room and asked him, "Was she a tad upset? Because there are a few things I get upset over, but one thing is if you don't know, then don't classify me as anything. Since she called me a bitch, I decided I'd show her what a real bitch is." Now that she had said this, she realized that she should apologize for her actions. Carlos stood quiet and just looked at her. He turned his back and then asked her to go to her room.

"I never noticed what a beautiful woman you are. Even though I'm a man and we are working together, I never mix business with pleasure, you know that. To keep respect and a decent working atmosphere, it would be best for us if you would return to your room while you're dressed like that."

Egypt felt awkward but in a good sense. She saw that he had a lot of respect for her and even more so for himself. And this was exciting to her. She had heard so much about him. Mr. Carlos Montana, the man who was known for passion, pleasure, and excitement. But on the same token he was known for destroying what he would create, for crushing those who stood in his way, and more so for denouncing those who betrayed him. He was not a toy-man in every sense of the word *man*. This was a man.

She found this totally attractive, but she knew that there was no chance at this time to make that approach. She didn't dare. She already had seen a display of his temper and had no intentions to have that happen to her. She smiled and went to her room.

While preparing her things for the following day, Egypt began to feel an emptiness within her. She picked up the phone and placed a call to the states to Columbia University. As she waited to be connected, she started to smile as she heard a voice so familiar to her.

"Hello? Hello, who is this?" She didn't speak at first, but she whistled into the phone.

"Hey, sis, how the hell are you? I'm so glad you called. It's never been this long since hearing from you. Well, say something?"

"You were on a roll, Jose, so any news for me about the grades?"

"Come on, you know that my education in high school compared to theirs is so vast it's hard to believe we all went to public school in the same state. Makes a real difference, Egypt, where you live and what they teach. Girl, I grab every free tutoring class I can just to try and break even."

"I told you, Jose, if you need the money for tutors just let me know when I call, and I'll give you the number, just call collect. I know the struggle. You forget I already went down that road. How is tu madre?"

"Well, our mother is holding up pretty good, but she just doesn't want to talk about you yet. She knows that you still help and that bothers her. Let me tell you, she didn't use the money that you put into her savings until she had to admit that your money made a difference then and now. I gave her your address before to see if she would send you a letter. I can only assume that she didn't."

"I really don't care so long as you and Gina are fine. How is Noel and Dioni?"

"As well as you would expect. See, we already knew what was to happen, and let's just say what was expected did happen. Cool, so what about you and your singing career. Can I start bragging about my sister who is corporately involved and also is a famous singer?"

"No, no, Jose, don't tell anyone about that. I'm trying to get Carlos to let me come out with a different name: Angel de la Noche, Angel of the Night. But he won't even go with the thought. Have you read anything about Baron in the social section of the paper?"

"I really haven't been reading anything outside of a textbook. I don't want to sound rude, but I have to go hit this free study group. Don't worry, I'm not giving in anytime soon since you've invested so much in me."

"You don't owe me anything. Just do your best, and I'll be sending some money to give you a hand with your extra load. I love you, Jose, and give the family my best."

"I do too, and just take it easy and don't get stressed out. Ciao, sis." And they rang off.

A couple of months had gone by and it was finally time to put the finishing touches on her opening act for the tour. Egypt was always told she would make it as a performer. This was her chance to find out. The feeling of achieving a goal had come true for her.

As everyone discussed the final arrangements of the financial situations including hotels, limos, and her diet and exercise programs, they all departed on the first flight. Egypt's first single had become a smash all throughout Europe and the Far East. All her new fans wondered what she looked like. They all wanted to see this mysterious and very talented woman. She had been away for just five months, but to her, it felt like five years. She sang tunes from the start of her career up until now for light entertainment. But she never dreamed that she would be the opening act of the concert tour for one of the hottest American male groups. The New Men in Town were very hot, and this was her chance to really be heard.

After several successful shows, Egypt had to sit back and asked herself, *Is it worth all that I have given up?* So much time had gone by, and the only one she kept in touch with was Jose. She wasn't about to lose touch with her brother. Everyone, even her mother, was proud of her. She wasn't the same woman she was when she left. Her appearance had changed along with her lifestyle; she was becoming adjusted to the fast and flash. Yet she knew deep inside she was still the same woman who loved Baron even though she was becoming physically interested in one of the members of the group.

They had completed more than half of the tour, and Egypt was still flying high on adrenaline. Eureka, the woman who had made the scene at Carlos's house, was also on the tour with them. She was the choreographer and one of the best in her field.

Eureka still felt like there was something going on between Carlos and Egypt. But throughout the entire tour, Egypt talked of nothing else but Baron and how much she loved him. Eureka approached Egypt and asked her if she had seen her true love Carlos. Egypt replied to her, "If you are talking about my true love, no, I have not talked to him since I left." Deep down she was getting tired of Eureka's smart-ass remarks about her and Carlos. She wouldn't mind a small affair with Carlos, but he runs on such a professional note that she wouldn't hold her breath. She began wondering if Baron was reading about her in the paper and saw the article where she told them why she did what she did. In the states there was plenty of talk about her. Especially about the conflict of interest of allowing some other label to promote her. She made statements which clarified why she did it exactly the way she did. She didn't want people to think that she only wanted her company created to build her up, so she went off on her own.

When Egypt opened in Paris, she began to feel very weak and light-headed. When she finished her number and went to her dressing room, she couldn't understand why the queasiness came and passed so quickly. Carlos walked into her room in a rush asking if she was okay. She replied, "Everything's fine. I'm just a little weary."

He sat next to her pulling her hair out of her face and sat there. She felt somewhat at a loss for words, so she asked him, "What did you think of the show so far?" He lifted her chin in his hand, looked down in her eyes, and said, "You are some kind of woman." He softly began to kiss her lips several times and then from nowhere got intimate with her. He laid her down on the bed in the dressing room and took off her costume, what little there was of one.

Carlos looked at her breasts and began to fondle them. He looked in her eyes and slid his hand from her breasts to the side of her neck and began to kiss her with every intent to seduce her. And this he did. Egypt wondered what this would feel like; she no longer had the wonder. It was happening. She was overwhelmed. He wasn't like any other man she had been with. He was a passionate and demanding lover. Before she knew it, she was on top of him looking down and not believing that such a forceful and overbearing man could be so gentle and fulfilling at the same time.

Unbeknownst to them, Eureka had seen Carlos go into Egypt's dressing room and not come out for some time. She didn't hear any talking, but she knew that no one had come out of there. She turned the doorknob very slowly, and when she opened it, she looked straight ahead and saw the two of them through the mirror.

The room was brightly lit; she could see everything and was shocked by it. She had a knot in her stomach because she still felt for Carlos. The sight of the two of them embracing in rapture tore her apart. As anger and rage ran through her veins, she ran into her room and grabbed her camera off her desk. Papers, tapes, and her small recorder fell to the floor. She looked at the mess and smiled as she grabbed the recorder. She set it to record and slid it in the room and she managed to take several pictures without either of them knowing. She hoped that they wouldn't notice the recorder. It was small, but the microphone was very strong. She closed the door. They never knew what happened since they were so involved with each other in their lustful pleasures; they were unaware of what was in store for them.

Carlos grabbed a hold of Egypt and told her, "There is no way that I'm going to give you up and let you go so easy." She started to kiss him on his chest, which was very masculine. As he sighed in ecstasy, she told him how wonderful he was and how she felt at that moment. He rolled her over and kissed the arch of her back and held her buttocks tightly. As he held her by her waist and up on her hands, he continued to please her. She shrieked in completion as she felt a warm sensation from her head to her feet. At that moment, Carlos grabbed her waist tightly, arched his back, and lowered his eyes as he responded to her erotic sounds; he no longer could sustain or endure the passion running through him. As he released the rapture within him, he collapsed on top of her back. As they lay there motionless and speechless, they continued to breathe as if there wasn't enough air.

Carlos rolled Egypt over and lifted her in his arms and walked her to the mirror, his foot just missing the recorder lying there. He made her look into the mirror just so he could tell her that he wasn't letting her go no time soon.

"It's time for you to decide whether you want Baron or me, and I say it's me."

Egypt didn't say anything; she was confused. She never realized that Carlos even thought about her in that way, yet she was so happy. There wasn't much she could say. He got dressed and grabbed her by the arm and pulled her close to him and told her, "I'll be back to take you." There was a knock at the door, and since she wasn't completely dressed, he gave her a towel, and he sat in a chair and told whoever it was to come in.

Eureka and a few others came to tell Carlos that some things needed his okay. Eureka asked Egypt, "Are you feeling much better?"

"Much better," she replied.

"I bet you're feeling much better now," chuckled Eureka. Eureka stayed behind while Egypt took a shower and Carlos attended to his business. She waited a few moments and took the recorder and got out of there in a hurry.

Daimon, one of the boys from the New Men in Town, walked in her room and asked Egypt if she was feeling any better. Egypt explained what happened to her. He stressed that she should see the doctor when they returned to the states. She agreed because she could no longer go on feeling that way. He also told her that they only had until the next morning when they would be in the states. So that if she wanted him to go with her, he would. She was glad because she didn't want to go by herself, and she couldn't trust anyone else. She definitely didn't want the press to get hold of this. That was the last thing she needed right now.

Before she knew it, there was a knock at her door. By the time she said come in, they were in. It was Manny, Bach, and Jayme dancing their way into the room. Egypt laughed and said, "Aren't you missing one? If anyone else tries to get in this room, they better take a number because there isn't enough room to even pass a light case of gas."

Suddenly a voice came from the hall. "If I can't come in, I guess you can't have this. La, la, la, la, la. So what do you say?" replied Neil, opening the door slightly waving a yellow sheet of paper at her.

She ran to the door to get it, but he told her, "First a kiss." She kissed him on the cheek, and he handed it to the others as they broke out into a chorus of the song that was on that piece of paper. The lyrics were the song that she composed about her love for Baron. After they finished, Neil in a deep voice said as he read the enclosed telegram from Baron, "I hope you enjoyed the song. They agreed to sing it for me to you since this was from you to me. I've been sending you flowers, but this time I wanted to send this singing telegram to tell you something. Also I'm returning something that was yours and hopefully you will have it on when I see you again. That is if you still want me. Many things have happened but nothing that we can't overcome together. Hopefully you will say good-bye to everyone else and come back to me. Never stopped loving you. Baron."

"Stop."

Egypt started to cry, and she began to feel a little sick and ran into her bathroom. The guys started getting worried because as long as they have been together, they have never seen her this way. Jayme told them that he would stay behind and help her out. Daimon told him, "Remember—don't."

Jayme looked him in the face and told him, "Not to worry. I knew it was over, that it was just her loneliness."

Bach walked over and patted Jayme on his back and said, "You've got a lot of heart to sing that song knowing how you still feel for Egypt." Manny and Neil just shrugged their shoulders and reassured Jayme that they were all hoping he would wake up. Jayme just smiled and reminded them of his magnetic style and his melting words, and he shoved them out the room.

He glanced at all of her pictures, and there was a picture of them together along with photos of her with other people. He opened a book that had a picture of Egypt and Baron embracing each other on it. As he closed the book and turned around, there stood Egypt smiling at him. She reached out her hand for the book, and he gave it to her. She said, "It doesn't pay to be nosy because you could get hurt that way."

Jayme reached out to her and asked, "Why has it been so long since we've been together?" He understood that she wanted to keep their relationship a secret. She was confused about it and told him so, but as far as a true relationship was concerned, she wouldn't be able to honor it properly.

"Look, Nobu Tanaka, I care for you, but you can't expect me to just stop and begin something with you that I'm not sure of. Please, I really do care. I told you before I'm still confused, and I just need to think," she said and began to cry.

"Do you realize that I felt for you since the first day I met you? Can you understand what it was like to sing something to you from some other man? I have to pretend how I feel for you and act as a friend. We've been seeing each other for three months now, and for the past two weeks, you've distanced yourself from me. I know that there's no one else that you could've been with, but I can't hide it much longer. All the guys know. They saw you leave several times and saw me kissing you, so I couldn't lie to them any longer," said Jayme.

"Tanaka, how could you? I trusted you, damn!" she yelled.

"What is with you, Egypt? I can't figure you out. Why are you calling me by my Japanese name? What—to remind me of who I am? I know that I'm Japanese. One who is in love with you and wants to spend time with you and wishes to make you happy. But I see that's not what you want, so before I outstay my welcome, I'll leave you now. *O-yasumi-nasai*," said Jayme.

"*Iie matsu.* Jayme, I said no—wait! *Kuru koko*—I said come here. Or don't you understand your own language?" asked Egypt sarcastically.

"*Sumimasen*," said Jayme as he turned around slowly. "Just in case you didn't grab that, I said excuse me. Where did you learn Japanese?" he asked.

"That's a long story, but I do. So realize what you are has nothing to do with what I am trying to say about you," she said and reached over and held his hand close to her face and kissed it. "Jayme I've found love and lost it. I'm to a point where I don't know what love is or if it is real. What I do know about is confusion, lust, and frustration. What is lovemaking? What is real love? What we did, was that lovemaking, or was it two people who were lonely and working close together and in the heat of the moment just released sexual desires? What do we really have? Tell me, Jayme. Is it love, or is it loneliness that brought us together? Because loneliness has played a big part in my relationships, and if it wasn't that, there was a great chance that it was pure lust. When has it really ever been love?" she said. She looked him up and down and ran out the room and down the hall, out of the door, and into her limo.

By the time it sunk in, he ran down the hall after her. When he reached the back door, there stood Daimon putting his hand up and telling him to stop. Daimon told him, "Leave her alone. Just let her go to the hotel and relax." Jayme pushed him out of the way and went out the door only to see the taillights of the limo departing.

Jayme held his head in wonder and took a deep breath. Daimon held him by the nape of his neck gently, then patted it and told him, "Bear in mind that she's ill and let her rest. Tomorrow we'll all have a long flight ahead of us."

Jayme looked him straight in the eyes and said, "Love never rests." He walked over to their limo and got in.

In the limo no one spoke at all for almost the entire trip. Bach then asked everyone if they wanted to have a sing-along. As he began to sing a short chorus of "Row, Row, Row Your Boat," they all looked at him and started to throw various things they found in the car at him. Bach had broken the tension among them.

Manny replied, "Well, thank God, I don't have to go through any of that shit. Everything is going just fine in my life."

"Of course everything is fine. You're going out with my sister, and I'm sure as hell not going to let you screw that up now, would I, Manny?" said Jayme.

"That's funny, Nobu," said Manny and snickered.

"Keep that shit up, Nobu, and I'll break you in half because I have a few things on you myself, Manuel Antonio Rodriquez Delgato Santiago," replied Jayme as everyone began to laugh.

"Well, you can kill that noise too," said Manny angrily.

"You need to simmer down considering I have a few things on you myself, Manny. Several extra visits in France and a few in Italy. I don't think Tamara would like it very much. By the way she said she would be at the airport, so if you have any blotches, you better get started with that comb on your neck and any other areas, my comrade," said Jayme.

"I think you need to get a grip," said Daimon. "Look, you need to get your two cents out of my life and mind your own business and stay out of mine. Maybe you'd have some business of your own to worry about. So take some of my advice and mind your own p's and q's and get a life," Jayme replied.

"You need to chill with all that. Listen to what I'm telling you. You should forget this whole thing with her," said Bach.

"When have I ever told you what to do? When have you ever heard me tell you, 'Bach, I think you should be taking care of all those kids you got'—your private legacy," said Jayme.

Jayme turned to Neil and stared him straight in his eye as if to say that he was next on the hit parade. Jayme asked him, "What do you have to add to this?" "Jayme, I couldn't care less. I have my own trials and tribulations. I don't have time to contemplate yours. As far as I'm concerned I don't care so long as it doesn't interfere with the group because that feeds and clothes me. I let nothing come or anything stand between me and this group, and I have little to no respect for anyone who lets anything stand between them and their goal."

Jayme swallowed hard and said to everyone, "The group means a whole lot to me, and I'm just a bit frustrated." Daimon refused to look Jayme's way until Jayme reminded them, "No matter what, Neil is right, and it's time we all began to act like we are together instead of just acquaintances."

Everyone cracked a smile. "But when you're right, you're right. So I'll be the first to admit that I was wrong for forgetting that we're a team, and we must function as one and not like we can just do whatever we choose to now. So let's cool out because we'll all be home soon, and no matter what, I'm not going to stop caring for her, but I will open my eyes and make sure that I'm not interfering with what our main purpose was in the beginning."

By that time they arrived at their hotel and ran through it like wildfire. They all made sure that they enjoyed their last night there. They got dressed and hit the streets.

As they talked to some of the local people and took pictures, they began to start acting like they were friends again, an unbeatable team. They forgave each other's shortcomings and realized their friendship was truly an important thing.

Neil, Jayme, and Bach decided to go in the park and run through a flock of pigeons. They ran into each other playfully and laughed. Daimon and Manny ran behind them spraying them with water. They got together holding each other by the shoulders and began to sing their favorite song as they headed back to the hotel.

On the way, they stopped near a wishing well and grabbed in their pockets for change to throw in. They put their hands together and threw a penny over their shoulders. Like all for one and one for all. They turned and watched the water make ripples as the penny sank to the bottom.

By the time they got back to their rooms, it was almost morning, and they had to finish packing. When Jayme went to Egypt's room, she was already gone. He went to check with Carlos to see where she went. Carlos explained, "Egypt is not returning with the rest of us. She received a call from the states only this morning while you were out having fun. Her mother has taken ill, so she just wanted to be alone for now. I guess there wasn't too much more she could take with her father just passing away recently.

Jayme looked surprised because in the whole time that he was with her, she never mentioned anything about her family, much less that her father had passed away. Carlos added, "That is one of the main reasons that prompted her to pick herself up and get going with her music career.

Her father always wanted her to do that. He wanted to be a musician himself and was very talented I heard. He found there was no steady money in that. He had children and a wife to take care of, so he had to put it on the back burner. He hoped she would be his legacy."

Jayme thanked him and walked away like a wounded bird. He was so hurt and caught between tears. All this time he felt so close to her until then, and he realized that there was so much more of her he really didn't know. When he returned to his room, everything was packed for him and on the way to the airport. Bach went looking for him and found him sitting by the windowsill. Bach put his hand on Jayme's shoulder. He stood up and stared with so much pain in his eyes that Bach felt it too. He hugged Jayme and held him by the shoulders as he led Jayme down the corridor.

While at the airport there was a silent moment before Manny stood up and started to sing, "I'm leaving, on that midnight train to Georgia." As the rest joined in, Jayme sang out from his feet to the deep corners of his soul. When they boarded the plane, they left behind Carlos and a few others to wrap up their stay. Most of all he hoped he left behind the pain he had experienced. He began to wonder, was it love, or was it what she told me? But he felt that loneliness could never feel that good. It had to be love. Love. Well, love on his side anyway, he couldn't speak for her. As Jayme looked out of his window, he reclined in his seat and drifted off to sleep.

Back at the watering hole, Eureka walked up to Carlos and began to get very passionate with him. Carlos kept trying to move her out of the way, but she pressed herself against him and kissed him. Carlos stood there not moving. She told him, "Stop trying to act cold. You know there was a lot that passed between us." Carlos still said nothing to her and continued to finish what he was doing. This angered Eureka to no end, but she acted as if it were nothing to her.

She felt that he didn't want her anymore. She decided to get more aggressive. He snatched her by her hair and pulled her up against him. He kissed her like he was a savage animal. He even bit her. He tore off her blouse and manhandled her breasts. She shrieked in pain and pleasure. That he couldn't fathom.

He grabbed her and made her look in the mirror. As he held her tightly, he screamed, "Eureka, why don't you have any pride in yourself? Why do you insist on being with a man that wants nothing to do with you?" Eureka stayed silent. He turned her around and stared at her.

"Eureka, what's wrong with you? Can't you see I don't love you? I don't even want to sleep with you. The thought of even picking up where we left off is too depressing. So don't even. We had nothing, and we have nothing. You're a damn good choreographer and we work well together, but besides that, there is nothing there. Do you hear what I'm saying!" he yelled.

Eureka screamed, "Let go of me! I don't want you either. All you ever think about is that damn Egypt bitch anyway. But you'll never be happy with her because she's still in love with Baron, you fool. There's nothing that she wants to do with you, so don't you feel like me?"

"Not really, I'm not like you. You don't see me knocking my head on the door where I'm not wanted. Am I chasing after her? No. But look who's chasing who! So are you all that hard up, or am I just that good?" he asked as he broke out laughing.

Eureka went to slap him, but he caught her hand. Before he got ready to hit her, he turned his back to her. He sat down and put his head in his hands. She cried out, "Why are you doing this to me?" She touched him. Carlos pulled away, and she cried more. There was nothing else to be said, especially when love was never there in the first place. He really didn't want to hurt her like that and it hurt him too, but she needed to wake up. He felt that if he hadn't said those things, the silly game would continue.

Eureka heard those same words, but it meant nothing to her. She still felt that it was Egypt's fault for what happened. Carlos had his back turned to her, and when he turned around, he thought she left. But she was right behind him, completely naked. He just looked and felt he was weakening. If it wasn't for his self-respect, he would be tempted to reach out and allow his carnivorous ways to begin to devour her whole.

She approached him and took hold of his hand and placed it upon her breasts. Carlos regained his senses and took a deep breath. While she unbuttoned his shirt, she kissed his chest and gently nibbled one of his nipples and caressed him. He turned from left to right, very bored, and asked her, "Are you finished?" As he moved her out of his way, he took the things he was working on and walked out of the room, leaving Eureka standing there naked and feeling very cheap and alone.

She dropped to the floor and wept. She lay there holding herself in a pool of tears while Carlos was preparing to leave for the states. He had to make sure all the arrangements for the rest of the tour were handled properly, and he couldn't be bothered with Eureka now.

When Eureka got herself together, she went to Carlos's room and walked in. He looked totally disgusted with her. He said, "When the tour is over, there's no reason for you to stay around. And if you want to leave now, I understand."

Eureka said, "Carlos, wild horses couldn't drive me away. Most of all I'll tell you something, sweetheart. Remember what goes around definitely comes around, and sometimes just a little push is needed."

"I'm warning you, Eureka, not to sabotage the show because there is more people involved than just us. And you better not harm Egypt. Remember that she has been through a lot lately, and now that her mother has taken ill, there is no telling where her mind is presently," replied Carlos.

"Look, baby, that's not my problem, and I don't really care," she said.

Even though he was angry, he couldn't understand why she was telling him this. When she left his room, he slammed the door. He wondered about her actions and why she was behaving like a spoiled child. She was never like that when they were together. She was a pain in the neck sometimes and a bit dizzy. Not like the way she was acting over Egypt. He couldn't make heads or tails of what was going on in her mind, but he felt she was going to be nothing but trouble. With this on his mind, he couldn't concentrate on anything else.

As everyone else got themselves together, the last few people behind made sure that everything was ready and off. They were all happy to get to the states, and this trip was awaited by some of them since they had never been to the states before. Eureka sat a few seats behind Carlos on the plane. As he tried to read, he felt her eyes piercing through his back. He turned once to face her, and she was glaring into in his eyes and smiling. This worried him because she was angry with him and acting too friendly.

As the stewardesses walked past Eureka, she stopped one of them and gave her a message to give to Carlos. The woman handed him a drink and the note. He read it and sent back the drink, explaining it wasn't necessary to send a drink and that he was too busy to talk. He then asked for a phone to call Egypt to see how she was doing. An answering machine picked up the call and he didn't leave a message. He got up to stretch his legs and back from the long ride. Eureka reached out her hand to stop him from passing. She expressed, "I'm sorry, and I've had time to think things over. I want a good show, and if there was tension, it would show in the performance."

Carlos didn't know whether or not to believe her, but she was absolutely right about the effects of tension on a performance. He nodded his head and returned to his seat.

People noticed the change of behavior between them. Before they could talk, but now they had steady eye contact with fire in their eyes. Eureka's fury had just begun, and her rage was sure to follow. This was a scorned and very jealous woman. But what's worse is her obsession with becoming Mrs. Carlos Montana. It seemed she was not going to stop no time soon; she was a woman on a mission.

The announcement came over the loudspeaker that they would be approaching New York's La Guardia airport and would be landing shortly. Several of the passengers started applauding. Eureka walked up behind Carlos and touched his arm. Carlos nearly jumped out of his skin.

"Just for the record I said I was sorry, but I never said I would stop loving you. Plus more than anything I know that deep down inside, Carlos, you're very much in love with me too," she said and kissed his cheek.

"Would you please control yourself and stop this? You're taking this too far now. You don't believe me, do you? Listen, for the last time, I don't love you, and furthermore I'm beginning to worry about the way you're acting over this," he replied tensely.

There wasn't too much left to say after that except that he needed to get rid of her somehow and real soon. When he heard the plane was getting ready to circle the airport, he asked for the phone. Carlos made several calls. He made sure that his car was ready for him by the time he stepped off the plane and left messages with several people about getting a new choreographer. The show wasn't scheduled to go on for a little over a week, and he hoped that he could replace Eureka and make sure she was sent back overseas. He had every intention on having her held there for psychiatric treatments. He was starting to believe that she was losing her mind slowly.

By the time he was done with the calls, the plane was preparing to land, and he had to return to his seat. When the entourage had collected their luggage, some headed for their cars and some hailed cabs. Carlos saw the car for him, and as the driver opened the door, Egypt stepped out of it.

"Welcome, darling. I'm so glad that you arrived here safely," she said and kissed him. They held the kiss momentarily until he remembered Eureka wasn't too far behind him. When he looked over his shoulder, she stood there looking at him as if he had committed adultery.

"Babe, isn't that Eureka over there? Why is she standing over there and doesn't come and say hi? Tell her to come here."

"No, don't even do that. Please, that would be like inviting disaster and a lot of trouble over here. Just get in the limo, and I'll explain everything on the way to the hotel. Please believe me. Hurry in before she gets here," he said and pushed her in the car.

"Look, Egypt, I don't want to alarm you or anything, but Eureka is acting as if something is going on between us. How she got that idea I haven't the foggiest. All I can tell you is that she had a sixth sense on this. She is beginning to give me the willies. The creeps. Everything about her is beginning to make me wonder. I feel as though she has just begun something, and when she finishes, it'll be something we both will never forget," he said distraught.

"Carlos, I really think you're making a bit too much out of this. You make her sound as though she is obsessed with you or something," she said.

"Well, if you want to call it that, you can. As a matter of fact, I think you hit it right on the nose. Tell you one thing, I'm gonna hurt her if she continues with her shit. She's becoming a pain in the ass. I've known her for a while now, and I do recall her always planning a future together, but I've always set her straight and she would agree," he said as he drifted back in time.

"Is this your ego talking, or do you really believe that she's capable of creating a lot of problems for us as well as the show?" she asked.

"There is no telling, and I really don't know her anymore. She's set on believing that I want you. She's right, but I know that has been kept between us. No one knows except us," he said.

Meanwhile Eureka was listening to the recording she made of Carlos and Egypt in the dressing room. As she sat in her cab on her way to the hotel, she didn't know that Carlos changed her hotel reservations. When she arrived, the desk clerk informed her of the change and that she was in a neighboring hotel. She was furious. She asked the clerk who made the change. He told her it was a Mr. Montana. She grabbed her belongings and started to leave. She suddenly turned around and asked if there was an Egypt Acardi registered. The clerk said there was no one by that name there. She sighed in relief.

When Eureka had gone, Carlos and Egypt walked through the lobby. He spotted Eureka first and grabbed Egypt, and they hid behind an advertisement. When he saw her leave, they both walked quickly to the door to make sure that she had gone.

Egypt said, "I'll see you in a few days because there's so much I've got to do. Regardless of how you think, I feel you're making a big deal out of this. And anyway I wasn't ready for a commitment."

Carlos turned his head and asked, "What made you come out and say that?" She looked him in the face and told him, "I haven't forgotten that day, and it meant a lot to me, but I have a lot of things in my past to get in order first and then I can begin with my future." She left him and went home.

When she arrived home, there was a message on her answering machine. When she played it back, she heard Baron's voice telling her that he still loved her and so much has happened to him while she was gone and he missed her very much. She was so excited to hear his voice. He wanted to see her that evening. She ran around trying to prepare herself because she longed to see him.

Chapter 8

"Angelica, Angelica, what are you doing now?" Franco laughed.

"I'm trying to get the kitchen in some sort of order. You could help, Franco. Baron wants everything perfect because Egypt's coming over. Did Athelia fix upstairs?" asked Angela in a frenzy. "Just calm down and relax. Hey, beautiful, I noticed something. When the time is right you're gonna make a wonderful mother. Right now you're a damn good wife, except for a few things. You're too noisy sometimes and a bit rambunctious, but other than that, you are fantastic," said Franco while helping her pick up the groceries off the floor.

Angela was rushing so much she dropped the groceries again. As they both straightened up the kitchen and started to cook a light dinner, Franco kissed her on the cheek. She gave him a pinch on the rear end. Franco turned and grabbed a hold of her behind tightly and kissed her.

Baron was standing there watching and shaking his head. "So are you two cooking food or each other?" he said as he laughed. "You know, Angelica, it feels so different to see you this way. Sometimes I wanna rip him apart for touching you. And in the same note you're his wife. Lucky for him!" and they all laughed.

Angela reached out to Baron, and they embraced. She said, "I love you dearly, Baron, and I hope one day that you're as happy as me and Franco are." Franco said to Baron, "There's a woman out there for you, and I sincerely hope the day will come soon." They started getting the house in order.

Baron was hoping that after tonight Egypt would stay home, but he had a bad feeling running through him. The phone rang, jarring him out of his thoughts. He answered it; Francis was on the line.

"Baron, it's Francis. Bad news, you have to come over here right away, and I'm telling you there could be trouble."

"Okay, Francis. I'm on my way."

137

He told Angela, "Look, that was Francis, and I gotta go. If I'm not back in time, send the car for Egypt and tell her to wait for me and I'll be back in a few." Baron ran to his bedroom, and when he headed for the door, Angela grabbed him by his waist and asked, "Baron, where are you going, and why? I know you're strapped, I felt the gun. Please, stop this craziness!" she pleaded. "What happened to Father was enough, and we can't handle anything happening to you too."

Franco pulled her away from Baron despite her protests. She slapped Francis hard on his face and screamed, "Stay out of this, this is between me and Baron!" And she walked away. Franco asked Baron, "Do you want me to go with you?"

"No, I think it's best that you be here with Angelica and be here for Egypt when she comes and that way I know they'll be safe," he said and he left.

For a while, Angela had no words for Franco. He took her by the arm and sat her firmly in the chair. She finally said something intelligible to him and yelled at Athelia. After she made a complete ass of herself, Franco walked into the yard with his whiskey sour. Angela ran out behind him and slapped up the drink in his hand. Franco raised his hand to slap her, but a voice from out of the darkness said, "Don't even think about it. If it's that kind of party, the both of you can go back to Italy because none of us are going for that here."

"Who the hell is that? Show your face!" said Angela.

"Tell your sweet love to back away from you now, and I'll be more than happy to show my face. First of all, Angelica, that wasn't a smart thing to do. I think I would have knocked the shit out of you myself. But see, you're family, so I just couldn't stand here and watch, right, Tigre?" said the voice.

"Oh shit, damn you hell, it's you, Joseph. Where the hell have you been hiding? The whole family has been worried, you little shit," said Angela.

They embraced, and Joseph wiped away the tears that were forming on her face. He picked her up and spun her around in the air and put her down. He walked over to Franco and put out his hand. Franco took a moment to receive it because he didn't care too much to be threatened. But he shook his hand firmly, embraced him, and slapped him on the back just like he would family.

They returned to the house. Angela told Joseph of the family happenings since he's been gone. Joseph said, "You know, Angelica, I never told anybody this, but I figure I should let some of these things in my head fall out. When I and Francis was growing up, we never really got along. Uncle Nunzio always was spending more time with Francis than me. I guess I figured it was because Father always was spending his time with me and distanced himself from Francis. I guess we just grew apart because of Nunzio's interest in Francis and me being with Father all the time. Francis is really close to all of you guys, right?"

"Remember, Joseph, we didn't used to get along either. Then Francis broke up that fight we had when we were teenagers, remember? Francis was always family oriented, that's one thing I can say about him," Angela said. *Whereas you, Joseph, are all into yourself,* she thought. "Francis taught me a lot about what 'family' means and how important it is to keep the ties strong, considering all the scrapes he saved me from."

They were getting in a deep conversation when Athelia reminded Angela about Egypt's arrival. She stood up and ran upstairs to get dressed and told Franco to do the same. As she dressed, she thought Baron would be happy to see Joseph again. She was glad she had invited him.

After dressing, she made a quick phone call to one of Joseph's old girlfriends to see what she was doing tonight. She thought she had a great surprise for him. By the time everyone was dressed, a phone call came in from Baron saying he would be there shortly. Angela told him that she'd invited Marilyn.

"Angelica, that's fine and all, but you know I wanted everyone gone at a certain time because I'm hoping to convince Egypt to come back home."

"I think you should take it slow for now, but I know you're not going to listen to me anyway."

When she got off the phone, the doorbell rang, and she knew it couldn't be Egypt yet. When she turned around, there was her old friend Marilyn.

"Damn you've changed, for sure. Just yesterday you looked like the world had come to an—"

Marilyn cut her off to say, "Well, that was yesterday, and this is a whole new day and things do change. Has Egypt gotten here yet? I've read so much about her."

Joseph replied slyly, "No, but I'm glad to see you. Hi, Marilyn, long time, baby. I know that you're going to say we have a lot to catch up on. So before you say anything, Angelica, please excuse us. Come with me into the garden. I know it real well . . ." He reached out his hand and guided her into the back.

Franco asked Angela, "Are you gonna talk to me or not?" *Simple question,* he thought. She ignored him and went into the kitchen, and he headed for the front door. Angela ran after him and grabbed him from behind and said, "Don't be angry with me. I just don't like the thought of my brother going out like that. I wish you would've tried to make him stay instead of agreeing with him. I forgot that there's so much of Baron in you." She held him tightly to her and added, "All those qualities are what made me fall in love with you—the fact that you can't be molded. You are your own man, not your family's man, but your own. That's a quality that I admire in my brother too. He really is the only male in my family that would defy Father." Franco held her firmly and kissed her passionately on her lips, and the doorbell rang.

Angela pulled away and looked at him strangely and kissed him again, and the doorbell again rang. "Okay. Franco I know it's love, but am I going crazy? I keep hearing bells when we kiss." The bell rang again. "Now that's the doorbell. I thought I was going a little, mind you, just a little nuts."

Franco rubbed the top of her head. She stuck her tongue out at him. She answered the door, and there was the shock of her life: her mother and father. Her mother wheeled Nunzio into the foyer, and Angela said nothing. All she knew was this was going to be a very interesting evening.

Franco turned around and saw Nunzio and was tempted to walk out of the room. Angela looked him in the eyes as if to say, "don't." He caught her glare and remained put. *There is definitely a stillness in this room,* thought Franco.

No one knew what to say. As the waiter went around to give out the drinks, Nunzio cleared his throat, and the bell rang yet again. Angela went for the door thinking, *saved by the bell.*

There stood Egypt in a beautiful chic outfit, a lovely pink-and-white chiffon affair. She thought she would wear something sexy yet simple to this semiformal dinner. Her shoulders were bare, and she wore the pearl necklace and earring set Baron bought for her a long time ago. As she walked in with Angela, she looked around to see where Baron was. Just when Angela was about to tell her where he went, he walked in through the garden with Joseph and Marilyn.

With his arm around Marilyn, Baron was talking and laughing about something, and they walked into the living room. He looked up and saw Egypt standing there, and his mouth opened wide with awe at her loveliness. In a very innocent way, she had a womanly appearance about her. Egypt felt a knot in her stomach when she saw him with his arms around Marilyn. Baron released his hold on her and walked over to Egypt. She was more concerned with Marilyn than noticing Baron. When she saw the man next to Marilyn hold her and kiss her, she breathed a sigh of relief.

Baron took both of Egypt's hands in his, stepped back, and they gazed at each other. He led her away in amazement and delight, never noticing his father and mother were there.

The Don cleared his throat again to mention, "Egypt, you look very lovely tonight. Baron, did I tell you that I'm glad that you and Egypt are back together?" He said to Egypt, "It was hard on the family while you were gone. He wasn't himself, and he made everyone's life topsy-turvy. So I'm glad you're back, so he could be himself again because he was beginning to annoy me and everyone else in here. So, everybody, let's drink a toast to the reunion of the family and the strength we have. If I'm not mistaken, my nephew Joseph has found his way back home also. Raise your glasses, for we are all together including my daughter Angelica and my son-in-law Franco. Raise them up in hope."

They all took glasses from the passing waiter and raised them up. "Now this is a family," declared Nunzio.

"Father, do you mean this, or is this another one of your ways of working around us? No, or are you sincere this time?" said Angela.

"You were always the spicy one. You're so strong and loud, and you speak what's on your mind. Baby, come here, that's what I've always loved about you. Unlike your brothers and sisters, you didn't care if you knew that it was right, you stuck by that. I love you and that's why I came by, and I wouldn't do anything to harm you. Most of all I feel as though I let the family down. I should have known better than to go out there with everything that was going on. I knew that they had a hit on me. I guess after a while you begin to feel invincible. So, Baron, let's eat and drink," said Nunzio.

As everyone gathered and began talking, Nunzio signaled over to Baron to come over to him. Nunzio asked Baron how Francis was doing, and Baron told him, "That guy probably knows more than you do yourself." Nunzio smiled and replied, "I'm very proud of him." Baron asked his father, "Why all these years were you so close to him?"

Nunzio didn't reply but turned his wheelchair around and asked everyone if they were enjoying themselves. He knew he had to get in with his children in order to get close enough to Franco. No matter what, Nunzio did not want any daughter of his with a Delucco. *But for now,* he thought, *I'll play along with it.*

Baron watched his father, and he wondered what he was up to; he knew his father all too well. This definitely was not him, and he hated to see what was up his sleeves. He knew that he had to stay close by and keep an eye on things. He thought, *When the shit hits the fan this time it's gonna stink from heaven to hell.* Baron hoped that it wouldn't, but he knew that it was too much to ask for. Angela walked over to Baron and told him that she felt the same way. Baron looked at her like he didn't know what she was talking about. She pinched his face and told him, "Don't even try and play like you didn't know what I meant."

"Baron, I could see right through that man. I can see beyond the wheelchair, and so can you. Mother and the rest can swallow that shit, but I know better and Nunzio doesn't change that easy. And nothing is that important to him other than his vendettas. Franco is a Delucco, and he is from the opposing side. Father isn't going to take that and throw it away. Trust me on this one, Baron," said Angela.

"Angela, does he have any idea that Franco's sister is coming? Because all hell will break loose if something goes wrong. Did you ever find out why Father hates his family so much?" asked Baron.

"I have some ideas I found out while I was living in Italy. Goes back before we were born and had something to do with a misunderstanding. Franco's uncle was accused of raping and killing Father's sister. But it was proven wrong, and he was set free. Uncle Nicholas went wild and killed Franco's cousin, an eight-year-old girl. He missed Franco's uncle and hit her instead. Right after the shot, he stood there in shock, and they gunned him down while his friends fled, leaving him to die. When the news traveled, they had to get out of country. They headed to America where they already had family living there for some time. But before they got away, a lot of Father's family was killed. Much blood was shed over that. Even though Father knew that the guy was innocent, he was very upset over the bloodshed of his family. Franco's family has buried it behind them, but for some reason, it seems that Father wants to start the whole thing up again, but over here on his own turf. The power Father has over here is as equal to the power that Franco's family has over in Sicily. Baron, I don't want the bloodshed to begin again," explained Angela.

"Hey, don't even sweat over that," said Baron. "Don't take it so lightly, Baron, because you wouldn't understand it unless you could see those faces and hear those voices like I did in Italy. They weren't joking and, Baron, neither is Father."

"What's the big secret over here you two? I know better than to trust two Gianelli's in the same corner, especially talking very low. So tell all man. Something ain't right," said Joseph as he approached them.

Before Baron could utter a word, Egypt started walking toward them. Baron had almost forgotten about her. He glanced at her; she was so lovely. She asked if they could talk because something was troubling her. He grabbed a hold of her hand and walked her into the yard.

As they held hands and walked by the water, they admired the moonlight which lit up the evening sky. It was very romantic and peaceful around them. She asked, "Why is there so much tension in there? I feel so much more at ease outside here with you." He just stared at her and tried to look away before she would notice that he was staring.

She smiled and said, "What's wrong, Baron? I see what you're doing, and you're making me a bit nervous. I'm not used to you acting like this. So talk, that's what I thought this evening was for anyway. For us."

Baron couldn't help but laugh. "Egypt, this evening I just thought it would be best to have a few people here because I didn't want you to feel as though I was trying to make a move on you. So voila! There's a crowd. Except one thing, I never invited my father or my cousin and his ex- girl. You could imagine what I planned for this—"

Egypt cut him off to reach over and place her hand across his mouth and gazed into his eyes. As they embraced with passion, shooting sparks flew everywhere. She began to explore Baron's body. As she started to devour his neck, he guided them over to a lounge where they both sat down. She confessed all the feelings she was holding back. He stopped cold in his tracks, pulled her back, and looked her straight in her eyes as if to say, he couldn't believe what he was hearing. "Egypt, you sound as if all you're concerned about is the sexual part of the relationship. Now I've done a lot of thinking since we weren't together about how I feel about you."

"Baron, can't we talk about that later," she said, and she unbuttoned his shirt and kissed his chest. As she attempted to remove his dinner jacket, he grabbed her hands and pulled them off and looked at her, and then he stood up.

"You're not the same as before. You're more beautiful than ever, and I'm so attracted to that. But," as he paused, "you're not the same. Butter, what happened to you? You weren't so—I don't want to go into it. Please let's just take it slow. Don't get me wrong, butter, I love you. I just want to make sure you're still you."

"Get away from me. I'm going home, and I don't ever want to see you again. I come here, and you just push me aside like I was no one. What the hell is wrong with you? You invited me here to insult me. First, no, I figured it out."

Baron reached out to grab her. "Get off me! Don't touch me now, you son of a sea cook, inadequate, impotent, no good satisfying, self-centered, egotistical, Italian bastard! By the way, you're acting more like your father every day."

Baron became furious and grabbed her, dragging her to a glass door. She struggled all the way there. He slid the door open and slapped the curtains away. As he pulled her in, she was somewhat tangled up in the curtains. He threw her into the room. She was missing a shoe, and her hair was all in her face and she kept pushing it up and blowing at it.

"Don't you come near me or I'll scream. Baron, look don't make me hurt you. I'll beat the living shit out of you," said Egypt.

"Oh, you will? Come on, Egypt, you're mouth has just about overridden your body's basic desire to stay alive!" yelled Baron.

"You take another step closer to me, so help me from the heavens above I'll kill you dead. I'm not playing, you poor excuse for a man," she said with a tone of disgust. "You'll be the 'Italian Gelding' when I'm through."

"Shit, that's it. I've had enough," he replied. He grabbed her and threw her down on the bed and yelled at her. He unzipped his pants, tossed them off, and looked at her with fury. "I'll show you how impotent I am and how manly I can be."

He held her down, and she began to cry out but he was not himself. As he continued wrestling with her, he just stopped, looked her straight in her eyes, and rolled off of her. He sat at the edge of the bed and just held his head as if in pain. Egypt was lost in a pool of tangled emotions. He reached for his pants, and she could hear a quiet whimper, or was it tears he was wiping off his face? A broken voice spoke, "Just go. Please get your stuff, and I'll call the car for you. Please." Baron sighed, "I'm sorry."

Egypt heard so much pain in his voice. She sat a little behind him and turned his face in her hand. He turned away, and she reached again. He asked her to stop.

"Please don't turn away from me, Baron. Listen to me, and look at me please. I'm so confused, but I know I love you. I just don't know why. I'm so afraid of you and this power that this love holds. It sometimes frightens me. I do love you too. What hurts me so much is to know that I have been through so much and that I still love and need you. Why, is what bothers me. To see you hurting at this moment is cutting me like a knife." As she wiped off her tears, she leaned over and kissed off Baron's tears.

"Oh, Egypt, I love you, and this circle that we are putting each other through is tearing me in two. When you left me—"

Egypt covered his mouth and shook her head as if to say, "don't speak." She lay down and placed his head by her shoulder and covered him with the sheet. "No, Egypt, I have to finish. When you left me, I was lost and didn't know what was going on. Out of nowhere you up and left without a word or clue. I was left to run a whole business, and it was your dream." He sat up and held her by the arms. "It was your dream, and I wanted it to come true for you. I wanted to show how much I loved you by letting your dream come true. And what do you? Leave me. You left me so humiliated and embarrassed just standing there. Making an excuse for you not being there. When that wore off I was just taking care of Egyptian Labels and wanting you back. Wondering how was I going to find someone who doesn't want to be found. Most of all you left me with an album of us to tear me even more. So many nights."

Baron zipped up his pants. "You wouldn't believe the nights I lay there with that album and a bottle trying to see if there was a clue in it to help me find you. But there wasn't till I ran into Fatima. She came to me, and if she hadn't, I guess I would have heard from you when I read about it in the papers. On tour, the Queen of the Nile. Why did you have to go like that? I need you, Egypt, but I guess we both know we can live without each other. But how happy are we?" he asked.

"Are you finished?" she said and walked toward the door. "No, you're not walking out of here without talking to me about it," said Baron. "Egypt, god you have changed. If you want to go, then go, but I can't take this game of 'merry-o-round-the-love' emotions because I'm getting off this carousel now. Either we walk on solid ground or you wear your seat belt tight as you ride up and down the carousel alone. I'm getting off here." Egypt opened the door, and he didn't say anything. She turned to look at Baron, and he was right behind her.

Meanwhile at the party, Angela was running rampant through the yard looking for Egypt and Baron. Franco caught up to her by the poolside. He took her hand in his and asked her, "Why would you be looking for a man that you know in the first place wanted to be alone with Egypt? It doesn't make any sense to go hunting for them. Baron is a big boy, and he can handle himself."

They went back into the house. Joseph and Nunzio were talking about Joseph's father. The tension subsided a little, and everyone had finished eating and were enjoying their coffee. Nunzio asked Margherita for some anisette for his.

"Where is Baron? How long are they both going to take, all night?" Nunzio laughed. "Please ah, 1 . . . 2 . . . 3 . . . boom, bang, get it over with and you're back together. Then you tell her to make some food, right? Ah, with all this, make me a drink. Angelica, come here and find your brother for me. I wanna discuss something with him. He can finish up later. I came here for business and not to just sit around and wait until his funny business is over. Yeah you, ah, Franco, come here. Wheel me over there so I can look out onto the porch," bellowed Nunzio.

"No, he won't, Father, and neither will I. Baron is a grown man. I didn't find it amusing that you spoke of his relationship with Egypt like that. You carry on like this because she won't have anything to do with you, right, Father? You can't stand for anything or anyone to stay in your way. I'm your daughter, but I'm not your little girl. So don't talk to me in that tone of voice," yelled Angela.

Baron walked in the room, and Egypt followed soon behind. While all the talking was going on, they stood by quietly and listened. "So I see who wears the pants in this marriage. Do you share razors and swap locker room tragedies?" Nunzio laughed.

Franco stood up and looked down at Nunzio and said, "You're so lucky that your fat ass is in that fuck'n' wheelchair because I would have tried to dislocate your ass from your back. This is my wife, and I don't care who her father or her family is. Angela and I, we're our own family now, and furthermore, if you ever talk to her in that tone or attempt to think—"

Suddenly a laugh burst out of Nunzio. "I hoped that somewhere in your pants was a sign of a man. So you think you would've spoken up a little sooner to the Don if I wasn't on my, what was that?"

Angela spoke out, "Fat ass."

"Thanks, yes, fat ass. I don't like you or the oak tree you blossomed from. I remember when you were living in New York a while ago. You were too damn feisty then, and your ass is too hot now. If I had my way, you'd be going back from where you came from on your feet or on your back. Makes no difference to me which one," said Nunzio and spun his wheelchair around.

Angela took hold of the chair and spun it back around to face her and looked at her father in disgust. "You ever let me think that you have any intentions on hurting him again, Father, you'll be kissing the edge of my .25 caliber, and just for the record, Father, I'll never forgive you for the death of my baby. Don't open your mouth because if it wasn't for Mother, I would've killed you myself. But it seems that someone got to you first."

"Stop it all of you please! I am so sick of hearing everyone fight and argue in this family. That's if it's what we really are. I feel as though you're all fighting and you probably don't even know why you are. Nunzio, I had enough of this, and I'm leaving and going to a hotel. And as far as I'm concerned, I need a long vacation from everyone. Yes, I'm talking, and maybe I should even get a divorce from all of you. You all talk about yourselves, but you never hear me say anything about what I ever needed or wanted. So everyone just shut up. Angelica, I understand how you feel, but you're wrong and you're right. No matter what he is, he is your father, but he has no rights in interfering with your marriage. Nunzio, if I ever find out that you had something to do with it, you can definitely kiss me good-bye. Because indirectly you caused our daughter to miscarry our grandchild. Your blood. Mr. Gianelli, you do disrespect your children. If you were to treat me that way, I would have walked out years ago. But, Nunzio, you sure knew better. I'm leaving."

As Margherita walked out the door, Nunzio laughed and reassured everyone that she would return. As an hour or so had gone by, the car came to pick up Mr. Gianelli. He was hot under the collar, and everyone kept their distance. When he left, Angela called her mother to let her know that Father was on his way and that his state of mind still hadn't changed. When the housekeeper answered the phone, she informed Angela that her mother had packed and left. She didn't tell anyone where she was heading.

Angela became worried and went to talk with Baron. When she looked for him, he was standing outside of the bathroom door. When she asked what the matter was, he just replied, "Egypt is very sick."

When Egypt opened the door, she said, "I'll be okay, Baron. I've just been going through this for the longest since Europe." She walked out and went to get her coat. "I think it's the change of water and everything. I'm feeling very light-headed, so I need to get some rest. Baron, thank you for an interesting evening. As for the carousel, when I ride, I sit in the coach."

As Egypt left, Angela looked at Baron and said, "I guess I missed something somewhere. I wonder what's wrong now. For two people to be in love, you sure didn't look it just now. Is it her new life of glamour and handsome men at her feet? You didn't ask her if that story was true in that trashy paper? So how many guesses till you speak?"

"Angelica, till the cows come home."

Angela shrugged her shoulders and said, "Nothing new when the Gianelli clans get together. Mayhem and havoc hold hands."

Angela walked over to her cousin Joe. He and Marilyn looked at each other and decided it would be more entertaining at her place. So Angela let them out, and Franco grabbed Angela from behind and wanted to go home. She said, "I just can't leave my brother feeling bad. He might need me." By the time they cleaned up, Baron asked them to head out because he needed time alone. Angelica kissed Baron and got her stuff together. Franco said a few things to Baron and told him to take care of the flight arrangements. Baron almost forgot that he still owned a business. He hadn't been keeping up with the company lately. Baron thought to himself that Egyptian Labels was about the only true thing sticking by him. It's the only tangible part of his life.

When Franco arrived home, Angelica had reminded him that he was to have put the dishes away and finish their kitchen. He gave her such a look. He went into the kitchen, and she went and did a few other things. Angelica was getting some chilled wine and two chilled glasses ready from the bar. She jumped into the shower while he was getting his share of the housework done. When she got out, he walked into their bedroom. She was standing there with her towel on and her hair wet, and he became aroused. Angelica told Franco to take a shower—that he had a stress-filled evening.

Franco sensed an eager thrust within him. But he knew it would be best to refresh himself before a full course feast of "Angelica under sheet." He stared at her and removed all that she was wearing (which wasn't much) with his eyes.

She stood there amazed at his silence, and this made her feel very attractive and quite sexy. She couldn't move. His eyes were like that of a cobra and she the prey—mesmerized. He reached over and moved her wet hair from her brow and kissed her. Angelica's towel fell off, and he grasped her buttocks and pulled her close to him. Franco stopped just as sudden as he started and chuckled, "I guess I better take a shower, right? Hold my spot." He walked abruptly into the bathroom.

Angelica grabbed her robe and toweled her hair and tried to make it look nice. Then she ran around the room setting up candles. She lit them and went to get the wineglasses. She placed everything on a small table and then laid out a beautiful comforter on the floor. She then raced into the kitchen and gathered a chilled bottle of wine, grapes, cheese, and a flower. Even though it was a fake one, it still set the mood.

By the time she returned, the water had just stopped in the shower. She jumped in her lavender lace negligee and lay on the comforter. When Franco came out of the bathroom, he glanced down toward a wiggling foot and naked calf. As he walked further, he encountered a vision of beauty. There lay his goddess of love. She lifted her hand upward, and he so gently held it with the tips of his fingers. Franco kissed her hand and lay down beside her.

"Was I supposed to dress for the occasion?"

"Somewhat, except we can do without the towel. It's too dressy for this occasion. Instead of black tie and tails, this is more on the natural note," Angelica said as she pulled off his towel.

As they embraced, the room was filled with desires and love. The candlelight enhanced the romantic mood. As he lay his head on her stomach, she played in his hair. He began to express what he was feeling; Angelica placed a grape into his mouth. Franco grinned as he returned the favor.

They both made a toast to their love. As they caressed one another and ate cheese and whispered sweet words to each other, suddenly the flames from the candles began to flicker wildly. The two of them stopped and watched the flame from this one particular candle in amazement.

"I can only assume that it's telling us the next step," said Franco.

"Franco, you make me feel like a queen and my body is screaming out . . . ," said Angelica. Franco began to kiss her passionately, caressing her neck and kissing her earlobes. She began to hold his chest and engulfed herself within the excitement that he was bringing out of her. Angelica sighed, for Franco was not himself; he seemed to have an extra tender touch. As if the scenery had enticed him to release the passionate side he kept deep within.

Franco fondled her breasts and looked at her virtue and embraced her as he rolled Angelica above him. He held her from her shoulders as he just stared starry-eyed. She only grinned slightly then blew a kiss at him.

"I want to gaze at you with the candlelight enhancing your beauty. Angelica, you're my love, beautiful, and most of all, my precious wife. No man is as happy as I am."

Angelica had a tear in her eye; she leaned down to kiss him as her hair covered his face. He laid her next to him; she then placed her fingers in his mouth, and he began to kiss them sending chills up and down her body. She placed his hands on her breasts. When he had least expected it, she had taken him. Franco's mouth opened and not a sound came from it. He opened his eyes, and Angelica looked like Lady Godiva on her stallion riding strong and proud. Her back was arched, and her hair fell behind her. The light of the candle flickering off her smooth skin was magnificent. The sight was indescribable. All he could do was engross himself in the pleasures she was bestowing upon him. They were truly making love. It was an exhilarating feeling rushing through his body. For a moment Franco felt as though he had stopped breathing. As for Angelica her body became stiff, and her heart felt like it was about to burst. She sunk her nails into him, and Franco didn't feel a thing. He was experiencing a sensation that his toes were tightening, and every muscle in his body froze for the moment. He opened his mouth, and a sound of pure exuberance bellowed out.

Angelica sounded as if she ran a marathon; she was unable to regulate her breathing. They both collapsed in a pool of sweat. Angelica gazed at the flame from the candle and drifted into sleep.

As morning arrived it found the two of them entangled on the floor. Franco reached over and moved her hair from her face and kissed her. She opened one eye and began searching with one hand for a sheet. Unable to locate one, she tried putting on her negligee, covered her face with her hands, and asked, "Are we still in heaven?"

"I am, but it's time for you to get up and do your womanly chores in the kitchen," he said as he chuckled.

"I'll give you some womanly type chores," she said as she got up and grabbed a pillow. She swung and hit him with it. He just laughed at her. She looked a mess; her hair was all over, and she stood there with the negligee all twisted. She caught a glimpse of herself in the mirror.

"Oh yeah, I look a mess, right? That's what's so funny, right?"

"No, you always look a mess, nothing funny about that," he replied as he continued to laugh.

She went to the small table she prepared last night and took the glass and poured the last bit of wine in it on him. He rolled, but it still got on him. She placed the glass down and started to walk away, but he got her leg and pulled her down. He didn't let her fall onto the floor because he caught her in such a way she was mostly in his arms. He went to kiss her, and she closed her eyes and he said, "Oh, morning breath," and he rolled on the floor, got up, and ran into the bathroom.

"Oh yeah, okay, you think you're cute. I got your morning breath when you come out of there."

Then the phone rang. Angelica told him if he wanted it, he had better get it because it's not the morning breath's job to answer the phones. Franco came out and answered the phone. It was Francis and Baron on the phone. "Angela, go ahead and take your shower now because I'll be on the phone for a while. Babe, hold this end while I take it in the den."

When Franco reached the den and picked up, he told her he had it. But she didn't hang up right away because she heard familiar voices. Baron spoke and then Franco repeated again for her to hang up. She finally did. Angelica went into the shower. As she stepped out, she was wondering who the other voice was besides Baron on the phone with Franco.

Francis was telling both Franco and Baron that he wanted them both, Angelica and Egypt, to be his and Karessa's guests that weekend. Baron wasn't sure if he would be back in time from his business meeting but said he would definitely try. Baron told them that he had a business trip he had to go on in reference to Egyptian Labels, but he would try and see if he could change a few things. Just in case he couldn't, he would send a message to the hotel upstate where they were to meet. Franco said he knew that Angelica would love to go upstate, especially for an occasion like that. Francis was pleased, but he was hoping that Baron could make it also.

Francis told everyone he would be looking forward to seeing them. Franco told Angelica the news. Since they were both eager to finally have a change of scenery, they were going to pack. After they all hung up, Francis began to finish his packing.

"Darling, are you sure this is the right thing to do?" questioned Karessa.

"I'm a grown man, have you not noticed? Whatever my mother's problems are, they're hers. I'm not living my life for her or anyone. Do you think she's the only one? No, she's not. There's my uncle, Nunzio, and he'll hit the roof. I really don't care so long as we're together. I don't need anyone else. Come here, Karessa." He held her close to him and softly touched her skin. "Karessa, I don't see your color. I see a soft, gentle woman who brings the best out of me. Before you, I never ever felt the things I hear on songs or read in poetry. I would hear of friends and family speak on it, but it never hit me. It took someone special to make me see and feel this word spoken—*love*. It took you, and I'm not about to let you go for somebody else's idiosyncrasy. Not on your life. Maybe apparently you're willing, are you¿" asked Francis.

"Let's get something straight. I know how much I desire to be with you. I know I'm doing it for all the right reasons. I'm not trying to prove to myself or anyone else I can stand apart and alone and not fall. Sometimes I've wondered if you were doing this for love or to defy your mother. Don't get riled up, sit down and hear me out. I didn't imply that you don't love me. I'm just saying maybe you're pushing into this commitment to show you'll do as you please regardless to who gives their blessings or not."

"I understand, but it's because I love you, and I want you all to myself. To begin my family, my legacy. Come here, let me hold you for a long while. Come, my darling, come with me to the Casba," he said as he laughed.

Karessa reached out her hand and said," Oh, oh, strong, vibrant man, I'll go with you to the ends of the world. So long as we are side by side."

"Okay, let's get packed and head out before we have guests waiting for us to arrive. I made all of the arrangements for the flowers and everything okay. One thing though, I couldn't find your dress."

"I already took care of that. It's bad enough that you're seeing me today. I also think you shouldn't see the dress. I have to leave some sort of surprise to this blessed event. My parents will be there and a few other family members and friends from my side. What about your family and friends¿"

"Don't worry, they'll be there. I thought this was supposed to be small¿ I told the caterers how many to expect."

"Don't worry I already called yesterday and gave them the new list. I want to enjoy this moment to the fullest. I wish you would have told me about your mother."

"I don't want to talk about it. I'm too happy."

Meanwhile, Mrs. Antoinette DiBenedetto-Gianelli, Francis's mother, was having major coronary fits. She was trying her best to reach Nunzio to inform him of Francis's intentions. She never thought that his relationship with Karessa was anything more than curiosity.

Antoinette came from a very well-renowned family on the outskirts of Florence. All of the DiBenedetto's were known for their family traditions. The men for being very ruthless and their women not to be trusted alone with a man regardless if he or she was married. Most of all this family was given the utmost respect. You hardly read about them or even have seen them on the television. Not many of them came over, and those who did back in the twenties conducted themselves in a way that nobody suspected them of anything other than being a business-oriented family.

Antoinette married Dominic Nicholas Gianelli. He was not like his older brother Nunzio. Dom worked hard, owned a business legally, and was a drinker. She could locate Nunzio, but she turned to Dominic and asked what he was going to do about it. He looked at her and replied, "Why should I do anything to stop it? Francis is a grown man. Since when have you ever come to me concerning Francis? It seems to me you should continue to do what is your normal—call Nunzio. If I recall correctly, you only knew me for the other four children."

He lifted up his glasses and looked his wife straight in the eye with a big smile, and he finished his drink with one gulp. Antoinette was pissed the hell off. She was disgusted in him and in a fury with Francis. "Don't you care your son wants to make a black a Gianelli? She'll be entering in on the DiBenedetto's also. Or have you forgotten that your children are of a fine line? Would you put down that damn bottle and listen to me!" she screamed. "You're nothing more than a spineless frame of a man. Dominic Nicholas Gianelli, come back here while I'm talking to you," she said with rage.

There was nothing she could do with Dom. He was totally offset with everything. This was annoying her. Whatever she wanted, she seemed to always get. Except one thing, but that was something she had let go of many years ago. But in her heart she at least had a piece, maybe not the whole thing, but a piece. She was determined to get a hold of Nunzio; he was not going to sit still on this matter.

Dominic walked back into the room and yelled, "Antoinette Marie DiBenedetto Gianelli, what in the hell is your problem? So what the girl is black. My goodness, what a sin for her. Oh, at least you should be proud of the fact Francis fell in love with an intelligent beautiful black woman. You act as though the lady is stepping from the slums and using Francis to make her marker. You of all people should be able to spot a woman like that. The money-hungry, eager-to-move-to-the-top type of bitch. I could have sworn you've socialized with many black people, or should I say colored folk? You're blind mannerisms kept you from seeing what was really happening with Francis. He knew how you would be, so he lead you to feel this woman wasn't a threat, that it was a simple friendship. I applauded Francis, if this wasn't a swift kick in your ass what was! I'd like to take this moment to say, 'serves your ass right.'"

"Are you finished? Because you may be laughing now, but I'll have the last word and laugh. You mark me well, Dom, when I finish with Francis, I sure will have the last word," she said angrily and left the house.

Evening has come, and all the way upstate in a beautiful hotel, Karessa sat looking into a mirror. The phone rang in her room, and as she walked to the phone, she stood paralyzed. The phone stopped ringing, and there was a knock at the door. She jumped out of her skin. Karessa didn't say a word.

A voice called out her name. It was one of her sisters, but she still said nothing. She heard through the door her sister saying, "Maybe something happened to her." She went to get someone to open the door. Then Karessa acknowledged their presence. She asked them to give her some time alone. So they left but not soon enough for her. She was dwelling on the type of problems she was heading into. A mother-in-law who disliked her because of her color. What would that bias attitude do to their child? She knew this would create an absolutely undesirable atmosphere to raise it in. Karessa knew she loved him, that was without a doubt, but that damn word *but* keeps popping up in her mind. *What was going through Francis's mind*, she wondered. Did he know what he was getting into loving her? Did he really think it would come down to this, losing his mother? Even though the majority of his family seemed to support his decision doesn't necessarily mean they like what he is doing. A voice from her door kept saying, "Karessa, Karessa." It was a deep toned, "Karessa, Karessa I await you, and I do love you." She knew it was Francis. He didn't realize it, but he had given her the strength to finish dressing and follow her heart and not her fears.

Down in the ballroom of the hotel they had begun to allow the guests in to be seated. Everyone was dressed to the max. Francis was greeting all of the guests. When Franco and Angelica walked in, Francis was so relieved. Angelica looked ravishing in her soft blue sequined dress with a plunging V-back. And her hair was in an old-fashioned basket weave with hair loose in the middle. One of his groomsmen, a family friend named Lotario Scalise, walked over to Angelica; but Francis stepped in and grabbed a hold of his cousin's hand and kissed her, shook Franco's hand, and thanked them for coming. Francis's brother Vittorio, better known as Vitto, walked over and escorted them to their seats. Angelica asked Vitto if anyone else from the family was coming, and he said only their sister Ann Marie. He wouldn't be sure if his brother Joseph was coming. He figured Dominic Jr. wasn't going to be able to make it because he wasn't sure he could get a flight in from Venice. He and his family moved there a year-and-a-half ago. Angelica and Franco were on the groom's side which only had three pews were seated with a few people. Karessa's brother Donald, also a groomsman, was chatting in the rear with Lotario. He and Donald had much in common. Lotario owned several very elaborate restaurants in New York, Las Vegas, and Miami. Lotario was young and wealthy, courtesy of his father, well-known as John Rosco, who was recently gunned down. Donald and his father owned a company called Cafe de Supplies. Donald's father was the sole owner of Karessa Fragrances, which—little did Karessa or Francis know—he was giving them a large share of the company as a wedding gift.

Kevin Divine and his wife were in the room with his daughter talking about things. Karessa felt they should know. She then threw the news at them quickly and told them that Francis didn't know yet. She said she would tell him during the honeymoon in Rio.

Vitto walked back over to Franco and Angelica to tell them that his father knew about the wedding. Angelica looked and smiled as if to say, "what did he have to say about this?" Vitto told her to wipe the grin off because Dominic Sr. was coming but without Antoinette. She would definitely ruin the evening. She went as far as telling Francis if he goes through with it he lost his mother. So with that note, he didn't give her any of the details so she couldn't destroy the ceremony.

Franco just looked to them and interjected one important thing. "This is a wedding, and who would want anyone to turn it into a fiasco?" He had hoped that at least Francis's father would show up. But Franco realized that if he did, how would he get away from his wife?

Vitto came back to the pews where Angelica was seated and sat his brother in front of them. Dominic Jr. and his family were all there, much to Francis's surprise. When Francis was told, he rushed up to see him. He and his brother talked for a while, and you could see how excited Francis was. He finally felt as though he was getting some support from his family. He wondered if Joseph would show up considering he was the outlandish one. Joseph always would stir up their mother's feathers every chance he got.

When Francis turned around, there stood in a tuxedo, next to Donald, his father. Dominic Sr. put out his hand to his son and told him the best of luck. He too began seating people, and Francis was so happy that he came. His cousin, Ignatius DiBenedetto, is his mother's brother's son. He and Francis both had married non-Italians. Ignatius married a woman by the name of Mary Silverberg, which was just as bad to their family. So Ignatius knew what tension lay ahead for these two. Just when Francis felt the walls tumbling down on him, Ignatius walked in.

Francis and he went into the waiting room where Dominic Sr. joined them. They all started talking, and then Vitto showed up, and they began to get ready for the wedding. Francis wasn't nervous. As they all went to stand in front, he whispered to his father, "Where's Mother?" Dominic Sr. said, "Doing what she does best, hunting down Nunzio." They chuckled, and much to his surprise, many of the people he had invited came. When Francis glanced at Karessa's mother, she blew a kiss at him, and he returned it with a big smile. Baron even showed up along with Antonio, his girlfriend, and Nunzio Jr. and his wife. Francis just stood motionless when the music began.

Karessa had her close friend, an Irish girl as her matron of honor, open the ceremony as she strolled in wearing a royal blue shape-fitting gown. Her bridesmaids were in the same color but wearing a totally different style of dress. Everything looked radiant and enchanting as if it was a fairy-tale wedding. When the bride walked in, all eyes were on her. She was utterly enchanting, totally breathtaking. Her wedding gown was lily white and had a high collar and an opening near her cleavage where tear-shaped pearls were dangling. It was fitted to her shapely curves and flared out from her knees ending in an extremely long train. Karessa's veil was extravagant; it completed the entire ensemble of elegance.

Francis was mesmerized, and when the priest asked who gives this woman, her father removed her veil and kissed her. Francis opened his mouth and whispered, "I love you." She winked her eye as to say, "ditto." When the priest asked Francisco Lazzaro Gianelli if he took Karessa Irene Divine, Francis answered before the priest could finish. Karessa giggled out loud, and several guests did also. Francis didn't care. After Karessa said her piece, Francis stopped the ceremony to say something that was not rehearsed, which came as a surprise for Karessa. He spoke of his feelings. "The road that lies ahead will be rocky at times, but with the love we both share, it shall be our fortress. I may not be able to tell the future, but as far as I'm concerned, you are the woman for me."

She also added a few words to that. "Never before in my life was there a man that I loved as I love you. We are faced with much hypocrisy and prejudice. If it were another I would be worried, but you have taken me to the light at the end of the tunnel, and what I see is euphoria." The priest finished the ceremony and introduced Mr. and Mrs. Francisco Lozzaro Gianelli. They kissed again.

While the entire wedding party went to take pictures, the guests started sitting at the tables in the ballroom. The waiters brought out hors d'oeuvres and drinks. Franco, Angelica, and Baron were enjoying themselves. Baron was speaking about their Aunt Antoinette's behavior. She wasn't too thrilled with Egypt either. Nobody really understood her; she had something mysterious about her. Angelica told them maybe her closet was overflowing. Franco didn't understand what they were saying about their aunt, so he asked for them to get to the point. Angelica said, "Look, since I was young, I thought I saw my father leaving Antoinette's bedroom, but mother always told us not to repeat it. So I never did. As I got older, things started to fall into place. Antoinette was a class A number 1 whore. Baron and I one time saw a man we knew called dad leaving her house, so we thought something was going on. Do you remember, Baron?"

"Okay, Angela, I get what you're saying, but come on, it's Francis's wedding. This is not the place for that shit. I don't want to think of that bullshit, I came to enjoy myself. I plan on it."

"Franco, look here they come. Doesn't Karessa's sister look good?" said Baron. Franco looked and lifted up his brows and smiled. Angela hit him on his shoulders. He and Baron broke out in laughter. Karessa and Francis had their first dance, and after they danced, his father danced with her. The evening went well. When everything came to an end, the groom and the bride left to head for Rio de Janeiro.

That morning Baron left to head back to his office because he left a file that he needed to take back with him. Ms. Jackson left word with Heather to get in touch with him. There were a few particulars she felt he should be aware of before walking into the meeting. When Baron walked in, before his very eyes was Fatima. She approached him with caution and asked if he had a moment. Baron walked into his office and started fumbling through some papers on the desk. When he turned, she was so close to him his shoulder hit her.

"Baron, please, I've helped you, and I realize that you kept your part of the bargain. Now I need you. What will it take for you to help with one more step?" asked Fatima very seductively.

"Get off it. What the hell do you think I am? Let's get this shit straight. One: I got up in this world by myself, and if you choose to climb the ladder, I think Mr. Stout has enough authority to move you. Two: if you're worried about me saying anything, I'll give it to you in full thrust. Bitch, you do little to move me. Your methods disgust me. Fatima, your tactics are the reason why women have such a hard time in business. Three: If it was up to me you'd be out on your flat ass. Egyptian Labels doesn't need a sneaky slut like you to be a part of the corporation, especially a lawyer. By the way, I want you to know someone is always one step ahead of you. I know about your kind. So get any smart-ass ideas to tamper with things, and you'll never have to worry again about what you'll wear in the morning," Baron said sounding very much like Nunzio. "You really don't mean that," she said as she placed her hands in his hair. "I can tell you're a bit nervous around me. Oh, it's musty in here. The air conditioner mustn't be on." Fatima began taking off her cape. Underneath was more skin than clothing.

Baron felt a bit flushed at that point. No one could deny her exotic beauty, not even Baron. He held his composure and started to say something, but she cut in. "Now a man like you would definitely understand and appreciate good conversation. So I will converse, and you just listen carefully." She placed her hand firmly on his masculinity and slowly began to feast through his treasures. The sounds she was making affected Baron. He needed to release some tension and felt himself falling slowly under her spell.

"Get the fuck off of me," he snapped, and he pushed her to the floor before she could open his zipper. "I'm a man not a weak bastard. Get the hell out of my office and try keeping your clothes on your ass. Don't make me hurt you. Fatima, wipe off your knees and work on another floor. I don't want you. You're not even good enough to do that for me." Baron spoke so loud that Heather knew what was going on.

Fatima got herself together and left. Heather had her face inside of some paperwork, trying to act as though she was busy. Heads watched Fatima as she waited for the elevator. She felt awkward; she knew that Heather must have made a few calls. Fatima was thoroughly pissed with Baron. Running through her mind was that he didn't have to bite at the bait, but was it necessary to humiliate her? She stepped into the elevator as Mr. Tad Millson was getting off. Fatima gave him a dirty look just before the door closed. When he turned toward Baron's office, he asked Heather what was that all about.

Heather replied, "It was a tough conversation that wasn't turned on."

"Okay, I'm totally lost. Where's da boss? Did he leave for California?" asked Tad.

"No, he's inside. Do you want me to buzz him?" "Yeah, babe, and while you're at it, sugar, why don't ya plant a rosy one on me?" he said as he puckered up his lips.

"Humphrey Bogart, you're not. So, my dear sweet peasant, leave the tablet with me and return to thy moat."

"Oh, fair maiden, just one touch from your soft rosy lips would make one lone day seem to be ten glorious morns."

"Give unto me thy tablet of notes, or you both shall receive the gift of pink slips," replied Baron with a chuckle.

Mr. Millson handed him the papers for his meeting. He turned around and asked Heather out for lunch. She kept signaling with her eyes to go, and he finally realized and said he would pass by later. Baron told her he would be returning in two days. He walked back into his office to pick up the remainder of his work. He caught a glimpse of Egypt's picture. He picked it up and asked her to come home and stay. He held the picture close to him for a moment and then placed it back down. He grabbed his attaché case and luggage bag and rushed out of the office.

Baron hailed a cab to Laguardia Airport and caught his flight to California. While boarding the plane, all of his thoughts rested on Egypt. Not a moment went by when he wasn't trying to figure out what was running through her mind. He seemed to have everyone in an uproar. Mrs. Jackson had placed all of her eggs in one basket with these men.

Chapter 9

Egypt lay down thinking to herself of all the things that have transpired in the last two years. She realized so many of the problems were actually her fault. Like the people's lives that she had turned upside down to get what she felt she needed at that time.

Egypt at this point felt lost, and everything that once was good has been proven to be sour. This was like a bad dream from which she wanted to awaken. So much has happened and so much time has gone by; there wasn't much she could say for what she had done. But all she could do is try and correct it and that was going to be the hardest thing to do. Knowing that Baron still loved her excited her, but did she want to start over with him? The thought was wonderful until reality knocked at her door reminding her that there would be a lot of problems. One: Would he be able to trust her after all she had done to him? Egypt knew that love is strong, but how strong can it be? How strong was he?

She got up to make herself a cup of tea. For the longest she had been carrying a sick feeling inside of her. On her way to the kitchen, the light on her machine was blinking. When she turned it on, she heard Jayme's voice. The sound of his voice made her nauseous, so she just kept walking and didn't even listen. There was a good-looking and talented man who could have any woman. She thought, *Why does he continue to lean on me?* She was starting to feel dizzy, so as she sat down, the phone rang. It was too early in the morning for people to be calling her, so she snatched up the phone.

"Whoever you are, make it good!"

"Well, I see you're in a damn chipper mood. Well, I'm going to be the icing and cherry on your day." "Oh, hi, so what's wrong now, Bach?"

"Word, there's been no living or working with homes since you cut Jayme off. He doesn't say much, but he bust out the work. But the slammin' same sound isn't coming out of him. Yo, I'm probably the last one anyone would have thought would worry about him, but I don't like the change."

"I don't know what to say, hold on, my bell is ringing." She placed down the phone and opened the door, and there stood Gary of all people. She signaled him in and to be quiet. "Oh, it's a friend of mine, like I was saying I don't know what you want from me. I care about him, but I told him that I couldn't give him what he wanted from the beginning."

"But don't you want to kick some words his way to see what's got him acting so busted?"

"Bach, all of you are important to me, but understand maybe he didn't tell you, but I expressed that what we had was because of me being so lost and hurt. The pain is gone like it was then. He got me through a bad time. What can I tell you, that was it."

"Oh, man, I never thought you could be so foul. The shit you're kick'n' is off the wall, man. Homes was good enough to be dessert, and now my man is yesterday's trash. I hear you, I hear you now. Don't even bust a sweat and worry about my man, Jayme." Bach hung up the phone on her.

She looked at Gary and said, "I can't understand what he wanted from me."

Gary looked at her with a grin and replied, "Don't even ask me, my darl'n' because the answer is the same. I see you still have men as your invaluable pawns." She started to open her mouth. "No, Egypt, don't say anything okay. Remember many of the great chess players have used pawns to achieve victory, so get your values in order. As for me I was one of the fortunate ones, I knew I was stepping in the widow's web, so I kept my trusty scout knife to set me free. One more soul for your Pandora's box. Beware, a strong—"

Egypt raised her mug and smiled. "Hurray, Gary has all of his smart-ass remarks at 9:33 a.m. I only thought that part of your brain worked at this hour. Or are you allowing the top half to give the bottom half a rest? I'm sick of your mouth and would appreciate it if you left me alone before I keep on devouring all the men like a black widow spider. Get the picture? So since your mouth has ran on overtime, I'll let you out here." As she opened the door, he got up and looked totally surprised and walked out. He turned around only to see the door getting closed in his face. Gary wondered if she was losing it. She walked into the kitchen to get something to eat. When she opened the fridge, looking at the food upset her. She didn't know whether to eat or get sick. What Egypt did know was she wanted to go back to bed and sleep away a couple of weeks. But she had to get out because Carlos would be screaming as usual if she were late. That put a grin on her face. This man never let anything stand in his way at all.

The many times she glanced at him from a distance she would remember that very special moment they had spent in her dressing room. Egypt would smile a silly little grin, and she too knew he felt it. But he has never spoken on it since. A quick thought hit her: What would her beloved Baron think if he knew of her torrid escapades? She shook her head as if it were a bad taste in her mouth. Egypt put on a jacket and went toward the door. As she stepped out, her phone rang, but she allowed the answering machine to get it. It was the doctor's office they all went to. She decided to get the call when she returned.

When Egypt got to the studio, there stood Carlos with a screwed-up face. "Well, Ms. Arcardi, late today again I see. No, no, don't disrobe because you aren't staying. The doctor tried to reach you, but you weren't in. Go there, and call me."

"Okay. That's it, sire?" asked Egypt.

"No, I would appreciate it if you would come in on time, and before you come back to rehearsal, call in," bellowed Carlos.

"What's wrong with you today, is it me or what? This isn't like you, Carlos," replied Egypt.

"No, it's not just you, but now everyone's tests have to be done over which takes time from rehearsals, Egypt, and time we don't have. For the last few practices you've been sick and sleepy and draggy."

"What do you want? I don't feel good."

"That's not my problem. So go to the doctor and get it fixed."

Egypt started to walk out, and she saw Jayme. She thought, *What the hell else could go wrong?* She tried to walk by like he wasn't there.

"So, babe, I thought I would have heard from you at least. Don't say a thing, I know what you wanted, and I'm not pushing for anything. But I never said I could just stop loving. I miss your sweet smell and your fruity taste. I can only hope that something of me keeps popping up on you. So you can always sit back and think of me."

"Oh, please, Jayme, not today, I'm sick and just feeling shitty. I have to go."

"Okay, I'll go with you. I have to go anyway, so just lead the way, darling."

As they arrived at the doctor's office and Egypt gave her name, the nurse told her to go straight into the room and the doctor would be in there momentarily. As she went in the room, she was very impressed by the medical school he attended and the honors he received. All the plaques were nicely displayed on the wall and pictures of his family on his mantel. She touched his desk; the wood was of a quality grain. Egypt was starting to feel tense and a bit offset with why she was there, even though she knew it couldn't be all that bad. There was a lovely chair right in front of his desk; she sat down. All in all, she thought to herself, *Everything will work out fine.* She felt funny and placed her head in her hands. The doctor stepped in and saw her do this.

"So, Ms. Arcardi, is there something wrong? Feeling a bit tired?"

"Worse, I think I've caught a stomach virus or something. Like right now I feel lighted-headed. Anyway why have you summoned me?"

"I have your chart right here. Around when was your last menstruation?"

"What are you trying to say?"

"Answer the question?"

"I guess it was . . . when I think about it . . . it was . . . so much has been going on I have to look in my little booklet. It had to have been last month." She paused and took a deep breath and replied, "I didn't write anything down. Oh shit."

"Are you regular?"

"As regular as night and day. It always comes on time. Oh, oh, oh, here it is. Oh, shit, shit, shit it was around . . . and the only man was, oh, not his! It was two months ago."

"Ms. Arcardi, I have to ask this question, and I don't mean to offend you, but I see you're not married. Do you know who the father is?"

"There was only one man that my protection broke with. Of all the times in my life I would have loved to have been pregnant. Why now and him?"

"So, Ms. Arcardi—"

"Would you please just call me Egypt, thank you."

"Okay, Egypt, from the way you sound, I realize you're not thrilled, so am I to believe you want an abortion?"

"Every damn one broke. Come to think about it every time we had sex. That is strange, and it's not like he was all that. I'm going to have to get back with you on my decision even though I already know what I have to do."

Egypt began to weep into her hands, and through her teary voice, she cried out, "Why now of all times? Why in the hell now? What is wrong with me? How could I allow this to happen?" She jumped up and repeated, "What in the hell is wrong with me? Of all the men in my life, why him? No, there have been worse, but this is too close to home. Shit, that old saying, 'You play and you will pay.' Let me get out of here, and he's, huh, I just have to act as though nothing was wrong. I wish I could say it was a pleasure."

"Egypt, just take it easy," replied the doctor.

"Easier said than done. I have to keep up with my work, Doctor. I lift weights, run, exercise hard to keep fit for the show. I just can't stop."

The doctor shook his head and walked into the waiting room with her. She looked over, and Jayme stood there grinning from ear to asshole. He walked over to Egypt and held her hand.

"Is there anything I can do for you?" asked Jayme.

"Trust me, you've done enough, please give me a break. I'm going back home to get some rest. I sure need it after today."

"I understand, Mommy."

Egypt turned her head and looked right through him. If looks could kill, Jayme had died several deaths. She spoke with a firm but muttered voice, "How the fuck did you know? I just found out."

"Well, when you stepped into the room, your file was resting on top the receptionist desk. I asked her to do something, and she had to step away and I glanced inside."

Before he could say another word, Egypt slapped his face and walked out of the doctor's office. She heard him calling her from behind and yelling that he loved her and this was going to bring them closer. Egypt ran into the street to get away and nearly got hit. A taxicab came to a roaring screech and lightly tapped her. She wasn't hurt. He ran over and held her while professing his love.

"Get off of me, you lousy piece of shit, leave me alone."

A few people started approaching them and realized who they were. Some young girls yelled out his name and began to run over toward them. Egypt got away from him, but his fans caught him. Jayme couldn't get away from them.

Egypt reached her loft and met Sharla on the way and began discussing the day's events. Egypt went into the back to get something for her head. Meanwhile the bell rang, and Sharla asked should she answer. Egypt told her yeah because Jayme wouldn't have balls enough to be on the other side.

Sharla opened the door and yelled to the back that they (meaning the balls) were larger than she must have thought. Jayme asked her to leave because he and Egypt had to talk. Egypt told him he had no right to ask Sharla to leave. Sharla excused herself and left.

"That was really on the money. Sometimes I think your ass plays a major role on top more than at your bottom." He looked so hurt with that, all she could do was try to avoid eye contact. Considering she never saw him look so crushed.

He yelled, "Enough is enough! I didn't ask you to love me, and damn it I can't help it that I do. Ever since I met you I've dreamt of you. I daydream of us being together. No, I'm not crazy. I just have a bad case of unrequited love. Something you must have never tasted." "Look, I never said I didn't care about you, but I was honest about my feelings.

You know that there are two men in my life that I can say I love, and one of them way more than the other. Baron is my love, and yet Chai is my heart. I never lead you on. I care for you but not enough to have a baby that would make me lose what I love dearly, no. *Do you hear me? No, no, no, I just won't!* So don't even fix your lips to ask."

"You don't have to say another damn word. Okay, whatever the hell you decided, keep to yourself. I'll stay the hell away. Shit, what in the hell is wrong with me? Shit, am I blind or stupid? See ya on the flip side." He walked out of the door and turned back. "Regardless of what you do, I'll get over it. *Dreams are for fools.* You've showed me that. The love for you has occupied my mind, and I lost my priorities. But now I'm found, I sure was blind because all of the signs were right in my face." He walked down the steps and yelled, *"Actions speak louder than words!"*

As he walked off, Egypt felt so sick inside. She wanted to reach out to him but knew it would fail. The love and tenderness she could not give freely. This is want he needed, but it wouldn't and couldn't come from her. She shut the door and melted to the floor and cried like a lost child.

The street noises made her think of days in her youth when she would feel lost and unloved. There was no feeling worse than that. Jayme was hurting; she knew it wasn't all her fault, so why did she feel like her hurt was torn in two? Can being nice do so much damage? No, sex can when you use it to satisfy a desire instead of for love. *Love,* she thought and cried even louder.

She cried to herself, "Father, Father, I need your words. Your strength, your touch. I need you now more than ever. Why did you leave me here alone? Damn you, why? Why? It's so unfair. What did I do? I tried, I tried to be everything you wanted, and still I am lost and alone. How do I go on? I love you and miss you so much. I didn't even get to say good-bye, Father. Father, please reach down to me and hold me close and don't ever let me go. I'm so scared. Never did I think I would need someone as much as I need the comfort of your words to make everything all right." Egypt lay on the floor crying until she fell asleep.

At the meeting, Baron couldn't concentrate on business, so he told Mrs. Jackson to just give them the last offer to take it or leave it. They had spent over two weeks there doing business with several groups and production managers. But this one in particular was creating so many problems, he had to stick around longer than he had expected.

He realized that Egyptian Labels was growing so quickly, and they didn't have to be bothered with them. He felt if they could do better elsewhere then go, but get one thing straight. He stressed to her to tell them if they wanted to return, the contract offer would be changed for less money and a longer period. It would be their choice. Mrs. Jackson looked at him in a confused manner. She knew this wasn't her job to do, but realized he was under so much pressure and needed a break. She just questioned the action lightly because the company never worked like this before. Baron made a firm point the business was going to make a lot of changes beginning now. He wanted to break away from Stout so he could work without being watched.

He called for Daniel. He was in charge of contract negotiation. Daniel got on the line and took all of Baron's orders without a second thought. Daniel was busy reconstructing a new contract which was going to grab a lot of people by the balls. He was tired of being walked all over by everyone. A side of Baron was sliding out with a vicious taste in the mouth. He called the office and talked with Heather, informing her many pink slips were about to be handed out. The company was going to flow from a calm stream into the devil's triangle. Heather couldn't believe what she was hearing. Baron made it a point with Egypt's office to have the locks changed on her door with only one key to be left on his desk. If she was to show up needing anything, she was to await his arrival back to New York.

Heather asked, "When will you be coming back because Mr. Gianelli called and said it was urgent that he speak with you." Baron asked, "Which Gianelli was that?" She replied, "Your cousin Francis." He became enraged and yelled, "Why didn't you reach me with this message? She had just taken the number and hung up.

When he reached Francis's house, he had already left with Franco. Karessa was worried. She told Baron, "He didn't say a word except to tell you 'cafe de noche.' You know I'm still curious about why our honeymoon was cut short after a certain phone call. Then he just had to return." Baron tried to comfort Karessa by telling her everything was all right. Just do what she normally does.

Baron went back to the conference room where Mrs. Jackson gave him the news. She began rambling off on how it was so easy to get them to sign up. She just wasn't quite sure how just a few words shuffled off could throw them off. He really didn't care. His mind was elsewhere. He told her, "Thanks for filling in, but leave all the rest of the details to the production manager.

As Baron approached Heather's desk, he informed her he was leaving on the next flight out but wouldn't be returning for several days. He left for the airport and caught a flight to Miami.

When he arrived in Miami, he met up with Lotario Scalise. They discussed many things, but Baron was more interested in who actually tried to murder his father. Lotario answered, "When the time is right for you to know, then you'll know." Francis and Franco were awaiting

Baron's arrival. Lotario and some of his followers met up in the rear of the restaurant. Several things had to be taken care of first. Baron looked around and noticed that someone was missing. So he asked, "Where's Benny?" Lotario looked down and said, "Sometimes the answers we seek are right in front of our faces."

While they all were talking amongst themselves, a man appeared at the entrance along with two other no-nonsense-looking men. He stood there watching and never said a word. Everyone ceased to talk and rose to their feet. As he walked past, a chill entered the room. One of the men who walked in with this gentleman removed his coat for him. He placed both hands on the edge of the table and said, "This meeting will come to attention." At that point everyone spoke in Italian because there was no English to be spoken there. This was one of the stipulations of being able to sit where they were. No Italian, no entrance. Simple, with no questions asked.

After everything was taken care of, Baron still didn't know who ordered that hit on Nunzio. If one thing was going to be achieved, it was that. Baron walked over to Lotario and asked where Ignatius was. Lotario told him that he was unable to make it since he was finishing some loose ends that had to be cleaned up. Baron knew what that meant, nothing else had to be said.

"Look, Lotario, we have known each other too long to play games. I'm going to find out with or without your help. So how about it," asked Baron

"It's not me, babe. If I could I would," said Lotario.

"That means that the hit came from inside. So what did he do wrong and whose foot did Nunzio step on? At least tell me that."

"What's wrong, Baron?" asked Francis as he walked over.

"An old friend who's acting like an old clam," replied Baron.

"Baron, come on. Now remarks like that aren't going to get you anywhere. Francis come and put a cool rag on your brother." Lotario laughed as he stepped away.

"Baron, listen to me. Don't start here okay. This isn't ours. I understand what he's trying to say," said Francis.

"The hell you do. That bastard isn't your father. He's mine no matter how bad he is or what he's done. See, Francis, Nunzio may be many things, but I'd never leave a man alive on earth if I knew he wanted to harm my father. So don't tell me you understand. Uncle Dom doesn't even have enough backbone in him to run your mother. As a kid I always did wonder where you and your brothers got their backbone. But it's obvious you got it from the DiBenedettos," said Baron angrily.

"You lousy son of a bitch. Where the hell do you get off talking about my father like that? Remember Nunzio wished you could only be more like me. I'm the one who stood by his side, so where the hell were you? Out in bum fuck Egypt. When he needed you to come in, you stayed out. Now here you are, courtesy of me. See, you think it's you, Baron, but quite frankly, bastard, it's me," said Francis.

"Yeah, yeah, give the opportunity to tell it."

"Tell shit. While your nose was up Egypt's ass, your father and I were taking care of things," Francis said while turning away.

Baron grabbed him on the shoulder and went to throw a punch. Francis blocked it and laid Baron down flat. Franco heard the rumbling and ran to the back. The two men were on the floor at each other's throat. Franco couldn't handle this alone, and he called to the front. A few others tried to help break it up. The two of them looked a mess. Both were bleeding, but the worse thing was that they were family. This was not tolerated.

"Franco, get off of me. Everything is all right, just leave us alone," said Baron.

They looked at Francis, and he nodded his head. "So what now? I don't have time to fuck around with you, Baron, because I've got my own problems."

"I've got a lot of shit on my back, and one thing that makes me flip is Egypt. I won't have you, Father, or any other bastard say anything about her," Baron said with an evil look in his eye.

"Who said anything about her? I was talking about your behavior. Who am I to speak on her with my own situation? Look at me with Karessa. She's black, but she may not look it. That took me by surprise myself. When I met her, I thought she was Spanish until I realized who her family was. By that time I was already in love. I had slept with her and now I'm married to her."

"What are you trying to say? That if you knew she was black, you wouldn't have gotten serious with her?" asked Baron.

"I don't know about all that, but what I do know is it threw off everything my family believed in and now there's so much talk amongst my friends. See, now that Nunzio is down for a while no one dares to say anything to me. And my mother, forget about it, because when she finds out that Karessa is pregnant, I don't know what's gonna happen. I am lost for words, but what I do know is I love her. Baron, please, this conversation is to be kept between us," said Francis.

"You're going to be a father? I can't wait for that day. Francis, trust me. When I came to the realization about Egypt, my biggest concern was my father and what he would try to do. He did everything. He even tried to sleep with her, but nothing worked so he walked away. He even tried to push women at me. Francis, it's hard to be different in this family because not too many people understand the love we have for the women we've chosen. The family interferes. Hey, I'm sorry about blowing up on ya. Let's take a shot." "You know I don't touch the stuff anymore. The last time was my wedding, and I barely made it through the wedding night. That's where I found out about the baby. When she told me, every feeling of doubt just left. Baron, I do love her, and like you, I would challenge anyone to stand between us. A son is what I hope for."

"A son, Francis? Why not a daughter."

"To tell you the truth, just in case he comes across fools, he can defend himself. I realize our child will have many people who will be against him," said Francis.

Lotario walked over to them. "I see you both have calmed down. Between you both I could never see you two as enemies. You both know I have always believed that brothers shouldn't fight," he said and began to laugh. "I don't understand that man," Franco said with an eerie look.

"I still don't know who tried to hit my father. If I stay here and continue to shoot the breeze, I'll never find out. Franco while you were out there, didn't you—" Baron had to cut it short.

John walked in and asked, "Is there a private tea going on?" Everyone laughed and walked out of the room. Baron kept it in the back of his mind what Lotario said about Benny. Benny was always a part of things. Francis pulled Baron aside and told him not to question about Benny again because when they were alone, he would explain.

John looked at Francis and asked him, "How does it feel knowing you're going to have a bouncing baby bunny?" Francis jumped up and tried to grab John, but two other thugs pulled out guns. Baron held Francis back asking, "How the hell did you know she was pregnant?"

John replied, "She had to go to a doctor, and we have our ways. Now the other reason for this is you now are undergoing retirement. Tell Nunzio that it seems his family is beginning to crumble." He said the usual offering will commence, and the meeting would come to an end.

After everything was over, Baron, Francis, and Lotario walked off. Lotario explained, "John Scala is running things, and the voting went against you." Francis was not perturbed.

"Nunzio will take care of this, you all know this. But John and the others see things in black-and-white. So does Nunzio in many ways, but when it comes to you, Francis, I know no one fucks with you." Even Baron knew that there was a strange bond between the two of them.

Baron held Francis by the shoulder and whispered something to him. Francis nodded his head in agreement. They went to the hotel, and a message from Ignatius was left for Francis. They were told to meet with

Joe (Mustache) Giogani at Romano's on Bay Terrace in Boca Rotan. Joe Mustache held a lot of weight when it came to things. His words were very much like the Pope's—when he talked, everyone listened.

Franco stayed behind because Joe Mustache didn't believe in too many people in the "family business." As far as he was concerned, Franco belonged to the Deluccos. Franco's father is well-known in Sicily. He is very powerful there as well as in the United States. Franco knew that just by being with them would create problems. He stayed behind and called Angelica to ease her mind.

What a mistake that was. Angelica jumped up and down on the other side of the phone. She demanded his return and an explanation. Franco told her to calm down because he was unable to discuss anything with her. She told him, "Don't talk to me the next time the urge hits you because you can talk to my brother since that's where you spend most of your time," she yelled and hung up the phone. Franco picked up a glass and poured whisky in it and said, "Here's to marriage."

Around 3:37 a.m. Baron and Francis arrived back at the hotel and told Franco everything was taken care of. They had to return to New York quickly. Baron was to have been back and at the office several days ago. Francis was eager to get back home to Karessa. They all had different flight plans, and each left to go their own way. Franco was staying an extra day.

Meanwhile in Greenwich Village Egypt lay in pain and spotting. She didn't know what to do. Egypt couldn't figure out what could have caused the pain. All day she was experiencing difficulty but didn't think much of it. She looked for the doctor's card because he had written his private number on it. She called Jayme and left a message that she was in trouble and to meet her. The cramps were getting worse and the spotting heavier; she knew she was losing the baby. Egypt found the number and called. He said he would meet her at the hospital, but she refused to go. She knew if she stepped into the hospital, Chai would get wind of it.

It was 4:12 a.m. When the doctor reached her house, the door was unlocked. She continuously pleaded with him to just take care of her outside of the hospital. Egypt told him to take her to his office because she hoped Jayme would be there. He consented and took her to his office since she was in so much pain.

Egypt lay down on the examining table. He informed her he didn't have enough to numb her very well. She stressed she didn't care. He inserted the speculum to open the passage. Egypt started to moan loudly. He told her, "Stay calm because if you become tense it'll only make things worse."

"Okay, Doctor, I'll try," she replied even though she was scared stiff.

Jayme arrived and banged on the door. He started to yell for someone to open.

"Just go and open the door and hurry back here," Egypt said while crying.

"What in the hell is going on? Shit, what are you doing?" asked Jayme incredulously. "Egypt you called me to watch your—" The doctor cut him off telling him she was having a miscarriage and that he didn't have enough painkiller to get her through it. "So what do we do for her? She can't just lay here and suffer, let's go to the hospital."

"No, no, just hurry up and finish. The pain is too much . . . oh shit," she moaned. "Jayme, it hurts, it hurts," she cried out.

Jayme held Egypt's hand as the doctor inserted the instrument to scrape the walls of her womb. As he placed the fetus that already disattached itself from most of the wall of her uterus into a pan, Jayme began feeling sick. The doctor said, "Hold on a minute because I have to check and make sure I got all of the afterbirth." Egypt screamed as the doctor placed one of his hands into her vagina while pushing down on her abdomen with the other. Jayme held her down with both hands. Egypt never thought pain like this could exist. All Jayme could do was say he was so sorry to see her go through this kind of pain.

"Okay, it's over, and I hope you realize we all can never bring this up because something like this has to be reported. I'll discard this then I'll give you a prescription for you to start in the morning," he said. "You should go home now and get plenty of rest and watch yourself for a couple of days. You know, take it easy. I want to see you back here in three days so I can do a follow-up. This wasn't the best of circumstances because we should have gone to a hospital, but other than that, I think you'll survive," he said with a grin.

They helped her off of the table, and Jayme helped her to the car he was renting. He drove Egypt home and helped her into bed. He tried to express his sympathy, but she couldn't hear him through her pain. She started to cry again.

"Egypt, I don't think you should be alone tonight. I think that I should stay with you to make sure you're all right."

Egypt glared at him and thanked him but said no. She reached for the phone and called Sharla and briefly explained to her what had happened. Sharla took a few minutes in getting to Egypt's, and then Jayme left. It was a muggy Sunday morning, and he had to get back home, he knew the others would be wondering if he was okay since he left without a word. Sharla filled Egypt's prescription later that morning and came back to find her up making some eggs and tea for them. She walked in and asked Egypt, "Did you lose your mind while I was gone?"

Sharla took the spatula away, and they laughed. Egypt expressed her thanks for coming without any hesitation. The two women relaxed and laughed together.

"You know, Sharla, the thought of having his child bothered me, but I couldn't make up my mind. If I kept the baby, I was sure to lose Baron," said Egypt.

"What do you mean sure to lose Baron? You would have lost him, and you know it. At least this whole ordeal is behind you. I wouldn't have been able to do what you did without any real medication to kill all the pain. The pain must have been intense. Why did you tell him to do it?" asked Sharla. "I couldn't go into a hospital because of the press. I couldn't even take the chance of Chai getting wind of it. It's fine if a man makes a mistake, and we're supposed to forgive him, but if a woman makes one, that's a totally different story. Anyway I'm supposed to meet with Baron for a dinner engagement with his cousin and wife. I hope that I'm up for it," said Egypt with a worried tone. "Why are you worried?" replied Sharla.

"I never said I was worried."

"Okay, you didn't actually say it, but it's your tone of voice. If there's a problem the keyword is *cancel*."

The afternoon had slipped away, and the evening was beginning to slide in. The doorbell rang, and Sharla answered it. When she opened the door, a woman was standing there. She was roughly five feet seven, brunette, with beautiful green eyes. There was an air about her that you knew she was someone very important. This was Donna Magaddino, a very influential woman because of her father. She was originally from New York, but her and her family now lives in Chicago.

Sharla looked at this woman as though she must have been lost. She asked the woman who she wanted. She replied with, "Lady Luck." Egypt overheard the woman say this.

"No, that's not Magaddino. Donna Magaddino from Columbia University?"

"In the flesh."

"Come in. I haven't heard that name in years. Your brother Salvatore named me that. Donna, how is he?" she asked and let her in.

"Hi, I'm Donna, and if we wait on Egypt, I would never know your name," she said and extended a hand to Sharla.

She reached out her hand as well. She said to Egypt, "Considering you haven't seen Donna in so long, I'll step out. I have some things to catch up on anyway," she said and grabbed her bag and headed out the door.

"As for Salvatore, I told him I was going to hunt you out of hiding, so he sends his regards. It wasn't hard to find you. You're in all the papers, and I must say I was shocked. First I wasn't sure if it was you. Anyway I have a proposition for you," said Donna. The two of them talked for a while until Egypt realized it was running late and pulled herself together. She was still not feeling too well, but with Donna there, she couldn't show it. They both agreed to meet within the next three or four days.

Egypt left her house somewhat late. When she arrived, Baron had yet to come. He left word with Karessa that he would be late. Karessa and Egypt talked for a while. But Egypt felt uncomfortable and was constantly looking at Karessa's stomach. Karessa remarked on how much more time she had left. Egypt only could keep smiling, but the pain of what she had gone through rested on her face.

Karessa asked, "Is there something wrong, Egypt?"

She replied, "I can't stay any longer because I was sick earlier." Egypt quickly got up and left the apartment. When she was leaving the building, Baron showed up. He approached her and noticed that she wasn't well. She said, "I'm sorry that I have to leave, but these days I'm so busy that I have to keep long and late hours. I have a rehearsal tomorrow at seven in the morning so I really have to get going."

"Well then, can I take you home?"

"No, that's all right," she insisted.

He hailed a passing taxi. Baron kissed her and assisted her into the car.

Six days had gone by, and no one had said anything about the meeting in Miami. Franco and Francis had to work without Baron for a while. Egyptian Labels was beginning to occupy a lot of his time. The office was undergoing a total transformation. All of them had to cool down for a while. A few days after the meeting, several of Joe Moustache's men were gunned down. They missed their actual target which was Joe. So things were in an uproar.

July was hot and muggy. Karessa was home counting down the months in front of the air conditioner. She hadn't been seeing much of Francis since he was always away. She was just thinking of how she was missing Francis when the phone rang. "Hello? Yes . . . no problem . . . what time and the address . . . give me a few minutes . . . I didn't expect to hear from you . . . don't tell him? Well, okay a surprise . . . he'll be so happy," said Karessa.

As she was ready to step out of the door, she stopped, turned back, and wrote a brief note for Francis that she was going to a meeting in the park, and left it by the nightstand in front of her picture. When she arrived at the park, there stood a tall and elegant woman with dark glasses. It was her mother-in-law. No sooner than Karessa could open her mouth, Antoinette put her foot in it.

She explained, "My son only married you because of the pressure from the family. Ever since Francis was a child, he would always rebel against me." Karessa started to get angry. "Look at your marriage. What do you see, a marriage or a man doing the right thing? I think you got knocked up just to hold on to him and waited to spring it on him."

Karessa's only answer to that seemed to be, "He says he loves me." But Antoinette seemed to have an answer for everything. All Karessa knew is that this woman was going to make life miserable for them. The point that Karessa and he were in love didn't matter. The fact that she was black was the main problem. Antoinette made it a point to pull out the reason why Francis didn't mind so much her color. "It's only because you don't really look black so much. He even admits that you look more Latin than Black, or is the term 'African American' you people want to be called now? Nobody would know until you see your parents." She continued, "Karessa, was your mother a whore, and you're the product of a white man who just wanted to sample a darker cherry?"

That was it for Karessa; she flew off the handle and began to tell her off. She exclaimed, "Your son is the one who came to me first. He is the one who wanted to 'sample a darker cherry.' He's the one with all the sexual fantasies. All the personal things you don't know. Francis would do anything for me. You don't know half the things he says about the family. Telling me all kinds of things. Things he would never tell you in a million years. He loves and trusts me because he knows I'm not like you. The time he tries to tell you anything, you either turn your back on him or you run and tell it to the whole house." This was not Karessa talking but a very distraught woman.

Antoinette slapped Karessa, catching her off guard. She fell to the ground. By the time she got herself correct, Antoinette was halfway across a busy intersection shouting behind her back, "He's going to leave you anyway for his own kind." With this Karessa rose to her feet screaming, "You bitch, come back here!"

Karessa ran into the street. Before she realized it, the sound of screeching brakes filled the air. She was struck down by a delivery truck. The man got out of the truck yelling at other onlookers to come and help. "Miss, Miss, are you all right? Oh heavens above, she's pregnant. Somebody call an ambulance quick. Okay, Miss, everything is going to be all right," said the truck driver.

"Ann . . . A . . . Antoin . . . Antoinette," muttered Karessa as her eyes rolled up and her head fell back.

The man's shirt was full of blood. He tried his best to continue to wipe it from the side of her head. When the ambulance arrived so did the police. Bystanders told the story that the woman ran out into the street chasing after another woman. One lady explained that the other slapped the hurt woman to the floor. The police took all the information then looked into Karessa's handbag and found her identification.

When Karessa arrived at the hospital, she was said to be in critical condition. The police reached Francis, and he and Baron went straight to the hospital. When they arrived, she was still in surgery. It was a couple of hours before they heard anything. Francis was a wreck. He couldn't understand what had happened. A man in greens walked out of the two very large doors designated for surgery. One of the nurses pointed over to Francis's direction. He approached them from behind and called out to him. The two of them turned, and the doctor proceeded to explain Karessa's situation. "Mr. Gianelli, I'm Dr. Elliot Gordon, your wife's surgeon. She suffered a severe concussion and fractures to her skull. On top of that, she also had massive internal injuries of which I'm sorry to say that we couldn't save the baby. She'll need to stay in ICU where they'll watch and monitor her progress carefully. Again I'm sorry for your loss."

Francis took a deep breath and asked, "Was it a boy or a girl?" The doctor replied, "It was a boy, and he only lived for a very short while. Your wife is in very critical condition."

Baron asked, "What are you going to do for her?"

The doctor turned to Baron and explained, "There is nothing else we can do except to watch her closely. The rest is up to her and her inner strength. The only good thing is she seems to have a strong will to live." The doctor walked them to her room and explained that Baron could not go in. When Francis saw her lying there, he walked back to his cousin. Baron grabbed him and held him telling him it was gonna be okay. Baron tried to convince Francis to return home because there was nothing he could do for her there.

"Damn it to hell some fucker is gonna pay and pay dear. My son is dead. My son is dead. I wanted a son because he could be strong. He didn't even get a chance to open his eyes. Baron someone is gonna feel the wrath of a true Gianelli. All that pussy playing has ended. Whoever wants to play now is gonna taste my balls," Francis said in a furious tone.

Baron told Francis, "Don't dwell on it. I'll take care of it. I have someone in the area that's on top of everything." Baron left and went over to Costas Street. Karessa lay there helpless with an IV in her arm and tubes and wires hanging all over her. The machine just continued to beep, and all of this was working on Francis's last nerves. He needed to reach out to someone, so he called his mother.

He expressed to her that he wished Karessa's note said more than just a meeting in the park, but all his mother seemed to be worried about was if anyone got a good look at who she was with in the park.. Francis was a bit surprised because she never was interested before about who or what his wife was doing. But he chalked it up to her hearing his pain and was concerned. He told her that whoever it was was going to pay dearly. She thought to herself that he sounded just like Nunzio. She remembered that people used to say that when Nunzio would get very angry, he tasted blood in his mouth; she felt this is how Francis was sounding. Antoinette began to worry and asked Francis if he wanted her to come down there with him.

"No, that's okay since I'm not going to stay long. I want to make sure someone is on it. I have got to know who did this to her. I know that Nunzio and them don't like the idea, so it's going to be up to me alone to find out who tried to kill my wife. I know she just didn't run out into that busy street for nothing." He hung up and walked toward her room and stayed outside the window looking in. Looking at her was like a dagger in his heart. The fact that his son was killed was tearing him into small pieces.

At the police station, the woman was asked to sign a statement. There was someone waiting for her in front of the station when she exited. As she walked down the street, a small car followed next to her. A gentleman walking beside her pushed her into the car.

The woman began to plead with them not to hurt her and that she didn't have much money. One of the men asked her, "Do I look like I need money?" She got quiet. "When you finish answering our questions, we'll let you out. The quiet gentleman sitting next to her spoke. "An easy way to meet your maker is to say we talked."

They arrived at a predesignated intersection where Baron was awaiting them at the corner. After they had walked and discussed the information, Baron seemed puzzled because what he was getting wasn't what he wanted to hear. He thought just maybe there was an error somewhere. He prayed that it was. He got into his car and drove out toward the Verrazzano bridge, but before going over, he stopped in Bay Ridge Brooklyn. He waited for his cousin Giuseppe Scala at Giorgio's. Giuseppe stepped in very large. A big man in Staten Island and every bit as crazy as his name and reputation. This was a man who could gut out your heart and eat pasta right next to you and not give a shit. Baron always said his cousin only stacked twenty-six cards. After the informal greetings, they rode off towards Staten Island. It wasn't much to Barons surprise what Crazy G told him what he heard from the vine. Baron was pissed because he couldn't tell Francis this. Giuseppe offered, but Baron told him not to interfere because there was no love lost between his father John and Francis. Giuseppe agreed because he heard what went down in Miami. He stressed to Baron that his father's opinion is his own. Baron didn't want Crazy G's side to get involved because even though the two factions did not get along, they were all his blood.

"You know that John got it out for Francesco. He can't stand his mother too. Till today the shit doesn't sit right with me," said Giuseppe.

"You aren't giving me front page news because the shit is old. Uncle John has a bad taste for Nunzio too. From the vine, it's been going on before me. So it's some old shit. Your father hasn't touched Nunzio because he's married to his sister. I think if my mother said go for it, Nunzio wouldn't be able to sleep without one eye open," replied Baron.

"Come to think about it, the Scalas are an old family. They just stayed under cover till I came out. I threw pepper on the name, and a bright light now shines on us." Crazy G. laughed.

"That's why your father laid you out," laughed Baron.

"No, don't even bring up shit like that 'cause Nunzio ran through the town yelling that his son was a pussy. I heard that's why Francis had to step next to him. So, Baron, tell me, didn't it bother you that Francis was there and not you? Come on, inside you gotta admit you're glad that they knocked him down so you got the seat. John knew what he was doing, and there was no way he could let Francis continue to be a figurehead for shit. Get with it, Baron, look who he married," replied Giuseppe.

"For one thing, Karessa is a lovely and very intelligent woman. Second I'm not happy that Francis was knocked down. He put more time in this than I did. Let's get one thing straight before I leave. The information about Karessa, keep it quiet. I have to figure just how to tell him," said Baron.

"Your problem is you're too soft. Damn, tell him straight and step away quickly. The man has a temper, one hell of a temper."

"Okay, just take care of what you have to. I'll be by on or about the following week."

Somehow Baron knew Francis had to be told. But who would take that chance and tell him? A sudden thought came over him. He'd set up the person so Francis would run into it. He just needed the right patsy. *Who would that be,* he thought. First things first. He knew he needed assistance from Franco.

Franco had to get his shit together with Angelica. She was the daughter of the Don, not the Don himself. There seemed to be times where she acted as such. Baron knew that many times Franco wanted to knock her down. Franco was trying to avoid family interference. Angelica was a rare type of woman, he thought, and then his car phone rang.

"Yes¿ ... where did he go¿ ... has anyone heard from him¿ ... Okay, okay, don't worry, I have an idea. Didn't I say I had an idea¿ So shut up. I'm almost home ... don't worry about where I am. Franco's your man, so save the twenty questions for him. Look I ... I said ... would you ... all right, all right. When I get there, you and I have to talk." Baron hung up in a frenzy. Even though Angelica was his heart, Baron felt that she should realize that there is a certain place and a certain time for everything. He couldn't help but wonder how his father would handle things. What he did know is that Francis definitely knew how.

Back at the hospital, Karessa took a turn for the worse. The attending physician was Dr. Dennis Brazen. He was in the ICU with Karessa. Even though he didn't perform the emergency operation initially, he was well aware of her condition. Francis had returned and heard all the commotion. When he reached the room, they were desperately trying to keep her conscious. She whispered Francis's name, so Dr. Brazen allowed him in so she could speak. She looked at him and asked in a soft voice, "Francis, does color matter¿" He had no idea what she was saying.

"Do you love meese," she whispered, holding on to the words as if each word and breath were meant to linger.

"Of course, you know that. What happened¿"

"My baaaaby. Where is it¿ Did she hurt it¿"

"Who Karessa¿ Did who hurt it¿"

"Nooooo, gimme, gimme my baaaby ..."

"Karessa, who did this¿" Francis said as Dr. Brazen ordered the nurse to give her a sedative and take him out. Francis fought them, but they got him out of her room. He yelled, "I just wanted her to hear my question."

The doctor walked out after a moment or so to explain her condition again. Francis understood, but he tried to explain to the doctor that someone did this to her and how else can he find out unless she tells him herself. Dr. Brazen stressed, "Her condition is very delicate, and any more outbursts could result in her going into cardiac arrest or worse. If she comes through, don't let her know she lost her child. In her condition every positive thing helps her to strive to stay alive. You see," he explained, "the desire to live is sometimes stronger than any form of medication. Especially a mother, they have a maternal instinct to survive for their children."

Francis knew the doctor was right, but he wanted her to answer him because if she didn't make it, the answer would leave with her.

While they were discussing Karessa's treatment, all of her vital signs dropped. Her heart rate all but stopped, and her blood pressure followed suit. Dr. Brazen was called in. Karessa regained consciousness again yelling out names and saying in the barest of tones, "Make her go away . . . yes, he does." Suddenly she flatlined.

Over the intercom the message, "Code blue in ICU stat" echoed through the halls. Baron left one of his men there to stay with Francis; no sooner had Karessa first come through, he called Baron to inform him.. Baron was still nearby the hospital, so he sped straight over.

When he arrived, everything was in turmoil. Francis was trying to get into the room. Dr. Brazen grabbed the hypodermic and inserted her with Hemprin to thin her blood; they had detected a blood clot. When it hit, they were trying to hurry and put in a pacemaker. He grabbed the electrodes and yelled, "Clear!" When he hit her with the electrodes, her body rose and fell with no reaction. He waited momentarily and repeated it. Finally he got a minute, irregular heartbeat, but it was so weak that it stopped again altogether. They tried to keep oxygen flowing to her brain, but all they could do was hope the Hemprin dissolved the blood clot. They once more gave her heart the final shock, but her heart was just not strong enough. Francis watched through the glass as they made every attempt to revive Karessa.

Dr. Brazen looked back toward the window and saw Francis's bleak expression as he realized nothing else could be done. Baron touched his cousin on the shoulder lightly. Francis walked into the room and held her hand for a moment then covered Karessa with the sheet. They did everything for her. Francis tried to hold back the tears, but one slipped out. He never made an attempt to wipe it off.

Francis walked over to Baron and whispered, "My child and my wife. What else could go wrong?" Baron knew that he couldn't tell Francis now who was with Karessa. Francis asked Baron to take care of the arrangements for the baby, and he would take care of Karessa. He hadn't seen the child and didn't want the memory to linger.

The nurse at pediatrics informed Baron that they had taken several photos of the baby before he died and that he had a birth certificate as well as a death certificate. She informed him that baby boy Gianelli was now in the morgue and expressed her sympathies. This was getting to Baron because he couldn't imagine how Francis felt.

Baron called Angelica who also was going to help with the arrangements. Francis didn't know how to tell Karessa's parents, so he called when he arrived home. Francis spoke to her mother, and she couldn't believe what had happened. She was so upset and cried, "Why didn't you call me sooner?"

"I honestly never expected her to die. Everything happened so quickly."

She began sobbing hysterically, and her husband came to the phone. She cried to him that their baby was dead. He couldn't say a thing. Francis explained all of the arrangements would be made for the two of them. Mr. Devine said, "It's bad enough you're connected to some very influential and notorious people. Whoever did this to her probably did it because they wanted you."

Francis couldn't reply. Mr. Devine said, "Francis, I want you to release both bodies to me, and we'll take care of everything." Francis said he would sign the papers.

"I never thought it was a good idea for her to marry your kind in the first place," said Mr. Devine.

"What do you mean by that 'your kind'?"

"What do you think, that black people are supposed to be happy that their child marries someone white? Think again, Mister. The difference between your mother and I is I love my child more than my dislike of you. If this was to make her happy, I would abide by it. But as I said to her, just because I'm smiling doesn't mean I'm happy," said her father.

"So why now? Why didn't you say something to me sooner? At least you could have been man enough to—"

"Man enough! No, I'm more of a man than you or anyone else will ever know. I've had to deal with the white man and his trash before I reached here. And I used yall's money to get this far and threw your ass out of my way also. So need you? No, I've just about finished with you's. As far as I'm concerned, the blood of my child and grandchild is on your hands. Somehow, someway it had something to do with you," he said angrily and hung up the phone very abruptly.

By morning all the paperwork was made out. The funeral home had the papers sent to Francis, and he signed them. Baron was told not to do anything because her parents wanted to handle all of the arrangements. Her paperwork stated that she was married at her time of death, and she was being buried with her maiden name.

By the time of the funeral, very little of Francis's family was there. The Devines wanted it to be a one-day thing. No wake at all, just a simple ceremony at the church and from there to the burial grounds. Francis was just numb and confused. With the death of his wife, he saw many different sides of people. He heard from his mother three times asking if he was going to be fine. She kept pressing the issue of "everything happens for a good reason." He was too unbalanced to reply; he just stayed quiet.

Everyone treated Francis as if he weren't there. That is until he opened his mouth. Once again, Mr. Devine expressed, "My daughter and grandson died at the hands of the underworld." Francis too had a gut feeling and was thinking the same thing. He walked to the front and said a few words and was seated.

At the burial site, after everyone walked from the graves, he stayed there by himself. He swore that he would find that lady with or without Baron's help. When he stepped into the limo, he asked the driver to take him to Lotario's Café.

A few drops of rain fell over the evening with a cool breeze. While Francis was on his way, he felt strange—so many things were running through his mind. He was in overdrive, and he felt as though he wanted to explode. The rain began to fall rapidly. He could barely see his hand in front of his face. When he got to the cafe, Francis walked in, removed his coat, and shook the rain off. A lady took it from him.

"Lovely weather," a voice snapped loudly. Lotario was sitting with Baron. He didn't think Francis would have made it. Baron and Lotario finished their business and left.

Baron and Francis stood out in the rain and talked. Francis told him, "Don't worry, I'm going to be all right in the apartment. I'll be moving as soon as I find a new one." Baron thought that would be best.

Baron expressed that he could not imagine Egypt dying. Francis replied, "I've never even seen my son and something inside me wishes I would have." Baron didn't know whether he should tell Francis of the pictures he had gotten from the nurse. Francis asked Baron, "Are you all right? You seem to be in another place."

"Oh, I'm okay. I just need to get out of the rain. Look, I'll get in touch with you in the morning."

"Yeah, I don't want either of us to catch pneumonia."

Later that evening Antoinette was very surprised that no one found out it was her there with Karessa. She poured a glass of wine and lay back on the couch. Dom walked in and asked, "What's going on?" She acted like she had no idea what he was saying. He stepped over to her and repeated himself. All she did was get up to make another. Dom very seldom stood up to Antoinette, but he had a lot of questions that he wanted answered, and he wasn't going to wait. She jumped up in his face and told him, "Get back into the drunken stupor you're usually in."

He came closer to her. "Get away from me. Answer me something, when will there be a man in my life? Now that you've grown some balls, do you think they'll find their way in the bedroom? Get the hell out my face," yelled Antoinette.

"You think I'm stupid, Toni? Please don't push me. Just answer me this, when Karessa died, where were you?" asked Dominic.

"Go lay your ass down and stop moving faster than your brain will allow."

"Don't walk off while I'm talking. Answer me, damn you. What are you doing?"

"Walking the hell away from you and leaving you in the room by yourself. So please continue without me."

"Antoinette, this one time my words will count. I have something to say."

"So tell your damn self."

He grabbed her as she pulled away from him. She said, "My, aren't we searching for some balls? Trying to be masculine. It would be nice to have a man inside of my husband. When will you be a man in the boudoir?"

He went to slap her, and she slammed the door in Dominic's face. He turned back to the bar and made another drink. She called Nunzio and began to cry. She broke down and tried to explain everything to him hoping he would try and help. He told her, "Calm down and don't speak on the phone." She continued, "I can't bear the thought of Francesco not talking to me."

"I'll stop by while I'm at physical therapy tomorrow afternoon. I don't want to talk over the phone. I don't think that you really did anything, but Francis will blame it on you. So first things first."

When she turned around, there stood Dominic asking her again, "Now why are you jumpy, my dear? Are you going to answer me, or do I go with you tomorrow? It's been a while since I've seen Nunzio unlike you."

"How long have you been there?"

"Wouldn't you like to know? Don't worry I'm sober enough to hear what was said but not ignorant to tell you what I heard. Good night, my dearest, and by the way, I haven't spoken to your son since the funeral."

Antoinette began to get fidgety. She lay there glaring at Francesco's picture and prayed that this wouldn't get out of hand. Francesco held a very special place in her heart. He was so much a part of her and looked just like Nunzio. He had a few features of Dom, but those were also similar to Nunzio's.

She leaned over and shut off her night-light and slid in between her sheets. The rain continued to pour, and then the sounds of thunder crept through her. She heard Karessa's screams and sat up straight in a cold sweat. Her mind was starting to work on her. Antoinette sat at the side of the bed and put on her robe and slippers. She went to the foot of the bed and heard a voice crying. She looked all around her and called out, but there was no answer. She felt as though someone was watching her.

Antoinette went over by the bar and made a strong drink. She sat by the window and gazed at the trees bending from side to side.

"Are you happy now? Are you happy now?" she heard a voice say softly.

The branches tapping on the window made her edgy. She again heard the voice say this time, "He'll never forgive you. He'll never forgive you."

"Who are you damn it! Where the hell are you? You son-of-a-bitch you. Come out and face me," yelled Antoinette.

"I can face you, but can you face yourself?" replied the voice.

"Shit, show yourself." She reached for a gun under the bar. "So where are you? Som-ona-beetch, come out. Are you afraid?"

"No, not like you are of the truth coming out. Francesco will hate you forever."

There was the sound of a baby crying, she thought. But she knew that was impossible. The crying got louder, and she held her head. Out of nowhere the voice repeated itself along with the wailing of an infant. Antoinette went to walk out of the room, but loud thunder sounded and a lightning bolt struck and lit up the sky. She saw a silhouette of a woman with a package in her arms. Another bolt of lightning hit, and the woman was gone. Was she losing a grip of things?

Over by the mantel she noticed Francis's picture. As she lifted it up, her eyes made contact with the mirror and behind her stood the woman and that package. She dropped the picture and emptied the gun at her. Before she knew it, she was gone. Then by the window, she saw clearly the woman laughing holding a crying baby. She screamed and fell to the floor. Dominic, Ann, and Vitto came down to find her a nervous wreck with Francis's picture broken on the floor.

Dom took the gun from her and made sure it was unloaded. He saw she emptied every last round into a wall. Something wasn't right, and at that point, he truly began to worry.

Through it all, he knew she was never there for him, but he did love her. They helped her to her feet and sat her on the couch. She held on to Vitto for dear life. Vitto pulled back and asked what happened. Ann ran upstairs to get one of her tranquilizers.

She placed the pill in her mother's mouth and helped her with the glass of water. Antoinette was shaking. The sight she saw couldn't be explained to anyone. No way could she share what she went through. Vitto tried to get his mother to tell him what happened, but she would just reply she was all right. Ann grabbed Vitto by the arm and said, "I feel Mom is hiding something because for the last two days she was on the edge." No one could figure it out.

Antoinette went to lay down upstairs. Dominic tried to comfort her, but she wasn't receptive. He held his arms toward her in bed, and she just turned the opposite way. Even during a time like this, she still hasn't lost her bitchiness, he thought. He should have known better because once a bitch always a bitch. Then he turned off the night-light.

Chapter 10

Morning broke, and the mist from the night rain passed leaving its mark behind. Jose continued to dial his sister to give her the news about Dionisia. Egypt just glared at the phone as if to say stop. She finally picked it up to only hear her brother's voice running a mile a minute. He told her that she gone into labor. Dennis called from California to tell Momita. Egypt was so happy, but in the back of her mind, she began to recall yesterday. Jose noticed that she started to drift and asked if she was okay. Egypt just sighed and didn't say anything. Jose asked again then he was interrupted by Noel, and he needed to use the phone. So he expressed his concern and told her he would call with more news later.

After a few moments, she smiled and thought to herself she was going to be a Tia. Dionisia was so far away. She wanted to be by her side, but she was committed to do the concerts. How could she get around Carlos? Mr. Montana really was crawling up her ass and sticking to her like flies to shit. Egypt made an attempt to call Dionisia's apartment, but there was no answer, so Dennis must have been at the hospital. In a few more months Gina was going to have a baby too. Everyone seemed to be having a family. Both had husbands and homes and now children. Egypt felt a certain emptiness in her life. It was full of excitement and money, yet it seemed so unimportant compared to what she deserved. Fame was going to be great she knew, but what about sharing it with someone?

The doorbell broke her concentration, and she walked over covering herself with a robe. Donna laughed because Egypt looked terrible. She pushed her hair out of her face and asked, "What species do you belong to?"

Egypt didn't find any humor in it at all. As Donna made her way to the kitchen, Egypt asked, "Are you our pep-up pill?" Donna replied, "There wouldn't be enough pep in the city of New York or in that fact the tristate area enough for the both of us." Egypt knew it was going be a delightful morning.

Out of her pouch she took a few tea bags, placed a teapot on the fire and walked straight to her fold out couch. Egypt was trying to fold it back in, but Donna made her stop and finished it for her.

The pot whistled, and she ran in the kitchen to turn it off. While making the tea, she talked of the things that had transpired within the last few years. She was very inquisitive about Egypt's past.

Egypt asked her, "Come from behind the curtain and show your face. What do you want?"

"It's not that I'm ungrateful, just what brought all of this on? Look, you would be questionable about a sudden appearance. Donna we were good friends at one time, but a lot of time has gone by. It's not like you kept in touch."

"All of this is true, but I am being sincere—"

"No one said you're not but there has to be a little more to it than what I'm seeing. Am I right?"

Donna stood up and went to get her coat. "If I can't help an old friend without an ulterior motive then I had better go."

"No, Donna, I didn't say that you should go. Look I'm going through some damn stress." Egypt began to cry, and she walked into her kitchen and Donna followed.

"I didn't want to hurt you, but I'm here for a reason. I'm depressed because so much has gone wrong with my life so I thought I'd search you out. I didn't think you were doing as bad as me. Emotionally distraught. So you see, Egypt, it's not like I'm trying to interrupt and disturb your life, just the opposite. I need the change and new atmosphere."

"So you wanted a change? A change. Well, this is the place to be. If it's not one thing it's another. Thrilling huh? My life has been so uprooted this thrill is about to give me a stroke."

"Come on, Egypt, it can't be that bad," replied Donna. They sat there over herbal tea, and she gave her some of the dirt that had been taking place. Donna was laughing as well as crying with her. The two women took a long look at one another and said it was time to clean house. The only problem was where to begin. While they were busy deciding what to do next, Egypt's phone rang; it was Carlos. She asked Donna to go along with her to a sound check. She was a little nervous because of Jayme, but she knew she would have to face him. The show was that evening.

A week has passed and Baron was called and told to be at the loading docks after midnight. Baron felt something strange going on, but he had to go. When he drove up, no one was there. He stepped out and walked near the water. Baron looked over the water, and it seemed peaceful. The overcast of the moon laid on the river. While gazing in he saw a reflection of some sort. He slowly opened his jacket. He didn't want to make a sudden move. As he stood there, a chill ran up and down his spine.

Not too far from him stood a man walking around double stacked barrels. As he stepped forward, he reached in front of his pants for his gun. The man crept slowly, and each step was made with prescience. So soft he couldn't be heard. Out of nowhere a hand came from behind and grabbed him placing a knife through the back of his throat. The man's eyes bulged with shock as he fell to the ground quietly. This mystery man then disappeared as swiftly as he appeared.

Another one of Benny's goons were making sure that he had a good shot of Baron. While placing on his silencer a strong hand covered his mouth. He was then turned around facing a man who resembled an android. Mystery man smiled showing his gold teeth. Benny's goon tried to get away, but his attempts were fruitless. He tried to pull the strange hands off his face, but one, two, three, the man broke his jaw. Then he reached behind him for his knife and slit the goon's throat. He fell on top of the gun.

Baron heard a noise, turned around, and saw nothing. This was working on his nerves—just standing out like a sitting duck. He strolled over toward his car. A voice spoke tensely. It sounded like Benny asking, "What's wrong?" Baron turned but didn't see him. He realized it was a cat and mouse game. As he inhaled he turned with his .45 magnum drawn and carefully scanned the area but Benny wasn't there.

"Benny, don't screw with me. What the hell are you up to? I'm not fucking around with you," said Baron. "So who said I was planning to fuck you? You're not my type," chuckled Benny.

"Step out into the open, or shit ass, are you afraid to face me and shoot me from the front or do you need my back," Baron asked.

"No, I may not want to shoot you, just maybe gut your ass out. But not shoot you," Benny yelled out.

As the voice carried across the air, there was a loud bang and a barrel fell to the ground and Benny moved just in time. When he did, he let off a round and Baron was hit in his shoulder. Baron lost his gun; as he tried to get up off the floor, he caught a glimpse of it. It was too far away to reach. He wondered where the hell was Boa. He felt a cold brisk breeze rush across him. Standing over him was Benny, looking evil.

"Get up, Gianelli. Get the hell up, you weak bastard. You're not from the same core as your father. It took a lot to get him, but he just got out of the car in time. But he ran out of time now! See we won't make that mistake with you."

Boa grabbed his shoulder and broke his arm. Benny called out to his thugs, but Boa just shook his head. Benny was yelling in pain. Baron rose to his feet holding his wound trying to find something to stop the bleeding. He looked at Boa as if to say, take him out.

Boa lifted him up by the neck and smiled. In the background Baron said, "Don't worry I know who the rest were so beware darling." Boa snapped his neck with one quick move. He tossed Benny to the floor like a wet rag. They both got out of there, and Baron had Boa take his car. He hoped that he didn't leave behind any traces of him being there. Boa was told to get the car washed and make a quick ride upstate. His parents were supposed to be up there. Something that Benny said didn't settle right with him. It kept hitting like an instant replay.

Baron needed to see someone about his shoulder. When he arrived home, he called and told Francis to come by. Francis was still very distraught over Karessa. He felt something was wrong and pulled his thoughts together and headed to Baron's. As he approached the house, there were several cars there of importance. He was positive that something went down because Baron never took a chance being spotted with these people.

When Francis walked in and saw Baron with a bandage and a drink in his hand he yelled, "You went out alone, damn it!"

"Calm the hell down. I didn't go alone, Boa went with me."

"So who did this? When I came up the drive, I saw the car was missing. Where is it?" asked Francis. "Take a seat Frankie man, cool off," said Baron.

They all gathered like they were the knights of the round table, but it was just as serious. When it was over everyone agreed on what had to be done. Baron didn't want to go along because it meant staying away from the family. He knew he had nothing to worry about because Francis was much more attentive to detail then he was.

Baron wanted someone to go behind Boa to make sure that his parents were okay. Francis told him not to fret, to just go, and he would take care of everything. While they were about to disperse, a call came through. Baron's face turned three shades of red. When he hung up he looked at John and said, "Fontaine's body was found."

All hell broke loose. Worse than that, Baron said he couldn't leave Egyptian Labels because there were a lot of contract changes and he had to be around. "There is no way possible I could leave." Both Francis and John tried to convince him to go underground for a while. But he refused to.

Francis phoned Franco and left the cryptic message, "WHEN THE ROBIN FLIES UP, IT MUST SWIFTLY COME DOWN." Franco replied with, "No problem," and hung up. Angelica asked who was it, and Franco looked at her.

She went up to him and hugged him. "Okay, baby, I remember family business is not for me to get into. But, Franco, all I want to know is Baron, okay? Just by telling me he's okay is not telling me the news."

"Angela, Angela, you'll never change, will you? If anything was wrong with Baron, I would tell you. But my personal pest, take my word for it, Baron's fine. Now I have some business to tend to. Get me my black tapered slacks." She didn't move. "Angela, did you hear me? Okay I'll get my own shit. Sometimes you get me so pissed. Move out the way. If you're not going to be productive stand out of my way."

"I'll stand where I please, and as far as your damn slacks or anything from now on get yourself."

"Angela, you're a spoiled bitch at times, and this is one of those times."

She grabbed her pillow and tossed it at him and stormed out of the room. She waited for him to walk out of the door before she said anything. "Franco, why? All I want to know is why? Isn't it bad enough I was raised up in this kind of atmosphere? I just don't want to have a family living like I lived. I want to raise my kids in a decent and moral home. Can you understand that? I just won't."

"You knew about me beforehand, Angela. Please don't act so frigg'n' melodramatic. I'm not Nunzio, so when the day comes for my children, it will be different. Look, Angela, you're starting to work my nerves. Let's discuss this some other time."

He stepped toward the door, and she held him by the jacket. Franco looked right through her. She felt a quiver run up her neck. She didn't let go though. "Listen, good buddy, as you put it. Frigg'n' walk out the door without finishing this and don't come home in the morning."

Franco pulled away, grabbed Angela, and kissed her on the cheek and told her to calm down. Before she slammed the door, she ran over to him and looked him up and down. "You look and sound more and more like that bastard Nunzio."

"You swear Nunzio knows nothing about you, that he never truly cared for you. You think he doesn't know you, but he has you pegged. You act like the immature brat he speaks of. You could never deny that again to me. Angelica, time tells all tales, doesn't it?"

"You bastard," she said as he drove off.

Early that morning as the beams from the sun warmed Egypt's face, she sat up with a smile, for the first time in a long while she felt good. She thought of Baron, and she reached for the phone but it rang before she picked it up. It was Donna. Both of their spirits were riding high on the horse. Egypt told her to come by later because she might feel like shopping later since it was such a lovely day. She stepped into her shower and began to absorb the water as if it was washing all her troubles away. She brushed her hair from her face letting the water run to her feet. With a swift move, she placed both hands into the stream of water making it hit her face. She then sat down as though she were under the falls. She felt reborn, and nothing was going to upset her day. After a while she lathered up and got out.

The rich aroma of freshly ground gourmet coffee beans enhanced the beautiful morning. Egypt was making a breakfast fit for a princess. After she finished preparing it, she sat at a small kitchen table. She watered the few plants hanging in the window. Then she sat and indulged. Much to her surprise, the phone didn't ring or the door bell.

Egypt opened her door and picked up her mail and sat on her sofa. She stretched out and went through the mail. There was a letter from her sister which she opened. Inside the envelope were pictures of the baby. Egypt was so happy to hear from her. She placed the picture on the mantel. The doorbell rang, and when she answered, it was Donna. They both ventured forth toward a fulfilling day of boutique attack.

Armed with charge cards and checkbooks ready to conquer all sales and sales persons, they both chuckled and exclaimed, "Are you ready? Aim, fire, and charge it!"

Donna and Egypt ran up and down Manhattan. In an out of stores. Egypt purchased a lot of baby gifts to send to her sister.

They stopped at Planet Hollywood for lunch and met some other friends there. Sharla too was hitting the shopping scene. After lunch they all overthrew a few more shops and then retreated to each his own fortress. Much to Egypt's surprise there stood Chai not too far from her place. He spotted her and smiled; she walked over to him and kissed him. They talked, and he helped her in with the bags. Egypt asked Chai, "What brought you over? I miss you and the office."

Chai explained, "I came by to say good-bye. I'm leaving for Japan to stay there with my family."

"I'm really gonna miss you."

He gave her a slip of paper with his new address and phone number. Chai asked, "May I kiss you, Egypt?"

She grinned and nodded yes. Chai went to kiss her. As she closed her eyes, Chai looked at her and couldn't kiss her. She opened her eyes and asked, "What's wrong?"

Chai replied, "I have never stopped loving you. A kiss would only intensify my desire for you more, so why begin what you would not allow me to finish?"

Egypt understood and kissed him. Before he left, he gave her a gift he took from his pocket. Egypt's face gleamed when he placed it into her hand.

She lifted it up, and it was the most precious jade necklace. Chai placed it on her neck. As she turned and faced him, the sun that was still out gleamed into her eyes. They seemed to sparkle; her eyes appeared watery.

"There will never come a day that I won't understand how I could've walked away from a good man like you, Chai. Can you hold me please?" Chai held her with such emotion that she began to cry and he felt a lump in his throat. He had to leave because it was getting too misty in there for him. After the embrace he walked to her door and just left without saying a word. She too couldn't say anything because all that was left were tears. Egypt read the letter. It read

"When you want me, just walk toward the red sun, and I'll always be there."

She walked up the ladder to her small bed to look out her personal little window. She felt strange that her life was finally moving forward. At least some of the chapters in her life are closing. She felt that when each chapter closes, it brings her closer to a finale. This man she knew who he was.

Egypt wondered what had happened to Baron. She hadn't heard from him in sometime. Somehow she was going to reach Baron, but she wasn't sure just how.

Several hours had gone by and the night air filled her place. She kept walking to and fro from the phone. Every time she lifted the phone, she dropped it until she just went ahead and dialed his number. There was no answer, but his machine came on. She wasn't quite sure about leaving a message, but she did. Egypt lay there drifting back into time. A glazed feeling took over her as she began remembering the last moment she spent with Carlos. Something just jarred him from the corner of her mind. The intensity of their lovemaking. The overwhelming sensation of it all. She couldn't help but take a deep breath as she recalled every sound and emotion. Egypt grabbed her pillow and took a deep sigh as dreamland tiptoed her away.

It was very late when Baron received her message. He wanted to get back to her but he noticed that it was after 3:00 a.m. He couldn't help but envision her next to him. Soon he was going to make sure that they would be together.

As Baron went into the bedroom his phone started to ring. He was startled, he thought it was Egypt. When he picked up the telephone his voice was filled with excitement. When he noticed it was Francis his voice dropped a few octaves. Francis asked, "Were you expecting a call from someone else?"

"No, I wasn't." Francis knew better. "It's important that we meet in the afternoon. It would be best if it was at Egyptian Labels." They both agreed, so Baron called it a night.

Baron was a firm believer in getting an early start on the day. He was at Egyptian Labels before his own employees. He sat in Heather's chair as he watched everyone come in. Heather was startled to see him there. Baron was so unpredictable. Heather laughed at him because he was mimicking her behavior at the desk. Even with all the power he had he still could relate to his employees, but when he meant business, don't even grin at him. Baron was not to be toyed with when it meant getting down to business.

"Mr. Gianelli, you have a call on two. He wouldn't give a name at all. He just said 'Sparrow,'" said Heather.

"Thanks, Heather. Could you please get me the files on the last three accounts Ms. Aguliar was working on?"

Baron picked up the line. It was Francis saying he couldn't make it because he felt it best to meet at a neighbor's place. This meant to go over Angelica's. Baron agreed and said to meet at the usual time. Francis went along with it.

Heather came in with the files, and Baron jumped right in on it. As he went over her expenses, he hit the roof. He called Mr. Stout and gave him the rundown, but he wasn't too interested in it.

"Don't worry about the dollars she over spent."

"It's not a few dollars, and if it continues, I'll bring it to the attention of the board."

"Baron, what's the problem between you and Ms. Aguliar? If by any chance you feel she's performing at a level of insufficiency, let me know, and I'll talk to her."

"If for some reason there was something I felt was unappropriated, I would get back with you at a later date."

Mr. Stout questioned Baron again, but he refused to answer. He ended the conversation abruptly. After that he told Heather to get in touch with Mrs. Jackson and Daniel McNair to set up a meeting for this Friday and get the last ten groups' papers on his desk.

"Have all the information ready by Friday, and make four copies of everything." Heather knew shit was getting ready to hit the fan.

Heather buzzed Serinah and told her, "Watch out for Mr. Gianelli. Boy is he hot under the collar."

"I just saw Egypt go to payroll."

"Great, let me make a subtle hint to Mr. Gianelli that Ms. Arcardi was on the phone with George from payroll."

"What does he care about that? You just don't understand the chemistry between those two."

Serinah's phone was ringing, so she had to go. Heather drifted over by Baron's door and acted like she was talking to someone and mentioned, "I just saw Egypt going to payroll . . ."

Baron stepped out of the office and said, "I'll be back momentarily."

Heather had an idea where he was heading. She just grinned and continued on with her work. Baron damn near broke his neck trying to get to payroll. Just prior to reaching the door, he came to a halt and got himself together. He brushed back his hair and straightened his attire before entering. When he walked in, he looked around and didn't see her. George walked over to him and asked, "Is there a problem?"

"There are a few things I want to know about the amount they're taking from—" At that moment he spotted Egypt. She gave a slight smile and winked her eye at him. Baron walked over and kissed her on the cheek.

"So have you eaten yet, Egypt? If not, there's a place I know that's close by. So how about it?"

"Why not, so long as you're paying. Remember, no after-lunch dessert, love," replied Egypt.

"What's bringing you to Egyptian Labels? Especially to payroll."

"I had a few problems with tax questions."

He put out his arm for her, and they left. They strolled through the streets laughing and rehashing old times. When they arrived at the restaurant, they looked like they were back together again.

"You know, Baron, I hadn't felt this good in a long time. I forgot how much fun we had."

"That hurts me, Butter, because I thought the good times were so many that it would be too hard to overlook."

"Well, I don't think this is the time to retrace the past. The day is too beautiful to think back just to enjoy. So I see you and Mr. Stout have done a lot for the company."

"Nothing that you couldn't have done yourself. So what'll you have? Go on, tell the man. It's not my place anymore to order for you."

Egypt looked over her menu and crossed her eyes at him. He chuckled and replied, "Well, it's not is it?" "It wasn't then either. It seemed sometimes I didn't have a choice in the matter. So I figured why argue, it must have made you feel macho. Okay, I'll have the chef's salad and let me see, how about . . . ah well . . . ah, bring me a . . . so I'm a little rusty at it."

"Give her the chef's salad and french dressing with no croutons and the salmon on wheat crackers. As a beverage, she'll have a Manhattan with a twist of lime."

"No, love, too early for that, just make it Perrier with a lime slice on the side."

"Very good, bring me my usual and a pasta salad, thank you."

"Now then let's get back to business. I've done a bit of research on Egyptian Labels and noticed that the dividends are strange. Look, Mr. Stout owns at this present moment all the controlling stock. And if we, Egyptian Labels, cannot give him back the money and buy him out plus the 13 1/2 percent interest in the set time allotted us he gets to maintain controlling interest. In which case we had might as well be called silent partners. So what do you plan on doing about it?" asked Egypt inquisitively.

Baron lifted his drink to her and took a tiny sip and smiled. They laughed for a while. Then he explained that sometimes things that appeared to be wrong, in turn may be correct. He reached over and gave Egypt her glass and made a toast to them. He added that his love for her was undying. Egypt felt very awkward, so she said nothing for the moment.

They both felt there was a certain emotion drifting in the air. As lunch was winding up Baron, asked, "Egypt, would you have dinner with me?"

"There is no way I could, but maybe some other time."

The look on his face showed total disappointment. Egypt saw this and grinned inside. This was making her feel more sensuous. To see him desire her still uplifted her. But she didn't want to seem smug.

As they walked back toward Fifth Avenue, she held on to his arm talking and laughing. Egypt wanted to give him some sort of security. Baron asked, "Do you still feel anything for me?"

"Are you silly or what? Of course I do."

"Then I insist that we spend the evening together."

She let go of his arm and stopped. *What could I say?* she thought. *This is a perfect moment, but is it time to tell him that I want to start anew? She felt since the day she left, she wanted to come home. Did she dare even entertain the thought of reconciliation?*

Baron awaited her answer and placed his hand on her cheek; while taking it slow, he again asked her.

"Egypt, I feel that it's time to place yesterday behind us and pick up now. If the love we shared before is still there, there is no need to go back."

Egypt lowered her head and still told him she couldn't. For just a moment Baron was angry and began to walk without her. He turned and asked, "Aren't you coming?"

Egypt replied, "I thought you were upset, so I was letting you go ahead."

"No, why would I be upset? You're your own woman. Egypt, what's good for you is all you should concern yourself with."

"Now, Baron don't make me out like that. On the contrary, I would love to have dinner, but I need my rest. I have a late rehearsal this evening. I already made plans to hit the z's soon after."

"So what are you telling me, if you didn't have to go to rehearsal, you would accompany me?"

"Yes, Baron, I would have loved to. My schedule is very tight right about now."

"Good, considering for the next few days I too will be quite busy. So we can make arrangements to meet tomorrow at La Magnatte around six-thirty or so."

Baron kissed Egypt lightly on the lips and escorted her to the elevator. As she got on, he remained outside the door. All he did was give a wink, and she blushed.

While going inside the elevator, she took a deep sigh and spun saying, "I still love him." No sooner did she come to terms with that she also noticed that she has closed the loose chapters behind her. She couldn't consider starting anew unless she fixed things between her and Jayme.

When she reached her floor, she went straight to Heather. Heather was on the phone with Baron, but Egypt was unaware of this. She was making hand signs for the key to her office. But Heather was instructed by Baron that under no circumstances should she be allowed in. Heather asked in a roundabout way if she should she give up the key.

Egypt didn't catch what was going on. Heather smiled and acted as though she didn't understand what Egypt wanted. Egypt motioned again for the key. She opened the drawer and said, "Mr. Gianelli must have it with him."

"Why is there only one key for my office?" She picked up the phone to call maintenance to have the door opened. Heather told Egypt, "Nothing like that can be done without the consent of Mr. Gianelli."

Egypt was too through, so she turned around and standing there with a fog around him was Baron's cousin. Joseph spoke with a cigarette in his mouth. Egypt kept waving her hand in front of her face. As she waved, he continued to puff toward her.

"Okay, if you don't kill that damn cigarette, I'm gonna shove it up your ass. It's your choice."

"So yeah, got a problem heh. Looks to me you could use some help."

"I'm surprised you can see through your personal fog. Do you know where Baron was headed?"

"Nah, I haven't seen him. Something wrong?"

"There's no extra key to my office."

"So sweets your knight is here. Show me where it is. Come on lead the way. You and Baron hitting it off or what?"

Egypt started to catch an attitude and said, "So who are you now, Scoop Leigh? Just get the door open."

Heather ran down the hall telling them they had no right to do this without Mr. Gianelli's knowledge. She called security, and they were on their way up. Heather hoped between her and security they could stall them till Mr. Gianelli arrived.

When security arrived, Egypt showed them who she was, but that didn't interest them. "Mr. Gianelli left strict orders not to allow anyone in that particular office," said one of the men.

"Please try to understand that Mr. Gianelli is nowhere around, and I need to get into my office for my briefcase."

"Well, can I get a light from someone?" asked Baron.

"Mr. Gianelli, I'm so glad you're back, please explain to Ms. Arcardi that I was acting on your orders," said Heather.

"Calm down, Heather. Joseph, what in the hell are you here for? There's not a damn thing here for you. Egypt. as for your office that you now want to claim, you'll have to wait for maintenance to come and put it together. Until then no one will enter that room."

"For your information only, Mr. Executive. Nunzio asked me to drop in and deliver something," Joseph said arrogantly.

Baron excused himself from Egypt and told her he would explain later and not to worry. He and his cousin stepped into his office.

Baron made a drink for both of them, and Joseph was very eager to tell Baron what happened. Baron sat down, lit a cigarette, and Joseph blurted out that all shit had hit the fan.

"Nunzio demanded that I make him aware of the happenings, but I flat out refused because I felt if he had to do that then Nunzio should take it back. But Nunzio didn't want that because finally he thinks he has his son where he wants."

The phone rang, and it was Francis. Baron told him his brother was there with him. So Francis wanted to set up a meeting. Baron agreed, but they had to contact Ignatius and the rest. As Joseph walked toward the door, Baron grabbed his shoulder and said, "Do me one thing, cousin, just make sure you always remember what side your bread is buttered on."

Joseph laughed and replied, "The side that spreads smoother."

Awaiting outside the office was Egypt. Baron knew he had to make this good. He told Heather to take a break. He held his arm out toward his office, and Egypt sashayed in. Baron finished his drink in his office.

"You better make another drink because I'm about to chew off your head."

"Before you even start, think back when it all began and where we are now as a company. Plus, where were you through it all? To come barging in out of nowhere and then begin as though nothing at all happened is totally offbeat. Now that I have said my piece, talk," said Baron.

"Can I have a drink?"

"Is that all you're going to say, can I have a drink? Don't try and upset me, Egypt, I know you too well. You're trying to buy time to say something smart-ass. Correct?"

"Can I have a drink?" she asked again.

"Yeah, but first, Butter, can I have a kiss?"

"Really, Baron you would think you've grown up by now. Using bribery to get a kiss. If you want a kiss, just ask for it."

"So can I have a kiss?"

"No."

Baron handed her the drink and raised his glass with a smile. She grinned and drank, but before it all went down her throat she gagged on it. He knew she was going to do something wise ass, so he made it too strong. They both began to laugh. As Egypt opened her eyes from laughing so much, Baron was standing right in front of her. He held her chin and approached her slowly. Before his lips met hers, she closed her eyes. This let Baron know that it was okay. They both felt warm and tingly inside.

Egypt began to undo her blouse while they were kissing. Baron walked her toward the couch. He leaned her back. They fell slowly down but didn't miss a beat. He began nibbling at her plump breast while muttering his pet name for her. She placed her finger in his chest and pushed him into the sitting position. Egypt lifted her leg over him and sat down. His face was in awe, but then his intercom went off.

It startled Egypt; he reached over to the end table where the phone was. It was Heather telling him that Mr. Stout was on his way up. Baron was pissed the hell off.

Baron thought to himself that this man's timing was all off.

He looked Egypt in the face with that "I'm sorry" look. She grabbed for her blouse and began buttoning up. Then Heather announced Mr. Stout was there, but before she could finish, he walked into the office.

Mr. Stout just looked at all the little signs. Egypt's hair was messed up. The back of Baron's hair was standing up on ends. She buttoned her blouse incorrectly. Worst of all Baron's zipper was still undone.

Baron asked Gabriel if it was important for him to just barge in without knocking. Gabriel Stout realized it was going to be time to push what Nunzio wanted done. In the back of his mind, he was so surprised that Baron was unwilling to contact himself and Nunzio. He knew that Baron would walk away. So Gabriel had to work on a fine rope.

He told Baron, "I just dropped in to pick up some paperwork. I didn't mean to disturb anything. When I was standing outside the office, I overheard that Ms. Acardi was in and I wanted to see if she would be joining the organization."

Egypt just smiled and told him, "No, I'm just interested in what was going on. You didn't interrupt anything."

Mr. Stout just smiled. He added, "It's such a pleasure to have such a lovely sight in the office. Please excuse me," he said without mentioning the zipper or the blouse.

Both Egypt and Baron smirked and started laughing after he left. Baron told Egypt, "Within those few moments before being caught, it made me feel so good inside."

She just smiled. He continued to speak about how he felt like a kid when they're about to get caught in the down stroke. Egypt blurted out in laughter. She agreed and said that she was tripping over her own feet, and fumbling over her fingers. He laughed saying, "If only you could have seen your face."

She walked over very, very slowly waving her jacket. She threw her arms around his neck, looking him straight in the eye, she said, "See ya'round, sailor." Without a kiss or turning back, she was gone.

This wasn't any woman this was *the* woman. He loved Egypt like bees love honey. So much more was needed to add to the species before she would return home. Baron was determined to find or create whatever was necessary. One thing was for sure he was in love and would refuse anything or dare anyone to put this asunder. After all he thought he was now where Nunzio was, so his meddling would be out of the way. He could keep a better watch on things.

Much to his surprise Gabriel Stout already ran the news to Nunzio about the office rendezvous. With this and the other meetings Nunzio was sure that these two were on their way back. Nunzio got on the phone and made a few calls. The wheels were in motion. At this point Nunzio didn't care what or how it was done just not to let it happen. It was time for the enemy search.

Mr. Stout and Nunzio knew that Egypt's success was too quick. On the way up it was inevitable she had to make some enemies. So they're out there somewhere, and they were determined to seek them out. "So just a little patience and cunning and we're apt to find the missing key to unlock Egypt from Baron."

While the devilish two were in cahoots, Egypt went to meet Donna not too far from where she was. Egypt and she walked down Fifth Avenue, and Egypt thought she recognized Francis coming toward her. She tapped him as he walked by. He turned and laughed. He confessed that he too spotted her but wasn't too sure.

Donna began to look him up and down hoping he didn't notice. But there wasn't too much that got past Francis's eyes. She cleared her voice, and Egypt introduced them.

After a few moments it seemed as though Egypt wasn't even there. The two of them seemed to hit off wonderful. Next thing Egypt found herself at a side street cafe having cappuccino and neapolitans and cannoli and baba. The baba caught Egypt's eye. It looked like a sponge soaking up rum.

As she bit down in it, they both watched her. She stopped and asked, "Is there a trick behind it?" But before she finished, Francis picked one up and damn near swallowed the whole thing.

Donna offered Egypt some cannoli. She said, "Baron never gave anyone a chance at that or the baba."

"That's true," said Francis. "When it comes to these things, he was truly greedy."

Donna commented to Egypt, "I noticed that Francis and Baron resemble like twins. Isn't that strange?"

"No, it's not that strange because they're cousins. Their fathers are brothers. Who's older, you or Baron?"

"I guess I'm the guilty party," Francis replied. "But my cousin is right behind me." They all laughed.

Francis looked at his watch and told the ladies he had to go because he had a meeting, and he's a very tardy man. Before leaving he handed Donna a card with his number. She grabbed his hand and said, "Here's my number for when you want to call." "Ms. Donna . . . what is your full name?" asked Francis.

"Donna Magaddino of Chicago," she said with a lot of pride. She looked up at him. He grinned as if to say, "am I supposed to be impressed?"

"Okay, Ms. Donna Magaddino of Chicago, it was my pleasure to make your acquaintance. Thank you for the number, by the way, I'm Francesco Lazzaro DiBenedetto Gianelli from Elizabeth Street," he grinned and kissed Egypt. He whispered, "When are you two gonna stop playing and make everything final?"

She hit his arm and told him, "As soon as someone does something about Naughty Nunzio." He laughed and went to the Maitre de and took care of the bill. When he looked back, Donna was caught red-handed watching his every move. So he waved as she turned red.

No sooner did he leave than she began drilling Egypt about Francis. So she answered every question. As Donna heard everything, it was like a light went off in her head. Until the part of losing his wife and child. She couldn't deal with another rebound relationship. Donna expressed how she felt like a perpetrator. "It seems that I always get the men who are hurt from their previous relationships then I build up their confidence just for them to leave and make it with another. That is something that can drive you to drink."

Egypt asked, "Why would you want to return to Manhattan? I thought after college your interest in New York would have died down."

"I just needed a change, and I remembered my good friend. So that's one of the reasons."

Donna wanted to know about Egypt and this Baron ordeal. Egypt was a bit reluctant. "As far as me and Baron are concerned, I learned my lesson with Fatima. Considering being betrayed once, a second time I'm not going for. But anyway there isn't much to tell about me and Baron." Donna didn't quite believe her, but she said no more about the subject. They continued to talk about Francis all the way to Egypt's apartment.

Donna couldn't stay too long because she knew that Egypt wanted to get ready to go out that evening. There was a message on her machine, but she didn't want to play it till Donna left. Donna made her exit swiftly. As far as Egypt was concerned, she just wanted to see Baron and enjoy the night.

But much to her ignorance, Mr. Stout and Nunzio were in cahoots to put a damper on things. Nunzio wanted Egypt more than ever, and his rehabilitation may never lead him to be the man he was. Even with his paralysis getting much better, he still had to use a walker. He stood up with the walker to go make himself a drink and he asked Gabriel, "What in the hell is going to be done about this?"

"Well, for the moment, I'm trying to figure things out. I think that the angle of her enemies will do fine. I have a few people beat the asphalt till they find someone. It shouldn't take that long for them to find women and men alike. Someone whom she crossed somehow.

"One thing about Egypt she didn't hold her tongue. People don't care too much for that, especially when it was straight on target."

What Nunzio didn't realize was that this woman was not like the rest of the women in Baron's life. He told Gabriel that he didn't want Egypt destroyed, just the relationship.

Nunzio couldn't understand Egypt's attitude. If she were in love, why hasn't she married him? He had to end their relationship before there would be a bastard in the family. Nunzio may have been one of the underworlds top men, but he was a good Catholic in his mind because he contributed to the church which was a requirement. Regardless of how his children felt, Nunzio made sure that his sons' spouses were the right type of woman. For his daughters, there wasn't a man for them. Angelica slipped through the iron fist. He wasn't going to allow Baron to try it also.

Gabriel received a call, and he sat there writing down some information. He turned to Nunzio handing him a slip of paper. Nunzio unfolded the paper and read Eureka Devalle.

He asked, "So what about her?"

"She has the untold story including reasons not to talk over the phone. I'm going to have a meeting with her during the week," said Gabriel Stout.

"Look, you work for me. I want the meeting done tomorrow. Give her what she wants if the information is worth it. No goddamn fucking bullshit this time. The Goya Queen is spreading her *sazon* on my son. So before she gets him all seasoned up, I want the shit ended, and now."

"Okay, before we go too deep, Nunzio, think about what you're doing."

"Think about it? Think about what? You listen good. Everything you have is from me and my know-how. Okay, you just stand in front of me while I do the talking. You and I aren't a team, got it? I am and only I am in charge. So you let me do the damn thinking. So see what this bitch wants and take care of that. Remember I know what's best for my family. If it wasn't for me, what the hell would my children have?" he said while chewing on his cigar.

The smoke filled the room as he sat there looking smug. Gabriel knew that he was no more than a marionette on Nunzio's knee. Gabriel wasn't about to protest against Nunzio. He had a feeling that all of this shit was going to hit the fan. So long as it didn't come back on him, he didn't care. He called Eureka back making the meeting that evening.

Little did Eureka know she was getting ready to jump from the frying pan into the fire. She wanted Carlos very badly. She had a feeling that if she lay low, her opportunity would come. *Now that it's here,* Eureka thought, *I'm not about to let it slip through my fingertips.* Never did she think what Carlos would do if he found out. She knew Carlos loved Egypt. He allowed her to get away with things that no one else could dream of, so she was an easy mark. Little did she perceive that she was the key to Nunzio's destruction of Baron's relationship with Egypt.

When evening fell, he was off. Mr. Stout headed out to meet Eureka

Devalle at the South Street seaport by the shopping area. Even though everything was shut down, Eureka stood standing near a street lamp. She was nervous, and she started feeling as though she might be in over her head. It was too late for her to turn back now. The limo pulled up and a balding fat man walked toward her.

Gabriel opened the car door and told her to get in. When she bent her head in and looked, she realized the game was over. *This is the real shit*, she thought. She took a deep breath and sat down. She introduced herself and waited for him to do the same.

He said, "Introductions aren't necessary. Let me hear what you've got." She played the recording.. Gabriel Stout's face grinned. "This is extra exceptional."

The fat man placed a manila envelope on her lap. She didn't dare open it in front of him. She didn't ask for any particular amount and she wasn't about to ask now. So long as Egypt was knocked down in Carlos's eyes she didn't care.

They let her off several blocks away. When she stepped out and turned to say good-bye, the door was shut and the car sped off. The dirty deed was done. All the wheels will be in motion shortly. Eureka began to smile because Carlos would be hurt and needing someone to comfort him. *That's when I'll make my move*, she thought. She ran down the subway stairs and awaited the train.

After several hours went by Gabriel and Nunzio listened to the recording. Nunzio told Gabriel, "I understand why Baron is in love. If I had a woman that performed that well, I would climb mountains for her too."

The two laughed together and made good remarks. This was it, he had hit the jackpot. He knew once Baron heard this, he would be humiliated, and his pride shot to shit.

Nunzio needed to make things a little more on edge. They plotted the perfect way of keeping them apart. All that shouldn't be shared with Baron, Gabriel would handle it all himself.

First he wanted to get those two right to the altar and then he would snatch it away. "How?" asked Gabriel. Nunzio continued to chew his cigar and muttered a few words. He couldn't make out his words, but it sounded like 'a truss.' He picked up the phone and had one of his goons get Egypt's number.

"Now it's time to have a little meeting with the little Goya bean," he said to Gabriel.

Back at the cafe, all who were supposed to be attending the meeting were there, except for Francis since he was running a bit late. When he stepped in, everything went as planned. Smoke filled the room, and

Daniel O'Connor came in with his 'skinny' cigarette. Baron jumped and told him that that shit wasn't permitted on the premises. They didn't need to give the heat any reason to step in.

O'Connor was pissed but put it out and threw it to the curb, "Yo get it straight. Five-0 ain't shit to me. You have me here for a reason, so you better get the shit rolling or I'm outta here."

"Shit, man, your attitude leaves little to be desired, so take some advice and plant it or lose it," said Francis.

"The only thing you can tell me is how does it feel to be inside a dark cherry? Is it true that the darker the cherry, the sweeter the juice," asked O'Connor with a nasty tone.

Francis leaped over the table and grabbed him, pulled his gun out, and shoved it in O'Connor's mouth. Baron and Ignatius pulled them apart, and Baron noticed that O'Connor's piece was out. Baron quickly told him, "Think twice because there's no way in hell I'm gonna allow you to walk out alive if you shot my cousin."

O'Connor looked deep into Francis's eyes and said, "Next time you won't be lucky, pretty boy."

Tempers rose and personalities clashed. O'Connor and Francis watched each other from the corners of their eyes. Baron felt the tension in the room, but a lot of what was said that evening was still not resolved.

Lotario stated, "There's going to be a bachelor's party to get underway soon." He was trying break the mood. Someone asked, "For who?"

Lotario stood up and slapped Baron on the back saying, "I heard rumors that Princess Egypt has returned." Baron looked around and Francis laughed. Lotario couldn't understand what he found so funny.

"I don't think Baron is up to feuding with Nunzio," replied Francis. "True, we all have gotten used to his voice not being here that we completely forgot his attitude," said Lotario. "I don't give a shit what the hell he has to say. If I choose to I will. He cannot control me because I'm far from Tony and Junior," said Baron angrily. "I don't think anyone meant to curl your hair, so calm down. Hey, man, have a drink," replied O'Connor.

Baron walked to the door of their private room. He whistled, and a woman came over and told her to bring glasses and a bottle of scotch. When he walked back to the table, everyone was discussing Nunzio's return. No one could believe his miraculous recovery. All the doctors said it would take a miracle for him to regain his manhood. The doctors said the nerves and muscles within his penis were damaged. But knowing Nunzio the nympho, he would regain the usage.

Baron stood up when the drinks came in and opened up the bottle and made himself a drink. The Irishman O'Connor walked over and put out his hand to Francis and expressed that he didn't know of his dual loss. Francis hesitated but complied. Francis's gut feeling told him to keep an eye on him.

As Francis walked over to Baron he asked, "What's in store for the enemy?"

"Since everything is quiet, just leave it that way and keep an eye on things."

The meeting ended with hardly anything truly done because everyone figured it would be best to await Nunzio's return. Since it would be inevitable, they knew he was coming back. Baron too was glad with his father's absence because things happened without a lot of violence.

Back at Nunzio's he had just finished talking with Egypt and expressing his enthusiasm of his son and her reuniting.

As the conversation came to an end, Egypt was very confused; she knew how he felt about her. Something wasn't resting easy with her. So she called Baron and left a message on his machine. When he arrived home, it was too late to call so he left it for morning.

Baron barely was awake before he dialed Egypt's number. She answered before he could say, 'jack be nimble.' She rambled off everything that Nunzio said. Baron was so surprised that Nunzio talked with her.

"Egypt, it's urgent that I talk to you."

"I can't, Baron, because there's a show to do. I'm leaving in the afternoon, and I won't be back for six weeks."

Baron sighed. "Baron, Baron? Are you there?"

"Yeah."

"Look, it was great the few days we spent together, but when I return it's only gonna be for a short time. We really do have to talk, mostly I do. Babe, I owe you an explanation in the fullest."

"All you have to say are three words, and everything that transpired will be forgotten," said Baron eagerly.

"Only if that were easy. Look, I have a lot of packing to do and other arrangements to take care of. I promise to wire you. See ya."

"See ya, Egypt," he yelled. He whispered I love you into the phone even though she had already hung up. Baron slammed the phone. Every time he got close enough to ask, something always interfered.

He grabbed his sheets around him and walked into the bathroom. While he was showering, the doorbell rang. There was no one to answer it because he sent away all the servants. Baron had planned to convince Egypt to stay over awhile since it would be just the two of them.

He leaped out the shower with a hand towel covering him. When he looked through the window, it was Fatima. He thought to himself, *What in the hell does this bitch want?* He opened the door, and she just smiled.

"I never imagined you having such sexy legs," she said with a devilish look on her face.

"Thanks."

"You look so attractive in soap suds."

He glanced down at himself. "Oh, let me finish I'll be down."

"No hurry on my account, need any help?"

"No thanks, I can manage," replied Baron.

He swiftly went up the steps as she watched from behind admiring the view. While he was in the shower, Fatima went up the stairs behind him. She drew the curtains, and the room was covered in darkness. She undressed and stepped into the shower while he was washing the soap from his face. He yelled, "I'll be right down!"

In her sexiest voice she answered him in his ear, "I just love a man when he's wet with soap all over. It's so inviting."

He was startled. Fatima caressed his thighs touching and kissing his most intimate areas. Baron attempted to stop her, but she consumed him like a hungry tigress upon a fawn. Baron let out a whimper like no other. His manhood was in full bloom. He grabbed her by the hair pulling her off.

He opened the shower door and carried her out and placed her on the bed. She was somewhat frightened by his harsh manner, but it was not unfamiliar to her. Fatima's breasts were plump and ripe and her skin, soft and perfect. Baron was hungry and frustrated after his conversation with Egypt. This was an outlet. He licked her from her naval to her chin. He had not yet placed his weight on her. As he leaned over her, they kissed passionately; her nails in his soft hairy chest.

Baron sat beside her touching her breasts. As she sat up, she asked, "Is that all you have?"

This worked on him. He knew what she was, and he felt he could have his way with her then. After that remark he rolled her on her knees, and with all the force he could acquire, he entered her. She yelled for him to be gentle, but he pushed her into the pillow muffling her whimpering. She kept trying to reach him from behind. He was well endowed, and this he knew and took advantage of it. A few moments had gone by and she quieted down. He stopped and rolled her on her back and pulled her legs over the edge of the bed.

"Is it enough for you yet?" he asked. "Have I fulfilled your curiosity?"

She was whipped and tired. Softly she replied, "Yes."

He smiled and nodded no.

"Fatima, my sweet, you were curious of this man's capabilities, and I don't think I should send you off without knowing it all. Bitch, curiosity killed the cat, but I'm the dog who'll give you a hurting you'll never forget." He again entered her with a violent cruel manner.

They were sweating, and the pain felt pleasurable. All the anger and frustration left him, and for a moment he noticed how truly beautiful Fatima was. Just lying there with her hair in her face, Baron slowed down and pushed it from her face. He leaned over, and they kissed like wild animals in heat. She held his neck and licked his face. This was a surprise and a turn on to him.

The two rolled over together, and she arched her back to its fullest and took over. Baron leaned up holding her hips. He moaned in total ecstasy. The two were in complete lust for the flesh.

He began to feel a sensation; his genitals were about to rupture. Baron sat up as Fatima remained on his lap. Baron placed his hands under her arms and around Fatima's shoulders. Pulling her down, the two both felt the warmest sensation ever. Their bodies were sweating, and sexuality filled the room. He grabbed Fatima's hair pulling her head back, and both began to yell and moan as they released their lustful currents.

Fatima fell to her back and smiled. Baron rose and went straight into the shower. She lay there in awe. He bellowed from the shower, "What are you here for anyway?"

"Just to make amends. You know you treat me as though I don't exist in the office. If you're wondering, I did what I did to Egypt all in the name of business. Baron, you ought to know about undercutting business deals to make them conductive to you."

She giggled and added, "With a well-oiled piece of machinery such as yourself, Egypt must be dead sexually or stupid." Fatima was slipping her shoes on as he stood over her. "She's neither. Is your curiosity satisfied, Madam Fatima?"

"No, but I'll settle for it," she said as she giggled to him. Fatima rose to him and placed her hand on his back. Baron swiftly moved away, and she was startled by his behavior. She made another attempt to touch him, but he stepped away.

"Look, get off me. I gave you what you wanted, or did I forget something? Yeah, silly of me. Shit I must have been stupid. I should have known what you expected afterward."

Baron reached over in his wallet and threw two hundred dollar bills at her. "It slipped my mind, bitch. Here's payment in full. Stay around too long, and I'll have to charge you. Wouldn't that be a first for your book?

"If I'm not mistaken, you came here for that, and I never had whoring days before, but I guess all these months going without it got to me. Is it possible you forgot how it goes, bitch? The john calls for you. I'll be watching you. Your first fuck up and you're gone. Unless you're blowing the boss too?"

Fatima couldn't take anymore and ran out into her car. She was sick to her stomach. In all her years of being a hooker, she never had been so ill-treated by a john much less any man. Baron called all the shots and gave her what he felt she needed to feel.

Baron didn't want to take any chance with her because she was about a blackmailing type of bitch. He refused to allow her any leverage. He knew her kind, just about moving up the ladder. He hadn't forgotten what she did to Egypt and how she melted her way around Mr. Stout. A woman like that can only bring trouble. So he thought the best thing to do is keep her at a distance and continue to show her that he was no piece of putty.

After he dressed, he went down to the kitchen to start some coffee and toast. He sat at the table gazing out the window. He had no desire of going in to work. He couldn't help but think of what just happened. Every time he closed his eyes for a moment, he felt Fatima's sensual body next to his. He tried to shake the feeling off. He went and got a mug and sat with a magazine. He drank it slowly, and for an instant, he reflected on those animal behaviors he had. It was a part of him that he had never dealt with, and he was ashamed that he enjoyed it.

He made a call to Franco, but he wasn't in. Angelica asked, "Are you okay because your voice sounds strange? Anyway, why don't you come over for dinner this evening. Francis is coming with a woman."

"I wouldn't miss this for all the tea in China."

When he hung up, the phone rang again, but this time it was his mother. She wanted him to stop by because it was important. Baron said he would be right over. He grabbed his keys and headed out the door.

Margherita was waiting for him in front of the house. She asked him, "What took so long?"

Baron laughed and replied, "Mom, Howard Beach is not connected to Manhattan. So what's the emergency that I rushed straight over for? Do I get to guess? Nunzio."

"Don't start okay. Baby your father is up to his old tricks again. What's going on, Baron, tell me?"

"Mom, you know better than I do about him."

"Come in. Did you eat, baby? I'll have Anna fix you something. Anna, Anna dear, make Baron his favorite morning meal."

"Hey, sweetie, haven't seen you home in so long," said Anna.

"Good to see you too. Where's my sister? It feels like I haven't seen my sister in an eon," said Baron.

They all walked into the kitchen. He and his mother sat and talked for a while. They ate and laughed. Elizabetta walked in, and Baron jumped to his feet and kissed his sister. They embraced, and Baron pulled her back to get a good look at her.

She was as lovely as ever. Only if she would go out, she needed some sun. Baron got a brilliant idea and asked her if she would accompany him to a dinner engagement that night.

She turned it down; and he held her hand, looked her straight in the eye, and told her to forget what Nunzio will say. He repeated, "I'm your brother, and Father wouldn't mind. She looked to her mother, and Margherita smiled and nodded her head yes. She turned to Baron and said, "I would be honored to be in your company this evening."

He told her what time to be ready and that they were going to Angelica's. As he walked toward the door, Elizabetta went with him. She didn't say much, she just smiled. He held her hand tightly as they walked to his car.

"Try and overlook Nunzio's ways and ignore him. Go out and meet people."

"Nunzio has a nice man for me to meet over the weekend."

Baron got sick to his stomach. "Why don't you wake the hell up? It's your life, and you should live it for you."

He forgot who he was talking to for a moment. She had tears in her eyes and cried out, "I would love to, but Father has such a tight hold on me. I'm so frightened of being left in the cold. I don't know how to really do anything because Father made sure it was done for me."

Baron held her tight and wiped her tears away. "You have a family, especially me and Angelica. We would never turn our backs on you."

She then lowered her head saying, "My younger sister has a better grip on life than I do."

"That's about to change." Baron lifted her chin to make her smile, and she did. They agreed on the time, and he decided to pick her up in his limo to drive Nunzio crazy.

"Father knows his limo."

"Not to worry. I'll rent one for the occasion and have the driver drop me off by my car, then from there we'll head out."

She laughed and said that would drive Father nuts.

Chapter 11

Egypt checked her bags and boarded the plane. She lifted the window shade so she could see out. When she began to relax, a hand touched her; it was Jayme. He kissed her forehead and asked if she was all right. She was angry because she wasn't up to flying from New York to San Francisco listening to him express his feelings for her.

He opened the compartment and placed his carry-on in there. Jayme asked if she would mind if he sat there. Egypt shrugged her shoulders and then closed her eyes. Bach passed by them and stopped for a second to say hi.

But much to Jayme's surprise, Carlos himself told Jayme he was in the wrong seat. He looked at his ticket and said sorry and removed himself. Everyone in the group sat first class, but this time Carlos had seating arrangements for Eureka to sit in coach. She was pissed the hell off.

She walked to the first-class section looking for Carlos. Eureka asked, "What kind of shit are you on, placing me in coach?"

"I'm sorry, Eureka, there must have been an error somewhere," Carlos expressed with sympathy.

She replied, "Error my ass," and she stormed to her seat.

The plane started down the runway. As it began to take off, Egypt clutched her chair. Carlos reached over and placed his hand over hers. She opened her eyes and smiled. The two talked about the change in her life since she met him. They couldn't stop laughing.

After a couple of hours of idle chitchat, they ordered their meals. When they were served, she kept looking at his plate until he took a fork full and fed it to her. She did the same.

Eureka walked up on this and said, "If you two don't make me sick. Here are the damn papers for the new moves to set up with camera blocking."

"This couldn't wait, right, Eureka? You're still up to your old tricks.

Why don't you give it a break. You nor anyone else is not my woman nor am I in search of one. Please, not on this trip will I let anyone annoy me to hell. Go back from whence you came, or shall I have them escort you to your coach seat?"

"You don't have to be a smart-ass. Guess what, Carlos my love? Your dear miss thing will shatter. Remember, sometimes one sweet taste of the forbidden fruit and the price can be devastating," she said as she laughed walking off.

"I don't trust that bitch for some reason. She's up to something. I don't know what, but I feel an itch in my stomach," said Carlos.

"Oh, I think you're making something out of nothing. You need to relax. I can safely say you've worked yourself into a frenzy."

"Aren't you the funny one. I think you should stop singing and become a comedian," said Carlos.

"Knock, knock? Guess what, I'm taking a nap now. Chow, love. Stop laughing, and can you get me a pillow because I want to call in some z's?" asked Egypt.

When the plane landed, he woke her up. After everyone got their luggage, they headed toward the hotel. They checked in safely until someone spotted them, and then the hotel was overwhelmed with fans.

That evening they had to make a switch. Egypt was high on all the attention. She and Carlos ran around the town like kids in a candy store.

They went shopping and the whole nine yards. By the time they returned, Egypt had to turn in because it was an early morning for her.

Carlos walked her to the room. He stood there and told her that tomorrow things go back to business as usual. That at rehearsals he was the same old ruthless workaholic. She leaned up and kissed him on the cheek and said, "I know it's business as usual." She opened her room and just closed the door.

She ran to her bed and started to cry. All the feelings were running all upside down and inside out. She cried so hard her makeup ran.

In New York, Baron was on his way picking up Elisabetta in the limo. As they drove away from the house, Nunzio was asking Margherita who was in the limo. She told him that Elisabetta went out. Nunzio sailed to the ceiling and down. He looked as though his face was about to burst.

He grabbed his cane and went to the phone and waited by the front door for his car. Margherita walked behind Nunzio and held on to his cane and asked, "Do you really want to send this child over the edge too?"

She awaited his reply, hoping he would hear through his fury. But it never reached. All he said was, "My daughter lives in my house and will abide by my rules."

"What makes you her master? She does have a mother Nunzio, and I said it was okay. Listen to yourself. You act as though Elisabetta was sixteen. She is a grown woman held in an ivory tower. Let go, Nunzio, before you lose her too," she pleaded with him."

"You don't know shit about shit. I've taken care of you. Damn it to hell, do you know the outside world? Have you ever busted your ass to make a nickel? So don't try and tell me shit about all that I have done for this ungrateful family. What, damn it? What the hell have you ever done, other than look after the house and children? Even then I had to step in like now on that," yelled Nunzio.

"No, Nunzio, I didn't do anything. All I did was just put up with your shit for many years," she replied.

"Don't you speak to me like that, woman," he said in a harsh tone.

"Woman? No, you never looked at me as a woman, darling. I was just your wife—someone you laid with when you were too tired to go to your others. Don't look shocked, I'm not as simple or naive as you think. I took you for better or worse. Things in the beginning were fine because I was your fine virgin lady till you took me too soon. You had to marry me Nunzio, and I figured that out some time ago."

Nunzio turned his back. "Don't turn from me. Damn, when I was young, you sang to me and wined and dined me. Told me of your intentions, love, and everything. Nunzio, all you wanted was to sleep with me then. You never thought I would become pregnant. Many nights I wished I hadn't bore your child."

"With age, Margherita, you're starting to fantasize," said Nunzio, but she cut him off quickly.

"You fuck, don't you patronize me. I know that there are many woman, and rumors state you have a son out there. Nunzio Gianelli, I didn't divorce you because of the children. What do you think, I'm dead? I can't sense a touch that changes."

"How would you know about a touch changing? All you had was me," he said.

She smiled and turned her back. "Don't smile at me, and what are you trying to say? I thought you were finished with those hot and cold flashes. What are you going through now?"

He grabbed the handle of his cane and swung it at her. "Since when do you swear?"

"Since when do you walk without the cane?"

Nunzio caught himself; he hadn't wanted anyone to know how well he recovered. He went to lean on the cane again, but Margherita snatched it from him. She threw it on the floor.

She asked, "Are there any more surprises up your sleeves?" She went upstairs.

Nunzio was having a severe headache. He yelled for Joey, and he ran in. Nunzio sat slowly in his chair, and Joey gave him a drink. Joey asked if he wanted anything; he sent him off on a small errand. Nunzio didn't worry about the remark his wife made. He knew no man alive would be dumb enough to sleep with his wife. So he thought and then he laughed out loud because he knew Margherita didn't have enough spirit in her to do it.

But what he did feel is the man who was with Elisabetta may say all the right things as he did many years ago. His daughter would not bring a bastard into the family. He said out loud, "She will not bring a bastard into this house."

Margherita had returned and threw her last statement at him. She told him, "Don't worry because you added enough to the family. If our daughter made a bastard, it would just get lost among yours." She slammed the big heavy sliding dividing doors shut.

Baron and Elisabetta were having such a good time. Donna was the life of the evening. Francis and she hit it off lovely. Angelica called Elisabetta to the side. She said, "I'm happy that Father let you out of the castle."

Elisabetta replied, "Father doesn't know."

All of a sudden Angelica yelled Baron's name. He ran over there in a hurry. She asked him, "Are you in your right mind? Nunzio probably was having conniptions."

"Lighten up. I was gonna bring her home after 1:00 a.m. to just press it with him."

"Baron, Father, is going to lay you out for this one."

He laughed and hugged both his sisters. They looked so happy. But this time Baron bit off more than he could chew with his father. He knew it deep down that the moment of truth would come about when he took Elisabetta home. Until then it was party time.

Baron was under the impression that it was going to be a quiet dinner party, but it was far from that. Franco had so many people there Baron got caught in the crowd. He walked off to Franco's private quarters, and there were people sniffing cocaine. He walked over to the table, and there was Franco taking a hit. Baron was shocked. He rested his hand on Franco's back. This startled him, and he looked up, but Baron looked disgusted.

"What the fuck has gotten into you to do this shit? What have you blown, a mother-fucking fuse?" said Baron.

"Get off it. You act as though I'm hooked. Now and then I take a hit of blow. It's not like it's a daily vitamin with me," replied Franco.

"Does my sister know?"

Franco walked into another room with Baron. "No, she doesn't. Did anyone say anything to you the times you got toasted beyond recognition? No. Look, Baron, I'm not a junkie, and it's not like I lay with the white lady every night okay. Everything is going great. Come on, Fontaine is gone, and things are falling into place."

"Keep your mouth shut about Fontaine and lay off the sniff. It's not good for things. Just watch your ass. The heat would love to get their hands on one of us. All they need is one and the chain links began to fall."

"Look you're worrying about nothing."

"Listen. Sssshhh . . . listen close because if you start getting sloppy, you're history. I fall for no man. Got that? Make fucking sure you do," he said as he walked out of the room.

As he stormed past the guests, he grabbed one of the mirrors with the white lines on it and threw it in the air. He turned around seeing Franco in the doorway.

"Fucking history, man, let Nunzio get air to this, and I nor anyone else can help because you're on your own. Nunzio and drugs are like water and oil."

Angelica was walking toward the back room asking Baron if he had seen Franco. He was about to say no, but he pointed to the door.

It was getting late, so he found his sister. She really enjoyed herself, and Francis and Donna too were getting ready to break out. Francis noticed something was wrong with Baron. He asked Donna to keep his cousin company while he and Baron had a drink. Baron took the double scotch straight down nonstop. Francis asked him what went down. He told him without hesitation. Francis said, "I thought you knew about it. Damn, it's been going on for some time now. I thought Angelica was the only one that didn't know."

"Well, I'll make sure she finds out."

Francis made another drink for himself and Baron. They talked for a good half an hour. Franco walked over and asked Baron, "Is it necessary to tell Angelica where I am?"

"You shouldn't lie to my sister. She has a right to see what's going on in her life."

Francis stepped in and told Franco, "Think hard that everyone is looking out for you because in the end you'll be the one hurting."

Franco was too angry to see until a loud rumble went off in the back room. Franco ran back there. Francis pulled out his piece and followed.

There were two men getting ready to kill each other. When everything was brought down to a minimum roar, it was over the blow. Baron started harping off that this was what he was talking about. Franco looked dumbfounded, his personal room was torn apart, and things that went way back into his family history were destroyed. He was so skied up he couldn't think right. Franco reached for the shotgun and turned it toward the man. He was next to the door, and Angelica was trying to make her way through it.

Francis saw her, and he saw where Franco's aim went. He leaped over and butted the gun upward and it went off. Angelica hit the floor. Franco almost shot her. If it wasn't for Francis, shit would have definitely hit the fan.

Baron took the gun and smacked Franco across the face with it, and he hit the ground. Baron kept hitting him until they pulled him off. Angelica held on to Baron as he helped her out of the room. She began crying and fell to her knees asking Baron, "What's happening to me and Franco!"

Francis walked over and expressed, "Now more than ever Franco needs you." But Baron was leery of that. He had seen so many friends get hooked and lose all grip of things. He didn't want to see Angelica get hurt, but he cared for Franco too. He didn't mean to hurt him like that, but he almost blew his sister away.

Angelica looked so confused and worried that Baron told her go on but to be careful and if things get out of hand, she should come to his place. She walked slowly down the hall, and there stood Franco. He walked up to Angelica and held her telling her, "I don't want to lose you."

He glanced at Baron and put his head down. He moved Angelica aside and walked straight to Baron. He put out his hand and as he did, he said, "Baron, I know you're right, and don't fret because it's over, and my family means a hell of a lot more."

The two embraced. Franco said get the party rolling, and it seemed as though nothing had transpired.

Franco knew that Baron was going to watch him closely. He just hoped deep down that Nunzio wouldn't get air of this. Franco knew what his father would do if that was his daughter. The thought ran through his mind like wildfire. How in the hell could he have done that. The music was playing loud, and he walked into his bedroom with Angelica. She was still a nervous wreck. Angelica didn't say a word just stared. Franco asked her, "Do you think Baron or Francis would let Nunzio know?"

"They aren't like that. Besides, it wouldn't take much for my father to find out anything. Listen, are you okay?"

He nodded yes. She knew better, so she tried to talk to him, but Franco just wanted to come down and sleep. She went to tell everyone to go, but he didn't want her to leave his side. So she didn't.

Francis knocked on the door, and she let him in. Francis approached Franco calling him cousin. Franco said, "You'd give me more than I would you if the tables were turned."

"Trust me, my cousin is downstairs climbing the walls. Give him some time, and he'll calm down. Angelica, go talk with him. You of all people know how much Baron loves you. So to keep peace and keep the two men in your life without choosing, go talk. Franco, you truly fucked up. Go on, Angelica, I would like to speak with your husband alone. Go on, I'm not gonna do anything. Gimme a break."

"I didn't say a word. Franco, you want anything, babes?" said Angelica.

"Nah, I'm all right, go ahead and see Baron," replied Franco.

As she walked out the room, Francis closed the door behind her. He sat across from Franco and lifted up his hands. "We warned you that you were in over your head, man. One thing you should have learned is never touch. All the Feds need is to have this leak out, and they're on us like white on rice hoping you fuck up again. They'd haul your ass in so quick your other ball would drop. One thing for sure is if Nunzio was here, you would've been a dead man," said Francis.

"You act as though I don't have any sense. I know what the hell I did was wrong. I'm sorry, I didn't mean it. Damn it to hell, what do you all want from me?"

"Are you going to do something about your habit? Don't even fix your face to say you don't have a habit because I'll finish where Baron left off. See, Angelica is my heart also, and just because I'm calm, don't misread it. Because, Franco, man, you're family to me until you cross the line with blood. Until now everything was copasetic, but you've rocked the boat. I'm gonna throw you the life preserver once, after that you're shit out of luck."

"I got it."

"You damn right, you got it. And screw up again and you'll get it."

"Okay, okay, how many damn times you're gonna tell me. I heard you loud and clear. Listen my head is pounding, and I just want to sleep, is that okay with you?"

Francis told him to sleep tight and walked out of the room, and Angelica was coming down the hall. She gave him a kiss, and they embraced. She expressed that everything was settled with Baron. As he went down, everyone had just about left. Baron stood there with Donna. Francis apologized to her.

"Look I thought you had better manners than to leave a ravishing woman waiting for you."

"Donna, I tried, but somewhere I failed," said Baron.

"Give it a break. If anyone taught anyone, it was I who taught you. If it wasn't for my fine teachings, you would have never come across Egypt."

"Baron, now I remember the name. For the life of me I couldn't pull it all together. Egypt's Baron," she said.

"Why, you know her?"

"Very well. She and I attended college together," she said with a smirk.

"So now that everyone knows everyone, it's time to go, Donna," said Francis eagerly.

"I assume so if you must. Catch up with you late in the afternoon?"

"I'm not sure of that. I think the best time is the following day. It's five twenty-four in the morning, and I have a very busy morning planned for us back at my dwelling," stated Francis as he winked at Baron.

"Have a happy," replied Baron as the couple walked out. He gave a laugh. He knew he had to go home, but he was a tad uncomfortable after what happened. He walked out toward his car and the phone rang. It was Francis. He told him, "Business calls."

"Is it Nunzio?"

"Who else?"

Nunzio very seldom let Francis go too far before buzzing. Baron asked, "Did my father also want me?"

Francis said, "Even if he did, I know Nunzio could smell trouble on you. The way you're acting, he could read right through it, and if you don't speak, someone else would. This we don't need, too many things going on at the same time." So Baron headed home; it was an eventful evening.

Francis and Nunzio embraced tightly. He asked his nephew what was new. Francis told him everything was roughly the same. Nunzio felt the air get uneasy between them, so he gave Francis a chance to simmer down. Francis walked toward the window and glanced at the moon. He said to Nunzio, "The sun'll be rising soon, and I need my sleep."

Nunzio looked at him strangely. Francis tried to act as though he didn't notice. Nunzio lit his cigar and called Francis to his side. A lump was in his throat as he approached Nunzio. Even though he was a grown man, there was still that childlike feeling like the lie was written on his forehead. Nunzio stood up, walked away a bit, and turned, grabbing at Francis's neck which took him by surprise.

"Calm down, son, but always stand on your guard because even family will fuck you. Tell me, how have things been truthfully since my retirement?" asked Nunzio.

"As far as we can tell, Don, everything is about the same," replied Francis.

"Well, then, that means you nor my son can handle things because I expect to hear improvements. Progress. Look, how the hell do you think I got this far? By sitting on my fat ass behind a damn fucking desk? If you assholes don't take chances and some risks, we'll fall to the floor. Of all my blood, you, Francis, I was sure would come through. You're my mirror in youth," he said, and he swung his fist and took it across his desk knocking everything to the floor. "When anything is in your way, you knock it the hell out of the way. If you don't, someone will do it to you. No matter what the risk is, it's called strategic planning. If you have money, that's the key to success. In this country money can make a man kill his own son. You don't have to steal, but your money can do anything for you. Why did I have you next to me, Francis? Huh, why in the hell do you think you were next to me?"

"Then why in the fuck did your family pick Baron? How the hell do you think I felt? Then to have him come to me and ask for my help and to be his mouthpiece. What made it worse is when I tried to be the mouthpiece he still put his two cents in. I'm not saying he didn't know, he did, but not as much as he should have. So tell me, Uncle, what was I to do? Just take over just like that. I'm no ass either, Don. Simple, I wanted to know who left Tony and Junior to screw up and pick Baron anyway. Somehow they got away with it, but you didn't input shit. Don't even hand me any shit. Besides your interest in me had side effects," said Francis angrily.

"What?"

"Forget it, it goes back too far to lash out now."

"What did I do to screw your life up, Francis? I had you with me always, and there wasn't a damn thing I didn't do for you. You're like a son to me. Francis, you're right and it's getting too late and you're talking out your ass."

"Maybe treating me like that caused problems. Too much for you to grasp at one time, right? The things you did for me you didn't do for no one else, so don't hand me that shit. I'm your first nephew. Why don't you give me the truth, Nunzio? What is it about me, am I your patsy? Am I your silly putty kit? Why all the interest in my life up until now? Damn it to hell, Don, Baron belongs here talking with you, not me. He's in charge with your world, not I. I love my cousin a lot, and I don't want you to think I'm shooting him down because I know how you play one against the other. Not the wise man. Get it, Nunzio, the wise man. I can't work like this. It's either straight up or count me out. If you want someone to play the role, it won't be me," Francis said and threw his trench over his shoulder placing his hat on.

"So that's that. You said what you had to, and no one else gets a word in edgewise. Go on, big man, sometimes there's more to it than what lays before us," Nunzio said while puffing rings into the air.

This blew Francis's head all out of whack. He walked out slamming the door. Everything in him wanted to reach out and play ma bell with Nunzio's face, but for some reason, he loved this man more than his parents. Before he left the house, he stood by the door looking back at the office and walked back. As he opened the door, he saw his uncle gazing out the window.

"Are you looking for something?" Nunzio was startled as Francis continued, "I'll find out what you wanted and that's it."

"I can't ask for anything more than that. Just watch your ass till I come back and stick it out if you can. I'm coming back sooner than you think. Go in peace."

Francis left, but before he reached his car, the skies opened up and it poured. As he pulled off, he glimpsed to his left and saw Nunzio standing there. He couldn't help but wonder why. Is there something he should know, or is there something to the rumors he remembered as a child? While driving home he thought if it were true, it would have surfaced by now.

Elsewhere worrying about Nunzio sat Baron in the garden. He sat there in the rain trying to make heads or tails of the situation. He has gotten much better. Okay, he has a slight limp, but everything else is back in order. Why hasn't he come back? Most of all if he has a problem, he should discuss it with him, not Francis. What was so important that he needed to see Francis tonight? So much he thought was awkward, but no one would dare fix their lips to ask.

He stood up and pushed back his hair as the rain fell off his face. Baron couldn't rest with what happened at his sister's, then his father, and so many other things. The wind and rain was too much for him, so he went inside. The water continued to drip off his face. Baron went to his room to dry his hair with a towel and drapped it on his shoulders. He stared hard into the mirror as if he were waiting for someone to say something.

He turned to his bed and sat on the corner just thinking about Fatima and why she too came by. Then Egypt's face appeared, and he lay back closing his eyes. Baron pictured her soft and round breasts upon him. A deep yearning ran through him, and he decided that it was time and she had no say at all. He was finally tired of the shit.

Egypt was becoming Mrs. Gianelli sooner than she thought. With that he fell asleep.

When Egypt awoke, it was time to get up and head out to rehearsal. She jumped up, washed, and got dressed. She ran to the elevator, and when the door opened, there stood Damion, Bach, and Manny. She looked around and asked where was Jayme, but they didn't know.

The coliseum was packed with people working doing all kinds of jobs. Far away there was a man yelling his head off. It was Carlos complaining about everything. Everyone did what they had to, people ran from one end to another at Carlos's is beckoning. The music started, and he began to give directions for Egypt to follow. The rehearsal was going as well as any other.

Except Egypt and Carlos both noticed how extremely nice Eureka was acting toward them. This kept Egypt on guard, but Carlos was too busy and aggravated to truly care. As the afternoon approached and the caterers had all the food laid out, Jayme appeared. Egypt spotted him and he her. She lowered her head a bit and looked up with just her eyes. Jayme came close and held her chin up.

"Hey, friend, how goes things?" said Jayme as he kissed her brow.

"Fine," she replied with a tear falling from her eye.

"Even with discomfort, you look beautiful, my rose, with the heart of a raven. You plucked me naked, and yet when I see you I still see a half-opened rose. I can't say I'm happy about all the turn of events, but I'm glad we remain friends."

"Jayme, I hurt inside every time I see you because I too know of the love you feel for me, but I with another. A few hours around and dramatically people listen to us. But straight talk—you'll always be special to me. More than you could imagine."

The two went to eat when a large bouquet of flowers came for Egypt. She opened the card; it was from Baron. Several hours after that, a man brought a box for her. She was so impressed; she opened it in front of everybody. It was a diamond broach from Tiffany's. She wondered how in the hell did it get to her because it was only 5:12 p.m. There standing in the corridor was a man resembling Baron. The man resembling Baron walked over to her. She recognized him immediately.

"I took the first flight out here just to ask you," said Baron.

"Ask me what? No, Baron. No, not in front of everyone."

Baron got on one knee and pulled out a rock that would make your eyes roll back from the glare. Egypt was astonished with Baron's behavior. It sent a hot streak right through her. He was being totally open and free with himself. She reached down and pulled him up by the hands. She smiled, and he placed the ring on but no further than her nail.

"In front of God and all these witnesses, will you marry me?"

"If never before I wanted to be Mrs. Gianelli, I do now."

He put the ring on her hand. One of the musicians turned on a soft jazz melody, and Baron kneeled kissing her hand. He stood up and taking her by the hand walked her slowly in a circle. Egypt smiled as they danced as though no one was there. She let go of his hands placing hers on his face, and she kissed him gently on the lips. Baron embraced her in a kiss of lust. She felt the heat from him race through her body. They wanted each other right there.

Egypt got a grip on the situation and hugged him. A few people applauded, and the rest joined in. They both felt awkward. As they walked over to Carlos, he didn't care too much for the disruption, but rehearsal was almost over. Egypt asked, "Is there a seat available for Baron for the next show?

"Don't worry, I'll take care of it."

Baron extended his hand out to Carlos. The two men shook hands, but unknowing to Baron, this man too was in love with Egypt.

The couple walked off embracing one another. Carlos looked at them thinking back. For a short moment he recalled them in the meadow. As he stood there in a daze, Eureka tapped him on his shoulder.

"Where are you?" Eureka felt that something was wrong with him. She turned and noticed the direction he was looking. She smiled and said, "There's a lost sheep that won't ever come back."

He looked at her with animosity and told her, "Disappear like water on a hot day." She glided off snickering.

As Carlos journeyed back to the hotel, he decided to take a walk on the beach. A large tear was caught in his eye. He strolled on the sand, and the wind blew his hair in his face. As he brushed it away, he thought of Egypt and many others that touched his life. Watching those two brought back a time Carlos put far behind.

When will the pain die away? he contemplated. Carlos sat on a small rock as the waves reached his feet. *When will there be a time for him?* he pondered. Never had he felt so empty—tall in the saddle yet lost inside. Avoiding much needed fulfillment. He realized that Eureka loved him, but no way at all could he give what he had for Egypt to her. The total essence of Egypt brought a feeling of completion; like no other before. Carlos couldn't handle the emotions. As his eyes collected tears, he quickly removed them. Deep inside he hoped she'd leave Baron, but she had no idea how he felt for her. Carlos was unable to exhibit his love to her. With all his emotions bottled up inside him, he went to his hotel room. Carlos tried not to dwell on Egypt, but it seemed futile.

He called room service and ordered a bottle of scotch. After he finished drinking the bottle of scotch, the thoughts of Egypt still lingered in his mind. Carlos picked up the phone and dialed Eureka's room. They talked for a moment then he told her to come to his room because they had some details to discuss. Eureka could hear his state was weakened by liquor; she knew this was her moment to succeed and conquer. She grabbed her sexiest negligee, put it on, and covered herself with a sheer robe.

Eureka knocked, but before she could knock again, the door opened swiftly. He turned his back to her and picked up the scotch asking her, "Why did you come dressed like that?"

"Why, is there something wrong with my night wear?" asked Eureka.

"No, the outfit itself is lovely, but you're in it, and that leaves much to be desired," replied Carlos in a harsh tone.

"Here are the new schedules since we have to make some new arrangements. I can only expect Egypt to want to take some time off, after her news."

"If I didn't know better, it sounds like you're having problems with Ms. Thang's decision. Or maybe I'm out of my bounds for saying it (as she let the robe fall from her shoulders). You sound as if you could use some emotional healing."

"That is the farthest thing from my mind." Eureka smiled, and with a high-pitched voice said, "If I remember you well, you never had a problem before. What happened, after Egypt your manhood went with her?"

Eureka walked over to him placing her finger in his glass. She put her finger in her mouth making a suggestion. Eureka looked him straight in the eye, and without looking down, she undid his pants, placing her hand inside, holding his manhood. He stepped back, but as he did, she also moved forward. Eureka began fondling his chest. This was too much for Carlos right at that time; he felt weak.

"What in the hell are you doing? Get the hell out of here. It must be the liquor because you're not even worth a wet dream. So take your shit and go," said Carlos.

"Too bad, Carlos, too bad. I never thought I'd see the day you couldn't get a rise. I was sure a man like you could hold his scotch. My girl left you less than the man you were," Eureka said placing her fingers across his mouth.

She turned from him. He glanced down and realized he was looking at her buttocks. She had bent over and picked up the top to his scotch bottle. While she was bending over, he began feeling sensuous and aroused. He reached for her sheer robe and tore it off her. He lifted her off the floor and poured the scotch on her chest, licking it off. Eureka sighed and became overwhelmed. He then sucked her lips while carrying her to the bed. He collapsed on his back. She wrapped her legs over his chest.

Carlos looked up, and he saw a vision of Egypt; he smiled and whispered something, but Eureka didn't understand. He sat up with the look of hunger as he pulled open the rest of her clothing. He shook his head, and he saw it was Eureka.

Carlos was in a drunken state, and the thought of Egypt made him wild. Carlos then started having hard wild sex with Eureka. The force of it was totally exciting to her; her body tingled. He rolled off the bed and stood looking down on her, and he grasped her legs pulling them to the edge of the bed. Carrying out what he began, he continued forcing himself on her, and her groans and moans made him drift; again he saw Egypt. Eureka glared at him; she knew him, but this was vibrant and exhilarating.

Eureka made more noise, and as he heard the voice, the more he thought he was with Egypt. He called out Egypt's name. Eureka looked at him and asked him what he said. Carlos just told her he missed her and awaited her return. Before she could say a word, he called out Egypt's name again. "What did you say? Carlos, what did you say?"

Carlos looked down, and his vision cleared up; it wasn't Egypt. It was Eureka, and this upset him. As soon as he noticed her, his desire immediately retreated back. He lifted off quicker than a bat out of hell. He pulled her to the floor and walked away telling her she was sick in the head. "How could you lay with a man that didn't want you and is drunk?"

"You're a sick cookie, Eureka, you couldn't be my toilet cleaner. You don't have any self-respect. Just to get what you want from who you want, you don't care how you do it. You don't have any pride. Was I what you wanted? Did I perform well for you? Get the hell away from me, you tramp. I'm stinkin' drunk, and you lay with me. No self-respecting woman would do that shit. Mind you, you wench, don't come back talking you're pregnant because I would rather have a four-legged bitch carry my child than you. My people wouldn't accept you or what may spurn from your womb. Get the hell out of here. I had my way with you. Be gone, you submissive bitch," yelled Carlos.

She gathered her strands of cloth and weeping, ran out of the room. But not without swearing revenge on him and his precious Egypt. She slammed the door on her way out and hurried to her room. She called down for room service and asked for a martini. She jumped into the shower, and while she was in there, she heard a knock at her door. She told the steward to come in. She placed the towel around her and gave the man a tip.

As she sat on the sofa she sipped it down slowly. All of a sudden she thought of Mr. Stout and started to grin. She ran to the bed and jumped up talking about Mr. Stout is the answer. She rolled in her sheets laughing about Mr. Stout would make everything all right. As she drifted off to sleep, Carlos was drinking himself into an oblivious state. Just the thought that he had sex with Eureka made him sick.

The weather was ugly. Winds were moving garbage cans and branches from the trees were falling. A midnight type of sky overhung the morning. Instead of day it seemed like early evening. There were no birds flying, just hiding. There was a severe storm watch out.

Baron rolled over to find his Egypt was gone, but there was a note on the mirror. He walked over in his underwear to the mirror just waiting for it to say she was gone again. But the note read:

Baron, with all of the things happening at one time, I realized that through all the shit, you still loved me so. Until we marry, this was the last time we make love until our wedding night.

Baron laughed and looked at his watch and noticed he had to hurry to catch his flight out. He called down to the rehearsal hall and left a message for Egypt to get in touch with Francis if she needed him.

When he left, the rains began; he scurried to get a cab to the airport. Yelling behind him was a woman. Through the heavy rains, he couldn't tell who it was until she approached closer. It was Egypt drenched to the core. They embraced kissing. He tried to move her hair from her face, but the wind was so strong. They kissed and felt a strong physical attraction. He looked down at her and said, "Let's go back to your room."

Egypt laughed and said, "You have a plane to catch, and I have a show to do tonight."

"I guess that means no, huh?"

"That's what it means, no," replied Egypt.

"I guess no means no, right?" "Right!"

"So I better go before the rains drown us. Let me get in this cab and get back to New York."

They kissed again, and he got into the cab. She waved as he pulled off in the downpour.. She pulled her cap over her head and ran back into the hotel. Egypt went to her room to change into something dry. There by her door was Carlos Montana, standing with a glass in his hand. Egypt didn't know what to do, so she invited him in. He sat on her bed and told her to change before she caught her death.

She went into the bathroom and removed everything. She noticed that she left her dry things. She asked Carlos to hand them to her. He walked into the bathroom holding her robe. When she reached for it, he pulled away dropping it to the floor. He caressed her and kissed her neck while he grasped her buttocks in both palms. She gasped, and Carlos covered her mouth with his.

Egypt pulled away, swiftly moving out of the bathroom. She noticed that for a moment, she gave in to the feeling. But she knew if this got out, she would sure enough lose Baron. Yet the taste of Carlos was on her tongue.

"Egypt, don't run from me, just one last time, that's all I want. You would never know how much I do care. Just hold me in your arms," said Carlos.

"I can't as much as I want to. I can't, it's wrong," replied Egypt and pushed her hair off her shoulders. "I didn't ask you to love me. All I want is for you to hold me. Hold me adjacent to you."

"Don't you even hear what the hell I'm saying?"

"Don't you hear all I'm asking is for a hug? Not your life, not marriage, but a simple damn hug." She walked closely to him and held him. At first he didn't do anything but held her tightly. Slowly he started moving like to a slow dance. Egypt didn't see any harm in that. So they danced. Carlos wasn't leaving it at that. He licked the side of her neck. Goose bumps appeared, and she shivered momentarily. She stepped back and he kissed her. That was it for her—that quality he had began taking over.

As the two slid to the floor, she got on top of Carlos and acted as though she was going to take over, but she got up quickly.

Near the nightstand, he caught up to her and pushed her on the bed nestling her chest. She wanted to get away, but his touch excited her. She couldn't resist, so as the foreplay commenced, Egypt reached to the night table and took out a condom and opened it. Carlos undressed and got on his knees as Egypt placed it on him. This time Carlos didn't complain.

Egypt wrapped her arms around him. As he gratified himself within her womanly charms, he released a cry of pleasure which engulfed the room. She too was in a euphoric state. He made her feel as though they were the only two on earth.

After it was all over, she looked in the mirror, and tears fell. How could she have done this to Baron? she thought to herself. There lay a man that was everything she needed in a man except she knew that Baron loved her just the way she was. With Mr. Montana it was physical.

The rains were still falling heavy, and she grabbed her cap and went out.

Egypt walked through the drops making a desperate attempt to wash off everything she had done wrong. Egypt walked all the way to the coliseum, and one of the guards recognized her. He let her in. As

Egypt took off her cap, she stood on stage and began to sing and cry. A gentleman walked over and listened. He applauded when she finished, wishing her much luck that evening. She walked toward someone giggling; it was Eureka. Egypt asked, "What do you find so funny?" Eureka just giggled saying, "Sooner or later everyone will pay the piper." Egypt thought Eureka was losing a grip of things. She shrugged her shoulders and watched Eureka leave. Then she headed back to the hotel where she could rest before the show.

A part of her was hesitant to return. Egypt knew that Carlos was waiting for her to come back. Egypt wasn't too sure what to say to him.

Baron's name continued to run in and out of her head. As she strolled through the lobby, a voice called her name. She quickly turned to see who it was. It was Jayme, and she just started to cry. He grabbed her arms asking what was wrong with her. She couldn't say anything. She just told him she needed some rest and would go to her room shortly.

It appeared that her entire sexual past was out to haunt her. She closed her eyes and thought about how good it was when she was with Baron in the beginning and what the hell possessed her to walk out that door. It had been so long she seemed to have forgotten.

Egypt knew that this was a lie; she knew just why she left Baron. She pondered through her mind if she would have done it again. Within a blink of an eye she said no. She went back to her room and relaxed for a while before that evening's show.

Waiting for Baron in New York was a hell. In the day or so he was gone, he was to hear some dumbfounding news. He arrived at home, and Athelia told him that Nunzio left word for him to go to Café Cappuccino. When he reached there, people were just leaving. Francis walked up on him asking why he was back so soon. All Baron wanted to know was why didn't anyone get in touch with him.

"Look, there wasn't much time. One minute everything was all right and the next bullets were flying. For the first time I was frozen. So much was happening. My brother and Joey are dead and twelve others. All from different families," said Francis.

"I don't give a shit what anyone thought. I should have been told. Who else was hit? Does anyone have any idea who fuck'in' did this shit?" asked Baron.

"You know, Baron, that was my brother I saw get popped trying to keep Nunzio's ass out a casket. So many damn men died for him, why my fuck'in' brother and not one of his son's? Dominic is all out on a wire. My mother is wrapped up in Kleenex. So there's no one more than me who wants to know," replied Francis in a contemptuous tone.

"Okay point made and well taken. Let me speak with Nunzio. He has to know. He has to have some sort of an idea," said Baron.

"I don't think you ought to go in right now because my mother is speaking with Nunzio. He's the reason for everyone going. He wanted to be alone with her. If I know him well, it's the revenge speech, but for one thing, I know he means it."

Baron walked halfway in and Francis followed. Danny was standing guard. When they approached Danny he stood in front of them, as to say they couldn't enter. Baron and Francis smiled as Danny refused to move so they clobbered him on the sneak.

As the two walked in they felt like kids tiptoeing to hear what Nunzio and Antoinette were conversing about. Nunzio's voice was sweet and soft. A side neither of them heard before. When Francis looked in, his mother's head was in Nunzio's chest and his hand on her buttocks. Baron also caught a glimpse of this.

"Nunzio, I can't believe I lost my son and almost lost ours."

"Don't say that too loud, Antoinette, walls sometimes have ears," replied Nunzio.

"Regardless to all the years that have gone by and all the stolen moments, I never regretted having your son. Just that you can't acknowledge him has driven me crazy," said Antoinette.

"Listen I was always there for my son. I kept him by my side always, and many times Margherita asked if he was in fact my son. She used to claim the way I cared was out of the ordinary."

Francis and Baron couldn't believe what they were hearing. Baron stared at Francis and whispered, "It must be you. You're my brother. Holy shit."

"Holy shit my ass. They can't be meaning that shit. We must have missed something. Shut up and listen, I want to hear all of this to the end."

Nunzio walked away from Antoinette turning and saying, "One thing at a time. First I'm gonna have to put an ear to the ground to get wind of who did this. Second thing is for you to keep an eye on Dominic. My brother is a boozer, and he'll go out and get into some shit. One in the family is enough."

"It could have been two, Nunzio. Let Francis out, or I know I'll lose my only love child."

"Come on I've heard you say that for years. If there was so much love, why in the hell did you marry my brother? You stayed with him all these years and had children with him. Give me a break. I'm not disputing that at one time we both felt for each other. I can remember many good—"

"What in the hell are you saying to me. Why? Why did you wait so many years to tell me you loved me? When I was pregnant if you cared so damn much, why were you offering to send me away. I married your brother in the heat of the night. I knew he loved me, and you were married to Margherita. But professing your love for me and how soon we would be together? So you give me a fucking break. At least Dominic was compassionate. I was two weeks late, so I slept with him. He thought Francis was his child, so he married me right away. You should have been glad because you had no shame in sleeping with me when I was his wife. But as soon as you saw Francis and he was your spitting image, you played Uncle beautifully. So don't give me that crock of shit. Don't even try it. You have fucked my life up since I was young. Every time I felt something for Dominic, here you would come, the devil in a tweed suit. You screwed me up with those lies," she said as she started hitting his chest. Nunzio snatched her hands quickly. He threw them to her side, and she stumbled back a few steps. "Don't play that holier than thou shit with me. Ms. Smart Ass, I did my own checking up. From out of the blue your name popped up," said Nunzio.

"For what? I haven't done anything," said Antoinette.

"You would have me to believe that now, wouldn't you? Your daughter-in-law, terrible how she passed like that. That mystery woman too. Isn't it strange how she fits your description? I wonder how long will it take for me to find out who it was? And if it would be worth a trip to my son."

"You wouldn't dare. I didn't plan that not at all. I had every intention on telling her the truth. Francis didn't love her I know it. He was so much like you marrying the only woman he felt everyone would dislike. She was about to have his baby.

Someone in a higher place took care of that for me," said Antoinette." Someone in a higher place? Or should I say you? Antoinette you wanted to talk, so let's talk about the issue at hand. Because get this straight. Before you could destroy me, I just say one thing and you're history. From Francis on down. Everyone will expect this kind of behavior from me. But, Antoinette, such an upstanding woman like yourself, no, no, no. Mustn't try to play in the big leagues when you're only in the minors," he said and grinned.

"Bastard, what the hell did I ever see in your ass? All of my time and dedication I gave you," she slapped him.

While holding her face in his hands, Nunzio said, "Because you know you love the way I treat you. Most of all the way I lay with you. Every night your body lays next to Dom's, your heart wishes it was me." He kissed her.

Antoinette took a simple kiss and made it a passionate lust arena. Her hands and his were wrapped all together. Suddenly a sound came from the hallway, and they stopped. It was Baron; the sight of it made him stumble. Francis grabbed his cousin by his shirt, and they moved out of there with the quickness.

"What the hell happened to you in there?" asked Francis.

"What the hell? Didn't you feel like you wanted to bust in there? I could have killed both of them." Baron looked at Francis, and in a totally different voice said, "You're my brother."

"Tell you the truth I had a feeling about that. I remembered Uncle coming over many a times when Dom wasn't home. My mother used to send us out with the neighbor. But many a time I sneaked back and I would see Uncle putting on his pants, but I didn't understand."

"So why didn't you ever say something?"

"Oh, give me a break, Baron, who the fuck could I tell? Yeah, my younger cousin. I've got more on my mind than their ideal love affair. My wife, I can't believe it was my mother," Francis said distraught.

Nunzio and Antoinette came up to them. They asked if the two were back there. Neither of them answered. Baron turned and started to walk out. Nunzio called his full name, but Baron continued to leave. Francis walked up to his mother and slapped her. Antoinette's face was in total shock. The sound even made Baron stop in his tracks. Nunzio hit Francis. Francis told Baron to stay out of it. The two knew it was over.

Francis called his mother a murderer. She jumped toward him exclaiming, "That's not what I had in mind. Please listen to me! Just stop and look at me." Francis stepped to his cousin, and the two left.

Antoinette didn't know what to do. Nunzio held her close and wiped off her tears. She asked, "What are we going to do?" Nunzio told her to say nothing.

"The cards are in our hands, and however Francis and Baron want to play them, I'll still know what to do."

Francis asked Baron what he was going to do. But he didn't know. All he expressed was a need for a drink. Francis said he felt like talking to Karessa and his son. Baron asked if he wanted company, but Francis said he'd do it alone. He had to put some space between him and his mother and his companion—Father-Uncle figure. Francis got into his car and headed out to Long Island.

As he arrived there, the sun was orange and created such a lovely scene over the tombstone as if to welcome him there. He sat next to Karessa's plot and spoke for a while before crying. He found all the words to describe how he felt for her. The words he couldn't say when she was alive. He sat for a couple of hours until dusk, and then he went home.

The sky was lit by the stars that evening as though it were a very special night. Francis reached home and sat with a drink listening to music. A knock at the door abruptly awoken him from his daze. Francis rushed to the door because he thought something else went wrong. He opened the door quickly, and there was Donna. She walked right in as though she were at home. Dropping her coat on the sofa and removing her shoes, she sat down on the floor and smiled.

"Amazing, you looked as though the worst thing in the world happened. Now you're smiling. Hey, one for me. So don't stand there, sit back on the floor. Isn't that where you were?" asked Donna.

"How did you know?"

"The evidence is right before me. So what's a girl gotta do for a drink around here? I'll have a Manhattan, but if not a nice glass of wine," she said.

"Wine I have right on hand. So what brings you to my doorstep at this hour?"

"I don't know, just had a strong feeling. You believe in strange feelings?"

"Sometimes, so what do you want to talk about?" replied Francis.

"Francis, once in a while silence is in order when words don't work." Donna lay her head on his shoulder. The music was so heavenly the two noticed a difference in their mood. He laid her on the floor slowly. As he slid his hand from her leg up her skirt, she became tensed. Francis brought his hand back to her face. Placing his hand over her mouth Donna kissed his fingers. He lifted up her skirt, and she was wearing the most chic undergarment. The sight alone made him horny. The lace garter belt and fancy stockings were a complete turn on. As he gazed, much to his surprise, she was wearing crotchless panties.

Donna's hands unloosened her skirt, and it opened right up. She looked at him asking to take her. At that moment Francis didn't have to be asked twice. He thought to himself, her stomach is so flat and her hips round and delicate. He slipped off his pants and lay on his back. Suddenly he felt he couldn't do it. Donna sat up leaning over him. Her breasts were in his face.

He said, "It's been a long while and—"

Before he finished, she said, "I understand why it's so hard for you. Do you want me?"

"I do in the worst way ever."

Up and over she went beginning where he stopped. Francis in a matter of minutes took over. The two rolled from the floor to the sofa until Francis carried her to the bedroom. The two laughed, and each enjoyed one another to the fullest. Donna felt vigorous and exuberant and in love. Francis too was feeling all of the above and then some. They talked for a while.

"Donna, what do you expect from me?" Donna just knew it was time for that talk: "This was just a physical thing. I'm not ready for any one person in my life, I don't mind a friendly sexual thing but no more."

But much to her surprise, he asked her if she were interested in sticking around with him. Francis admitted it was soon, but he was having tingly feelings inside. "So are you in or out, Ms. Donna Magaddino?"

"Oh, everyone wants to hear what you said. But I can't help but say yes," she said and kissed him again. Both of them went for round 2. When Francis finished with Donna, she was a limp pool of sweat. He looked down on her saying, "I needed that." She hardly opened her eyes to acknowledge him. All she did was whisper, "I see."

Chapter 12

Baron called Angelica early in the morning. He caught her in her second dream. She could tell by the sound of his voice that something was truly wrong. She sat up so vigorous and alert. Angelica wasn't about to sleep until she found out what the hell was going on. Baron told her he would call back later, but she wanted to know. It seemed to her that he was about to say something she really didn't want to hear. But she pressed on until Baron reached a certain part of the conversation. As he continued, she dropped the phone to the floor. Angelica's mouth couldn't close.

"What the hell is going on, Angelica? Angelica, who is it?" asked Franco. He reached for the phone and she quickly grabbed it. "Okay now, who is it? And why don't you want me talking on the phone?" he asked with an angry tone.

"Just give me a minute, damn it, just give me a minute. I can't handle this. Baron I cannot digest this shit. Francis . . . and Nunzio . . . were what? Get the hell out of here. You've got to be kidding. How long did it go . . . are you going to talk with Mom? I haven't even eaten yet, and you've got me heaving. How did this all happen? Look, Baron, I can't keep the conversation going because I just want to puke and fall out. Bye," Angela said with a lost sense.

After Franco realized that it was his brother-in-law, he calmed down a bit. He was just trying to figure out why Angelica was carrying on like that. He wiped the tears from her eyes as she stood there mumbling what had happened.

Franco made her get quiet because he couldn't understand what she was saying. It took her some time before she got a grip on herself.

"So what did your father do?" asked Franco.

"It's not so much what he did it's more like why so long and why hide one of the products thereof?"

"Enough riddles, Angelica. Angela, start making some sense. What did Baron tell you to make you so damn burnt out? Something happened to Nunzio or his usual something he did?" asked Franco.

"Nothing great. No big deal. Well, if you think adultery is a small thing."

"For your father, baby, that's no big shit. Oh, I thought it was something worse. Did you really think that he was a saint? Please. Out of all his offspring I would have bet you knew pretty damn well. So you had me thinking it—"

Angelica cut in. "Oh, Francis is my half-brother and my slut aunt is his mother, and my dog of a father is his father too. Do you want breakfast? How about eggs and bacon on rye bread? Or, love, what about some pigs in a blanket? Just the thought of the two of them under the sheets gets me sick. All these years they knew but never said anything about it. It had to take the death of my cousin to find out this shit. Oh my god it just dawned on me. Francis, damn, he must be all fucked up. Shit, this news and his brother," Angelica broke down in tears.

"Come here, calm down, calm down. I didn't want to say anything while you were on a roll. But you have to imagine what the hell Francis is going through. Let me call him, maybe he needs to talk," said Franco.

Franco walked over to the phone and tried calling Francis, but there was no answer. He then tried to reach Baron at E. L., but Heather said he hadn't been in. He left word to await his call because he may be taking a plane out. Franco asked her where was he going but she had no idea. She told him that his voice was cracking as though he had a head cold or something. With that he jumped in the shower and told Angela he'd call as soon as he had some news.

She was worried for everyone. This was some sticky shit. Worst of all Francis was always accused of being Nunzio's favorite. Little did it come out to be it would be his son. Angela wanted to talk to her mother, but she didn't have a clue what to say. But deep down she felt as though her mother knew all along. Angelica couldn't help but to tear. Her mother had been through so much with Nunzio and she stayed. Angela only hoped that she never goes through that with Franco.

There was a light tapping on her patio door. She looked, and it was Vittorio. She opened the door and just stood there. He opened his mouth, but nothing came out. Again he did it and said, "Joseph's dead."

Angela held him; she loved Vitto so much, and there was nothing in the world she could say to mend that pain. He asked her, "Has Baron called you yet?"

She became angry, and she hoped that Baron wouldn't run the news like fire. She told him yes.

Vitto informed her, "Francis went to the house early this morning and talked to Dominic. When I walked in, I heard what was happening.

"I stood to the side. While they were talking, my mother came in and began yelling at Francis saying why did he have to run straight here.

"Francis told her that he had just gotten there, and where the hell was she all night long? She told him she didn't have to answer to him. With that my father stood up and asked the same question. My mother walked away, but Francis pulled her back into the room."

Angelica went and got something for Vitto to drink; she was all distraught. She told him, "If it's too much to talk about, you don't have to."

But he insisted, "I have to get it out, and you're the only one left I could trust. After the overall confrontation Francis called my mother every name in the book. She slapped him so hard the sound echoed. My father flew to his feet and began man handling her. She scratched his face, then he smacked her from one end of the room to the other. And that's when I knew I had to make my exit. So I headed here. It only took several minutes to get here. The shit is still going on," said Vitto.

"So what the hell are you doing here? Come on, Vittorio, you can't leave. You have to make sure they don't get out of hand. I can't tell you what to do, but you came here so I have every right to speak. *Go back now*," replied Angela very seriously.

Vitto agreed and started back to the house. He had no idea what would be awaiting him when he arrived. Vitto walked in at the moment when Francis went to stop Dominic from hitting her, but he suddenly stopped and she leaned against the wall weeping into her hands. Vitto couldn't handle what was going on so he went straight upstairs..

Dominic began yelling, "I had the thought years ago, but I couldn't bring myself to believe it. How the hell did you two hide this for so long? I live here, yet I was so blind. I knew that my brother had been with you, but that didn't stop me. I knew he left you for Margherita. I thought I was your friend. I helped you. I thought you loved me." After that he laughed and asked her, "If you loved Nunzio so much, why did you stay so long with me?" He just looked at her and spit on the ground.

She began telling him shit that he wasn't man enough for her and that the only reason she stayed was so Nunzio could watch his son grow. Then she said as far as you being a man, she could get better loving from a dead one.

Dominic quickly turned to her and reminded her that if she spent some time home, she would have found out how much of a man he was, and before she could handle a man she would have to learn to be a woman.

All of this was getting too much out of hand for Francis, so he wanted to leave. As he started to walk out, his mother yelled, "You're man enough to start the fire, but you can't handle the heat in the kitchen, huh, Francis? Was this necessary? Damn it was it? Who else did you tell?"

"Don't worry about me. Worry about your nephew because his collar is hot. As far as starting the fire, no you did that many years ago. Deception, Mom, deception. Oh, Mom, by the way if Father didn't or should I say Uncle now, well, I would have knocked the shit out of you myself."

"Francis, you had better never come to my door again in life. I was cursed the moment I conceived you. I gave you the best of everything," she said.

"The best of everything? If you don't shut the hell up, I will hurt you. You, self-righteous bitch. How can you stand in front of me attempting to portray concerned love after you caused the death of my family? You and Nunzio do deserve each other."

Francis started toward the door. He opened and looked back to say, "Never worry about me, just worry about your conscience. You and your lover both killed their grandchildren. Live with that, bitch." He spit in front of the door way and walked to his car.

Francis head was running wild, and he needed to disappear for a while. From his car phone he made arrangements to head out that evening for Miami. Before he left, he knew he had to get in touch with Baron. As he glanced at the time, he knew approximately where Baron should be. He dialed, and sure enough Baron was in his car heading to the office. Francis gave him all the information. Baron agreed that Francis needed some time to think.

After they talked, Baron headed up to the office, but before he could fully get out the elevator, people began bombarding him with paperwork. As he pushed them away and ran past Heather, grabbing his print out, Heather opened his door as he slid past her, she held out her arms and said, "Safe!" The two laughed; it was a little minibaseball play. Out of nowhere he became serious. She wondered what was wrong but didn't question it.

Heather buzzed him again and told him Egypt was on the line. Baron picked up the phone and asked how she was. She knew right off the bat something happened. Egypt asked, "Is everything all right?"

Baron told her too much had transpired, and he needed to talk. The two stayed on the line for about two hours. Heather buzzed in and asked Baron was he going to the meeting with the Harlem Boys IV U. He had completely forgotten about it.

He apologized and rushed off the phone. Egypt understood and said she would be home, they could talk then. Baron grabbed his work and headed to the conference room.

Egypt realized that shit had gone down and she had to be there for him. She called Carlos to come to her room. When he arrived, Egypt explained she had to go back to New York. He jumped on her ass about who the hell did she think she was, but by then, she was closing up her suitcase. He tossed it across the room. Egypt didn't know what had gotten in him.

"Carlos, you better get a grip. See you're acting asinine, so I think you had better go," said Egypt. "Egypt, everything is at its highest, don't break the link. You just can't walk out on everyone. We're supposed to be a team," replied Carlos.

"I realize that, but Baron needs me for the first time, and I feel a need too, Carlos. Damn you don't even play with me. Don't try now to act so concerned over me. You've acted everything but, except when the mood was right. Come on, I love you, but not the way I love Baron. Okay I can't up and go. I won't, but the moment my last note is done I'm Audi 5000."

"Fair, but as far as your concerned you knew how I felt and why I had to contain myself. I don't and can't show emotion," said Carlos.

"So die lonely. Because sooner or later your ass is going to need that sensation satisfied so get over it. Let's talk about do what you gotta, and I do what I gotta do. Just don't try to protest a fraud, if you do that tell it to some other ass. I am not with it. I'm out of here, so end of conversation," Egypt said and walked Carlos to the door.

She grabbed the phone and made the reservation and finished packing. For once she felt like herself and didn't want the feeling to get by her. She felt in Baron's voice that he didn't know how to ask her to come home. She lay across her bed and began giggling. She couldn't believe the dynamic emotion running through her. She sat up and dialed Gina's number. Gina was so totally flabbergasted and she couldn't believe it was her sister's voice. She expressed her delight in hearing Egypt so happy. When Egypt explained why, Gina asked her, "When is the date for the wedding? And you better not forget to tell us." "How could I forget when you and Dionisia are in it?" They talked for hours, and then the big question came, their mother.

They stopped laughing. For a moment they both were worried. "Leave Mother in Jose's hands," said Gina.

"Ignorance," Egypt said defiantly. Jose had a way with Carmen. When they both hung up, she quickly dialed Jose. He was very aware of Egypt's feelings about Carmen because of their past history together. They spoke on Carmen, and he told her, "Just relax, Egypt. There's not going to be any problems, considering she probably feels lonely now that almost everyone is gone."

Jose continued telling her about Noel and his problems. The two laughed, and Egypt promised as soon as she returned she would stop by. He reminded her that it was their mother's birthday coming up. Egypt told him, "I already made arrangements for you two to go out on the town."

"Instead of just us, why not Carmen and you?" asked Jose.

"Jose, at this point, I could do without a stress-filled evening."

Jose chuckled. "I understand, but why should I be the only one having stress-filled days with her?"

Egypt complied. "I'll try and go but not without you there."

Jose asked her to hold on because someone was on the other line. When he returned, his voice dropped down low.

"Why the sudden change in pitch?" she asked.

"That was Matilda. Man, that port-o-rock is working my nerves."

"So why are you calling her a port-o-rock?"

"Damn, Egypt, she tries to flip the script on me. Like she's the one in control and I ain't with it." "Through this whole conversation I've been dying to ask you, do you talk like this in school?"

"Yeah right, Egypt. I plan on walking in, 'Yo, what up, what up, profess?' Get real, Egypt. If I come off at home all correct, I'll have static, so just cool out. Like I was saying from the getty up, this bitch be working my shit to an uproar. Worst of all, I know I must love the shit out of her because I would have stepped a while ago."

"What's the lowdown on school?"

"I'm telling you one thing though. You know the answer to that one cause there ain't no way I'm gonna fuck up with that. Check it out, I'll send you my transcript. But back to Matilda she wants to get married, but I'm not down with that."

"Matilda and you have been seeing each other for only what, three or four months at the most, and you're saying that you love her? What makes you feel like that. Did she say or hint anything about marriage?"

"No, but—"

"But what? Okay, then sit with her and talk. If you care so much for her and you're sure and all, hey, Jose, are you using protection?" asked Egypt. He was quiet on the phone. "I'll rephrase that—are you wearing a raincoat? Why so quiet?"

"Well, we haven't done anything yet. I can't even if I wanted to since these tests have me in an uproar. She swears I'm fooling around, but yo, Egypt, physics is kicking my ass. I can't think about sex. Please, I got too much on my mind. Besides that I'm considering pledging."

"Before you go off on a tandem, first things first. When I come home, you and I and Matilda are gonna get together for Momita's compleano. I have to go because this is my last show on tour before I go back to the studio."

"Egypt, was this a whim, or are you serious? I thought Egyptian Labels was your true dream."

"I can't answer that. I'll call you when I get back. Love you, Jose. Don't forget to invite Matilda," said Egypt.

After they hung up, Egypt placed a call to her brother Noel. He was quite surprised to hear from her and was a little on the smart-ass side. She expected that considering she hardly called him.

"So, Ms. Rich, how goes things?" asked Noel.

"Don't start okay. I can admit I was wrong, but I don't agree on how you earn your money. But that doesn't mean I don't love you. Come on, Noel, peace."

"You didn't like how, what? Please, Egypt, who are you bullshitting, me or yourself? It's okay for you to live with that Guinea, and his family is so well connected? Don't play yourself, Egypt."

"Noel, what makes you keeper and distributor of all knowledge? Do you really believe I always knew?"

"If you didn't it's only because you chose to be blind. So don't judge me," he said.

"I'm not judging you. Damn it, shit, can't we ever talk without this bullshit? Can't you understand maybe I just don't want anything to happen to you? I couldn't bear the thought, Noel."

"Not you sounding like Momita. Egypt, Egypt, Egypt, are you crying? Stop it come on, don't do that. Nothing is going to happen to me. Egypt, I'm okay, why did you call?"

"I just wanted to hear your voice. I can't help but cry. Hold on okay."

Egypt went to answer the door; it was a messenger. She opened the envelope as she continued to talk on the phone. "Noel, I have to go, but I'll call again soon." As she was about to hang up, she quickly added, "Noel, I love you, bye." She hung up.

As the evening came to an end, Egypt gathered everything, and she said her good-byes. Jayme walked over to her and in silence the two said good-bye. Although he had so much to say, he knew it wouldn't be reciprocated. Jayme reached for her hand slowly. She wondered what was wrong with him. He kissed her hand and smiled. She held both his hands, walked up close to him, and kissed him. For just one moment she felt something. Afterward she just winked an eye and walked away. Bach and Neil watched from the sidelines.

Manny stepped to him asking, "Is everything cool, man?"

Jayme laughed telling him, "It couldn't have been better."

Egypt arrived in New York, but by the time she reached her apartment, she was exhausted and she wanted to talk with Baron. Egypt heard a knock at the door. She wasn't about to get up to answer it. She glanced at the clock, and the knock continued. It seemed whomever it was they weren't leaving.

She opened the door swiftly not asking who it was. She gasped for air; she was very surprised.

Baron grabbed her tightly. She gleamed, and the two kissed passionately. As he walked in, Baron closed the door with his foot. They were still embraced.

She asked, "How did you know I was home?"

"I called the hotel, and one of the crew members told me what time you left. I also called the airlines and found out what time the plane arrived in New York. You look out of it. Tired, babe?"

"Yeah. Baron right about now I could use a hot bath. And a good massage."

The two looked deep into each other's eyes and saw a passion that had been left kindling for a while. She walked into the bathroom and drew a tub of water and poured bath oil into it. She turned around to find Baron there standing tall and masculine. He had put on their song, a very seductive and vibrant jazz melody. He removed his clothes and wrapped a towel around himself.

Baron looked at Egypt, and with the ray of sunset falling on her, made the moment more sensual. He began slowly removing her blouse from her shoulders. Stepping close to her he kissed her down her neck. While letting her blouse drift off her arms, he slowly bent to his knees nestling his face within her voluptuous breast. She held him tight to her and—as her tears fell she slowly—whispered, "Sorry."

She knew the hurt she caused, and with that, he undid her trousers.

Egypt guided Baron upward, and the two caressed and kissed as they both felt like making love right there. Egypt stepped out of her pants into the tub. She sat slowly into the water, and she pulled Baron's towel off. He got in. They both made love. As Egypt sat upon Baron, he called out her name; this turned her into a tigress.

He grabbed her pulling her down to him. He kissed her as if he were trying to suck the life from her.

After a moment or so, the two ended up in her loft bed. For the first time Baron wanted to talk. He asked, "Egypt, do you love me or the sex?"

"No, you didn't say that. Are you funny or what? Stupid, now you're acting like me."

"Think about it. I have gone from hell to high waters to show I care and wanted you back. You left me . . ." "So that's what you really want to talk about, me leaving you, right?"

"No, not exactly just tell me what made you go and what made you stay away so long? I think those are fair questions," said Baron.

"Fair enough. I don't want to talk about it. What difference does it make anyway? What are you asking me, did I sleep around? Is that what's eating at you? So tell me, babe, is it that frigg'n' pride of yours?" asked Egypt.

"So I guess that means you did. I just wanted to know how you felt, that's not asking much is it?" he asked.

"Yeah, but it wasn't the same. I thought it would help to forget you, but it didn't," she replied as her eyes began tearing.

"No, Manteca, don't," he said as he wiped her eyes. "Because I slept with one woman, and it was wrong. The reason why it was wrong, was because I knew I loved you. You could never imagine how I felt when you said yes you'd marry me," replied Baron.

"You only slept with one person?" She felt strange inside. She finally saw him in a totally different light. She broke down into tears, and he held her by her arms asking, "What's wrong?" All she could utter was, "Hold me tightly."

As they embraced, she gazed into his eyes, and for just one moment, Egypt felt the urge to say I love you to him, for the first time in a long time. Baron pulled the pin from her hair. As she shook her head from side to side slowly, her hair fell past her shoulders. He grabbed her by her hair forcing himself on her. Egypt not resisting fell to her back like a wilting flower. She was soft and gentle against his rugged masculine ways. He awoken her with erotic passion as he became one with her.

Thunder and lightning sounded, awaking them. Egypt clutched Barons arm, and as he held her, she asked, "What happened between your parents?"

Baron really didn't want to talk about it, but he knew sooner or later he would have to. He briefly explained everything. Her mouth was open the entire time he spoke. Egypt was in shock; she was positive about Nunzio's infidelity but never would have dreamed that Francis was his son.

Baron got up and went to the kitchen. Egypt followed him without talking; she didn't know what to say. As he sat at the table, she started coffee. When she finished, she turned to see his head in his hands. She approached him massaging his shoulders. He sighed with relief, and he held her hand pulling her to his side. She then sat on his lap. Egypt wrapped her arms around him laying her head on his chest. He whispered, "I love you. Do you know when the big day will be?" She smiled and replied, "As soon as possible. Right about now, we could use some happiness around us."

"You still haven't answered my first question. When?" he asked.

She grinned and pinched his face. She jumped up and ran. He grabbed her in the living room. "Quickly, okay?" she answered. "As soon as I could get fitted in a gown, and you pull together a reception place and church, don't worry and I'll be there."

Egypt looked at the time. "Oh my goodness. I almost forgot I had to make arrangements for tonight because I'm going out with my family."

Baron was surprised and asked if he could come. She thought it would be just what the doctor ordered. He went and got dressed to head out. She walked him to the door in her robe. They kissed, and Baron started to get a bit carried away. She had to remind him that they were standing in front of the door, and the neighbors had good seats. He laughed and patted her bottom as he walked out.

By the time she was done getting ready, it was running late. She first made a list and started calling everyone she wanted to have in her bridal party. Then something dawned on her. How many ushers was Baron having in? She called his car phone, and the two got everything straight. She called the caterer and the church. She took the soonest available date they could get. It was right around the corner. Egypt was going to ask Jose to give her away and tell her mother about it now, before she heard it in the street. Tonight would be the perfect time to tell her mother.

After this evening, Egypt hoped that peace would come between her and Momita. The bell rang, and Egypt saw what time it was. It must be the limo she thought. She looked ravishing. Her hair was in a french roll with a long strand falling onto her face. Her dress fell off her arms and was black trimmed in gold. She was wondering as she stepped into the limo if Jose was able to convince Momita to use the money she gave to buy a pretty dress. As they drove off, Egypt dropped her head in shame. Why would she even worry about what Momita wore? It's her mother, and she shouldn't be ashamed that she was poor. But she knew people would look at Egypt wrong because she didn't help her family. But the outsiders could never understand her mother's pride which keeps Egypt from truly helping. After all, when her father was alive, it was easy to sneak and help. She thought of her father, and tears filled in her eyes. She hadn't taken the time to visit his grave, only to arrange for flowers to always go. Egypt knew that was no excuse for not finding time to go to the cemetery.

As they rolled up, there stood Jose by himself. Egypt's nightmare had come true; Momita was never going to really make amends with her. Egypt stepped out, and all eyes were on her. She felt a bit naked but spoke to those she knew and walked to her brother. Jose strolled over to her differently. Egypt didn't quite understand until she noticed a girl was walking along side of him.

"So, Jose, where's Momita?" asked Egypt.

"Don't sweat. I have everything under control. This is my lady Matilda. Matilda, this is my sister Egypt."

"Hi, I never met anyone Spanish with a name like Egypt. It's pretty and different," said Matilda.

"Thank you, and I haven't come across anyone with that name myself. Where is Momita? Oh, Jose, when we arrive at the restaurant, don't act surprised, Baron will be there. I hope. Because we're going to tell Momita . . . here she comes. What do I do?" Egypt was nervous and just gave her mother a kiss and hug and led her to the limo by hand. She didn't even notice what her mother was wearing.

"Well, Momita, it's been a long time. I hope this evening is wonderful for all of us." Egypt didn't know why she said something so dumb. She then knew she was nervous.

"So where we go?" asked Momita.

"I made reservations at a small restaurant at Julian's on Fiftieth. Matilda, you're quiet over there. Everything all right?"

"Don't worry about me, I'm absorbing the sights. When you're in a limo it seems a bit different. So how did you like your tour? Was it as wonderful as the papers made it?" asked Matilda.

"No, it's a lot of hard work, but I would rather hear what everyone else's is up to."

Egypt turned toward her mother and attempted to make conversation with her. Carmen asked Egypt a few things, and polite conversation came about. Jose and Matilda were having an under-the-breath argument. Matilda wanted to know who Jose was seeing on the side. He continued to ask her if they couldn't talk about it later. Matilda noticed that his mother was looking at her, so she said later would be fine.

Jose was stressed now. But he played it cool because he saw that Carmen and Egypt were finally calm with one another. When they arrived at the restaurant, as soon as Jose stepped out, Matilda made a flip comment. He told Egypt to go ahead that they would follow shortly. Egypt knew something was wrong but wasn't about to butt in. She and her mother went in.

"Damn it what in the fuck is wrong with you?" yelled Jose as he pulled her to the corner.

"Don't talk to me like that."

"You want to act like an ass I'll treat you suchly. Matilda, this is not the place, nor trust the time for you to be showing your ass. What would make you happy if I threw you on the floor and fucked you? Damn, it will that prove to you I'm not sleeping around?"

"You don't have to sound so nasty. I'm just asking you are you fucking around on me. Man, I'm not stupid. We don't sleep together, and we been together for how long now?"

"Matilda, I keep telling you school, man, school. That's all I want to concentrate on. If I didn't care for you, we wouldn't be here together, or would I find time to call. I must love you in a special way. Yo, I'm not sure if it's true love, but, Matilda, open your eyes before I go, man. Because I can't take the pressure from you and my books."

"So nobody making you stay. I just want the truth. Look at you. You're fine and becoming a doctor. Look at me, Poppy, I'm a project girl and barely got out of high school. I work the marketa. My family is poor, and look at the life your sister is living."

"Where the hell do I live? Same place I thought."

"You know what I mean Lindo? Since you can't see, I'll spell it out for you. You live there by choice and not by force. Your apartment is bueno, my people's place is wreck."

"Matilda, tonight you and I speak no street, and tonight please believe me I do want just you and no one else. Come here," said Jose.

"No, I don't feel like it. Jose, do you find me attractive? Do you ever think about making love to me? What kind of a relationship are we in?" asked Matilda. "The kind we're in is a straight-up relationship. Just the physical is not playing a role in it yet. What's wrong with you? Are you a nympho or what? Shit I'm getting tired of going through this with you. I'm not telling you again. If you need it that bad damn it, go sex someone. Just get the hell off my fucking back. So for now, smile, act happy, and let's go in before Momita looks to see what's wrong."

He snatched her hand and went in. They were immediately seated with his family. Sitting there was a man. At first he didn't really think Baron was going to show. When they greeted each other, the waiter came and serviced everyone. Dinner was finally served, and they all ate and laughed. Baron and Carmen got along lovely. They hadn't all been together like this in such a long time. Which he promised would never happen again. Baron ordered some champagne and kneeled by Carmen.

"Momita, if there was ever a woman on this earth I would give the world, it would be to your daughter. I have asked many a times for her hand in marriage, but she was always so hesitant. Now I want your blessing. Momita, I love her and want to spend my life with her," said Baron.

"You're everything she had spoken of. I can't give you happiness, but what I can do is give you two my prayers. Loco, you have my blessings," said Carmen with teary eyes.

Jose raised his glass and said a toast. Everyone was so excited about the occasion and began imputing ideas for the wedding. Momita wanted to know when. She also wanted to know how the wedding could be pulled off with such short notice. Egypt was in such good spirits that she had forgotten to mention she had already made the plans for everything.

Egypt hugged her mother asking her to help her through this. She had already made reservations for her sisters to be home and paid them that afternoon.

Just then the waiter walked over and asked Egypt if she would grace the band with a song. She didn't want to, but her mother smiled, so Egypt said yes but only if Jose would sing with her. Egypt told Baron, "If you want to hear a voice, listen closely to him." Jose blushed.

They both walked up, and people clapped. They told the band to play a very simple song. By the time they were finished, the place was full of tears. When they walked to the table, Baron asked, "How come you never tried to take your singing further?"

Egypt quickly jumped in and said, "He wants to be a doctor and not a singer."

"At one time all of us used to sing but for parties and weddings in the neighborhood. From Egypt on down to Dioni, we all sang and played instruments. Egypt, how come you never mentioned it?" Jose took out his wallet and showed Baron pictures of various shows and contests.

"Why don't you just come down to the studio and make a demo for at least the fun of it?" asked Baron. Jose seemed interested, but Egypt hoped that Jose would turn it down. Matilda asked Baron, "Could he come down with some of his friends?"

Baron said, "No problem."

"Oh yes, it would be a problem if it interfered with school," replied Egypt.

Matilda quickly said to Egypt, "I agree. Nothing or no one is gonna come between him and school. Be it physical or mental, all that Jose does is eat and breathe school." She added, "Not to worry because everything takes the back burner anyway."

Everyone could tell that there seemed to be a problem. Jose was embarrassed so he stood up and excused himself, took Matilda's hand, and stepped out. Egypt got up, and Carmen told her to sit. "Jose loves her, and he has to learn if he can deal with her."

But Egypt didn't like what she was saying. Baron asked what was going on. Egypt briefed him on it. He laughed and said, "Most women would be happy to have a man that didn't always think like that."

"My brother had a very big reputation with the ladies. Since Father passed, he started taking school, and his degree a lot more serious. Until he told me he met Matilda. He said she was special. but he doesn't know why. He truly cares for her, but she's making it hard on him. I'm not going to let anyone detour my brother."

"When it comes to Egypt and her brothers and sisters, no one bothers to stop her. She'd do whatever she could for them. Especially her little brother."

"I understand and I'll stay clear, but I still want Jose to come to Egyptian Labels."

Carmen smiled and sipped her drink. Egypt asked her mother, "Would you like a tour of the company? Considering how old the company is and you have yet to see it." Carmen felt that the wedding was more important. She told Egypt that this was going to be the event of all events. She wanted to give her full attention to it.

When they finished their after-dinner drinks, they all got ready to leave. As they walked out to the limo, they didn't see Jose or Matilda. Carmen glanced a block or so away and spotted them. Egypt started to walk that way, but Carmen snatched her and told her to leave him.

"You know it's hard for her too, but we have to let him make mistakes and go on. Just be there when and if he falls. They aren't too thrilled about you living with a man, but no one stopped you, now did they? No one caught an attitude until it seemed you forgot them." Baron kissed Egypt and her mother on the cheek and left.

Matilda and Jose walked back smiling, so Egypt was happy. On the way back the conversation was just about the wedding. Egypt told her mother that it was up to her to get in touch with all her aunts, uncles, and cousins. She would take care of all her own friends. Egypt tried to stress that she didn't want too many people from the old neighborhood because she didn't want any problems with anything. That day meant too much for her to have havoc and mayhem accrue.

By the time Egypt got home, even though she felt sleepy, it seemed she had no time to sleep. She had stayed up at her mother's all night. After everything was settled and she checked the apartment, she returned to the loft. She was happy, but she had a small feeling of remorse. The only thing bringing her down was that her father wouldn't be there. She wished she hadn't been so fickle and had married Baron years ago. But Egypt knew that nothing about life is that simple and easy.

She started to drift away and noticed that the answering machine light was flickering. She thought it had to be her Baron.

Much to her avail it was Chai. Egypt grabbed her pillow and covered her head. She thought to herself, *When will all this shit come to a quiet storm? Now what in the hell does Chai want?* she pondered. It was almost time for her to get up, but she wanted to at least catch two hours sleep. When her head hit the pillow, she was out for the count.

As the sun beams lay upon her face, she snatched the covers over her head yelling, "Not yet! not yet!" Then the alarm went off, and she slapped it off the wall. When she realized the time, she jumped to attention. She was off to the shower, and the phone rang while she had just finished toweling her hair. She rushed to get it.

"Hello, oh yeah . . . but it was too late to call you. No, I'm pretty much booked today . . . Okay late lunch, but I can't, okay. Where? All right 1:30 p.m. Chai, I don't really think this is a good idea, why can't we talk over the . . . Okay, see you at one-thirty," said Egypt. She hung up the phone totally astonished. *What brought this on? Oh my good*ness, she thought, *he could have found out about Baron. No,* she said to herself, *that couldn't be it. I hope I can get through this day in one sane piece.* She called Baron but got his answering machine. She got frustrated, and the day hadn't begun yet. As far as Chai was concerned she was worried that it wasn't a bombshell.

Mr. Baron on the other hand was running around making arrangements with his family and called his mother telling her of his attentions. Margherita said, "Baron I sure needed some good news, but I'm not sure how Nunzio is going to handle it."

"As far as I'm concerned, my father couldn't say anything to me."

"Have you spoken to Francis?"

"No, not yet." She was very upset with him. "Son, he had nothing to do with it. You can't be angry with him. He has to be hurting more than any of us. Have you considered his feelings?" asked Margherita.

"No, worst of all, Mom, I'm angry with him and myself. I thought something was going on, but I couldn't bring myself to bring it up. I've acted like a child. I can't believe what I've done," said Baron.

"So I guess, baby, I don't have to tell you that by you running around telling everyone you could see our business, you hurt a lot of people. Airing out the dirty laundry isn't the best thing to do. Enough of that, this wedding I'm so looking forward to and I'm so glad," replied Margherita.

"Well, I have to get in touch with Tony and Nunzio Jr. Egypt is going to call Angelica."

"But Angelica is married."

"She said it was her wedding, and she'd have it however she chooses. Let me hang up and call Tony because he's gonna call . . . no, I'll stop by Francis and talk. That would only be right . . . Okay, Mom, let me go," Baron said and then hung up.

When Baron finished his calls, he checked up to see where Francis was. After he found Francis, he drove over for that much needed conversation. Francis had no idea that Baron was on his way. If Baron would have told Francis, he knew that his cousin wouldn't stick around.

When Baron pulled up, Francis noticed the car. Francis went to the door. As he approached his cousin, Baron said "Is it possible for me to get a cup of coffee around here?"

Francis just stood there for a moment then replied, "Depending on who wants it."

"Okay. Shit, are we gonna stand out here and talk or go inside?" asked Baron. "I only let in family and friends, not strangers. I'm not sure if I know or in that case care to know." "In that case, my brother, I should be allowed in."

Francis went to slam the door on Baron, but Baron stopped the door with his hand. Asking for Francis to hear him out, Baron apologized for what he just said. He let Baron in, but they stood by the door. Baron said, "Look, please understand why I lost it for a moment. Just hear me out, okay? For one instant I only thought about my own feelings and disregarded what you could have felt. When I realized that my own sister was more concerned for your feelings than her own or even her son's, I knew that I went thinking about things the wrong way."

Francis asked, "Why do you care now?"

"Because you're my brother damn it and my close friend. I can't imagine not being buddies."

For a moment Francis felt like crying because he too didn't want to lose the bond they have acquired since childhood. Baron asked, "Francis, would you be my best man in my wedding?"

Shocked, Francis hugged his cousin patting him on the back. "Come on in, brother. Sit down, and I'll fix us a drink."

Meanwhile Margherita told Nunzio of Baron's intentions. He turned every color under the sun. Nunzio hung up the phone and called Gabriel Stout at Micdele Corporation.

Within the hour Gabriel was in Nunzio's office. He was yelling to the point that his veins were showing. Gabriel had to do something because Nunzio was not allowing this to happen.

"I need a few moments to gather my thoughts. There has to be a way to destroy this marriage. No matter what, Baron is not the one to work on. How about if we forced Egypt's hand into not going through with it?"

"How in the hell would we be able to do that?"

"Look, Nunzio, just relax. I'll get the ball rolling and fill you in later."

Nunzio stated, "It had better be good or else you'll be wearing the same suit for a hell of a long time."

Gabriel had to make his move quickly. His game plan was not too hard to achieve. He knew that Egypt's weak when it comes to pressure dealing with Baron or his family. A few phone calls he made and the ball was in order, but to make it more dramatic and permanent was what was needed, he thought. He pondered several ideas until he began to grin. To himself he thought how mean and ruthless he could be if given the opportunity.

After everything was set he went back to see Nunzio and told him of his plan. Nunzio was ecstatic. "Gabriel, my boy, it took a while, but I feel that you've finally came up with the solution. I just want to know how you came up with the idea."

Gabriel told him, "The place, the time, and the atmosphere will help make it more permanent."

Back at Carmen's place, neighbors and family gathered to plan this day. Egypt called her mother and told her to come to the loft, bring her aunts and take a cab. She explained that in the best interest of a good marriage she felt that they should included Margherita.

Carmen gathered a few people and went there, and Egypt called Margherita. Everyone was eating and planning for the event. The women all got along lovely. Angelica and Elisabetta even showed up. The date was set and so was the church and the reception hall. Egypt said that she had met this wonderful designer some time ago and that she wanted him to design her dress. Everyone wanted to know what she wanted, but Egypt loving to keep people in suspense, told them it would be a surprise to all. She laughed and went to the phone.

She called Carlos Montana just to ask how he was. Much to her surprise a woman answered the phone. Egypt hung up quickly. She was totally surprised; she wondered who the woman was. She didn't know why, but to even think of another woman with Carlos somewhat upset her. She felt she was somewhat irreplaceable. She called the man who she wanted to make her dress. She stayed on the phone for a while until Carmen tapped her.

When Egypt returned to the living room, almost everyone had left. She apologized for the long absence, but they told her there was no need for an apology. Everyone understood the reason for her being so anxious. Little did they know it was more like she was bent about being replaced.

After they all left, she called Carlos's house again. This time he answered the phone. "I never expected to hear from you after our last confrontation." She noticed there was some worry in his voice. She didn't know how to ask, but she wanted to know who it was on the phone earlier. "I just called to say that I hoped we could still be friends. You know, after all we've been through. I called about an hour ago and thought I had the wrong number."

He replied, "So that was you who hung up of Elisa."

"Elisa? You mean Elisa Taylor from United records?"

"Yes. I didn't know you two had met. When was that?"

"The first time was when I went with my friend Sharla to a meeting of the Black Women's Business Movement. She was either president or chairperson something in that order. If I'm not mistaken she is one of the top black business women in the recording industry."

"Well, I see you do your homework now, don't you?"

"At one time she was an adversary of mine until we merged with Gabriel Stout."

"Gabriel Stout from Micdele—didn't you know he's involved with the underworld? I would have imagined you knew that too."

"You must be mistaken. Stout may be everything under the book, but he is very legitimate. That much I think I can vouch for. He is nothing like my future father-in-law," replied Egypt.

"By the way, when is the happy occasion?"

The two talked for a while, and she invited him and a guest. Carlos told her, "I guess I'll bring Elisa."

"No problem," she replied. "Matter of fact Eureka is on my guest list. Well, I kind of did that so she could see everything with her own eyes."

"Do you mean to say that the reason you invited her was so that she would feel she was wrong about us?"

She laughed and said, "You got that right on the nose. Look, I'll see you at the wedding, and you take care of yourself. And also good luck with Elisa. Bye, Carlos."

She hung up the phone and walked through her apartment. She suddenly realized that soon this place won't be hers alone anymore. She was so accustomed to being on her own. A few moments of fear entered her about marriage, especially having Nunzio as a father-in-law. Life with that man would be hell. She thought to herself why does he always make sexual remarks and innuendoes. She took a deep breath and started to cry out of nowhere. She just couldn't stop the tears. She jumped up and grabbed her coat and went for a long walk. She hoped the air would clear her head so she could sleep well.

During the early morning hours, Baron received a call from Lotario to meet him down by the packaging warehouse. He also told him to be alone. Baron wasn't too sure about what was going on, but he knew he wasn't going alone and he didn't tell Lotario that. Baron called Francis, Franco, and a few others. He explained the situation of the phone call from Lotario to Francis, and he took it from there. The feeling that something just wasn't right ran through Baron's head.

Francis arrived within the half-hour. He told Baron everyone will be in place by the time they arrive there. Baron asked, "Where's Franco?" "He's waiting in the car," replied Francis.

When Baron arrived at the warehouse, he walked in with Francis. Lotario stood up and asked, "Why in the hell is he with you?"

Baron looked around and told Lotario, "If I thought that you were alone also, I would have obliged you." But Baron knew better.

"So let's get down to business. Why in the hell did you want me here and alone at that, Lotario? Francis and I are inseparable, so today look at it as a 2 for 1 sale," said Baron.

"Better than that we call this street sense. Again, Lotario, why did you want him?" asked Francis.

"Nobody was a talk'n' to you, so shut your face. I have nothing at this time to say to you, Francis. Baron, I can only think that your people are here also. So why don't we all come out and speak," said Lotario.

"I think we need to say what has to be said and do what has to be done," replied Lorenzo to one of the elders.

Francis whispered to Baron, "Where did they dig him up from?"

Baron shrugged his shoulders saying, "I thought he died years ago. What the hell is he doing here too?"

"Baron, come closer," said Lorenzo. "Are you crazy? First why are we all here?" "Come here, Baron, now," said Lorenzo.

Baron knew better than to get close. Instead he walked to the side, and Francis stepped up. When Baron moved, he saw the guns waiting, so he stood still. In his mind he was trying to plan an escape route. But there were only two ways in, and each end was heavily guarded.

Franco was beginning to get impatient and headed toward the warehouse. He told them, "It seems this is 100 percent real. Lorenzo's format is leave no man alive. A living man tells tales."

Franco's stomach too was in a knot. He couldn't understand why they called for Baron. He had to watch his brother-in-law's ass. Lorenzo signaled to his goons to take care of them.

Baron was busy staking out the place. He saw that there were two forklifts, one to the rear right where one guy stood near. The other was right by the front entrance. Directly above them was a giant crane and barrels to the left of them. All the equipment was on layers and layers of shelves to his left. So far he had nothing. When he looked to the right, they attacked, hitting his neck and shoulder. Francis tried to respond but was punched on his cheekbone making him sway. Quickly they hit him on the back of the head laying Francis out to the ground.

Baron held his head and felt blood. He looked up at Georgio, one of Lotario's men. Georgio was ready to strike again, but Baron quickly moved out of the way and kicked him in his side. Georgio fell to the floor, and Baron rolled him over and began to swing and connect with every blow. From behind, a man pulled Baron off and swung hitting Baron below the eye and again with a fast left to the nose. Momentarily Baron couldn't see clear. Francis was fighting to get his way over to help Baron. But before he knew it, two more men surrounded them.

No sooner did he hit one, two others were knocking him to the ground. Francis's arms were pinned back while one muscular man used him as a punching bag. Francis tried to get away, kicking the man in the face. This pissed him off, and he backed up and ran toward Francis butting him with his head. Francis was knocked out cold.

Baron saw Francis fall and fought his way through to help him. The huge amazon hit Baron in his back with a pipe sending Baron into the barrels. The barrels fell over and a liquid seeped out. Baron, limp and full of blood, was tied up.

When he came to, he was hanging from the crane and Francis was tied to a chair in front of him. Both their mouths were gagged, so there was no way for Franco to know what was going down. Franco's stomach made a flip, and he couldn't wait any longer.

He had Johnny and O'Conner take out the two men out front. O'Conner climbed up and over some crates waiting for one of the guards to come near. As soon one of them was directly underneath him, he jumped down. Before the man could say a word O'Conner knifed him in the throat.

One of the other guards heard a sound but moved in the opposite direction and spotted Johnny.

Franco saw the movement and noticed that it was Bobby, and he knew Bobby was cold-blooded. Bobby tried to sneak up on Johnny with his gun drawn. "So knock, knock, guess who mother—," said Bobby, but before he could hit Johnny, a fine cord was wrapped around his neck. Bobby dropped the gun, and Johnny hit the ground and rolled. Franco strangled him; Bobby held on to the end of the wire trying to pull it off the front of his neck. Franco pulled and tugged on the wire harder. Johnny took the butt of his sawed off hitting Bobby, then he pulled his knife putting it right into Bobby's heart.

Bobby lay there with his mouth open. Johnny looked down and said to him, "Knock, knock, fucker," and took the gun beating him in the face until it was no longer recognizeable.. Franco tried to stop him, and when he pulled him away, Franco pushed him onto the crates.

"What in the hell is wrong with you? Keep it down before you have everyone out here," said Franco.

"I can't help it I can't handle a gun to my head," replied Johnny. "Everything is clear, Franco, so what next? I looked into the window while you two were tickling ass. I have some bad news. Baron is strung up, and Francis is tied to a chair. They're not dead yet, but they are both badly beaten. So if we can get out were gonna have to be able to carry them out," said O'Conner.

"Damn it, how many are there ten, twelve, fourteen?" asked Johnny.

"It doesn't fuck'n' make a difference because it's more than what we brought. If I measure it out, it's three to one, and there are only six of us not including them. So what's next," asked O'Conner.

"How the fuck do I know? Damn it, shit all we can do is go in fighting. Except before we do that we have to create some type of diversion, so we can get them out of there," said Franco as he wiped the sweat from his forehead.

Inside the warehouse they removed the gag from Baron's mouth. "Lotario, why, and what the hell is going on? We don't have a beef."

Lorenzo walked from behind the table at which he was sitting. He approached Baron and then lowered the crane till Baron's face was level with his.

Franco was watching through the window and told O'Conner to look at the controls of the forklift. O'Conner nodded and knew what to do. Franco called over Danny and Phillip and told them to take the rear-door exit and come in after the first shots and not before. Barry already knew by the way Franco was looking up that he was to take the skylight. Johnny told Barry that he noticed some rope around and told him where to find it. So it was just Johnny and Franco by the front and Danny by the window.

"Baron, it's not you I want, but I have to bring him down to his knees. Nunzio has gone too far," said Lorenzo as he walked over to Francis pulling his head up. "So I get a two sons of the bastard. The night is so eventful. See, my compadre, it's not you, but you will pay so with you dead and I planned such a nice way for you to go. I put it together, so Nunzio would know you suffered into death."

Francis's face was full of blood, and he was weakened by the loss of blood where Joe Mustache stabbed him. Francis attempted to lift his head and opened his eyes as if he wanted to say something. Lotario ordered, "Remove the rag so he could say his last words."

One of their goons pulled his head up by the hair. Francis uttered, "Lorenzo, come close, I'll see you in hell."

Lorenzo slapped Francis's face so hard blood flew from his mouth onto his suit. Lorenzo took out his handkerchief and wiped the blood from his hands and tossed it at Francis.

"You're a dead man. Take Nunzio's bastard and find a way of swinging him like his dear brother."

"You dirty bastard. Leave him the fuck alone. It's me you wanted, you said so, leave my brother alone," cried Baron.

Franco gave the signal, and Barry waved to let them know he was in place. Franco knew it was on him because he had to get in without being heard or they would be dead men.

When Franco was ready, he snuck in through the front, and O'Conner whispered for him to come. O'Conner noticed a window slightly ajar but couldn't see anything in front his face since his sight was blocked by barrels. "If we can't see them, they can't see us." Franco told him to go on and check.

When O'Conner climbed in, he noticed that they were very well hidden. He went back to Franco and joined him, but he went around the side of the barrels. Much to his surprise a few barrels had been turned over, and the substance was running down the floor between Baron and Lorenzo.

While crouched over, Franco lost his balance. His hand fell in the liquid. He noticed the aroma and smiled. He went next to O'Conner, and the games were about to begin. He looked up and saw Barry was in place.

Franco took a deep breath and shot his gun into it. It ignited into a bright orange flame. The fire ran right between Baron and Lotario. Franco and O'Conner moved quickly from the barrels before the substance would go off. Barry jumped down while this was going on shooting his semiautomatic, gunning down several of them. He got himself off the rope and made his way to cover.

Lorenzo and Lotario fell to the ground. It was like a miniwar in there. O'Conner ran to the switch to bring Baron down further. As soon as he could, he lifted his arms and hit the floor. O'Conner took a shot to the shoulder. Franco got Francis to safety. He could barely walk.

Johnny busted in through the front with his sawed off pump. As if he couldn't be hit, no one noticed that there was one of the goons caught by the flames on their side. He came up from behind with a hose putting out a part of the fire. Johnny spotted him and blew the side of his head off. It was too late, that's all the space they needed.

Joe Moustache was the first over. He got into the forklift and headed for Johnny, but O'Conner was next to the forklift and had climbed up from behind. O'Connor was bleeding terribly. He reached toward Moustache, and the two fought until they both fell off. Johnny ran toward the forklift and got on it screaming for O'Conner to move. When O'Conner glanced, he saw the forklift coming right at them. He fell to the ground, and by the time Joe Mustache caught a glimpse of the approaching vehicle, it was over. Johnny ran the lift right into him straight to the wall. When he reversed, Moustache was still caught on the lift's forks.

Johnny went to help O'Conner when a bullet caught him in his side. Danny was trying to work his way from the barrels in the rear. He noticed Lotario's men weren't shooting too much at him until he realized the odor he smelled was oil burning. Phillip pulled out a knife and threw it across the room and caught Lotario trying to get out. As Lotario pulled the knife from his lower back, two of his men got him out of there.

As the heat began to rise, the sprinkler system cut on. The situation was so filled with bloodshed and destruction that in the background you could hear the engines still roaring. Danny stopped for a moment to see if he could get a fix on where everyone was. He heard a voice yelling but wasn't sure what it said. Out of nowhere, a punch from hell came and he landed on his ass. As he tried to rise again, a boot kicked him in the face. Danny rolled and got up, but this man was no joke. He grabbed him by his hair and gave Danny the uppercut of his life. He sent him up and across. When he went to leap on Danny, he quickly pulled out a small blade stabbing the man in the back of his ear. Danny moved him off and pulled himself up using the crates. Danny tried to stagger away, but the man had him by the pants. Danny was frantic, and he took a crate and slammed it on the man's head. Danny saw this didn't do a thing. Danny fumbled around for his gun but then a loud *boom*, from Johnny's sawed off took the man's head and spread it all over the floor.

"Felt like he was fucking Jason, huh, Danny," said Johnny while he brushed Danny off.

"Fuck'n' a right, the fucker didn't want to die."

"Oh yeah, he did. He just didn't want to go by himself," said Johnny as the two laughed a moment.

Barry had his hands full until Phillip came to the rescue. But much to their avail, three of Lorenzo's men were waiting for them, and Barry and Philip were cut down. At that point Johnny saw this and went into a crazy rage. Danny limping, also went wild. Franco heard the commotion and went over yelling, "Get out of there before the black gold blows sky high!" He continued, "Leave them! There's nothing you could do!" There was too many hurt, and it was just a matter of time before it would go up. Johnny, O'Conner, Danny, and Franco, got the hell out of there. Franco, the only one not injured, helped Francis while the others, limp and lame, helped one another. Baron suggested they had to go to one of his father's hideaways.

Franco didn't want to leave the others because he felt that Barry could still be alive, but he knew Philip was wasted. He ran back, but the fire was bad, and because of the sprinklers and smoke, he couldn't really see. He heard Barry crying out for help. This tore him up inside, so Franco went in through the back since the fire was bad up front. As he went in, he put his gun in the front of his pants as he walked toward Barry's voice. Franco didn't want to make his presence known.

"Franco, man, I thought I was left as a goner, man. I'm hurt bad, man," said Barry.

"Don't worry, we're outta here. Just gimme the piece. You look like shit, man. Fuck'n' Rambo bastard. You're a crazy ass. Come on, Barry," said Franco.

He turned his back, and before Barry could say a word, one of Lotario's men shot Franco in the leg. He fell to the ground with Barry. Franco took out his pistol and looked him hard into the eyes, and the man's gun let off a click. Franco smiled, then said, "Have a nice life," then *double tapped* two to the bastards head. The two got the hell out of there.

Everyone got in different cars trying not to leave behind anybody. Baron had to make an attempt in driving. Francis could barely sit up on his own. Baron told everyone what time and where to meet. First things first, and he called Nunzio and informed him of the event. Nunzio was hot under the collar. He made a few calls and set up a meeting. He told Baron to go home and take Francis to their doctor and anyone else to the hospital where Nunzio owned a few influential doctors. They all went and did as they were told except Baron had to meet up with Egypt that morning and knew he had to explain what happened to her. He had to talk with her early because that evening everyone who was anyone would be at that meeting.

By morning Egypt was still hyped up after the evening's preparations. Her phone rang, and it was Jose and his friend Carlito. They had everyone ready, and they wanted to know if Egypt heard from Baron. She realized he hadn't called her. So she asked why they wanted him, and Jose told her that they wanted studio time. Egypt told them don't worry, she'd make a few calls, and everything will be set up. Carlito and Jose were too excited.

Egypt quickly cleared the line to find out what happened to Baron. Her stomach turned in knots. Something was wrong. His machine picked up at home: no answer on the car phone. She tried the office it was her last hope.

"Hello, Heather? This is Egypt. Has Baron called in yet? Do you have any idea where he'd be?" asked Egypt.

"Ms. Arcardi no, he hasn't made an appearance as of yet, but he does have several important meetings. If he isn't coming, he usually calls in to tell me who to send."

"Who is the meeting with?"

"Mr. Stout wanted to go over the financial status, and Mrs. Jackson will be there also."

"Have all the information sent to my office and tell Mrs. Jackson to meet me there in an hour-and-a-half. I want her to brief me on what's been happening. Also make studio time available for my brother Jose. You know, you sound very hesitant, and I just want to tell you not to worry because Baron already gave it the okay. By the way, Heather, don't forget to get in touch with me as soon as you hear from him," said Egypt.

Standing next to Heather was Fatima, and she overheard her say Egypt's name. She put her hand out for the phone. Fatima said, "Hi, stranger, how are you?"

"Fatima, what in the hell are you doing?"

"I just wanted to talk with you okay. I wanted to say sorry, but you have to understand, my logic—"

"What damn logic? Logic doesn't tell someone my whereabouts. Thank goodness no one was looking to kill me. You betrayed me, how can you justify that?"

"Sure, it was wrong, but you were stupid. Do you know how many women would die to have a man like Baron? Even for Baron to give them polite conversation?"

"So I know this. He's a handsome man, so what does that have to do with telling him about me? Do you know? I really would like to know."

"Egypt, you're a blind bitch. Can't you see if it wasn't for me knowing you really loved him, you would have lost him? So I tried to override your damn stupidity. Egypt, I would leap, bound, and run the marathon to have a man like him. You know just how much he loves you, and you treated him like trash," said Fatima.

"First of all, it's none of your damn business. Second thing, lady, at this point in time, I don't want to say a damn thing to you."

"Sure. Why would you unless you were going to say thank you?"

"Thank you, thank you, for what?"

"Thank me for telling Baron or else you would have dug a hole so deep with your relationship Baron would have walked. Think not? If you won't admit it, then forget it. By the way, congratulations. I heard about your and Baron's engagement. Regardless to how you feel, I wish you the best," Fatima said very sincerely.

Egypt was quiet for a moment and replied, "So I guess you're somewhat right, put Heather back on the line."

When Fatima handed the phone back, Egypt said crossly, "Heather, next time you do some shit like that, I will give you your pink slip myself. Have a good day."

Late that afternoon when Jose, Carlito Power, Lourde J. C. and Hurricane Hector arrived at the studio, they found everything was set for them. Carlito's mouth fell to the floor when he found how modernized and extensive the equipment in the studio was, and they even had a small crew to guide them through it.

"Yo, man, this shit is pumpin'. Damn, Jose, your sister's living large," said Lourde J. C. "Sure the hell is, man. She has all this fresh shit," added Hurricane.

"My sister wouldn't have anything if it wasn't for Baron. He pulled it all together, and it was his money and connections. Man, all these props are his. Word, Egypt coldheartly dissed him. He thought that all of this would have held her. You know he was wrong because she stepped. Anyway he had to be doing something to her for her to go. I think the brother is probably doing something he ain't got no business doing," said Jose.

"Damn, Jose, what's up? Sound like you hate the brother. What's up with that? Look at what he's hookin' us up with."

"Come on, give me the reel so I can lay it down," said Carlito.

All of them got busy and were excited except for Carlito and Jose. Those two kept everything in order. Nothing seemed to get these two riled. When it came to work that's what they did. Jose was a bit on edge, so Hurricane started messing with him that he needed a good lay.

"Is Matilda holding out or what?"

"Man, you know with him, books and women don't mix well," said J. C.

Jose turned to him and went off telling him, "Why don't you mind your own business and worry about the crackhead bitch that's having your kid." J. C. jumped up at Jose, but Carlito grabbed him and told him, "Don't start none won't be none."

Lourde J. C. turned his head and said, "Jose just needs to get blown, that's all." Jose got up and walked out. Hector went to get him.

"Come on, Jose, don't let J. C. get to you. He's only fuck'n' with you, he's a dick, so let it go."

"We're ready to lay the lyrics, so come on," said Carlito from down the hall.

"I fuck'n' don't want to," said Jose.

"Jose, don't cold flip the script on me. I didn't do shit to you. So get your props together, and let's do this," said Carlito. As Jose walked back, he looked so evil. He mumbled a few words and walked in the booth. He turned to J. C. and just said one word, "Ignorant." Carlito said to Jose, "You and J. C. can take that shit into the street, but work has to be done and now. I'm fuck'n' pissed with all the bullshit around me."

Jose agreed and got down to business. But as soon as they played the tracks back and Jose heard everything, he walked right out. "Jose, what the hell is wrong with you, man?" asked Hector.

His beeper went off, and it was his girl, Ledia. Hector told Jose to wait because he had to make a call and wanted to talk with him. Jose went down the hall and showed Hector where the phone was. Hector only stayed on for a minute, and then he pulled Jose's coat and asked what was up with him and J. C.

"We all thought you knew. It was over Matilda. J. C. had been kick'n' it to her for a while. She wouldn't even return a smile. She's cold-blooded, man, and I don't know what to do. You know J. C. is a dog, and he'll kick it to any female with warm blood."

"I'll talk to him because this is fucked up, and we can't work like this," said Hector.

"Personally, Hector, I don't give a fuck," said Jose.

After their first session, they all left and headed back home. Jose had some studying to do, so he went toward Columbia U.

Most of the afternoon went by, and Egypt hadn't heard from Baron. This was starting to get to her. The way Baron appeared he was only trying to stay out of reach with Egypt until he looked a lot better. He knew he had to call in. When he did, he spoke with Serinah. She connected him to Mrs. Jackson who informed him of Egypt's intentions. He was all for her doing the meeting, but no one in the company was comfortable with her. Mrs. Jackson expressed that it's hard to understand someone to act so concerned, but stay away just until their boiling pot simmered down. Baron took quick offense and defended Egypt. Mrs. Jackson said that no one is saying she's not qualified, but she stepped in at an awkward time. Baron knew what she meant.

Right about now things were soaring for Egyptian Labels, which they hoped it could buy out Stout. That was all Baron was busting his ass for. To get his money to build with to give it back with interest. Everything had fallen into place, but the opportunity wasn't knocking yet. Not at the right door. Baron expressed his regrets, but there was no way he would get shown up. Mrs. Jackson said not to worry she'd make sure things flowed well. Baron leaned back in his Jacuzzi. The water was warm, and the heat relaxed him. As he reached for his drink, a hand grabbed his. "You know this shit's not over. I'm not laying low because I want it all even if I die trying," said Francis.

"Listen to me, Francis, if we walk out of here now we're dead men. I have every plan to get married, and I refuse to have this shit fall on it. I waited too damn long. You or anyone will fuck it up for me. So we will lay low until Nunzio takes care of it. Lotario and Lorenzo know that he's on the warpath. So for now we all are playing the waiting game. Sit back, get a drink, and loosen up," said Baron.

"The hell I will. You're too laid-back. What is up with you? I expected you out of all people would be ready to jump out for the next round."

"Why should I when they won the round. I'm not an ass. First of all I'll let someone else do it for me. Remember, ass wipe, think the police are bound to put it together and then want to ask questions. Let Nunzio and the elders handle this."

"No, hell no, you can lay there and relax, but I'm not forgetting what they did to me," said Francis as he walked out and down the staircase. Before he could get to the bottom, Lenny, one of Nunzio's men, walked in front. He told Francis of the words Nunzio had left. Francis was burnt. He turned and went back to the room.

"So, brother, back so soon? I told you just relax. The funny thing about it is I trust Nunzio with this one. Remember we're blood, and he doesn't let shit slide when it comes to that," said Baron.

"I'll lay low for a while, but if shit doesn't get fixed, I'm going too," replied Francis.

"I do know one thing is I have to call Egypt and meet with her somewhere and explain what happened."

"You mean she hasn't heard from you? Oh, you're in for it. I called Donna several hours ago."

"Let me get up and call now."

Chapter 13

It's been two months since the confrontation between Baron, Francis, and Lotario's men. All the wounds were healed, except Egypt's. She was very upset by what had transpired. That lifestyle wasn't for her, but she loved Baron and wasn't walking again.

It was nearing their wedding which was the talk of town. People from all over were coming to this event. Margherita and Carmen worked well together. Margherita wanted the best for Baron because she had never seen anyone move him the way Egypt did. And she admired Egypt because of her inner strength.

She walked over to Nunzio while he was reading and smoking his cigar. She removed it from his hand and just stood there. He ruffled the paper and put out his hand for it. She looked him straight in the eye and shook her head no.

"Margherita, I wanted it."

"You know, Nunzio, I want something too. I needed to know what were you up to. Because throughout this whole ordeal, you haven't said anything."

"What gives you the idea that I am up to anything?"

"Could it be because you have to have what you want no matter who it will hurt? I'm not an idiot, I know you, oh too well. Whatever it is you're going to do, *don't.*"

"Margherita, give me my cigar and don't do it again. As far as my son, he is a man, if he chooses to be with her, that's his business. He's a man and it's his life," replied Nunzio as he returned to his cigar and reading. He didn't even look up at her again. He acted as though she weren't there.

This made her mad, but she had a strange feeling he was up to something. She went to the phone and called Egypt and spoke with her. Egypt reassured her that there was nothing that Nunzio could do to her or Baron to spoil their moment. The two talked only momentarily before there was a beep on the line. She took the other call; it was Baron. He asked her how was she doing, but he didn't want to tell her about his trip but he had to.

He had to make a trip to the coast and wouldn't be back until the night before their wedding. She flipped, and he tried his best to make her understand that it was something he had to take care of. Egypt didn't want to hear anything, but she just made sure she got her point across.

"You better not be late or say you missed a plane just so we'll have to put it off. Nothing you could say would ease my mind, except that you'll come in a day early."

All Baron could say was he would try.

Several weeks had gone by, and Baron was still on the coast, and the days were numbered before the wedding, but Baron hadn't concluded his business. Egypt was on edge because her dress wasn't ready yet, and the rest of the wedding party still had to be fitted. Baron was going to be the only one missing at the rehearsal. This was working on Egypt's nerves. She was so tense and snapping at everyone. Her sister called her to the phone, and she snatched it asking who it was with an attitude.

"Hope that you don't always talk to people like that."

"No, just those who aren't here and their wedding day is in five days."

"I called with some good news. I'm coming in two days earlier, and I'll be leaving here on the eleven-fifteen flight, which means I'll be in early tomorrow. I'll call you when I arrive," replied Baron.

"Are you sure this isn't another false alarm?"

"Hey, butter, see ya in the morning and have the sheets warmed up."

"Don't count on the sheets. Remember not until the wedding night. I told you before and—"

"And nothing, I mean, it this time. See ya, be safe."

They hung up, and Egypt was so ecstatic. She couldn't help but smile and talk differently toward everyone.

Dionisia said laughing, "I guess he said something you wanted to hear. Now I see you're not acting like a bitch."

"Don't start with me, he's coming home tonight."

"Thank goodness he must have gotten the telegrams telling him you were driving everyone away," said Dionisia. "I know you're kidding me, but I couldn't have been that bad, could I?" asked Egypt.

"No, but we should have, right Gina?" said Dionisia.

"Well, now that you ask, yes, Egypt, you were performing like a spoiled brat. But that's nothing new now, is it? So old lady, Baron, finally trapped you, ha-ha. You know I'm not supposed to be in the wedding?" said Gina.

"Why aren't you?"

"Because I'm married."

"So it's my wedding and you're my sister and it's my day. So that's that, and if anyone has a problem with it, to hell with them," replied Egypt.

Dionisia and Gina with a few others started to get everything together before they were leaving. After everyone had left, she curled up with Baron's picture and fell asleep.

It was only 11:37 p.m., and at Nunzio's house, he was making the last nook into his master plan. He and Gabriel were making arrangements. Everything he wanted he always got, and this was going to be no different. Everything was mapped out to a tee, but now everyone just had to play their parts well and let the cards fall where they may. Nunzio didn't care if you liked or loved him after that, just the fact to do it and deal with the repercussions after. Gabriel finished on the phone with the courier and reassured Nunzio that nothing could go wrong.

Nunzio lit his cigar and offered one to Gabriel. Gabriel waved his hand to say no. He walked over to the bar and made a drink. As he swished his drink, he glared into the glass asking Nunzio, "Is this what you really want to do?" Nunzio looked him straight in the eye and told him, "I never regret anything I do." With that Gabriel raised his glass up and began to drink.

Now that everything seemed like nothing could go wrong, Egypt gets a call at 3:00 a.m. from Baron. His flight was canceled because of aircraft problems. Egypt's stomach was in a knot; she knew something would go wrong. Baron tried to make an attempt to comfort her. All she did was remind him that she was right and that Murphy's Law was going to go in effect with her wedding. She started to cry. She told him, "I feel like you really didn't want to get married anyway. I know you're having cold feet, and if you don't want to get married, it's okay. Just say so now." She rambled on that she didn't want to be stood up at the altar.

When she finally took a breath, he jumped in. There was nothing he could say to calm her down except that he'll be there. So instead he just made a bet with her, but she wasn't going for anything. Baron said good night, and they hung up. Since she felt that everything was going to go wrong, she couldn't fall asleep, so she just lay there in bed.

It was now three days before the wedding, and Egypt was getting fidgety because she hadn't heard from Baron at all since that evening. She was hoping she didn't push him. All she was doing was crying. This was a side of her she didn't know. The pressure was too much for her.

Baron finally returned and went straight to Egypt's loft. When she answered the door and saw it was Baron, she leaped on him. He just stood there with her in his arms surprised. Baron asked, "Will I always get a greeting like this when I come home?"

"No, silly, it's only because of the moment." She gave him a hug, got down, and said, "After marriage, you'll be lucky if I serve your dinner."

"So sure I wasn't going to make it right? Now what do you have to say for yourself? Let's get started with those warm sheets."

"No, I don't think so. You knew what was in store for you if you didn't make it. I'm on my way out." She started to get her coat and bag, looked back at Baron, and said, "Good thing you're back to make sure all the men are ready and have been fitted for their costumes."

"Costumes? What costumes? You mean tuxedos, right?"

"No, I made a few major changes which I must have forgotten to tell you. Sorry, just a little oversight. You know that can be expected from time to time. Arrangements and invitations and lists and people—"

Baron walked over to her and wrapped his hands around her neck acting as though he were about to choke her. He started to laugh and kissed her. He assured her that whatever she wanted to do was okay with him. She gave him the address where he had to go to be fitted. She told him that everyone in his party was due for their final fitting today. He was tired, but he went anyway.

He used her phone to get in contact with Francis. The two talked about the ceremony, but he wouldn't tell Baron what to expect. Baron wanted to know what the hell the big secret was. Since Francis wouldn't talk, he hung up on him.

Egypt said, "You know this event is being covered by magazines and the press only because of who we are. I only have one truly famous person in it. She's a good friend of mine going way back and she's pretty well-known. Her name is Conchetta Alverez. She's a tall dark-haired Latino woman with sparks just like me. We kept in touch mostly by phone and wire. Whenever she's in town, we run through Manhattan like two children in a candy store."

As the big day drew closer, Egypt was feeling those butterflies. It was getting too close for comfort, but everything she had planned was working to a tee. That also worried her. *Something had to go wrong, but what?* she pondered.

All of the costumes and accessories were ready, all but her sedan. She had several of Jose's friends including Gary who was to carry the sedan. Egypt was sure that this would be the wedding of all weddings. The church wasn't very thrilled about it, but Egypt talked from priest to assistant bishops, and finally they approved of her very unorthodox ceremony.

As she sat in her living room, she knew that the press was going to try to weasel their way in considering the many important people who were going to be there. So if they needed a story, she would give them a unique one at that.

Her doorbell rang, and she answered it. There was a delivery man there holding a large box. She signed for it, and when she read the invoice, she found out it was the ostrich feathers which arrived right on time. She was eager to open the crate, but as she started to open it, there was another knock at her door. She let Baron in, and she ran to the crate. As he walked toward it, she told him he couldn't look inside of it. This made him wonder what the hell was going on. He moved her out of the way and read the invoice sheet.

"Egypt, make it real good. What in the hell do you need ostrich feathers for and real ones at that? And whatever you do, don't stutter. Excuse me, I'm listening. You have my undivided attention," said Baron.

"Well, I wanted it to look just as real as possible, and not made from plastic," replied Egypt.

"Do you really think my brothers are going to go for this? I was surprised when I saw the getups and that went far enough for me, and now I still have to go back for a second fitting. But, baby, let's be honest. Aren't you getting a tad bit off track? It's a wedding, not a gallery show of ancient times."

"So now the truth be told. You hated it from the start .Why didn't you say that from the beginning? Now that money has been shelled out, you're gonna criticize."

"Did those words come out of my mouth? As far as I'm concerned, forget it, do everything your way, and I'll just show up."

"Wait a minute. What are you saying, that I took over? If I'm not mistaken you said the show was mine." "Next time I'll choose my words more clear. I should have said you're in charge of a sensible wedding. My mistake was saying the word *show*, right?"

"If you have a problem with it, we could just—"

"Why do you have to take everything to the extreme? Just do what you want, okay? My comments will be kept to myself, thank you very much."

"Make sure of that. I gave you a chance to do something, but no, not you."

Baron cut her off. "Egypt, I love you, but end of topic and nothing else has to be said on the matter. And before I forget why I'm here. You forgot one very important thing, darling, the honeymoon. Well, the flight doesn't leave until the following morning unless we leave on the flight before that which we have to be at the airport by 3:10 a.m."

"I don't care just so long as I'm Mrs. Baron Nicholas Gianelli," she said as she embraced him.

They kissed, and Baron explained that he had to go back to the studio for a short session with the *Harlem Nights*. He told her, "If you really wanted to," as he lifted his eyebrows, " you could persuade me to stay and I'll be late for the session."

She laughed and said, "Not until the wedding night."

"Well, it doesn't hurt to try. Oh, and don't forget that there is a meeting with Mr. Stout later also."

When he left, she went right back to the crate. She couldn't get it open, and she was getting impatient. It dawned on her to use a hammer. She ran into the kitchen and out like a bat out of hell. She pried it open and looked inside. She was amazed; it was so beautiful. The sedan chair was finished, and all she had to get were several bottles of baby oil for the men. She was deep in thought as she considered the four men she hired to carry the sedan when Egyptian Labels crossed her mind, and she remembered there was a meeting she had to attend.

"Where in the world are my stockings and my pumps? No, I can't find a damn thing around here. Okay, get a grip, Egypt, and take a moment to make sure you're getting everything. First things first. Paperwork, where the hell is my file? Okay, here it is, now trench, keys, and out the door," she said aloud to herself. She glanced around to make sure she had what she needed.

Mr. Stout was finishing the last of his arrangements for Baron and Egypt. He and Nunzio had just finalized their transaction. They toasted to their future success. Gabriel gathered his material and called his secretary to inquire about the week's meetings. Holly, his secretary, told him that the meeting with Mr. Gianelli from E. L. was canceled. Holly proceeded to say that Mr. Gianelli wanted to reschedule the meeting until after his return from his honeymoon. Gabriel told her he would get back with her shortly and hung up the phone.

"I refuse to allow him to throw a wrench in my plans, damn it," uttered Gabriel."

"Calm down. No matter what happens the only thing to remember is to let nothing detour you from the goal at hand. Relax, Stout, that bitch will not hang her Goya lifestyle on my son. That damn whore whored once too many times. What pisses me off is the way she acts so demure to me. All along she was out there fucking the world. Fix me a drink. Come to think about it, out of all my sons' bitches, she might have been the only one to refuse me.

"But her track record is amazing when you compare the rest. It was only because of the money. This floozy didn't even have enough sense to go for the money. That hot Latin lover is going to wish she backed off from my son when I destroy her in Baron's eyes. My son, Mr. Morals. Please, she will hit the curb so fast her head is gonna spin. Well, a toast my friend. To the end of the Spanish invasion. Viva la Gianelli's," said Nunzio.

"You have a way with words, my friend, you have a way with words," replied Gabriel.

Now it was narrowing down to the final count, and two dozen roses came to Egypt's door. She spun around the room a little and fell to the floor. She couldn't imagine what Baron could have written. She opened the letter and began to read it. Tears filled her eyes. In the bottom of the box was a disc. She finished reading the letter, then she played the disc.

His voice was tender and soft. It made things even worse when one particular song played. Egypt's tears flowed rapidly, and she slid to the floor. All of the memories and promises she made. Never did she think someone could love her so much. She reminisced the times they walked through Central Park. The time they made love on a park bench in the middle of winter. He even swore unconditional love. She never imagined she could have hurt him so bad. There was no way of rectifying what she had done. Egypt knew sorry could never be enough.

The phone rang; it startled her for a moment. She answered it with a tearful voice.

"Yes, can I help you?"

"What's wrong, Egypt, are you crying?" asked Baron.

"Yes, baby, but I'm happy," she replied.

"You really think I'm a fool. I would rather you just say you don't feel like discussing it than lie."

"All right I don't want to argue. Please, I'm about to get ready to head out to the office."

"Don't bother—"

Egypt cut him off abruptly saying, "Don't start. I said I was coming and I'll be there."

"Darling, that's why I'm calling just to tell you since the wedding is so close everything that was started will be handled by Daniel and Tad Millson. Anything that was to begin around the wedding and honeymoon will wait till we return. See everything has been taken care of."

"Well, I see, Baron. Job well done, but when will I take part in the decision making? This is not the time to go into it, but next time, please speak with me first."

"Egypt it's going to take a little time for me to do that. I'm so accustomed to just making my decisions and going with them. Since you weren't around, I became—"

Egypt cut him off. "Are you trying to tell me something? Are you holding something back? I'm feeling as though there is a lot more you want to tell me about my involvement or noninvolvement with the company. So speak. Why don't you speak your mind because if that's it, I understand. You really did do the work, and an idea isn't worth shit unless you go through with it," she said.

"Egypt, what in the hell is wrong with you? I can only assume you need to talk. I'll be over shortly," he said.

"Don't even worry, baby, because there's not a damn thing I want to talk about. Considering I feel as though you're only trying to appease me or shut me up. I'm not an ass. That blatantly seems to be a Gianelli trait. So, darling, if you have a problem with things let me know, and I will correct it. As for me I'm still going to the office and do a little work. Would you like to take some time off and let me handle it alone? There will be no problem. I can, you know, handle it," she said with a teary voice.

"Egypt, I've known you too long, so don't think a paltry argument is going to make me hit the roof and forget everything. No, my love, it seems you have some bottled-up feelings, and before we get married we're going to talk," Baron said in a very serious tone.

"I guess I can't stop you."

"Yes, you can just say no."

Egypt looked up to the ceiling, and tears were falling off her face. She tried to answer him without a tearful voice, but she could not. She uttered, "Do what you want. Knowing you I'll see you tonight, right?"

"Maybe," said Baron questionably. Little did she know Baron was getting tired of her indecisiveness and her sharp tongue.

Her gut was telling her that he wasn't coming. She quickly picked up the phone but remembered that she had no idea where he was. "Okay, Egypt, get it together because somewhere from point A to L, you got lost. Keep your mind focused straight ahead because, lady, if you didn't live that way you wouldn't be here," she said out loud to herself.

Downtown was in an uproar. The events of events, one of their own, climbed the ladder, and the wedding of all weddings was within a couple of days. People from her old neighborhood were so excited for Egypt even though many of them couldn't come, but this didn't seem to bother them.

Banners, flowers, and all sorts of Latino decorations were up to show their support and best wishes for her. Her mother never knew how many people there were who knew of her daughter.

Carmen sat at her window, and a sense of pride hit her. She could only pray that she and her daughter would never be at ends again. She knew that her husband would have gleamed with pride. She knew in her heart that Egypt had accomplished a lot. Since her husband's death, she hadn't had all of her children together in one place at the same time. Then she recalled that Noel wasn't coming, but she knew that she just had to have everyone there. She grabbed her sweater and went out the door. As she went out, Jose and Matilda were coming off the elevator.

"Que te pasa, Momita?" asked Jose.

"Nada, Jose, nothing's wrong," she replied, getting on the elevator. She went outside and walked around until she spotted Noel. She didn't like what he was doing, but she was tired of fighting and crying. He noticed her and felt like he was a child in trouble again. He raced over to her, worried.

"Is everything all right?"

"Noel, I know who you are and what you do, but I still love you. Please understand that all my babies mean so much to me, and just once I would like to be in the company of all of them before I die. Please change your mind and come to your sister's wedding." She knew how much Noel adored her, and she knew he would say yes.

"Momita, me amour. Yo querro mas, but that I can't give you. I lay my life down for you if you ask me to, but to go, no. *No! Si justa*, be fair, come on."

In a strong pain-filled voice she replied, "Que Dios te bendida porque yo no," and turned her back walking away.

Noel was in shock by what she said, and it appeared she meant it. He ran to her saying, "What do you mean by God be with me because you won't? Momita, you're kidding right?"

She stopped and looked him straight in the eye, said nothing, and left. He didn't know what to do with himself. He couldn't go, there was no reason he felt he should kiss Egypt's ass. What difference was there between the Gianelli lifestyle and his? Except theirs was a hell of a lot dirtier than he could ever hope to be. He went back into the bodega.

Jose was standing in front of the building waiting for his mother. When she turned the corner, he and Matilda raced over to Carmen asking her if she was all right. She didn't have much to say except that she lost her son to the *la calle*. Jose asked, "Has something happened to Noel?"

She shook her head no and said, "I don't want to talk about it."

Matilda fixed Carmen's sweater at the collar and kissed her cheek. She placed her arm around her shoulder and walked her into the building.

Jose put his hands through his hair and looked down. *What else is gonna happen?* he thought. Out of nowhere he heard his name called. When he looked up, it was Carlito and J. C.

"Yo, yo, what up? What's going down with the studio time? Bust this shit. Since your sister has all the pull, let's use it. With her you know we're gonna come off," said J. C.

"Get off my sister's tip. I'm not with it. I can't split myself from school and do that."

"Damn, Jose, man you gotta be the fucked up one in the group, right? Check it out just 'cause your ass is book smart and can't take that route don't mean I can't. Yeah, I wanna be down with the money posse and that's my only way out. You think you're the only homeboy that wants out? Fuck that I do, and the only way I can is kickin' lyrics. Are you down or not?" asked J. C.

"I don't know, just give me some time. I don't even know why I'm gonna think about it. You know Egypt is gonna cold flip on me if I fuck up."

Matilda walked over to Jose and held on to him and said hi. The one to speak to her was Carlito. J. C. just looked at Jose and told him, "Check you out later." He turned to Carlos and asked, "You breaking out or what?"

"Nah, man," he replied. When J. C. was gone Carlos said, "I told you it was because of Matilda he was acting like that."

Jose gave Carlos a pound and said, "I'll check you out later, man." He and Matilda went back into the building. When they got in the elevator, he looked at Matilda strangely. She sensed his inner repulsion too. She asked what was wrong, but he didn't reply. She began to speak asking him, "Why are you with me? I'm not as intelligent as you are by no means, and I'm not as pretty as the girls you usually had and I know it's not the sex, so what is it?"

"What? Don't be stupid. Why does it have to be beauty and brains or sex? Matilda, why couldn't it be just the total being?" he said as they walked in the front door.

"Come on, Jose, don't front on me. Tell me why?"

"Matilda, just shut up," he said and kissed her. Carmen walked out of the kitchen calling Jose and Matilda to eat.

"Why don't you call Egypt and see how she's doing," said Carmen. He called her, and they talked for a while and hung up. Egypt thought about her conversation with Noel. She knew he was right about Baron and his family, but she loved Baron regardless from where he came from. How could she hold it against Noel when it all boils down to Baron's family being involved in unethical activities?

She phoned Baron at home, but there was no answer. She noticed the time, and she was running late for her wedding rehearsals at the church with Conchetta, Dionisia, Donna, and Sharla and the rest of the wedding party. She rushed to get a taxi. When she finally arrived, everyone had already grown impatient. Egypt was very apologetic, but Dionisia called her to the side.

"Are you ready? The clock is ticking away. You'll soon be Mrs. Baron Gianelli. Did you ever think it would come to this?"

"I think if he wasn't such an ass at times, it would have happened a long time ago. But you know me, I have to take a simple thing and make it into a major problem. Mrs. Gianelli sounds real good, doesn't it? But I'm not trading in my Acardi for nothing. Who has the baby?"

"Who do you think has her? Daddy dear babysits."

"Come on, Egypt, let's get it on." Egypt and her wedding party were having the time of their lives together. They all seemed to get along well. Egypt didn't expect this to go so well.

As time progressed, the men started to roll in. But she was still waiting on Baron. It seemed as though he wasn't going to make it. When Jose arrived, he asked when the festivities were going to begin and when was Baron arriving. All she could say to him was, "He'll be arriving shortly."

Everyone took their places, and Baron came traipsing in. Francis walked over and familiarized Baron of what he was in store for. Egypt was thoroughly furious. The two talked and worked out their earlier conversation.

Tomorrow was the day of all days. The two walked out to the courtyard. Baron agreed that they both had premarital jitters. They decided that everything said should be forgotten, but Egypt still wanted to get a word in edgewise.

"Baron, it's important that I get my point across to you. I've been acting the way I've been—" Baron covered her mouth with his finger and said, "No explanations are necessary." But she insisted.

"Baby, you could never imagine what it's like to be a Latino woman. More so than that one who is willing to fight against the odds—to break ground for others. I went to school and worked my butt off. I always wanted to sing but saw too many of my friends get taken in. I just didn't want to be another statistic. When I came up with the idea of Egyptian Labels, you know I ran from one end of town to the other. I tried places in New Jersey and Connecticut, but no one wanted to get into it. You were right out there with me with the same idea, my idea. All ears turned your way. I couldn't help but be hurt, wouldn't you? So what do you expect from me? Egyptian Labels was and is mine. To know that if it weren't for you it would still be a dream.

Even though I knew you helped me because of your love for me, it still didn't matter. Why could people hear the idea the same from me, Baron? Why, because I'm a woman or, for that matter, Puerto Rican. All these years I've known it was because you were a man, and the business world seems to prefer a man's point of view before a woman's and especially a Latino one for that matter."

Why are you with me, Egypt? Please explain why are you with me? Can you explain why in the hell are you marrying me if you feel that way? Tomorrow is the day. Are you saying you don't want to?"

"Baron, I never said that I didn't love you. That never came out of my mouth. Be fair. You felt that it was important that you understand why I did the things I did. Of course I love you, babe, nothing could change that. I accept you the way you are including your crazy-ass father. Which brings me to the subject of why he was being so nice to me this evening. What's going on with him?"

"Don't worry about Nunzio. He is the least of our problems. I want to know why you took so long telling me you hate me for helping you."

"No, I didn't say just that. There is no one I love more than you besides my family. You are my family now and I don't think you understand the point I was trying to make. I'm just upset and furious with myself and a little bit with you."

"Oh, now the truth be told."

"You just seemed to be interested in my sexual techniques more so than my mind. Okay, in the beginning of E. L. you consulted with me, then you went off with it. I started to stay more at home or just sit next to you at functions. I should have said something then, but I thought since you had more business sense, I let you talk for me. Then you would just come home and jump straight into bed. You didn't even brief me about what was happening. Next thing I know we're merging with this Gabriel Stout person. Okay, great move since E. L. soared to the top which seemed overnight. But before that, you very seldom included me in—"

"What are you saying? That I demoted you from partner to only bed partner? Get off it, Egypt. You could have said it at any time that you felt left out. Like you don't know how to express yourself. Okay, but what after everything was done and finished, you were offered a seat on the board of directors and your own staff."

"A seat and my own staff? Damn it, do you hear what you're saying? I shouldn't have been offered shit since I own the bitch. Me, I started it, and with one swift move of a masculine hand, I seemed to be out and placed underneath you. Baron, say it's not true. Think hard about what was happening around then. Plus your horny-ass father was harassing me on a regular, and I just couldn't deal with it anymore. I'm only speaking out so we can start off on the right foot."

Baron reached out for her, and the two of them embraced. He held her tight and whispered, "We should never just walk away from each other without trying to express what we're feeling. You know what? I can't believe the marvelous wedding arrangements that you've made."

Out of curiosity he asked, "How much was all of this costing?"

She just smiled and replied, "I just wanted to get married, not have a funeral. Do you mind?"

"If you don't tell me, I'll have a heart attack right here and now."

She wouldn't say. "But I will tell you this: it costs a hell of a lot less than Princess Di's wedding."

"Thank you," he said with contentment.

Dionisia and Amber walked over to them. Dionisia wanted to know if everything was all right. Egypt was acting like she just gave Baron the old one-two. Dionisia asked Baron, "Are you ready to join up with our locita family?"

Laughing he replied, "No one's family could be crazier than mine." Soon everyone was laughing and having a good time. Nunzio walked over to them with Margherita. Egypt looked at Baron and started to laugh louder. This made Nunzio feel very uncomfortable. But in his mind he knew he would have the last laugh.

Dionisia walked past him as though he were a disease. Little Amber walked outside with Egypt and Baron. Nunzio couldn't look toward Egypt as he asked Baron if he could talk to him for a minute alone. Baron asked Egypt to take Amber back inside and give him a few minutes. When they had gone, Nunzio asked Baron, "Are you sure about what you're getting into?"

"I had a feeling that this was on your mind." Baron walked away.

"Baron Nicholas Gianelli," he said, and Baron stopped in his tracks.

"Why are you doing this to me? Why can't you just accept my love for Egypt and her love for me." "Don't worry. Your eyes will be opened soon."

"What is that supposed to mean?"

Nunzio puffed the smoke from his cigar and gently giggled the ice glass and said again, "Don't worry because your eyes will soon be opened."

This was beginning to get underneath Baron's skin. But Nunzio refused to elaborate. So Baron had no choice but to ignore his statements.

Egypt couldn't take it any longer because she wanted know what in hell did Nunzio have to discuss with Baron. She walked right in on their conversation and stood there smiling. Nunzio passed and said, "You smile is very lovely, but after tonight, it will be a long time before you do it again."

This sent chills up her spine, and she quickly asked Baron, "What is he talking about?"

"I don't know. I'm just as confused as you are." All he could do was shrug his shoulders. She felt like this man was up to something, and it meant she would have to be on her guard at all times. She didn't trust him, and she was damned by this man because she didn't play his game the way he wanted her to. So with all of the plans for the wedding tomorrow, she knew it would be a day filled with times worthy of her memories.

Baron held her by the shoulder, and they walked back inside. Everyone was enjoying themselves. His brothers and his friends were singing. It was closing upon the hour of twelve, so Georgina ran and got her sisters cape and placed it over Egypt. She and Baron kissed, and he told her, "Until tomorrow, my sweet."

Egypt left, but everyone continued to enjoy themselves. Angelica and Franco were dancing in the courtyard underneath the stars. Baron looked at his baby sister and began to reminisce. He walked out and saw Elisabetta talking to one of his employees. She looked different for some reason. Franco stepped up behind him telling him, "Another one bites the dust." The two laughed and started to tease each other.

Carmen told Jose to get Baron and to start sending everyone home. The beginning event was here, and everyone needed their sleep. Shortly after, the group departed to their own homes. Baron called Francis to talk over a lot that was on his mind. Not so much about the wedding but mostly them. After an hour or so they hung up.

As the sun light gently warmed her face, a tear fell on Egypt's cheek. This was it—the moment she had been waiting for. The phone rang, and it was her mother saying she was on her way over. Egypt hadn't even received her eyesight yet, and her mother was up and ready. Her sisters as well as Amber and Donna stayed the night with her, and the rest of the women got their wake-up call from Carmen while the men got their calls from Margherita. Even though the ceremony wasn't until that evening, no one wanted any errors.

Egypt's headpiece rested on top of her armoire. As she regained sight, the sunlight bounced off the gems encrusted on it. It was so lovely that Egypt couldn't help but put it on. She stood in front of her mirror, and Donna stood next to her.

"This is gonna be one hell of an affair. So are you ready or what? Or maybe I should just open the door for you to run out. Egypt, say something!" exclaimed Donna.

"Okay, ladies, are we up and moving? Oh, I see that the queen has arisen. Come on, get a move on it. There's only one bathroom, so before

I went to bed, I made a schedule. Here's a copy for you and you," said Gina.

"Did anyone call over to Angela's place, and what about Elisabetta?" asked Egypt.

"Don't worry. Everything's been taken care of. Mrs. Gianelli said she started on her end already and not to worry. And you know Momita is up on it. She already had Jose get the men on our side of the party together. So take a deep breath. Don't sweat it, girl, everything is going down just right. Except one thing. I forgot to remind Steve to bring my makeup bag which I forgot. Let me call him," said Gina.

She ran out of the room. Everyone that stayed over was moving all about getting ready. Over at Margherita's was just the opposite. The tension was so thick you could cut it with a knife. She felt something in the air but couldn't pinpoint it. Baron called his mother, and they talked over what he and Egypt had discussed.

Margherita went upstairs to her bedroom. As she sat at the edge of the bed, she asked Nunzio what was going on. "Baron told me what you said to Egypt. If anything happens and I believe even just a little bit that you had something to do with it, it will be over for us."

Nunzio looked right through her, grunted, and rolled over. She attempted another word, but the phone rang. She answered it. It was Tony making sure that everything was going all right. "I called Baron, but his machine just picked up."

"Oh, he just had some last-minute meetings to attend. He just didn't tell Egypt because he thought it might worry her." The two hung up.

As the day progressed, everyone was doing the jobs appointed them. The church was being decorated as well as the catering hall. The sedan chair arrived at the church. The only traditional garment would be the priest in his amice. Other than that it was going to be a spectacular event.

A tremendous amount of planning, hard work, and sweat went into this celebration. Even Gabriel Stout had to admit that. But he was certainly ready for his part in this play which took a fair amount of planning also. His date, Eureka, felt she should have a front-row seat to this gala affair. Gabriel gleamed. He made his calls and finalized his game plan. Everything was set for the church.

The time had come and all were excited. The church filled with photographers and all kinds of people from A to Z. The church's decorations appeared to take you back to ancient Egypt. It was breathtaking. The trumpeting sounds of horns announced the arrival of the groom and the groomsmen.

Baron and his man were wearing the traditional garb of ancient Egypt, complete with swords and headpieces. The costumes looked totally authentic and stunning at the same time. Flashes went off like crazy. The bride's party arrived with the same trumpeting music. Following behind them were four very masculine men carrying Egypt in the sedan chair. They set the chair down, stepped back, and kneeled with their heads down.

All was quiet; they were waiting for the grand exit of the bride from her abode. Egypt stepped down with the help of one of the groomsmen. The audience marveled at her grace, style, and beauty. She was dressed in the traditional wedding attire of the ancient queens of Egypt. Her eyes were so well painted with such artistic flair that they exuded elegance, pride, as well as a flavor of sensual and erotic pleasure. She looked so graceful and beautiful that she could put any of the Cleopatras to shame.

Her uncle kept his back to her as she awaited him to escort her to Baron. He turned to her with his head down. Tears filled her eyes, but she knew she couldn't cry because of all her makeup. He gently kissed her cheek; she looked him in the eyes, and she saw it was her brother, Noel. She was so happy to see him. In fact, she was quite surprised to see him after what Jose had told her.

As they proceeded down the aisle, several women dressed as slave girls fanned them with the largest of ostrich feathers. The vibrant coloring of the atmosphere and the costumes bewildered all present. No one expected to see as much elegance in one place, especially the news media. They had never imagined something so spectacular.

Baron looked back and saw Egypt, and his mouth opened in surprise. All the groomsmen stared at her also. Francis leaned over toward Baron and said, "You sure picked the right door this time." But off on the sidelines watching every move was Nunzio.

Eureka and Gabriel both agreed this wedding was fantastic. The priest asked, "Who gives this woman into marriage?"

Noel hesitating answered, "I do."

Carmen was so happy and proud seeing him there that she cried. When they had passed her, she got so excited and was awed by the grace of the occasion. She waved her handkerchief at them. Egypt turned, smiled, and threw a kiss at her.

Francis sensed Baron's enthusiasm, and he wanted to break the tension. "Get ready for the old ball and chain, pal."

Baron grinned and replied, "As gorgeous as my bride is I'd gladly wear that ball and chain any day."

"The love bug's got you bad, man," chuckled Francis.

Egypt was so preoccupied with the decorations around her. She stopped to take in the air of the place, and she noticed that the floral arrangements were outstanding. She told herself to take a pat on the back for this one. She never expected things to come out as wonderful as they had. She felt like this was her dream come true. Only three years ago if someone told her this would happen, she would have laughed in their face.

The priest spoke a few more words and presented the mass. While he talked, Egypt noticed a shadow to her side, and it looked like her father, Jose Sr. She whispered, "Poppie?" The image seemed to be smiling at her, and at once she felt a sensation of peace envelop her. She had felt her father's presence; to her, this completed today's affair. He had been the only one missing, till now.

She continued to watch this apparition from the corner of her eye until it disappeared. Donna held her hand and asked, "Are you all right?"

"I couldn't be better," she replied smiling.

The music began, and Conchetta Alverez began to sing in both Spanish and English. Her voice carried melodious tones throughout the church; there were no dry eyes. Since all of the bridesmaids could sing as well, they chimed in on all of the choruses. This song was written especially by Egypt describing her love for her new husband.

After the song Baron spoke to Egypt. "I really most sincerely and with all my heart love you dearly."

She answered, "I know you must love me very much since you were willing to stand here in front of hundreds of people in a skirt."

Everyone snickered or giggled in a low tone at her reply. The priest asked for the rings, and the two ring bearers appeared with a small truffle with a golden platter which held the wedding rings. The two boys were pulling on the platter, and they both swung around and flung off the rings which went rolling down the center aisle. Baron and Egypt glanced at each other, turned their heads, and watched their wedding rings roll down the aisle. They looked back at each other in amazement once again.

"Is it necessary that we have them?" he asked in an amused tone.

"Well, I'm not going to get them."

"So then, let's fake it. I've got a cigar band."

"Baron just go get 'em," she said trying not to move her lips. The two boys went down the aisle to find them with the flower girls in pursuit. In the pews you could hear the people chuckle under their breath. The flashes from the photographers' cameras were having a ball with the children and the confusion they were causing. Even the priest snickered a bit.

Then out of nowhere Evelyn, one of the flower girls, yelled out, "I found it, I found it!" Immediately after one of the bearers yelled out the same thing. They then raced to the altar, and each placed their find on the platter and returned it so the priest could bless it.

After the priest recited their vows to them, Baron and Egypt recited their own to each other. When the priest announced their union, they kissed as though they were about to make love right there on the altar. The guests stood up and applauded.

As the newly married couple walked back down the aisle, she winked at Nunzio. As a response, Nunzio lifted up the sides of his lip in a snarl. Margherita caught his reaction and asked, "What are you up to, Nunzio?" He just shook it off as nothing.

When everyone was on their way out of the church, Nunzio caught up with Gabriel and asked, "What happened?"

"I'm not sure. The messenger should have been here, but the backup will show up at the reception hall," replied Gabriel.

"I don't want any mix-up with this, Gabriel." "There's nothing to worry about, just take it easy. The package will definitely get to Baron one way or another."

"Nothing better happen to screw this up or your ass is out," Nunzio replied seriously. Eureka tried to utter a few words to him, but he looked right through her as if she were cellophane. This sent a chill through her, and she became nervous.

She spoke softly to Gabriel. "What's going on with the recording I made? You still haven't told me my part in this play."

"You have no part in this, Eureka. This little performance does not include you."

There was no doubt that she was angry. She felt that if it wasn't for her this whole setup wouldn't be happening because they wouldn't have anything on Egypt. With that attitude she departed for the reception hall.

The guests arrived, but Baron and Egypt were yet to come. They were busy in the Central Park vicinity consummating their marriage. They were laughing and joking around in the back of the limo. "There are a couple hundred people awaiting our arrival."

She grabbed him by the back of his neck pulling him down in the car. By the time the two had finished their lovemaking, Baron was struggling to put her gown back together. They couldn't stop laughing because her gown was lopsided.

When they finally arrived, the entire wedding party was restless. The photographer caught the two coming out of the limo looking a wreck. Egypt's mother was standing there giving her a look of disbelief. Baron put his head down; even though they were now married it was still a strange feeling, looking her in the face.

As they went in, the music began playing softly. All heads turned. But by that time, Egypt had straightened herself and looked as radiant as before. The brightness of all the flashes blinded them.

After all the pictures were taken, the food was presented, but Egypt wanted to throw the bouquet first. At her command, the single women gathered round for the chance to be the lucky one to catch her bouquet. Egypt tried to trick the girls by faking to throw her garland of roses.

"Are you ready? Okay, this time for real. 1, 2, 3, 4, . . . nah. Wait. 1, 2, 3," she counted quickly and threw it in the direction of Elisabetta, who caught it. She held it up high for everyone to see. Egypt hugged her.

"Okay, now make my marriage a success and get married yourself. By the way you look fantastic. Ancient Egyptian attire fits you. Well, let's go see who your match is. I'll get Baron to throw my garter belt. She ran up to him. "Baron, it's time for you to see who the mate is for the receiver of my bouquet. Baron, Baron, I'm waiting," she said as she lifted up her gown.

Her beautiful legs were showing, and his cousin said, "Those legs would never wait on me." Baron went over and squeezed her face, kissing her and saying, "Hide those legs because they're mine now. And do you have to lift it so high?"

"Don't start now, Baron, just lift the dress and pull off the damn garter belt."

"All you men can do is wish and pray you get a package so well wrapped. Okay, don't crowd around so close. Getting this doesn't mean you get my wife," he said as he slipped off the garter.

He tossed it up in the air, and out of nowhere Noel leapt up and caught it. Everyone stared in silence. Noel put on a silly little grin. Egypt hugged him and whispered, "Now behave please. This is my wedding day, you know."

"Come on, Liza, looks like it's you and my brother for this one." The two posed for pictures, smiling.

"Calm down, Baron, it's only a few photos. They're not having sex okay. By the way, what is so wrong with my brother? He's not good enough or Italian enough for you?"

"Why are you going to make an issue out of it? I know you're not going by a few facial expressions? If you're so curious about what happened, just ask. If you really want to know what I'm thinking, just ask and I'll tell you."

"Since you brought it up I will. So what in the hell, no excuse me, why in the hell don't you like Noel?"

"It's not Noel, it's what he does. The life he lives. I wouldn't subject my sister to a life like that."

"But it's okay that Franco has similar business but just on a larger scale. No, not today, Baron, not on this day."

She walked into the crowd, and several people gathered around. Matilda and Jose and a few of his friends were speaking to Egypt. Noel saw a stranger walking around looking lost holding a package tightly. This aroused curiosity in him since all presents for Egypt and Baron were handed to security who placed them on tables.

Why doesn't this man place his gift with the rest of them? he thought. This act was annoying him. A few wild thoughts ran through his mind. He thought of the family his sister just married into and hoped that this stranger wasn't there to bring havoc to the occasion. With this Noel watched him more closely, and this man ask for Baron.

That was it for Noel. If this man was invited, he would have known who Baron was. Someone pointed out Baron, but before this man could reach him, he grabbed the stranger pulling him aside. He said, "Make one false move and that's all she wrote." Egypt caught sight of this exchange and moved toward them.

"Who the hell are you and what is in this package?"

"Get the fuck off me," replied the intruder.

"I'll beat your ass homeboy. Gimme that." Noel grabbed the box the man had, and at that point, Egypt asked, "What's going on here?"

After Noel explained what happened, they opened the package. Inside, there was a mini recorder.. Noel put the headphones on and listened. After a few seconds, he snatched the headphones off and grabbed the man by his throat asking, "Who gave you this to bring here?"

Confused, Egypt wanted to know what it was he heard. Noel tried to keep it from her, but she was too fast and grabbed it from him.

She placed the headphones on, listening to these strange sounds; then recognition set in. Tears began filling her eyes rapidly, and she didn't know what to say. It was a recording of her and Carlos having sex like two dogs in heat. She placed her hand on the man's genitals while Noel held him down and covered his mouth. Egypt tried her best to make this man's genitals become one. With tears falling from his face in obvious pain, she asked him, "Who sent you and where did this come from?"

The man knew, if by any chance he was caught, where to place any blame. First he cursed them both, but Noel quickly turned the man around and pushed his face into the wall bending his arm in the back like he was twisting a pretzel. Noel repeated Egypt's question with more force.

Still the man did not speak until Noel used his head as a door knocker.

"It was a woman named Eureka," he screamed. Egypt's face didn't register any surprise at all.

"Egypt, do you know this woman?"

"Noel, just finish him off," she replied.

"With pleasure, sis," he said as he commenced to beat the shit out of the man. Egypt just walked away.

After Noel was done he went looking for Egypt. When he caught sight of her, she was in the process of snatching Eureka up by the nape of her neck and dragging her into the ladies room. But before Egypt could do anything, her mother-in-law walked in.

"Is there a problem, honey? Baron's been looking for you for a while now. Everyone is waiting for you and Baron to dance because no one can until you two do."

Egypt smiled. "I'll be right out in a minute." When Margherita left, to Eureka she said, "You can't hide from me, miss. Before this evening is over, you will not be leaving the way you came."

When she walked out the ladies room, Noel asked, "What was that all about?"

Egypt replied, "Just get your brutal bouncer girlfriend to keep an eye on the bitch in the bathroom." Egypt stood there until Nelsa walked over. "Noel told me what you wanted done. I'll see to it this bitch doesn't leave okay?"

Egypt thought to herself that this was some ridiculous shit happening at a wedding. But it was definitely happening at hers. She placed that lovely but phony smile on and ran to her man. She planted a passionate kiss on his lips, and he wondered to himself what happened to make her act so different when earlier she was pissed the hell off with him.

"Baron, when was the last time I told you I loved you? No matter what asinine things happened between us. I do love you. There is no man alive that I love more than you. Until we have a son," she laughed.

"Do you know one thing? I know you pretty well, so what the hell's going on?" he asked.

"What makes you think that? Just because a few moments ago we had a few words? Don't you expect that when two people just get married? So Mr. Baron Nicholas Gianelli, do you have anything you would like to add?"

"Only, can I have this dance, Mrs. Baron Gianelli? We can leave out the Nicholas part."

People began staring at the two since they were just standing there not moving. Baron placed his arm around Egypt and appeared to be in another world. That is, Baron was. Egypt was trying to figure out how and why would Eureka do this to her on this day of all days. Baron swung her around, catching her off guard, and her head dress slipped. When she straightened it out, she caught a glimpse of Carlos.

She thought to herself why Eureka was so vindictive. Didn't she realize that what was between her and Carlos was just for the moment? Even if it was to have lasted longer, Carlos still wouldn't have wanted Eureka anyway. She kept thinking to herself how in the hell did Eureka make that recording. She knew as soon as she could she would get to the bottom of this. It didn't make any sense for Eureka to have played this fiasco now. Why didn't she just tax us with it when it happened? She couldn't see the reason in it.

"Egypt, Egypt, where are you?"

"I'm sorry, baby. I was all caught up in the music and the mood. I just floated away a bit."

"Well, float right on back here because I feel as though I'm carrying you."

"When did everyone join in the dance?"

"That's it, Egypt. What's going on?"

"Nothing, damn it. Why does there have to be anything going on?"

"Maybe because this is our wedding day, and most couples are very attentive to each other, at least on this day. You're acting very peculiar."

"Peculiar? No, I don't think that's the word. Just spacey. Come on, let's sit down or something."

"No, we have to take the 199th picture. Here comes that blasted photographer again."

"Oh, I forgot about him. Who the hell hired him anyway?"

The wedding party lined up to take the photos. All the women on the one side and all the men on the other. The children which included Evelyn, Amber, Juan, and Miguel were still excited about the pictures and lined up in front smiling like angels even though the two boys would not stand still for long.

The photographer and the few paparazzi that managed to get in were having a ball. Egypt found a way of disappearing for a moment after the pictures were done. She retrieved the recorder from its hiding place. When she reached the bathroom, Nelsa or Noel weren't there. Someone tapped her shoulder, and she nearly jumped out of her skin.

"Relax, babe, they're both inside in one of the stalls," said Noel. Egypt walked in and called Nelsa's name. When she saw Eureka she asked, "Why did you try to give this recording to my husband? Do you have some sort of mental problem or what? Because if you do, you better take that problem back to where you got it. And anyway what could you possibly gain by this bullshit?"

280

"I didn't try to give it to your husband. I had nothing to do with it. You're barking up the wrong tree. I'm not denying I made the tape, but I had nothing to do with where it ended up," she said as she laughed.

Egypt turned beet red and punched Eureka so hard it looked as if her head would spin around on her neck. Eureka hit the floor, but Egypt told her to get up. Eureka went for Egypt making her headdress fall off. But before it could hit the floor, Gina walked in and caught it at the last second.

Stunned, Gina screamed, "What the hell is going on here?" To her, her sister fighting just turned the clock back. She instinctively jumped in and pushed Eureka down. There was no way she was going to let her sister fight it out on her wedding day. She pulled Eureka off the floor and started punching her all about her face and head. Pulling her hair, she swung Eureka around and gave her a knee to her face. She continued to beat the stuffing out of her until Eureka screamed she had had enough. Even though Gina thought that fighting was barbaric, Eureka was no match for her.

They left the bathroom, and Egypt explained to Nelsa and Gina what the stress was. "It was over some old bullshit that she felt she wanted to settle with me."

When Eureka pulled what was left of herself together and took care of her many bruises, she walked out the bathroom door and caught up to Egypt. "If you felt I was a threat, just wait. This is only just beginning, sweetheart, and someone closer will be trying till he succeeds." She strutted away.

Those words rang a bell. She couldn't help but to cry. She definitely didn't want word of this scuffle to get back to Baron. She wanted the reception to come to an end right now. She wanted to leave on her honeymoon and get the hell out of New York right away and just hide from this awful mess she was in before the shit started flying.

When Baron walked over to her, she almost jumped out of her skin again. He wanted to know why she was so jumpy. She didn't reply; she stayed quiet since there was nothing she wanted to say. Noel and Jose went over to see what had happened to their sister. Jose stared at her. By his expression, she knew Noel had told him. Catching on quick, Baron realized that they all knew something he didn't.

"Is anyone going to let me in on this, or is this only for the Acardi family?" he asked.

"Stop. Don't be silly, honey. Nothing is going on. We're just reminiscing about things you wouldn't understand."

"I wouldn't? Just try me."

"Look, if she said you wouldn't understand, then you wouldn't," replied Noel.

"Don't be arrogant, Noel."

"Baron, we were just talking about how my life has turned out. From then to now and how happy you make me."

"Oh, that sounds good," replied Noel mockingly.

"Oh, stop it, Noel. Why are you always playing like that?" responded Egypt quickly.

"Can't a brother still annoy his sister even if she is married?" "Well, because the husband of the sister doesn't look like he thinks you're kidding, it just may start some bullshit that would be very much unwarranted. Thank you very much," she said sarcastically. "And the husband of the sister would appreciate it if people would talk as if he were standing here also. Thank you very much and so on and so on. Back to the issue," he said with acerbity.

"I still want to know why your headdress and your clothes look all in disarray? Make it really good but better than your usual."

"Oh, go to hell, Baron. My brother and I were messing around and acting like we did when we were young. Then I started to talk with Gina and we then came back with Jose."

"Oh, please, Egypt. They came back after me."

"No shit, Mr. Genius. I didn't think I had to tell you when you walked over now, did I? Baron, what in the hell is wrong with you? You're making me feel like I'm on trial or something when I haven't done anything wrong."

"I just sincerely hope not. Come with me because I want to talk to you privately," said Baron.

The two walked out and into the back garden. "Egypt, I do trust you, but I believe something is bothering you, and I just wanted to know if there was, I would help you."

She could not look him in the face while he spoke. She held his hand swinging it while gazing into the stars. He knew she wouldn't say anything until she was ready. She turned to face him and kissed him on his cheek. He held her tight and thought she was in some kind of trouble and that she just hadn't figured out how to express it yet. On the sidelines watching carefully was Nunzio.

He was furious. If he were a volcano, he would have had an all-time eruption. Egypt saw the look on his face and stood there, paralyzed. Baron noticed this. He rushed over to Nunzio and said, "Is this going to be a regular? Because if it is, you might as well forget about it. She is my wife now no matter how much it bothers you to face it. It's not going to change a thing. There's nothing you can say or do to change my mind."

"Or is there, Egypt my dear?" replied Nunzio with a sneer. "Have anything to say about your time lapse?"

"Is there something in particular you're talking about, Dad?" answered Egypt with the straightest face she could muster. By the statement Nunzio said, it told her it had to be him who was in on it. She had to make her way to Carlos soon before too much of this gets out of hand. She led Baron by the hand back into the hall.

Conchetta, watching from one of the windows closed the drape and walked over to Egypt. She asked Baron if he would mind losing his bride for a moment. Baron conceded.

"Look, Egypt," said Conchetta, "I know that there is some major shit going down, and I want to help."

"Conchetta, everything is all right and under control. I just have the usual in-law bullshit." To herself she wished it was only in-law problems. Now she felt as though this matter had better find a solution before it becomes public knowledge.

"Hey, Egypt, we go way back, and this is not your style. So of course I'm gonna see right through this. By the way your husband is a doll."

Conchetta what would you think if I were to tell you to just trust me. I have everything under control okay. So let's enjoy this reception," said Egypt.

"All right. Let's turn this party out," agreed Conchetta.

Conchetta had the band play some salsa music; and Egypt went over to her mother, took her by the hand, and started dancing with her. The dance floor became packed. Matilda and Jose looked fabulous dancing together. They kissed, and Egypt smiled. Her mother winked and told her, "She is good for Jose. I hope to attend their wedding someday."

Baron waltzed over to cut in on the mother-daughter dance. Egypt stepped over to dance with him, but he wanted to dance with Carmen. This delighted Egypt seeing her husband and mother getting along so well. They danced and laughed having a good time.

Egypt walked over to her seat, and she caught a glimpse of Nunzio staring at her wickedly. The look sent a cold chill down her spine. She knew that from this point on, it was a silent war of the worst kind between them. She looked to Baron for support and comfort and looked back at Nunzio, but he had disappeared. This spooked her. She looked around to the opposite side, and there he was.

"Egypt, what's wrong?" asked Carlos.

"Oh, Carlos, it's you. You know what that bitch Eureka did? She recorded us in bed together and tried to pass it off on Baron. She even tried to say she had nothing to do with it. I don't believe that bitch for a minute. But I think I know who played a major part in it," explained Egypt.

"What? I can't believe that. Why in the hell would she do something like that? Or anyone else for that matter," questioned Carlos.

"In the face of sane people you would be right," said Egypt. "But we are dealing with irrational souls;especially my father-in-law. I know he dislikes me, but I would have never imagined in my wildest dreams he would try to really come between us. I don't know how I'm gonna handle this. What can we do?" she asked him.

"By any possible means, can you tell your husband the truth? Have you ever thought of that? If he really loves you, he'll understand it happened while you were both apart," said Carlos.

"Stop and listen to what you just said. Would you?"

"Okay, let's forget the truth for now. How can you explain it if it does get back to him? If your father-in-law has that much power as they say, then you're up shits creek without a paddle or a boat."

"Thank you for summing up that I'm about to drown. Do you have a life preserver for the both of us? Because I'm not the only one he may try to drown with this."

Carlos replied, "He has no interest in me. Or else—"

"Or else what? He may not have any interest, but we know Eureka sure in hell does. Depending on what our little jewel has acquired, we don't know if she has it in for you or not. Crewman don't just jump ship into shark-infested waters.. Carlos, we have to plan this out together. Like I've been saying, "what are we going to do?""

"Now that you've shed some light on the situation, I have no alternative but to meet up with the little psychopath and ask her what she's up to. And then play it by ear after that and hope for the best."

"How is it going to make any damn difference if you talk to her? I have to get back out there and mingle. So when I get back from the honeymoon. I'll have to get busy on a solution," replied Egypt.

"Carlos, Egypt, the party is in there," said Dionisia pointing at the dance floor. "Why don't you come join us."

The two walked in, and Dionisia held Egypt's arm telling her what she saw didn't look appropriate. .

"Dionisia, get your mind out of the gutter and wait till you're home with hubby." They shared a laugh. At twelve midnight the clock struck, and Baron lifted up his wife and they disappeared in the limo. Their luggage was already packed and waiting for them. When they drove off amidst waves of good-bye, good-luck wishes and thrown rice, they continued where they left off when they were around Central Park. When they arrived back at the house, they changed and left for the airport before they missed their flight.

No one was told where the lovers were bound. This they felt added a touch of mystery to their departure.

Chapter 14

Three months have now passed since the wedding. Things were turning out for the best for the newlyweds until the evening of Wednesday, the third. Baron and Franco were talking together when a hail of shots aimed at Baron hit Franco. Fortunately for Baron, Franco had successfully pushed him out of the line of fire. Since being in the hospital, Baron hadn't left his side.

Egypt showed up at the hospital with a change of clothes for Baron. He looked awful which worried her. She had wanted to tell him her good news, but she felt it wasn't the right time. She recently found out she was six weeks pregnant. She was so happy. And this time, she thought, *I'm not sick at all.*

She gave him his clothes, and he placed his head in her abdomen. She didn't know how long she could compose herself, so she told him, "Honey, he'll be fine, wait and see."

"I know, but I want to be here when he wakes up. If it wasn't for him, I would be lying right beside him or lying in a pine box."

Angelica wasn't taking the matter too well. "I'm sick and tired of this family and the way they live. I wish to hell I was never a Gianelli. They all make me sick to my stomach." She kissed Egypt and told Baron to go home and get some rest and that she would call if anything changed. Baron stood up, and when he did, Egypt noticed that he hadn't shaved.

"Come on, baby, you did all you could, okay? Let's go home. He's still in stable condition," said Egypt.

"Yes, go home, Baron," added Angelica. "What can you do? There's nothing anyone can do now except hope everything goes well, and believe me it will. I love you, Baron, now go rest."

"Okay, but please call me," he said. We walked over to Franco, held his hand, and moved his hair and replied, "Don't let me down."

As Baron walked in his bedroom, he sat on the floor. Egypt ran the bathwater for him. She coaxed him in the water so he could relax. But he was so distant she couldn't stand it. She didn't know how to snap him out of his depression. Suddenly she decided to remove all her clothing and get into the bath with him.

After she washed him down, she lay in front of him, and he placed his arms around her. She turned toward him and kissed him.

"Baron, you know I love you. So understand what I'm about to tell you. See what your sister is going through? That could be me. I know you haven't forgotten it because that's the reason why you're acting this way. Which is understandable. But I don't want to go through the anguish, hurt, or the loss. Please get out and now. We have a great business which is ours. There's no reason why you have to be like Francis or the damn Nunzio. It may work for them but not for you. Baron, do you hear me?"

"I was waiting for you to finish. Give me a day or so, and we can sit and talk about it. At this present moment I can't think straight, and I don't want to say okay and then not go through with it." Baron got up out of the bathtub.

After that exchange, she felt she would leave it alone. She also noticed that he might have pepped up a little, so she ran through the house naked to get some ice to fix him a drink. When she returned, he was fast asleep. She slid under the sheets and curled up under his arm. She missed the comfort of her man. It seemed to her any eternity since they actually slept in the bed together.

The phone rang, and she leaped up to get it before the sound could wake him, but he too heard it and grabbed it before she could.

"Baron, they're taking him in for surgery because he started hemorrhaging. A bullet still lodged inside shifted and that's what caused it. Baron, would you come up here? I need all the support and comfort I could get."

Baron was dressed and out before Egypt could say a word. She tried to get dressed and catch up with him, but he was gone. She was livid because she wanted him to stay away from there. She couldn't understand why Angelica would do this when she knew he needed his rest. She called a taxi to take her to the hospital. She certainly wasn't going to let him go alone.

When she arrived, Baron and Angelica were talking with Franco's doctor. He was explaining what they just did for him. "Everything is going well now, Mrs. Delucco. In time he will be up and moving about as well as before. If you want, you can go in to see him but only for a moment. You should be home and getting some rest because he'll need you strong to care for him so he can heal properly."

"Thank you, Doctor," she said and headed for the ICU. Baron looked over his shoulder, and there stood Egypt. He walked over to her. "You know, the best part of everything is that somehow, someway you're always by my side. Butter, what would I do without you?"

"I wonder myself," replied Egypt. "But I know I'd go crazy if this were to happen to you."

"Okay, I'm getting the feeling we're going back to the conversation I want to avoid. So let's just go home and skip the confrontation. Deal?"

"I have no problem with that. But we're gonna have to deal with it sooner or later. I'll hold back, but when the curtain goes up, you've got a lot of explaining to do."

"I'm hungry and tired. "I can't decide which one is winning," he said as his stomach growled in demand of food. "All right, there is our answer, hunger won. Let's go to Le Bleu."

"No, let's go home, and I'll cook. I can do that you know," she said sarcastically.

"You mean that's what you were doing? Could have fooled me." Egypt's made a face. "No, come on, you know I'm just kidding you. Home it is, Egypt."

They started for the exit.

"You know I'm only kidding you, sweetheart," said Baron. "You had better be only kidding. I noticed you eat my food when I cook it. If it's that damn bad, I'll just send you home for dinner. It makes me no difference what—"

Baron covered her mouth with his hand and led her to the parking lot. Egypt drove home in a wild frenzy and almost killed them both on the way. When they walked into the house, he started laughing.

"I can't believe that you took all that to heart. Can't you tell that I was only teasing you? Come here, my sick one." Baron held her around her head. "Gimme a wet one," he said seductively.

"Do you want it rare, well done or—"

Baron kissed her to shut her up. Her kisses felt a little out of sorts to him. She was acting strange, but most pregnant women do. He was slowly catching on to the fact that she was acting a bit peculiar. "What's been bugging you? You seem a bit tense and crabby all of a sudden."

This comment startled her. She quickly replied, "Nothing's wrong with me." She didn't want to let on to her condition—not yet. She tried to laugh it off, but somehow he was not totally convinced but he took her word for it.

"Baron, I'm just worried about you and everything that's happened to you so far. I'm just scared that something bad will happen and you'll leave me, and I don't want that." Her reply to him meant that she had to be more careful of what she was doing and saying until she felt it would be appropriate to tell him. With Franco and the fact that someone out there wanted him hurt didn't make pregnancy all that delightful.

Baron tapped her and asked her, "Butter, what are you thinking about?"

"Oh, nothing. Why, does there seem to be a problem or something?" she replied.

"No, I just asked a question. I can't do that anymore it seems. I know you said you've been worried, but it's all over now. Thanks."

"Why are you thanking me?"

"Because of your actions, you showed me a lot."

"If I didn't love you, you moron, I wouldn't give two fucks in a duck's ass. Now would I?"

Baron picked her up and carried her into the bathroom. He put her in the tub and turned on the shower. She screamed and he laughed. She grabbed the nozzle and turned it on him and drenched him. He entered the shower, and they both played a water fight until he caught hold of her and kissed her so passionately. She tore open his shirt and started biting his chest leaving small marks.

This turned him on, and he began to undress her. He looked as though he were a ravenous wolf about to spring on a defenseless lamb. Egypt fell to her knees and kissed the inner of Baron's thighs. The sensation was so overwhelming that he had to hold on to the walls for fear of losing his balance.

They hadn't lusted after each other in a long time. The two stumbled out of the bathroom still clutching each other unaware of their actions. They tripped into the bedroom where Baron pushed everything off the writing desk onto the floor. He sat her on the top and began to make love to her rapidly. As he held her buttocks she latched onto his hair pushing his face in her breasts. The two panted like a pair of panthers without enough air after a successful kill.

Egypt was sweating all over. Her nipples were covered with beads of perspiration. He licked them off tenderly. He lifted her off the desk and moved her to a chair. On the chair he moved soft and passionate. This sent a chill down her spine. He whispered to her, "Baby, you feel so warm and soft to me. I know this couldn't be feeling the way it does."

Egypt felt finally that things were falling back into place. From the chair he leaned her forward and gently to the floor. For a few moments he stopped moving and gazed down at her in silence. She asked if there was anything wrong, but he shook his head no.

"I just want to look at you."

"Why, have I changed in the last few hours or something?"

"Just for that, you sarcastic pain, have it my way then." Baron entered her hard and forceful, but she let out a sigh of all sighs. Holding him by his shoulder blades, she dug her nails deep within his skin, leaving cat marks from his neck to his buttocks. He let out a painful bellow, but this did not stop them from continuing with their feverish and hot escapades. This act brought him nothing but pure pleasure.

She rolled him to his side and got up. He was surprised that neither of them was finished. On the contrary, it was far from over.

She ran over to the door calling him to her. When he got up, she moved away; she felt a bit playful. He tried to catch her. Since she knew no one was likely to come by, she wanted to take advantage of it. She grabbed a sheet from off the floor, and as quick as lightning she wrapped herself in it. She looked like a Greek goddess which enticed Baron more.

She ran out the room and headed for the dining room. She lay across the table and reached for the long matches in the matchbox, struck it, and lit the candelabra. He watched the glitter of light flicker off her body. As he approached her, she began breathing heavy; the anticipation was overwhelming. He made sure he took his time. When he stood directly in front of her, he placed his hand on her thighs and slowly removed the cloth from over her. He pulled her up and put his head in her bosom. He loved her breasts the way a child loved his favorite stuffed animal.

He placed his mouth over her ample breasts and nibbled his way to heaven. She arched her back in pleasure of his tongue and lips. He laid her back down and began to kiss her inner thighs and approached her passion area. He stopped and whispered, "Do you love me for me or for the way I make you feel?"

"No, Baron, don't do this now."

"I guess if you have to think about it, I guess that's my answer."

"I know what you're doing. Baron, you know I love you, but if you want to stop and discuss this right now I'm willing," she said and laughed to herself. She knew Baron would never stop his lovemaking for anything in the world.

"What, are you serious?" He kissed her neck and placed his hands on her buttocks. "Take me, Baron," Egypt said. He didn't hesitate at all. They were at passion's delight.

She glanced at their silhouette upon the wall. She envisioned them in the wild among trees, vines, and exotic birds of flight. This set her in the mood even more. She pulled his face up by his hair and called him her jungle lover. They were at it so intensely that she ended above him and couldn't remember how she got there.

He called to her in a deep sexual tone. She told her stallion that his journey had just begun, and in the heat of it, she took him and made her way with him.

The beads of sweat rolled off her forehead to her chest. As she shook the sweat off her, it flicked on him. Baron's heart was beating rapidly in ecstasy as Egypt called to him in Spanish. This was the crème de la crème. Even though they were short of breath, their wild lovemaking did not slow their pace at all. Egypt appeared to be determined to exhaust Baron; he wasn't about to let that happen. They knew that neither of them would be able to last longer. It seemed to be an endless night.

Suddenly, a breeze from a slightly opened window sent chills through them. Baron let out such a bellow that Egypt thought he was speaking in tongues. Actually, he was lost in such a state of passion that he started speaking Italian to her.

"Baron," she said in a breathless voice, "I had no idea you could really speak Italian. Those words really turn me on."

He looked at her and smiled. Out of nowhere their bodies moved in sync, and the exotic emotions had reached their peak and the two crumbled in a puddle of sweat.

Amazement showed on his face as he awakened to the warmth of sunlight. He looked around to notice he was on the floor with Egypt under the dining room table. He moved some chairs so he could stand up. He glanced at her, and she looked a complete mess. He walked to the shower, stepped in, and felt a hand on his buttocks. Egypt had slipped into the shower to start another session.

"No, Egypt. I have to get to the office, and before I go, I wanted to visit Franco. Stop, I'm serious." Egypt's caresses went unheard. "Stop, we could do this later."

"Maybe I won't feel like it later. That's all right because I have a doctor's appointment anyway. So will I see you at two-thirty or what? Are we going to the meeting together, or is it going to be another separate type of thing?"

"What difference does it make if we're together or not?"

"Well, if I say one thing and you turn around and change it, that makes me look as though I have no say and this keeps people from trusting my word. Gimme the soap."

"Here's the soap. What do you mean that no one will trust you?"
"You're missing the point, Baron. Move out the water please," she said. She continued, "If I say I want something done in four days, they go to you and complain and you give them seven days without even confronting me to see if there was a reason why I needed it in four. The keyword is *undermine* me."

"If you felt this way, why did you wait so long to tell me? Could you let me wash the soap off me?" Baron continued, "Egypt, why couldn't you have brought this to my attention when it first happened?"

"I didn't know how to approach you with it. What the heck are you doing?" Baron splashed her with water again. "Hey, quit splashing water in my face. Stop it, Baron!"

Baron leaped out of the shower and turned off the hot water leaving her to freeze in the cold water. He laughed and grabbed a towel. All you heard was fowl language coming from the bathroom. She ran out also and chased him through the house. Baron continuously repeated for her to stop because he was running late for the meeting.

"Egypt, I already told you that I wanted to see Franco. What's wrong now," he said while putting on his clothes. She said nothing as she lay across the bed watching him dress. "Egypt, what's on your mind?" he asked. She didn't reply. She got up leaving her towel on the bed to fix his tie. She walked over the nightstand and stared at the phone as if he weren't there. He knew this was a ploy to make him feel bad. But in the frame of mind he was in, it wasn't going to work.

"Baron, you never answered me. Are you attending the meeting or not?"

"I doubt it. It truly depends on how things flow this morning. Look, if I can't make it, I'll have Heather get back with you. What do you want me to do?"

"If you don't show up, I'll just cancel it. I have no problem with that, do you?"

"Egypt, you seem to be trying to crawl under my skin, but it's not going to work today. So before we get into it, I'll eat out and see you later," he said as he gathered his things to leave.

Egypt was burnt, and she really couldn't put into words what she wanted to say. It felt as though what was in her mind couldn't come out properly the way she wanted. After she finished dressing, a sudden taste hit her mouth. It was a curdling taste on her tongue. Out of nowhere she ran to the bathroom. She began hugging the porcelain bowl. When she finished, her eyes were full of water, and her stomach ached. In the mirror she saw the first reflections of pregnancy. *How was she going to hide it from him?* she thought.

As she rinsed her mouth and face, she walked out and back in the bathroom again and repeated the ritual. She wasn't handling her little secret very well. She completed dressing and tried to leave the house, but she was hesitant to go. But everything seemed to be all right, so she left.

When she arrived at the office, she went to go see Ms. Jackson. As she passed Serinah, she told Egypt she seemed a bit flushed. This worried

Egypt, so she went straight to her own office and told Serinah she didn't want to be disturbed by anybody, not even Baron. It was nearing the lunch hour, and she made a call to the local deli.

She then told Serinah that she would be taking a long lunch and not to bother her until she was finished. When the delivery boy arrived, she leapt to the door. Catherine was there and said, "Mrs. Gianelli, I paid the delivery man, and I brought you the box since I wasn't going out to lunch." She placed the box on Egypt's desk.

"Are you expecting someone for lunch?

Egypt didn't want to explain all the food so she just smiled and offered some to Catherine. She declined and replied she was on a diet.

"I guess I got a bit carried away with the menu. Ha-ha. You know when your eyes get bigger than your stomach, ha-ha. Are you sure I can't convince you to join me, or did you bring your own?" Egypt asked.

"No, that's okay. I better just go outside for a little while and soak in some sun since it's such a lovely day. I would suggest that to you, but your lunch is a bit too heavy to be lugging it around. I'll see you in an hour." She rose to leave.

Egypt sat in her chair and looked like a child in a candy shop. She ate nonstop. When the door opened and she looked up, it was Baron and she choked. He ran to her and tried to help, but she signaled that she was okay. This was not a sight he was accustomed to seeing, but he had more important things on his mind.

He explained, "Egypt, I have some family things to take care of."

Her expression said a lot more. She never replied. As she finished eating, she looked up at him and asked, "If I said don't go, would that make a difference?"

"It's just one of those things that can't be helped. I have to handle it myself. This is a part of my life. Everything can't be planned to the exact second like you would like it to." Egypt rose and opened the door for him. "Well, go handle it then. You know how I feel about that," she said. Baron looked at her like she was crazy.

Egypt noticed that her stomach was getting that tingle, so instead of getting into an uproar, she closed the door behind her and quickly got on the elevator. When Baron got to the door and looked around, she had vanished. He wanted to go after her, but he didn't like running after her when she acted like this. So he waited in her office and sat there for about ten minutes.

He thought he would make some calls from there. As he looked around for Daniel's extension number, he came across a little drawer with a very modern lock. This sparked his curiosity, so he tried the lock. It was open, and he looked inside and staring at him was the shiny new barrel of a .22 caliber handgun and a mini recorder. He didn't like being nosey, but his interest got the better of him.

As he started to play the recorder,, Egypt's buzzer went off. It was Catherine asking him if he wanted to take a call from Francis Gianelli. He said over the intercom that he would and picked up the phone and placed the recorder on the desk.

"Catherine, how did you know I was in here?"

"Easy. I was walking back into the outer office, and I saw you entering while your back was turned. I didn't say anything because I thought Mrs. Gianelli was with you. Do you want the call or not?" she asked.

Baron took the call. It happened to be Francis calling from his car phone. Whatever it was that Francis said it made Baron get up and leave without realizing he didn't put the recorder back where he had found it. When he realized it, he was already out of the building. He figured that when he saw Egypt he would explain.

When Baron reached his car, Francis pulled up and told him, "Leave it and ride with me." As they pulled away, they noticed Egypt sitting near the statue in the front of the building. She saw them leaving and turned her back; Baron knew she saw them. He had a gut feeling that when he returned things weren't going to be the same. Francis noticed Baron's silence and asked him what the matter was.

"I saw Egypt sitting by the statue, and she knew it was us. I felt just a bit funny because I went into her private drawer, and I didn't put her mini recorder back that I had found. That's all."

"Well, all I can say is that the best thing to do is to get this over with and discuss it."

"That's easier said than done. You don't know Egypt very well, I see. She's a doll, but when you get into shit like this, she's a damn pain in the ass. She doesn't and won't understand that this so called business is something that you can't just walk the hell away from. If it were—"

"Don't say it because you know you couldn't leave it like that even if you were never interested in it anyway. After Nunzio was hurt, he would have stayed out. Who are you trying to kid, Baron? Yourself maybe but not me. Before Egypt married you, she knew this was your life. And when she was living with you, she knew this was your family. Unless you made the fatal mistake by telling her you would stop," said Francis.

"Enough. I don't want to get into that now. We have too much shit to take care of and I don't want to go into my home with any bullshit. Besides, what are we worrying about Egypt for? I have everything under control."

"If you had everything under control, why are you so worried? Forget about it for now. If we don't hurry up, we're going to be late. Call the airport and make sure the plane is on schedule."

As Baron made the call, surprise hit his face. "Plane? Oh shit, I forgot to tell her that part. I have to call the office first."

"Baron, you can call from the plane. We'll be there in a few. Don't even bother with the airline. How's Franco by the way? Is Angelica taking it bad?"

"I saw him this morning. He'll pull through all right, but I'm not too sure about Angelica. Francis, she's making arrangements to divorce him if he stays within the family. Nunzio is trying his best to make him feel welcome. He told Angelica that Franco was a man, and if he chooses to be in the family, that she would have to accept it," said Baron.

"He doesn't mean it. If anything, he's hoping Franco grabs his masculinity and stays where he is and Angelica keeps her stubbornness and divorces him. If I know Nunzio, and believe me I know him, he'll let Franco stay a while, get comfortable, and then he'll be a dead man. Your father is not the forgiving type," replied Francis.

"You would think after all that has happened, he would let the hell up? But who in the hell are we talking about? The demon of all demons, Nunzio."

"Come on. Before we miss the flight, did you make sure everyone would be there before we will?"

"Of course, they arrived there two nights ago and made sure that everything was secure. I could sure use a drink right about now," said Baron.

Baron was on his way to the airport, but back at Egyptian Labels, Egypt was nervous wreck. When she had returned to the office, Catherine had told her that Mr. Gianelli stayed behind for a while awaiting her return. Egypt sat at her desk and noticed something odd. Tears filled her eyes when she noticed the recorder left on her desk. Somehow he had found her secret drawer and had opened it. She didn't know how, but she knew that he must have done it.

The recorder that sat in front of her reminded Egypt of her wedding day. She always said that what you do in the dark comes out in the light. She just wanted to be the one to bring it out. She buzzed Catherine and asked her if she had any idea how he left.

Catherine had no idea what she meant. Egypt repeated the request. But to Catherine it seemed like she was talking Russian. Egypt asked, "What? Was he happy, sad, mad, glad, craved, or indifferent?" Catherine replied, "He just seemed in a hurry to get the hell out to me."

"Thank you, that's all." Catherine departed. Egypt just stared at the recorder on her desk wondering if he played it or not. She honestly didn't know why she saved it. Her private line rang. "Hey, babe. I'm flying over Philadelphia, and I just wanted you to know where I was and I wanted you to know that I'll be returning soon."

A lump grew in her throat. "What brought the trip on?"

"I'll discuss it when I see you." Egypt just knew he had listened to it.

"Egypt, are you still there? I'll call you this evening, okay?"

Egypt didn't respond at all. Not even a single wise crack left her lips. This left Baron worried. She was too quiet and understanding.

Baron walked back to his seat and told Francis what happened. He told him to let it rest because he had other matters to place his concentration on. Baron called to the flight attendant and ordered a double scotch.

"Francis, what worries you more than anything when there is a problem facing you?"

"When the problems seem to level out without a resolution."

"Right, my dear brother. The quiet before the storm."

Egypt sat at her window looking up wondering what was going through Baron's mind and if he were indeed coming back after hearing the recording.. She rested her head in her hands and began crying. She had her secretary cancel all her meetings for the day because she had to go home. As she left the office she ran into her brother Jose.

Jose grabbed her by her shoulders. "What's wrong, baby?" he asked.

She didn't choose to speak on her matters right then. Jose wasn't going for that since he could see how upset she was. "Egypt, we have a few minutes before the meeting with my lawyer. Let's talk."

She had completely forgotten that the meeting with her brother and his group was the beginning of a possible career for them and that was very important to them. But she simply couldn't stand there in front of him with her eyes filling with tears.

She told him, "Wait a minute. There's something I have to do. I'll have to see you later," she said, kissed him, and ran back into her office leaving Jose looking bewildered. She called on her assistants to take her place at the meeting and then ran for the elevator. Once inside she wiped her eyes and just gazed at the mini recorder she held in her hands. By the time she arrived home, the office had called and left a message on her answering machine asking her to get back with them. There was a breakdown in the studio, and since they couldn't get in touch with Baron, they needed her to supervise anything that needed to be done as far as repairs were concerned.

Her phone rang off the hook, but she didn't answer one call. Heather paged Baron. When he called and was told no one could reach Egypt, he really began to worry. He started thinking about her recent illness and erratic behavior and wondered if she were all right. "What should we do, Mr. Gianelli?" asked Heather snapping him out of his dreamlike state. "What about contacting Mr. Stout?" she continued.

"Heather, I know you know that our company is no longer affiliated with his, so it's none of his concern. Just tell the technician in charge to have everything taken care of, and if they need a signature, have them fax me at 1-800-555-5555. If anything else happens, page me then."

"What about Mrs. Gianelli? Should we still try to get in touch with her?" asked Heather.

"No. Whatever happens, just page me. She didn't leave a memo to where she would be, did she?"

"No, according to Catherine her next two days of meetings were canceled without reason or rescheduling," she replied.

Baron hung up and went back to his seat. He told Francis that he thought something was really wrong with Egypt. Unknown to him, it had more to do with just him going into her desk and retrieving the recorder. It was much more than that. This thought weighed heavy on his mind.

For what was about to go down in Miami he needed to think clearly. "You had better not make the wrong moves when we arrive because I don't want either of us to end up the way Franco did," stated Francis.

"That was only a fluke, and you know that," replied Baron.

"Just make sure that's all it was—a fluke. There have been too many slipups, and things are no longer working like clockwork. There have been way too many hits lately, and now there's an overload of police officials involved."

Francis threw more shit on Baron's shoulders. As for the officials, he forgot to tell him of the new shit which came up for the reason Franco being hit.

"Did I tell you about tap upon tap?" asked Baron.

"Baron, you really think I'm a fucking ass wipe. I didn't need to be told because I practice that precaution always," he replied.

The plane landed, and their limo awaited them. Everyone who was anyone would be there for just an hour long talk. This would be damn near to impossible to catch a recording. "Even if anyone did," said Francis, "it would be only one statement with no replies. It's either follow that statement or be prepared to fight. Simple, isn't it?"

No answer came from Baron. He was in a world all his own. When they reached the meeting place, it smelled of cigar and cigarette smoke, plus the unmistaken aroma of booze. The topic of discussion didn't sit too well with either Baron or Francis.

It's Franco we no longer trust, if I ever trusted him at all," someone barked. "His people have been getting too much of our business, and it must be him who's leaking all over the place," they added.

Baron hit the roof and began spouting retorts of his own. Francis grabbed him before he put his foot in his mouth and aroused the anger of the group, but he wasn't going for it. "Silence! I will have silence in here, or this shit is done before it's started," said a man sitting at the head of the table.

"Get the fuck off me, Francis," yelled Baron banging on the table. "How and who the hell do you think did this?"

Someone produced a handkerchief with Baron's initials on it. Baron grabbed it out of his hands and said, "All of you can go to hell!" Baron walked out steaming.

Francis stayed behind to try to calm things down. No matter what he tried to say to cover up Baron's response, the board didn't want to hear it. He asked for time to settle down Baron. They conceded, but Francis and Baron were fined because there was to be no replies on their part. Francis told them he would take care of Baron in his own way the best he could.

They got back in the limo. When they spoke, it seemed nothing could be said to calm Baron down. "It's not like I want to see anything happen to Franco."

"I know that it was Nunzio that was pulling trump cards from behind his back!" he yelled. He was very pissed off.

"Frankly I think it's about time to talk to the old Don. Too much shit is going down for me, and I think his hands are quite dirty," said Baron. "Francis, are you coming with me or what?"

"Baron, there is no way I would let you confront him alone. I definitely feel sorry for Nunzio right about now."

"Oh, how quickly we forget. I know he's our father, but you care more for him than I ever will. Besides the name, you are damn near his twin."

"Baron, I know you're in a fucked up state of mind with what's going on right now. So before you and I end up on opposite ends of the rope, we'll bring the note of Nunzio to a halt. Are we staying, or do you want to get back to New York?" "After I acted the ass in there, I think it's wise to leave because there's no way I'm ever going to hurt my sister." Baron realized there had to be a hit out either for him or his family or else Franco wouldn't be lying in the hospital. He didn't need to end up at odds with anyone. There has got to be a solution to this dilemma.

They arrived at the airport, and Francis was trying to book a flight back to New York. He was told there was one leaving within the hour.

There were a few seats left for first class, and he took those. They were on their way back in an hour.

Nunzio had received a call telling him the outcome of the gathering, and they also requested something be done about Baron. Nunzio knew this; the fact was that Baron was a young upstart just like he was back in the days and tough as nails to boot. To handle this one was going to take kid gloves and no trip ups. Baron wasn't going to crumble easy. He was going to be the puppet to play this game. He thought his wife was on his every move; worst of all she was voicing her opinion when it wasn't warranted. He knew Angelica was too upset with Franco's situation to give him any kind of attention. Who? Now who, he pondered.

Then it dawned on him. No one better than to get screwed by your right hand. Nunzio reached Dominic and spoke to him. "We need to talk family. Business, strictly business. We're brothers, and you can't let things linger on complaining that your life was short. This appeal he made to Dom seemed sincere. Dom wanted to know how in the hell did he know how to reach him.

"Are we not family? How could I let family disappear, especially us? We're brothers, and nothing come hell or high water can ever change that."

"Eh, true, Nunzio. What is there to talk about? Let's leave all that shit behind and move our way," said Dom. "Our separate way. How's that? Let some street dame do to me what they did to you without my knowledge. Shit."

"Nunzio, you know I didn't know she was pregnant with your child until a long time after. I didn't know," said Dom.

"Besides," said Nunzio, "it was way too late to tear us apart. I, eh, you know how I feel about your family, the whole thing. Come on, Goomba, how about some dinner. What do you say, eh?" Dom nodded his head yes. "Okay then, tonight."

"Tonight, Nunzio, tonight," replied Dominic.

He wasn't too sure of what his next move would be, but between now and tonight, it would be mapped out perfectly. Next thing was to set up another meeting, but he himself would go. *No messengers this time*, Nunzio thought to himself. Everything will be taken care of now. Nunzio lit his cigar and sat back in his chair. One of his men came in to let him know that he had some news that Pepito from Chicago was here in New York.

Pepito only comes in and out and just leaves a trail of bodies. The fact that Pepito was in town worried Nunzio because neither he nor the men on his side didn't call him here, and he didn't know who did. This man had a better record than Babe Ruth had home runs. Nunzio knew that if the Board hired him that he certainly would know about it. *If in fact he's here on business, then who is to be taken out?* he thought to himself. He had to send some scouts out and fast.

Late that evening, Nunzio received a call from Francis that it was urgent that they speak. He told Francis to come right away. By the time Francis arrived, Nunzio had heard from one of his people about Pepito. "He definitely is in town on business, but who I still don't know," said Nunzio.

Francis and Nunzio sat down like back in the old days and had a drink and talked. Out of nowhere Nunzio said, "I have a feeling that it's one of us who is going to be hit."

"That's insane, not one of us," replied Francis.

"Look, first of all, there were the few attempts made on Baron's life, the attempt made on mine and on Franco's life and plus the fact that now Pepito is here and nobody knows why. It all adds up to somebody over here being hit." This statement had Francis's full attention, and he put down his glass.

"How are we going to get Baron the hell out of here without anyone knowing, including his wife?" Francis said. Nunzio knew that this was the one time he had to put aside his feeling about Egypt.

If something happened to her, he knew that wild horses couldn't hide Baron. Francis said, "I have an idea where I could go for some information."

"No, I'll take care of everything. Bright and early things had to be done. This hit man is prompt as well as exact. One of the best. You gotta be very careful with him."

"Nunzio, why are you so nervous?" replied Francis. "It would be better to take care of him first than to go shifting and moving people around. There is only one of him, and look at you and all you own. Can't you pay him off or something like that?"

"I know it sounds so easy, but it's not. Pepito has a reputation of being thorough, and once he's paid to do a job, nothing stops him. He's like the fucking terminator or something. Why do you think he's one of the best? He works for the money, not for friendship. If anyone paid him, he'd kill his own mother for crying out loud. He cannot be bought twice. It's like he takes pride for what he does, that's why he gets hired."

"So what you're saying is that even with all your glory, you yourself can't get him to back off? Everyone has a price," replied Francis.

"Francesco, think. If he did have a price, he would have been bought off long ago, and his reputation would have gone right down the drain. No, more importantly is that we have got to do something about Baron. We have to get him out of here safely so we can deal with Pepito. Why take the chance of any negotiations falling through and he accomplishes what he sets out to do? Francis, go over to Baron's and tell him tonight."

"Why don't you tell him yourself? I've got a hot appointment this evening," he said with a grin.

"You're meeting a woman that late? She must be a nightwalker," said Nunzio. "I don't think so if she's waiting at my place. Don't worry who she is, just make sure you talk with your son," said Francis and walked out the drawing room. Nunzio held the door open and softly said, "Go in peace."

At that point, Nunzio knew he had to confront Baron and convince him to leave. He also knew that there was no way in hell Egypt would go with him. This continued to pop in his thoughts. Margherita came downstairs and asked, "Is everything okay with Francis? I heard his voice, and it's not like him to show up at this hour."

Nunzio walked away from her as if he didn't hear her. The two had been quarreling over Elizabetta recently, and he was in no mood to listen to her wails. Instead of having a full-scale argument with her, he went into the guest room to retire.

The phone rang, and Margherita answered it. It was Angela. Margherita took a deep breath; she thought Angela had some bad news about Franco because of the late hour of her call. Angela was in fact happy and gave her mother the good news. "Mother, he can speak now. He's doing great, but he will still be here for a while."

"That's wonderful news, baby. I hope he gets well fast. Tell him I said get well soon and give him my love."

Unbeknownst to either of them, Nunzio had picked up the extension and was listening. He heard Margherita say that she thought he seemed very worried. Angela didn't reply to that. But she said, "Mother, I'll stop by tomorrow afternoon to see you. I want to go home and take a hot shower and come back to the hospital. I'll talk to you later, bye."

She hung up. *She never once asked about me,* thought Nunzio to himself. This was starting to get to him, but he still felt that Franco was not the one for his daughter or that Egypt was not the one for Baron. "And in due time they all will see it my way," he said softly.

After a while, Margherita walked into the guest room to talk to Nunzio. Nunzio felt an argument approaching and tried to seem uninterested. She didn't care if he wanted to listen or not. She told him, "Look, Nunzio, I think I need some time and space for myself. I'm leaving you and I'm going now."

Nunzio sighed. "Look, Margherita, it's almost three o'clock in the morning. We'll discuss your leaving in the morning. I'm tired, and I want to get some sleep if you don't mind."

As she walked out of the room, she remarked, "There need be no discussion about this. I've made up my mind." She slammed the door behind her.

By morning Egypt was in her newest position, hugging the bowl. All that ran through her mind was where Baron was and what was going through his mind about the recording. After she got up off the bathroom floor, she went downstairs to get something for her craving when she saw clothes on the floor. Baron was sleeping on the couch. She didn't know what to do or think of that. She sat across from him and called out his name. Baron was on edge from the night before and almost fell off the couch when he heard his name called.

"Why in the hell are you trying to give me a heart attack?" he asked.

"I'm not," she replied.

"And?"

"And what?"

"And what my ass. You woke me up, remember. Your ass is gonna sit there and give me a fucking heart attack and then you look at me and say, *and what?* What planet have you just returned from? What?"

"Nothing, I thought maybe you wanted to talk to me about something." Egypt wanted to get the confrontation out in the open and over with.

"Talk, did it appear that I was in the conversation mood, or did it appear that I was in the sleeping mood? Egypt, you're acting awfully strange. If there's something on your mind, please speak or else let me get back to sleep."

"Since you brought up the topic of what's on my mind—"

"Brought up? Me?"

"Yes, about being in my office. I wanted to explain that it was while we were apart, and it seemed that we weren't going to make it. I was lonely and hurt and confused. I needed some sort of comfort."

"What in the hell are you talking about? Egypt, look, I'm tired and not in the mood for guessing games. I was sleeping you know. How in the hell could that possibly look like I wanted to talk? Huh? I have too much shit to get up to your bullshit," he yelled.

"Well, excuse the hell out of me. You go in my desk drawer, private at that, and then you have the nerve to jump down my throat?" she screamed forgetting for a moment what that recorder held.

"Oh, so you want to get into that now? So yeah, let's talk about that.. Yes, I took it out your drawer. And for that matter, why do you own a gun? And furthermore you never told me about it. Do you realize the trouble you can get into having a gun like that?"

"The gun? No, no, no, we must be lost. You're more concerned about the gun than the—"

"Yes, I am. And what about the . . ." It was then that he realized that the whole conversation was about the recorder and not the gun or even rifling through her private drawer. "Egypt, you're right, it's about what's on it.. It has me confused. Explain."

Egypt felt that something was going on because she thought there was an eeriness about the way he changed the topic so quickly. The mood was different, and she wasn't sure what to say next. She didn't know if he had listened to it or not. She almost sold herself out.

The doorbell rang, and she ran to get it. Standing there wet was Francis. He shook off his umbrella before entering, and Egypt kissed him on the cheek. "Hi, Francis, come on in. You look like a man who hasn't had anything to eat in a while. I'll fix you guys some breakfast."

"Egypt, I want to thank you for that lovely woman. Donna has been a pure delight. I just took her to the airport. She said she's going to call you as soon as she gets home," he said.

"She was supposed to call me this morning," she said from the kitchen.

"We were a bit tied up that's all," he said and smiled knowingly at Baron. "Where's Athelia and everybody else?"

"I gave them all some time off. They'll be back next week. Since I'm not in the office much, I can pretty well handle everything here. Baron, do you want pancakes or—"

"I want to know about what's on it ," he replied. "To tell you the truth, I want to finish this conversation, so don't get all happy." To Francis he said, "Why are you here so early?"

"Did I come at a bad time for you, lovebirds?" said Francis. "Because if you want, I'll make this quick. Let's go into your office, Baron, okay?"

"Yeah, let's go. Egypt sure has been acting strange for the last month or so. As strange as the shits."

They went in. They heard music and Egypt singing in the background. Baron tried to concentrate and talk to Francis, but her voice was too sweet and lovely and the words seemed so familiar. She came to the door with her hair flowing singing.

And when the rain begins to fall, this is the place we belong. Like those winter days all turn to spring, we belong together. La-la-la-la-ela-ela . . . I always wake with a smile knowing that you're by my side. Our two hearts belong together, and when the sun comes, greets your eyes, your smile warms my heart. In silent dreams you are the one who speaks the words I've known so well in

the moment we meet like two hearts. Somehow we know
that we were to be like the winter rain will turn to spring,
we belong together.

This brought Baron so far back that it was hard for him to stay mad
with her. He walked over to her, and they kissed. Francis knew that it
would be best for him to come back later, and he left.

The two of them began dancing to the instrumental sounds of the
music. They drifted into the garden with the rain falling on them while
she continued to sing to him. Baron moved her wet hair from her face;
they could not resist the tempting mood enveloping them. With all the
jungle sounds of the music and the jungle sounds she made to him, he
had to have her now. Baron took Egypt right there in the garden. She put
up no resistance at all. They made erotic love.

Francis was in his car thinking about the entire ordeal, and he
suddenly pulled off. He thought about Nunzio and of what had to be
done to prevent anyone getting to Baron. He couldn't quite get the whole
picture together, but he had to do something. Nunzio was thinking like
the old school, but Francis knew that Pepito had to be taken care of
somehow and to find out who was putting the hit on Baron.

First things first. He was going to make arrangements for Baron to
get out. Out of sight but still in touch with things. Francis picked up his
phone and made a few calls to his favorites. He knew that O'Connor and
Johnny would be the ones. He would have preferred Barry since he had
the same mentality as Pepito while still being loyal to the family. But
after that last episode, he wasn't too sure of Barry.

As Francis pulled up to the restaurant he thought it would be better if
he took matters into his own hands. He pulled away from the curb and
recalled everyone by pay phone.

The evening had come and almost gone by the time Francis got in
touch with Baron. After all was said and done, he gave Baron the final
move; he had to convince Egypt.

"Look, butter, I don't want to leave. This is only a temporary thing
until my family can fix things. I want you to understand that."

"I don't want to think about leaving without even knowing where
I'll be going. It's simply out of the question," she said.

Francis replied, "Look, Egypt, your life is in a lot of danger too. Think
about that."

"I told you I didn't want a life like that. A life on the run I cannot deal
with. I want my children's life to be normal. This Cosa Nostra bullshit
isn't going to be a part of my life."

"Egypt, you knew it was going to be rough from jump street because of who Nunzio was. And when it's all broken down, it sums up to leaving with or without you," said Francis to Egypt.

"I have no choice, Egypt. We're supposed to leave tonight, but with all the attempts to convince you to come, we're wasting valuable time. Now everything is off schedule. I've got to hide out until sunset tomorrow."

Egypt still could not understand the danger her or Baron was in. She was uppity and annoyed. She faked being tired and went to her room. Baron followed her and curled up next to her. He had a funny feeling run through him. He tried to explain, but she wasn't listening. "Hold me, Egypt," he asked. There was no response.

"Egypt, I never thought things would happen this way. You gotta believe me. I would never let anything happen to you. I love you." He waited a moment, and there was still no reaction from her. This cut through him like a knife. "Butter, just look at me, please?" he said painfully. She sat up and stared right through him in anger and misery. That was no more than tearing his heart in pieces. She rolled over on her side as if he weren't there. He couldn't express the feeling running through him because it was alien to him. It was dark and cold inside his mind. He couldn't sleep very well that night. He tossed and turned to no avail. Sleep never came.

When Egypt awakened, she found Baron with a drink in his hand looking out the window at the sky. She still didn't speak to him.

"So how long is this going to last? I'm leaving before sundown, and are you riding with me or what? By the way something slipped past me yesterday that we never finished. About that recording. What was on there that had you worried shitless?" He waited for a response; one never came.

"Since I overlooked that discussion, there is no need to continue. Well, silent one, what about it? Are you going to say anything to me?" he asked in a snide voice.

Egypt got up and went into the shower. She didn't respond to him. It was like he wasn't there. She knew that if he heard that recording, he would have done something off the wall, so she didn't want to say anything about it. She was so mad that he was still leaving even without her that she finished showering, dressed in silence, and left. All he could do was to let her leave.

Baron knew what he had to do no matter what transpired between them. He felt that she should have conceded just because of their safety if anything. Where they would have went they didn't need anything. Francis was ready anyhow, so he only had to bide his time.

Egypt rode to her doctor's appointment. When she talked to her obstetrician, the doctor told her, "Look, Mrs. Gianelli, you simply cannot miss your appointments because prenatal care is very important."

"I'm sorry. It's just that I have a bad case of morning sickness and some very heavy mood swings. I don't know. I'm just a little out of it, that's all."

"Look, morning sickness and those mood swings of yours are normal in pregnancy. I'm going to write you a prescription for the sickness and just try to rest and relax yourself. You're living for two now, and everything you eat and everything you do affects your baby. Just lighten up, and everything will be all right," she said.

After Egypt left, she went on a small shopping spree for her mother and sisters. She thought it would be a nice surprise for them and the relaxation of shopping would make her feel better. Before she knew it, it was almost time for Baron to leave. She knew that she couldn't make it home in time, so she just took a cab straight to the secret rendezvous. Because of the traffic, she knew it would take a while.

At home Baron had waited as long as he could. He thought that by her not being here was her way of objecting to his leaving. He had to leave, so she couldn't have her way this time. Francis was beginning to get nervous because things again were running late. "Come on, Baron, we have to leave now. I'm sorry that Egypt's not here, but what can I do?"

They rushed out the door and into the awaiting car that held O'Connor and Johnny. When they arrived at this small landing field, Egypt was standing there. She saw several men walking her way, and one looked like Baron. She ran to the waiting area's entrance calling his name which pissed Francis off because he insisted on anonymity. Baron didn't care. He ran toward her and embraced her. She was trying to say something, but Baron pressed his fingers over her mouth.

"Don't say anything, butter. Just understand that you have to come too because I love you and I want you with me safe. Egypt, no, don't," he said as he wiped a tear away.

"Baron, I'm not going with you. I want you to stay here with me. Everything will be fine. Just tell the police because they have ways of protecting people."

"Not people like me, butter," he replied. "Look, the rest of them are on the plane. Walk me there. Come on, it's still warm out even though the sun is setting."

Egypt said nothing, and she stood there like a statue. Baron went to kiss her, but she didn't move to return the kiss. He gently kissed her forehead and walked out the door toward a waiting jet. Egypt watched through tearstained eyes his progress toward the plane. She wanted so much to run after him. The pain in his eyes was unbearable to her.

A shiny reflection hit her through the window. She squinted her eyes to see what it was, and she noticed a rifle with a man attached to it. She started waving her arms and hitting the glass to get anybody's attention. She was trying to warn Baron of the man with the gun. He didn't understand her signals, so he just waved back and stopped to blow her a kiss. She saw the man take aim. She banged harder on the glass and screaming, "Look out, Baron, that man has a gun!" She felt so helpless in there because he didn't know what she meant.

A single shot rang out. When she saw Baron fall to the ground, her body slid off the glass slowly, and she fell in a heap on the floor. Nobody heard the shot because the jet was on. Egypt finally rose off the floor and ran screaming from the building for help. The pilot saw her and yelled, "There's a woman out there on the runway."

Francis turned to see what the commotion was all about. He spotted his brother ten yards behind him on the ground surrounded by a pool of blood. Egypt grabbed him in her arms hysterical. She whispered, "Baron, don't speak, don't move. Help is on the way. Don't worry, I'm here, and I'm not going to leave you."

Barry and O'Connor went looking for Pepito; they knew he had to have been the one. Francis yelled for the pilot to radio for an ambulance. When he looked back, Egypt was rocking him.

"Baby, don't say anything. I'm sorry it's all my fault. If I wasn't so busy trying to have my way and if I had just stopped to listen to you and went—" Baron raised his hand on her mouth and said, "Would you just be quiet for once and stop crying? I love you. Do you still love me?"

Egypt wiped his hair from his face, but she didn't notice that his eyes had closed. She went on talking, "Oh, because I couldn't love anyone else but you, honey, we're gonna have . . . ," and she stopped. She noticed his eyes were closed, and her blood ran cold. Tears swam on her face as she finished, "A baby . . ."

An ambulance arrived, and Francis took over. He told Egypt that it wouldn't be wise for her to ride in the ambulance. "Don't worry, Barry will make sure you arrive at the hospital safely."

When they arrived at the hospital, she was told by a surgeon, "Your husband is being flown to a trauma center by helicopter since his condition was serious and had worsened. But all that can be done will be done." The doctor left.

Nunzio was informed of Baron's condition and was on his way to the trauma center. There was no way that anyone would get near Baron, thought Nunzio. He had everyone that was under his thumb reacting. When he reached the hospital, the first person he saw was Francis. Francis had tears in his eyes. Nunzio shook his head and yelled, "No!

Not Baron," and hugged him. While he hugged Nunzio, he whispered something in his ear. The two went aside and decided what had to be done. Nunzio asked Francis to see to all the arrangements. He would take care of the intricate details. Francis asked, "What about Egypt? Shouldn't she know what's going on?" Nunzio shook his head no. He went to see Baron's doctor.

When Nunzio returned, he told Francis, "Everything has been taken care of. I'll make the call to Dominic. He knows someone." Francis noticed Egypt making her way toward them.

"Shit, here comes Egypt. Let me speak to her myself. Nothing you say will sit too well with her."

As Egypt approached Francis, she said, "Francis, where is he? No one seems to know anything. First they said he was in surgery, and when I get to the operating room, the nurses say that he was never there. I want to know what the hell is going on," she said. She noticed there was no response from him and that Nunzio walked off. Then she added, "No! Please don't say it, don't! Damn it, say something! Just don't stand there looking stupid. Francis, where is my husband? Where is Baron?"

"Egypt, I'm sorry," muttered Francis.

"Sorry for what? You're lying, damn it. I can still feel him. No, no, *no*. I can still feel his presence," she replied shaking.

"He didn't have enough strength to make it through the surgery. He died during the surgery of heart failure. We already have the mortician coming to pick up his body," said Francis mournfully.

"He doesn't even know we're having a baby," she said softly and broke into tears. Francis held her and told her that in her condition he didn't want anything to happen to her. He quickly reminded her of Angelica and her situation. She had to keep a grip on herself for at least the baby's sake. She agreed. She said, "At least, can I say good-bye to him in my own way?"

He decided to let her go. When he walked her back to the nurses' station, they informed them that his body was already in transit with the mortician who called for him. Egypt clutched Francis and collapsed into his arms, fainting. The nurses ran to help her and revived her with smelling salts. Francis told them she was pregnant, but he didn't know how far along she was. In fact, he was quite surprised and happy all at the same time.

As she came to, the nurses bombarded her with questions. She kept repeating, "I just want to see my husband, that's all I want. It just doesn't feel right. He can't be dead."

Francis signaled to O'Connor to help him with Egypt. "O'Connor, hold her while we try to give her this pill to calm her nerves. The doctor said it would put her to sleep, but it won't harm the baby. I have to meet up with Nunzio before the press and the media get hold of this. I want Baron's body in my custody and sealed before there's too many embarrassing questions asked. So take her home, will ya?"

"No problem," he answered. "But one thing though, Pepito is still out there looking for you."

"Right about now he should be in his glory over Baron's death. He'll want me to sweat it out. He realizes I won't run from this, so he'll wait for me during or right after the funeral. He loves the rush of the kill. His adrenaline will pump much better if he feels like he's making it a massacre. If he follows the time schedule, nothing should go wrong. Capishe?"

O'Connor took her home, unplugged the phones, and closed the windows. He didn't want anyone to think they were there. *She's sleeping like a baby,* thought O'Connor. Several hours went by, and he began to worry because she hadn't stirred yet. He heard the door open downstairs and pulled out his gun. The footsteps were light and soft, but he was not mistaken.

The person was walking as if they were trying to sneak up the stairs quietly. O'Connor stood behind the door. As the person stepped in, O'Connor cocked back the gun and was just about to fire a shot. Angelica gave out one yell and fell to her knees. O'Connor took a deep breath and put the gun back in its holster. She started fussing and yelling at him.

"You scared the shit out of me, you fool." She punched him square in the chest for it. All the commotion awakened Egypt.

"Baron, don't leave me!" she yelled waking up.

"Are you okay, Egypt?" said O'Connor running to her room.

"He'll never even get to see our baby," she answered crying.

"O'Connor, what in the world is she talking about?" asked Angela. O'Connor replied, "As far as I can tell, she's pregnant."

"You know damn well what I'm talking about."

What's wrong, and why would my brother leave her?" asked Angela.

"He's dead. Gone right in front of my eyes. Just like that, he's gone," said Egypt and started crying again. Angelica sat on her bed and put her face in her hands and also began crying. "Dead? Baron? No, not Baron. He can't be dead, there must be some mistake."

O'Connor said that he would rather have Francis or Nunzio explain what happened to them. Angela remembered what O'Connor said about Egypt being pregnant and immediately straightened up. She didn't want her to lose her nephew or niece. She held Egypt in her arms and rocked her. Tears fell like raindrops from both of them. Angela calmed her down and went to make her some tea to settle her stomach.

O'Connor was already downstairs. She asked, "Is there a reason why you're still here?" He responded, "Francis thought it was best if I stay here for a while, just until he gets here." The bell rang, and Angela went to answer it. It was Donna. She exclaimed tearfully, "How is she? Francis called me and told me to fly back out here to keep an eye on her." O'Connor followed Angela to the door just in case something went wrong. Angelica looked at him and asked, "Okay, O'Connor, how did my brother die?"

He didn't reply. Angela walked over to the phone, and Donna went upstairs to see about Egypt. She saw the phone was unplugged and plugged it back in. Angela called her mother, but the line was busy. Angela finished making the tea, and then she called Donna downstairs.

"Donna, if anything happens, or if you find out anything, will you please call me or leave a message? I have to get back to the hospital to see about Franco." She gave her the number to both Franco's hospital room and their home. She left and went to her car.

First things first, she said to herself. *I have got to know what happened. And to do that, I have to get to the big cheese himself, Nunzio. I know Francis won't budge or divulge anything where Baron is concerned. Now, Angelica, where would that fat piece of cheese be? One place I know he would have to go sooner or later is home.*

Angela arrived there to see the press and television cameras. When she got out of the car, they seemed to swarm around her like bees to nectar. She had to repeatedly tell them she knew nothing about it until one hotshot reporter mentioned something about her husband's family possibly connected to her brother's killing. This remark triggered a spark, and she looked that man straight in his face and hit him square in the jaw. He had already followed her onto the property and she yelled, "You were trespassing on private property, and if anyone wants to try me, just come on and you'll get the same shit. So, everyone, get off my property and leave!"

When she walked in the house, her mother was a nervous wreck. Angela held on to her mother and whispered, "Mother, Egypt is pregnant. Several months or so. We have to be strong for her and see her through all this."

Margherita stopped right in her tracks. "I don't know whether to cry or smile. Why didn't they tell us?"

"Egypt never even got a chance to tell Baron. So oh well. How do we handle this? Kid's gloves aren't gentle enough for this."

"You were always the sensible one out of all my girls. How would you do this?"

"Where's Nunzio?"

"He went to take care of all the arrangements. Baron will be buried tomorrow."

"Tomorrow? How could he be so hard-hearted? He never even tried to tell me or Franco, and he's off making burial arrangements. Do you mean there's to be no viewing of the body, no memorial, or nothing? How could he do that to his own son, Mother? How? And then, how will we be able to contact everyone?"

"Your father said the 'quicker the better.'"

"Mother, this doesn't sound right. Something fishy is going on, I can feel it. I have to see my brother to be sure. I still feel him next to me."

"So do I, baby, so do I," said Margherita.

"When and where is this funeral to take place?" asked Angela.

"I have yet to find out. Please, Angela, stop. Don't you think this is hurting your father too? It has crushed him so badly, and he wanted the arrangement done his way. All I know is that he decided to have the casket closed. He said it was mostly for Egypt's sake. I wonder why though."

"Closed? What in the hell happened to him that his casket has to be closed? I want to know what the hell's going on here. I'm tired of being in the dark. Shit, someone is going to answer some questions and real fast," said Angela.

"Angelica, calm down. Don't even think about approaching your father with that attitude. You are being inconsiderate of his feelings. That was his son just as much as it was your brother."

Not to say anything more disrespectful, she just said good-bye and left. Angela wasn't going to rest easy with the hush-up bullshit. She thought that if she went to Francis's, maybe he would be there. Maybe she could get some answers from him.

When she arrived at his house, he was not there. She was frustrated, tired, and hungry. She went back home to shower and to get back to Franco. *Franco*, she thought, *he has to be told. Damn, in his condition I hope he doesn't have a relapse. Still, maybe I shouldn't tell him right now. But I know soon he will have to know. There's no sense keeping it from him forever.* She drove back to the hospital.

Donna was worried about Egypt. She was walking around the house in some sort of daze, gathering up his insurance papers and starting to write a statement for him. She remembered that she hadn't called his lawyer. She called him, and he told her that Mr. Nunzio Gianelli had already taken care of everything and not to worry. "Prior to his death,

Mr. Gianelli changed his will. That's about it, Mrs. Gianelli. Take care of yourself," he said and rang off.

The fact that Baron had changed his will recently surprised Egypt, but she didn't care about that. In the state of mind she was in, all she wanted to do was wander around until everything became clear. But Donna wouldn't let her go out alone, so they went together. They walked around the garden for a while. Donna thought that if she brought up their old college days, it would take her mind off things for a while.

"It's okay, Donna, we don't have to go back in time. This walk eased my tension a bit. But there isn't enough walking or talking of yesteryear to mend my heart of Baron. I know I'm not ever going to accept this, but at least, I have a piece of him. I'll be all right, so don't worry about me."

"Are you sure, babe? I know if it were me I would have fell apart by now."

"The way I see it, I really don't have a choice. My baby comes first and that's that. All I want to do is get in touch with my father-in-law. He has taken over very fast, and I haven't gotten to say or do shit about my own husband's affairs."

"Well, Egypt, Francis and Nunzio just didn't want to put this burden on you with you being pregnant and all. I'm sure they were thinking of you, and they didn't want anything to happen to you or the baby."

"I am pregnant, yes, but that doesn't mean I'm incapable of handling certain situations. Furthermore that man should know better than to get in my business," she spoke angrily.

"Let's head back in the house. I think it's starting to rain. I felt a drop or two."

"No, you go in," Egypt replied. "I want to think about things alone. A little rain won't kill me," she said and walked further into the garden.

As the rain began falling harder, she continued to stroll in it. The raindrops were falling off her eye lashes, but it didn't seem to bother her in the least. She pushed her hair from her face to look at the little bridge. She recalled them making love right there on that bridge with the moon and stars as their candles. She sat on the bridge and cried hard and loud. She rocked herself, and a warm feeling came over her. "Baron," she said. "Baron, is that you? Damn, it still feels as though you're not gone. I love you, and no one could take your place, ever."

Egypt took several deep breaths and stood up. She felt a little sick and wanted to get back in the house. When she got in the house, she ran straight in the bathroom and assumed her usual position over the bowl.

Donna was jumpy. She became even more jumpy with Egypt's

pregnancy. "Egypt, have you ever thought that the man who killed Baron might come for you next?"

"Why would you even think that, Donna?" replied Egypt.

"Because then tell me why are there more of your father's boys outside the house?"

"That's it. Donna, help me pack a few things, I'm going back to the loft. When Baron went on his trips, I would go back there or if we wanted to be alone. So that's where I'm going."

"How do you plan on getting past the goons out there without being followed?"

"Was I not married to a man who was an expert on losing his father's men? How do you think we managed to be alone at my loft with absolutely no interruptions? Those idiots still have no idea where my loft is."

The two walked in the downpour to a stack of wood. Egypt revealed that it actually wasn't a stack of wood at all but a cleverly hidden compartment containing a motorcycle, helmets, and some riding gear. Egypt rode them down a small path in the woods in the back of their house until they hit a paved street. Donna was amazed. "Only a chosen few know of this secret road or the secret hiding place."

Egypt remembered that one of the chosen few was Francis. He anticipated her leaving like that, so he had Barry already waiting at her loft. Donna asked why weren't they going to her loft.

"How dumb do you think I am? We might have been followed, so I want to throw them off. We're going past your place." When they arrived, Egypt asked Donna to go into the store for a few things and then they would go to the loft. When Donna left, she drove off. She made her way to a phone booth and called Chai, not realizing he already left. She didn't know what to do, but she knew she couldn't go back to either place. She paged Carlos; he was her last resort.

He called her back, and she briefed him on the events of the past twenty-four hours. He told her it would be no problem and arranged a place and time to meet. She was off. Francis walked into her loft, but she was not there. She called her house to speak to Francis. "Where in the hell are you, Egypt?"

"Don't worry about me, Francis, I'm all right. What I want to know is where Baron's body is so I could make the rest of the arrangements. I'm his wife, damn it, and I should know the whereabouts of his body."

"I already told you that Nunzio took care of everything. His funeral and burial is tomorrow."

Egypt flipped her top. But she realized there was nothing she could do to change things. All she knew was that now she was carrying their legacy; Nunzio would be kissing her ass. And that she knew was a fact.

She gasped for air and asked Francis for the address and time for the services.

She would play the role that was neatly laid out for her. Francis didn't want to get into it with her, so he gave her the address. After she wrote down the information, she slipped up and made a comment to Francis that she shouldn't have. She told Francis, "Since this whole affair is being done so quickly, then that's all the quicker to get away from Nunzio."

Francis freaked. They couldn't let that happen. Her pregnancy had to be monitored closely and carefully. He tried to smooth things over with her, and he thought he had succeeded.

When Carlos went into the bedroom, he couldn't help but see how beautiful she looked sitting on the edge of the bed. He sat next to her and kissed her neck. She turned and wrapped her arms around him and wept. All the ecstasy had left him, and he felt guilty about what he had just tried to do to her. She had just lost her husband.

"I'm sorry for just coming apart at the seams like that," she said apologetically.

"No apology needed. It is I who must apologize."

"Why, you didn't do anything. Thanks for letting me come by, but I have to get home."

"No, no, you don't have to leave. You should stay here for the night. It's perfectly okay. Whatever makes you happy. You really don't have to go. Anyway you look pale and flushed to be out there in that weather. It looks as if you're coming down with something," said Carlos.

She chuckled. "Yeah, I am. It's called morning, afternoon, and whatever time it wants to be sickness. I'm only pregnant."

"You're what?" he replied shocked.

"Pregnant. That's when a woman has a swollen stomach and aches and pains and at the end of nine months, a cute and cuddly and crying infant comes out? You know, a child, a rug rat something we all were once. Pregnant, you dope," she said sarcastically.

"Close your mouth. Damn, you act like I was going to tell you it was yours. Give me a break. I realize that I still look good, but that's only because I know how to dress around the extra weight. And plus I have a small stomach, and I'm not really showing yet. Hello? Hello, earth to Carlos. Would you close your mouth for crying out loud?" she said.

"So how in the hell did that happen?"

"Dumb ass. What the hell, have you had a lobotomy or something? Have you been taking stupid pills again? Carlos, you're making me feel weird, so to cut to the chase, why are you acting like this?" asked Egypt.

"No reason. I have a meeting to go to, and there's an extra set of keys on the table," he said. He kissed her on the forehead and left.

Egypt went to lie down, but something continued to haunt her. She grabbed the keys and left her stuff and went back out. This time she hailed a cab. When she got to the hospital, she hoped to find out more than she did the first time she was there. But still no one seemed to know anymore than they had told her already.

Finally she had to accept what was happening around her. But it still didn't seem right. She felt that everything was not being told to her and that there were pieces missing to this puzzle. She went back to the house. She knew she couldn't keep searching for an answer when things had to be factual.

Nunzio walked into his home, and it seemed to have been transformed. He wife was dressed in total black, and the mirrors were all covered. He looked at her with trouble in his eyes.

"What's on your mind, Nunzio?" said Margherita. "You look troubled. I hurt too, and through my tears and prayers, I will find peace and understanding as to why this had to happen."

"Margherita, I hate to see you hurting like this." And said nothing more. He just put his arms out for her, and she sobbed. He had forgotten how warm she was. He couldn't remember the last time they had embraced like that, with her warmth. Margherita felt this as well, but she knew this was not the time to discuss their lost love for one another.

He pulled her away and wiped the tears off her face. She then remembered Angela's fury and sat him down to explain what was going on with her. Nunzio seemed not to be worried with her; he was more worried about what to do about Egypt and he said as much.

"Since when are you so interested in Egypt's feelings about anything? The last I heard you were out to get her," said Margherita.

He stood up angrily. "There will be no other man raising his Gianelli blood other than the family itself."

"It would be very unlikely that she would allow you to have any say about Baron's child," she replied.

Nunzio didn't want to hear that. He had to find a way of making her live in his house come hell or high water. "Besides," she continued, "Egypt is not the kind of woman who takes kindly to being pushed around. She's the rebellious type, worse than Angelica ever was. You had better not push the issue with her, Nunzio. You should leave that to me and Angelica. We probably would be able to convince her better than you could." Margherita too felt that Egypt should come to live there because she had a feeling that if not, they could lose her and their grandchild.

"Seeing how I lost my son, I don't want to lose my grandchild also." Nunzio couldn't argue with that; she was 100 percent correct. He sure didn't want his grandchild raised by a bunch of Goya beans. So he nodded his head and allowed them to work on Egypt.

"But if you two can't work it out with her, then I have no choice but to do things my way. But come hell or high water, she will be living in this house with the child, or if not, then just the child." Margherita knew he wasn't about to let up on this at all.

Francis was talking to Egypt back at the house. She handed him all the papers that would be needed to complete the business at hand. Francis took them; that was the least of all the problems. Most harmful he felt was Egypt's inquisitiveness.

"I can't help do anything, is that what you're saying?"

"Everything will be done by tomorrow," he answered.

"Tomorrow. Everything is about tomorrow, but you have yet to explain why but that's neither here nor there. Like I said I'll dress the part and even act the part. So did your dear Nunzio type my script for tomorrow? I hope it all comes off as well as you planned."

Francis couldn't take much more of this. He had to go through with this charade regardless of how it made him feel, which was like a heel. However he felt it was for the best. "Egypt, where's Donna? I thought she was going to stay with you?"

"Oh. I kind of tricked her and got away," she replied.

"Well, I don't want you to stay here by yourself now. We'll stay here overnight until all of this blows over."

"No need for that. I already made arrangements to stay with a friend."

"Egypt, it isn't wise to involve more people in this than it is necessary. Just stay here with your family."

Something didn't sit right with that statement. It was dark out, and she was feeling a bit woozy. She went into the kitchen and put something together for herself and then she went to sleep.

When she woke in the morning, she peeked out the door and saw that Francis and Donna were already up and dressed. In fact the entire family was there plus relatives from long distances. She didn't know what to do. She heard footsteps approaching, and she quickly closed the door and jumped back into bed. Angela looked in on her and asked softly, "Egypt, are you okay?"

When she didn't answer, Angela added, "I sent Donna out earlier to get you some new things for the funeral. I know you didn't have time to shop for yourself. I hope you didn't mind that I took the liberty of doing that for you."

The clothes were all laid out on the chair by her bed. Egypt felt herself getting sick again. She got up and walked into the bathroom and assumed that old familiar position again. Angela stood by the door asking if she was going to be okay. "Egypt, I'm not going until my mother and brothers arrive. Nunzio sent a car for us, and it will be here shortly. So when you're done hugging the bowl and freshen up, we'll be leaving."

This burned her ass. She felt so useless. She thought it would be best for her if she went to her mother's house for a while. She told Angela she couldn't sleep in the house anymore.

She prepared herself for the service and left for the church in the limo. She was definitely surprised. There in the church were the most beautiful flower arrangements. When she stepped farther inside, her mother was waiting at the back pew for her. It was then she noticed the casket. It was dead center of the church. She felt her knees weaken and clutched her mother's arm tightly. She started speaking Spanish explaining to her mother that something was wrong, that she couldn't find the tears.

Carmen whispered, "That's just because you don't accept it yet. Wait, it will happen, and when it does, you will feel relieved and at peace with yourself and with Baron."

After the priest expressed through prayer his words of comfort, Francis added his eulogy. Margherita and Elisabetta cried. Angelica, like Egypt, just hadn't accepted this.

At the back of the church sat Carlos Montana. When everyone prepared to leave, Nunzio caught a glimpse of him. He walked past him and waited by the limo for him to approach. When Egypt walked by, he stood up and held her hand. Noel walked over while they were outside.

"I really don't think this is a good idea him being here."

She answered, "Carlos is just being sympathetic. Nothing more than that, Noel. Please calm down, Noel. That's all over with. What can happen now?"

To Carlos he said, "Hey, look, man. Any other time is fine, but her husband ain't even in the ground yet. I have a feeling that father-in-law of Egypt's is watching us carefully." He shook his head in Nunzio's direction. He continued, "So I think it's best that you don't go to the cemetery with us."

"I think you're right," he replied. "Yes, I'll leave. And I'll see you back at the apartment. You still have the keys, right? See ya, bye," he said and kissed her forehead.

Noel caught sight of Nunzio watching like a hawk. He grabbed Egypt's hand and told her to be careful with Carlos. They didn't want him to get a pair of cement loafers. "Noel, you have been watching too many gangster movies," said Egypt.

But little to her surprise Noel was very much on track to Nunzio's thoughts. If Carlos was to be a threat, then he would have no qualms with taking care of him.

Egypt shrugged her shoulders and said, "Noel, I feel any minute that someone is going to jump out of nowhere yelling, 'Cut! Great. Everyone can leave the set early.' Because all the shit that's been going down I feel could only happen in the movies."

Noel reminded her that the movie began long before she was even awarded a role in it. "You knew what was in the soup before you bent down to sip it."

"Well, Noel, what a lovely analog," said Egypt. "Get away, you're no help at all. I'm hurt, and you're going to remind me like I don't know. Sometimes you can be a real ass, Noel."

"Look, Egypt, they're signaling you to go over there and stop looking so mysterious and letdown," he said.

"How can I?" she answered. How can I look a way I don't feel? I've been trying to get my point across. I was there when it happened. Nothing happened to his face or his head, so why is his casket closed? I don't think I've asked a lot of them, and plus I let them take over all the arrangements that I should have planned. Up until now no one has tried to explain any of this to me. Not even anyone at the hospital could tell me what happened and why his casket had to be closed." Francis walked up next to her.

"Egypt, we all thought it would be best that you don't see him on account of your pregnancy. I explained that already why we did this. Egypt, come on and get in the limo," said Francis.

"I hope you really don't think that I believe all that bullshit. But if I must, I'll go along with it. This will not sit easy with me," she responded.

She got in the limo without a sound. When everyone returned, they went to Nunzio's house. Margherita asked Egypt if she would like to lie down for a while. She walked Egypt through a beautiful hallway and into a very large bedroom. She lay down on the king-size bed, but something didn't rest with her. She looked around at the antique furniture, and curiosity got the best of her. She rose and went to the closet and peeked in. Her mouth fell open; there were her clothes hanging up. She opened the door and walked down the hall and straight out of the house. Her mother ran after her, calling her in Spanish.

Egypt turned to her with tears streaming down her face. Carmen held her daughter, and the two spoke in Spanish. Egypt told her she had to get away because they weren't about to trap her into living there. She got in Noel's car and waited for the rest of her family to come out.

Noel drove her home to the loft. When she arrived, she noticed lights on in the living room, and she swore she had turned them off when she left. A cold chill ran down her spine. She was shitting bricks but she didn't want to call Francis for help. She opened the door slowly. A familiar voice told her to come in.

It was Chai. She ran to his arms crying. He sat her down and wiped her face. She rambled on about losing Baron and what have been the aftereffects on the situation.

"Listen, all I want you to know is I'm here, and I'm not going to let you go through this alone. As soon as you're up to it, I wish to marry you and help raise your child as ours. I could never let you go through a bad time and not be there for you. May I kiss you?" he asked timidly.

"Why do you ask such a silly question?" The two kissed slow and gently. "I can't find the words to describe what's running through my mind. I still love Baron, Chai. It's not like I didn't love you, but I'm carrying his child. I couldn't ask you to put yourself into the trash that I'm sure would follow that decision. But thank you anyway," she said.

"I'm willing to wait until the baby is born. But, Egypt, I cannot willingly leave your side. I didn't ask you to love me. I just want to help you and Egypt, the love will follow later if it's to be," he replied.

"I don't want you to feel responsibility for my problems, Chai. You seem to have a way of always being there for me."

"Egypt, I could never explain what it is about you, except that it's hard to leave you. It's as though your essence runs through me."

"I know somewhere down the line you're going to want to make love like we used to, and I don't think that I—"

"Time heals all wounds," he said. "We will approach that subject later, so don't worry yourself with that now. Like I said already, the love will follow later."

"What's going to happen to me now, Chai? I'm so scared. His family isn't going to make my life any easier for me and my baby. This I know to be true. Do you really think they won't interfere if I married you after I had the baby?" she asked.

"Egypt, that's the last thing you have to worry about. So long as you have me, no one will harm you." He said those words like a Samari warrior. He stood up and went into the kitchen and made her a glass of warm milk and brought it to her. She smiled at him, and she drank it.

"So, my knight in shining armor, are you ready for battle? Because, my darling, you have just entered the war zone." Chai held her close to his chest and kissed her on her brow and whispered, "I'm armed and ready."

Christmas and New Year's had come and gone, and Egypt held herself together. But when Valentine's Day neared, she began to feel empty within. Several days before, she had received one single blue rose, and no one but Baron ever did that. She lay back and reminisced for the first time in a long while.

They had just met, and he was very attentive until he had to do some running for his father. "It's family business," he had told her. Months had passed, and one day waiting for her was a single long-stemmed blue rose. Egypt jumped up and waddled to a box in her closet. There she opened a handwritten letter from Baron.

> *Much time has gone by I must say*
>   *My absence seems like forever and a day, but unique as this*
> *rose so blue, is my love for you. So long as your love for this rose*
> *is true, I will always return to you . . .*
> *Baron*

Egypt doubled over in tears. *Who would play such a mean trick on me?* she thought. No matter what, she thought and stopped for a moment. She recalled that she had never told anybody about that. She thought, *How in the hell could this be happening to me?*

All of this started to get to her, and she found herself having lower back pain. She took a taxi to the hospital, but they told her she was fine. She was roughly about eighteen weeks pregnant, and she still had a long way to go. Her due date wasn't until July, and she was already as big as someone six months pregnant; she knew there were no miscalculations on her part.

She returned home, and Chai was sitting there patiently waiting. Egypt told him that she was feeling strange, so she went to the hospital. He asked what had gotten her so upset. She didn't answer right away.

"Could it have been the rose and the letter? Not that I was prying or anything, but I went into the bedroom, and since your closet wasn't closed, I noticed clothes lying all over the floor. That's not like you to be careless like that. I went in to straighten it up when I noticed the letter and the rose. I read the letter, and Egypt I'm sorry, but—."

"You had no right, Chai," Egypt complained. "You don't live here. This is my home. You were snooping through my most personal things. Who in the hell do you think you are? Where in the hell do you get off making my business yours?" she screamed. "I didn't ask you to be a part of this, you put yourself in. I don't need your help or anyone else's in handling my life or my child's."

Chai got up and walked to the door. He didn't say a word and left. She felt like the bottom of an ant's ass, but she tried to brush off the feeling as though it was solely his fault. Inside she knew who to really lay the blame on.

Egypt made an attempt to call her sister and talk, but she wasn't home; she even tried to call her mother but to no avail. She opened a miniature wine bottle and drank it and cried. The rose and the old poem along with her unjustly yelling at Chai. Add to that the fact there was no one to talk to and she felt lonely indeed.

St. Patrick's Day rolled in with a bang for Egyptian Labels. Several of their clients had hit the top of the pop charts. This news was great for Egypt since she had done so much work. She literally buried herself into the company. All had seemed bright from outside.

Catherine buzzed Egypt to tell her that one of the corporate attorneys, a Ms. Aguilar, wished to speak with her. Egypt was hesitant, but business is business, she thought. She told Catherine to let Ms. Aguilar in. Fatima was radiant as always. Egypt felt a little awkward being a plum. Fatima immediately paid her a compliment, but it didn't make Egypt feel much better. She knew she looked like a plum.

"Fatima, how can I help you? There has to be a reason for you to be here. Usually you have someone on your staff represent you. What's wrong?" asked Egypt.

"The company's financial state has taken a major twist for the type of company we are. We're bringing in a larger income than expected, so in order not to be taxed out the ass, we need to turn the money in other directions, meaning have the money work for us—"

"Thank you, there's no need for you to break it down into syllables for me, I get the picture. So what are you suggesting? In order for you to be here I know you must have some kind of treatment or proposal. So what are you saying? What do you plan we do?"

"To tell you the truth the only way I and everyone else sees it, we need to expand. Venture out beyond the aspect of production and the music video level. I picture Egyptian Labels expanding to movies and changing the name to E & B Gian Productions. This way if it doesn't do too well, it won't pull EL down. We could also take a new turn and try handling rock music. Rap, R & B, and pop is fine and has brought in a lot of money but let's open it up to new areas," explained Fatima.

"Good points, Fatima, but I can't see hiring new staff who specializes in rock music and also branching out in motion pictures at the same time. The concept is fine, and we're about due for a change of pace. So get everything in order, and we'll all gather round King Arthur's table and converse. Make sure you set it up with Daniel and Mrs. Jackson. I'm not sure, but I think Tad is on vacation but just double-check. Have it on my desk in a week and the meeting two business days later."

"Fine, in one week you'll have it."

As Fatima was leaving the office, Egypt called out, "Fatima, isn't this a bit out of your field? Or are you embarking on an exploration into new territories?"

Fatima took several steps toward the door and turned slowly to reply, "Could be," and continued out the door.

Something about Fatima still worked Egypt's last nerve, but she had to give it to her. She had already saved the company thousands and brought thousands in legal suits against other labels sampling music without paying. She was sharp and on the ball.

Egypt thought for a moment that maybe she ought to take a few classes in corporate management considering it was Baron's field. There were many times when she found her back up against the wall. This way she wouldn't have to depend on others' opinions so much.

Catherine buzzed in again and reminded Egypt that she had a meeting with Mr. Stout. She wasn't too thrilled with dealing with him again, but she couldn't give him the brush-off because, after all, he was there for the benefit of the company. She thought maybe she would bounce of idea off him to see what he thought. Considering he hired Fatima and stayed on after the separation. He always spoke highly of her, but then again, she thought it would be best to wait until Fatima had it all down on paper. She told Catherine to get her files ready, and she would leave in ten minutes.

A full day had gone by, and Egypt was very tired. She needed a warm bath and a good massage right about then. Before she could get her foot in the shower, the bell rang. She debated whether or not she should answer it. It rang several times more. When she finally reached the hallway she heard Chai's voice calling out to her.

"I'm fine, calm down," she answered.

"Why did it take you so long to answer the door?"

"Have you forgotten that I'm the size of a small cow or what?"

"You're not that big. Were you getting out the shower?"

"No, I'm trying to take a bath."

"Bath? No, you can't take a bath."

"Don't worry I'll be fine." She walked toward the bathroom and the phone rang. "Damn. I think everyone wants me to stink. Hello? Oh, Francis . . . No, I'm fine. Tomorrow? That'll be okay . . . lunch . . . You what? You didn't have to do that . . . no that would be fine. No, not at twelve. Can we do it one-ish or so? Fine, okay . . . tell her don't be a stranger. I'm glad the two of you are still together. She'll be joining us . . . great tomorrow then."

As she walked into the bathroom, Chai followed. Egypt asked sarcastically, "Yes, may I help you?"

"Yes, are you going out to lunch with Baron's brother, cousin, or whatever?"

"I really don't think it's any of your concern. And if this is going to be like last night, then I suggest you'd better go, okay," she said annoyed.

"No, I was just asking. Why? Can't I ask?"

"No, you can't ask, and I think you had better go before we or, should I say, I say something out of character."

Painfully, Chai replied, "What is it with you, I haven't done anything to you other than be here and keep loving you? What else do you want, blood?" She looked him firmly in the eye and replied in a deep voice, "I want Baron."

Chai's heart crumbled within. He didn't know what to do. He thought he was walking, but he was so stunned that he for a moment he couldn't move. Egypt realized what she had said and reached toward him. He stepped back, and this put a chill through her. She didn't mean that to sound the way that it did. Chai still couldn't move anything except his eyes. He looked her up and down.

This made her feel very uncomfortable. "Please don't look at me like that. I didn't mean it the way it came out." She ran toward him and held on to him and kissed him passionately. He never responded to her kiss. She stepped back and held him by his shoulders telling him how much he means to her and that she's been under a lot of stress lately.

It seemed as though he couldn't hear her. He reached in his pocket and dropped her keys to the floor and walked toward the floor. She couldn't believe this was happening to her. The vibrations were so real and frightening. She held on to his arm; he took her hand off him firmly and left.

She was emotionally distraught. She ran for her coat to go after him. She ran down the flight of stairs and out into the cold and blustery March evening. The trees were snowcapped, and the moon lit up the street very brightly. She ran down the street the best she could calling out his name.

"Chai! Chai! Where the hell are you?" She couldn't see a sign of him anywhere. It was as though he disappeared. "Chai, don't go like this. Please, Chai," she yelled in a tearful voice. She pulled the collar of her coat tighter around her neck and throat. She hadn't noticed the brisk breeze she was so upset. She called out again, but getting no answer and not seeing him, she turned back to her loft.

Tears uncontrollably flowed from her eyes. She was silent. Before she reached her corner, she received a warm embrace. She quickly turned around kissing and explaining her actions all in one breath. Chai walked her back to the loft and sat her on the sofa.

"Egypt, don't say anything okay, let me talk. First of all I too have feelings and experience hurt. Just like anyone else, there is just so much hurt and disappointment they can stand. Don't test my love for you because there is no need. It is very real. You, on the other hand, love me I believe, but it is different than mine for you." She opened her mouth to speak, but he stopped her.

"No, don't speak, let me finish. I'm not trying to make you forget Baron, and I'm not trying to fill his shoes. But, Egypt, treat me with the respect that I am due."

She leaned toward him, and they kissed and she began to caress him. Chai too felt the urge rising in him, and he wanted so much to become one with her again. She placed his hands around hers and she came closer to him. They felt a chemical reaction building up; she hadn't felt that way in a long time, and it felt foreign to her. As he kissed her neck, she felt a warm sensation from her head to her feet. When she looked up, it didn't feel right anymore. Before she could say something Chai had stopped on his own.

"You feel it too. I can't, not right now, and especially not like this. I do want to make love to you, but at this time it would be wrong," she said. "I'm still carrying the love I feel for Baron in my heart. Until I can separate the two—"

Chai kissed her gently. "Egypt, go take your shower, and I'll get something to eat."

When she got out of the shower, he had some Italian food for them. After they had eaten, Chai massaged her on the sofa as they watched cable. Egypt made him stop for a moment and kissed him.

"Chai, I have said it before that you're in a war zone, but I had meant with Nunzio, but lately it seems you have been in one with me. I have truly been acting the ass."

Chai held her and continued to watch the television. "Okay, but when I give birth is when we see who can be able to handle what."

She laid her head on his shoulder and fell asleep.

Chapter 15

Four months have passed, and Egypt was as ripe as an apple; the waiting was killing her. Now that she knew it was a multiple birth, she was just waiting to know how many. Due to the fact of the way the babies were lying, the doctor was unable to detect exactly how many she carried. She didn't want amniocentesis done to find out, so she waited.

Through the entire last month, Chai was very supportive. Nunzio had his comments and discussions with her trying to convince her to live with them, but that plea fell on deaf ears. Egypt didn't mind Margherita, Angela, or anyone else staying in contact with her; it was just that with Nunzio something didn't set right.

Egypt walked down to the pizzeria to pick up her mail and thinking that some things never change. There was a letter for Baron mixed in. It didn't make any sense to her, being a delinquent letter from his life insurance company. This seemed strange to her, but she didn't pay any mind to it. She went back upstairs, and she put the mail on the table, quickly dressed to go to the obstetrician, and then later over to her mother's place.

She began feeling stressed and wondering whether she would be pregnant forever. She sat back and thought what it is going to be like to be a mother. The thought frightened her, especially doing it without Baron. Now more than ever she thought of him; his absence made this ordeal awkward.

She turned to her window quickly. A funny feeling ran through her; she felt like someone was watching her. When she checked further, she saw no one. But the sensation was there, and it felt real. She walked downstairs to the door, and she thought she caught a glimpse of some man moving away from her window.

Egypt went back to get a thin jacket, and she left. As usual she was late for the appointment. She made sure she took all her personal information with her. By accident, she grabbed the insurance letter and placed everything into her bag.

After her appointment she went to visit her mother. It was warm out, and all kinds of people were outside sitting on lawn chairs playing their music and watching the children frolic and play in the open water hydrants. She walked along eating piragua which she bought from a vendor in the street. A little girl kept staring at her, so Egypt asked if she wanted an ice cone also. In Spanish the girl answered "Si gracias" Egypt gave her the money and she ran off. A little while later she returned with cherry piragua on her face smiling and eating happily; Egypt smiled back and laughed.

When she reached her mother's building, her brother and Matilda were outside. Egypt saw that Matilda didn't look the same.

"Hi, Matilda, *nina que pasa?*" To her brother she said, "Jose, Jose."

"Okay, you see," Jose answered.

"Why don't you just come out and ask and stop beating around the bush." "Are you two pregnant?"

"Well, I don't know about him," replied Matilda. "I know I am."

Egypt said, "Are we celebrating or what? How come Momita didn't tell me? I'm surprised she didn't have a fit."

Matilda's head dropped in anguish, and she said nothing. Jose put his arm around her and pulled her head to his chest. Tears collected in her eyes.

"Did I say something wrong?" asked Egypt.

"If you could have heard your mother. She cold flipped on Matilda as though she set out to get pregnant on purpose. Egypt, it wasn't like she wanted to keep it. I told her not to get rid of it. No, not my kid. I don't give a fuck, it's my blood, and I'll take care of it. I'm not stopping school, so get that look off your face because I'm almost finished anyway," stated Jose. "Momita didn't blame it on me, and what pissed me off is that Momita kept calling Matilda names until I couldn't take anymore and just walked out."

"Walked out?" replied Egypt. "Where are you staying now?"

"With Matilda's family for now."

"When did all this happen?" asked Egypt.

"Within the last few days. I'm not speaking to Momita. To hell with her. I've helped everyone try to understand her and deal with her shit. Fuck it now, she pushed me too far, and now I'm not trying to have her shit," he said angrily.

To Matilda Egypt said, "I'm sorry all this had to happen to you, and I'm not trying to make excuses for my mother. But she's just worried about Jose's future. She doesn't want him to fall into any trap," said Egypt as she opened her jacket and showed them her swollen belly. She continued, "She's always talking about how Jose is her last hope."

Jose exclaimed, "Momita said that it was Matilda's responsibility, and I tried to explain that it was my fault in a way too. She jumped right in with how Matilda has a baby she doesn't even take care of and a lot of other shit."

Matilda said, "I understand all that, but I think there's a lot more to it than that. It's probably because I haven't got college. It's fine if we were temporary, but the thought of us truly together, I'm not good enough. More than that, she seemed to keep stressing about my little girl. Carmen found out because my mother told her. She thought since you knew that naturally your mother knew also.

I don't have my daughter," continued Matilda, "but my oldest sister takes care of her up in Yonkers until I get myself together. I don't talk much about Jolinda. My baby is going on three." Matilda wiped her eyes. "She was born when I was nineteen, and her father died when she was about five months old. Matter of fact he got shot right over there at the bodega."

"Does she know all of that too?" asked Egypt.

"Why tell her when it's none of her business? It's Matilda's life like I told her. If it doesn't affect me, then it shouldn't bother her. If anything, the only person who should say anything to me, it's you, Egypt. You've taken care of me financially as far as my education is concerned. And for that alone, I promised I wouldn't fuck up."

"I know you won't," answered Egypt. "You're not going to live with Matilda's family, and if you want to be together, start planning what you want to do and I'll help you."

"Jose has asked me to marry him," said Matilda. "I don't want to get married just because I'm pregnant. I know better that it wouldn't work like that unless he loves me. I told him we shouldn't have the baby that we should wait."

"Shut up, Matilda. I know how I've always felt about you, stupid. It's just hard to express that's all. Look at the dysfunctional family I come from. Just look at Egypt, the prime example," he said and started to laugh. Egypt grinned and punched him in the arm.

"But seriously, Jose, I'll help the two of you." Egypt took a deep breath. "But as far as Momita is concerned, why don't you let time heal all that? Matilda, how far along are you?"

"I'm going on six months this week," she answered.

"You carry cute at six months. I looked like a beached whale. Jose, Angela called me to go to the beach. I started laughing because I asked her if she wanted to see me get harpooned or something. Seriously, coming up soon is my due date, and I'm surprised I lasted this long carrying a litter. But I wanted everyone over to the house for my early birthday bash."

"Egypt, your birthday is in August, not July," said Jose.

"Jose, be smart. I'll be having my little tribe long before my birthday comes around, and what can I do then? I'm gonna celebrate early, and besides I'll be on complete bed rest soon anyway."

Matilda asked, "I thought you didn't live in the house anymore and that you sold it."

"Oh, hell no, I plan on raising my children there. That's why if you two get your asses in gear, you can live in my loft and just pay me one-third the rent and handle everything else. I'll help, and as soon as you fuck up, you're both out. Jose, between us, the record deal was closed, and you'll get a nice sum of money, but—."

Jose made a face. "No, calm down, the keyword is here is *but*. You must live off the money and finish school because in your contract was a small loophole, and it lies on your education. Egyptian Labels has the right to drop you if you don't complete your degree. I'm sorry, but it's a part of love."

"That's fair," he answered. "So ah, Matilda, is there going to be a wedding or what? I'm not living with someone whom I'm not married to. You know I'm not that kind of guy," he said and smiled. "And for an engagement ring," he added, "let me see . . . I don't want a diamond. I'd rather an onyx stone set in 14 karat gold, no plated bullshit either. Considering things, we shouldn't have sexual intercourse until our honeymoon," he said and laughed hysterically.

Matilda grabbed him around his neck and shook him a bit as they all giggled. Jose held her face close to his and told her, "Matilda, I love you, and the fact that you're carrying my child makes things even better because it only enhances the love I already harbor for you."

He continued, "Things between us are rough right now, and many times I have treated you unfairly and without love, but you were always my rock and you stayed faithfully by my side. I know I gave you many tearful nights trying to figure out what you meant to me. Matilda then and now I knew, but I was just afraid of it. The thought of loving and losing it. I felt that it was better just to avoid the whole thing. But that was my stupidity. Remember this always, Matilda, I want you, my child, and Jolinda as a family. Don't say a word, just listen to me, and you also, Egypt.

Jolinda and my baby are blood and should be raised together. And on a serious note that's that," ended Jose.

Matilda's eyes were full, and he kept wiping the tears away. She asked if she could speak. In a tear-filled whimper, she said, "Jose, I love you. Can I have a ring too?" They laughed and embraced kissing.

Egypt's birthday party was the talk of the month. Everyone who was anyone would be there, stemming from the industry to very prominent political figures. Francis and Angela helped arrange things. Francis made the arrangements for uniformed and plain clothes armed security throughout the grounds. Anyone who didn't belong definitely would not be making it in.

The music blared. She had invited Chai but wasn't sure if he would attend since Baron's family would be there. Later, Egypt was having so much fun until she noticed Nunzio and Chai talking. There seemed to be some sort of problem, so she walked over to them catching an end phrase about his son's wife.

"Yes, Nunzio, I'm Baron's widow, not his wife any longer. I refuse to let you treat a friend of mine with your uncanny disrespect at my function." Nunzio answered, "I know more than you realize. Your Asian boyfriend isn't welcomed here. Keep that shit to your bedroom."

Egypt reached out for him, but one of his goons grabbed her arm. "You're not fucking with my evening, Nunzio. As far as I'm concerned, you can get the hell away from me and my babies. Nunzio darling, I think you don't realize that since Baron has passed, all I have to do is remarry and allow my husband to adopt my children and you couldn't stop me. So fuck with me if you want to because my ass is trumped down, and don't force me to pull a Boston on your ass. The name of the game is spades, baby. Spades." She held Chai by the arm and mingled in with the crowd.

She didn't realize it, but she had pushed Nunzio once too many times. This time he was determined to get his son's children. Francis saw Egypt's and Nunzio's exchange of words and walked over to him. "Remember, Nunzio, to be careful because of Baron's sake. Those are his children. Everything will be all right. Just a little more time, and everything will be back to normal."

Nunzio replied, "You're right. Let her keep going the way she is and she will be digging her own hole. Yeah, time is on my side. How many more weeks will it be for the transaction to take place?" he asked.

"B. G. said eight weeks or so it will be over and out in the open," replied Francis.

Angela asked Egypt about Chai. "I know, it's not like I expected you to stay alone forever or anything."

"Angela, me and Chai are just very good friends, that's all." Egypt's pager went off, and it was Fatima. This surprised her. She called Fatima back.

"Egypt, there's something going on with those insurance papers you told me to check out for you," said Fatima hysterically.

"Okay, Fatima, calm down. Meet me by the front gate," said Egypt and hung up. When Fatima arrived, they went off in her car. "To tell you the truth, Egypt, I felt that doing this favor was nothing until I kept running into brick walls. Until I found out that the insurance papers used to prove his death were forged. Every time I investigate further, people would clam up. So I asked a friend to overstep the legal aspect to try to find out more."

Egypt said, "So what are you saying? Make it quick, I can't stay away long."

"Egypt, my friend is in the hospital with broken bones and a concussion from asking too many questions relating to Baron's death. What in the hell is going on here, Egypt?"

"How in the fuck would I know? You're making me nervous here. What exactly are you saying?"

"Girl, you're on your own with this one. This is out of office business, and I'm not with it. I don't want to end up lying next to my friend or for that matter next to Baron."

"Just calm down. So what about the insurance papers, and why did they come back delinquent? When I called about them, they said everything was fine and thank you for the check, like they received payment on it or something. When I asked for more information, they asked my name. Fatima, when I gave them my name, they said they couldn't discuss anything because it wasn't my policy. What the hell is going on?" asked Egypt.

"I haven't the foggiest idea. But what I do know is we must be getting close because someone has noticed us."

"But who the hell noticed us, and what does this have to do with Baron? Fatima, I don't know, but deep down, it seems to always come back to the Gianelli family."

"Well, that's where I get out. You're one of them now."

"Gimme a break," replied Egypt. "This whole business seems to me to be highly organized, and I have to know. Why is the insurance all messed up all of a sudden—"

"Did you ever try to get the death certificate or obtain his medical records?" asked Fatima.

"Yes. That's what gave me the thought to start checking things out. The death certificate states that the cause of death was excessive loss of blood due to multiple gunshot wounds to the chest. The medical records are sealed, and I was told I have to get a court order to get them opened. I don't want people to think I'm bugging and can't accept Baron's death.

It's just too many things don't fit. I have to know the truth. There are too many loose ends. Fatima, I don't blame you for bailing out on me, but just give me a little more time."

"How much longer, Egypt? Until I'm pushing up daisies or sucking up oxygen through a tube? These guys mean business and not the kind I'm used to dealing with."

"All right, take me back to the party. Look, stay a while and relax. I'll figure out something. I'll talk to my brother. No, I don't want to bring him in on it too."

"Oh yeah, but it's okay for me to be in on it, right?"

Egypt laughed and told her to get a grip, especially at the party. As they walked up the walkway, she mentioned what had happened between her and Nunzio in reference to Chai.

Fatima mingled in the crowd and saw a lot of people that she knew. Margherita made her way over to Egypt asking how she felt. Egypt replied that they all were doing as well as expected. "

Well, if you all are fine, then why do you look so sad?"

"Didn't you ever feel there was a time when things seemed to be right but really weren't?"

"What are you driving at, Egypt?"

She didn't want to sound crazy to Margherita, so she smiled and said nothing. Franco and Angela brought Egypt a plate of food, and they sat down laughing and talking. "The food is great, especially the Spanish cuisine. Who catered it?" asked Franco.

"La cosina de mi mama," replied Egypt.

"Where's that?"

"My mother, Franco. Don't act like you don't understand Spanish. Your language is close enough to it, okay?" While laughing, he said, "Yeah, but it's good, and the decorations make it seem as if you're in Puerto Rico. It's so colorful."

"Hey, hey, what are you trying to say about all these colors?" asked Egypt playfully. "You both are nuts. But, Egypt, this is wonderful. You sure know the meaning of the word *celebrate*. Those ice cones are delicious. They remind me of the men I see all the time on the street except they are all wearing costumes."

"We call them piragua," she explained.

"What is this wrapped in paper? It's delicious too."

"Oh, that? We mostly eat that at New Year's. My aunt and cousins made it. It's called pasteles. All right considering you don't know, I'll explain." Egypt led them to a long table holding an array of treats.

"There is arroz con gandules y polo and pernil which is rice, beans, and chicken. There's roast pork, flan, and all sorts of other delights. Did you get to the international table which is serving West Indian dishes? There's roti, curry goat, peas and rice, pudding, and souse. Greek at this end with souvloki and shiskabobs and other things. Farther down, we have the basic Italian dishes which you know all about that. Indian, French, and German cuisines."

"You have really gone all out now, haven't you?" said Angela. "The decorative colors, blue, white, orange, and yellow and pinatas are lovely. My mother is having a great time. There's so many different things to eat and types of people to converse with. Even Francis is having a good time."

"I think Donna has a lot to do with that," replied Egypt. Noel stood up and began to make a toast to his sister and her children's health. After he finished, two men rolled out an enormous five-tier birthday cake. Egypt was expecting the cake she had ordered, but Noel surprised her with his cake instead. It was fantastic. She and her brother posed for pictures next to it. She was glistening and overwhelmed by the turnout. She then raised her glass and made a toast to all of those who helped her and stood by her side through thick and thin.

"Most of all I would like to say something, not to drop the mood, but it just wouldn't be the same if I didn't say:

Baron, I love you, and no matter what, I know you're near, at least in spirit though I feel different. I feel your presence always, and it gives me the strength for each day I face without you.

And to everyone, happiness and let's party on," said Egypt. The music went full blast, and people started dancing and Egypt cut the cake. Fatima walked over and tapped her on the shoulder. Egypt passed the knife to Carmen.

"Come over here, Egypt. I can't believe this, but I recognize two men here while I was out playing Columbo and my partner was dodging blows."

"Well, it doesn't seem to me he was dodging shit," said Egypt. "It was more like he ran head into them."

"Head into them, around them, underneath, or above them. The fact is we were accosted over your curiosity, thank you very much. The point still remains: Why are those two here at your function?" said Fatima in an up-tempo voice.

She continued, "Didn't I say some shit like I didn't want to end up lying next to Gordon? I want to stay in one damn piece from head to toe. Not head and toe as one unit. Got me?"

"Okay, Fatima. I can't help it if Flash didn't have enough zap up his ass. By the way, did he connect any punches? Did he get his point across like, don't hit me? Or did he just lay there and allow them to have their way with him? Damn, Fatima, of all people, Gordon? You know all they had to do was knock his fuck'n' coke bottles off him and he was out for the count. Shit, damn, Gordon. I would have done better in the state I'm in," Egypt said frustrated.

Fatima chuckled. "That wasn't nice."

"It may not have been nice, but your ass knows it's true. Gordon. I still can't get over it. Unbelievable. Just tell me why? That's all. Why?"

"To tell you the truth he was cheap labor," replied Fatima.

"Gosh, where did I go wrong?" said Egypt half to herself. "What did I do to deserve this? Huh, tell me what? When I paint a picture, it always starts out like Michelangelo did it, and by the time it's finished, it looks like Picasso fuck'n' jumped on my canvas."

"Huh?" said Fatima.

"Huh my ass. A simple question I had about some insurance papers, and it seems like we're uncovering the fuck'n' KGB."

"Come to think about it, it does. I think we had better back off, seriously, Egypt. I don't understand what we ran into, but to tell you the truth, we ought to back the fuck off."

"I know what you mean, but I have to know what's going on."

Fatima pointed to a man by the serving table. "Look over there. That man's looking over here."

Wait, that's him, come to think about it. That man came with Nunzio," said Egypt.

"Ladies, ladies, can I interrupt this gathering? Ms. Egypt please introduce me to your lovely friend."

"This is one of our best . . ." Fatima cut Egypt off.

Fatima continued, "Overseas clients, and I'm very much married and better known as unavailable, thank you." She held on to Egypt's arm, pulling her away. "That was one of them. They must have recognized me. Oh shit, what am I going to do?"

"First of all release my arm. You're stopping the circulation, thank you. Just stay close to me but not that close. Shit," said Egypt.

"Egypt, maybe I'm making something out of nothing. It could be a co-inky-dink. I'll relax."

"Good, because my water broke."

"Don't even play that shit with me, Egypt," said Fatima nervously.

When they returned to the patio, Fatima's face was pale. She was a wreck. People were staring at her as she yelled for someone to call an ambulance. Francis and Chai both ran toward Fatima, and she kept trying to convince them it wasn't for her.

Egypt was giggling, and she tapped them and said she was ready. Chai asked, "How long ago did your water break?"

"About ten minutes ago or so," replied Egypt.

Nunzio walked over, and people moved out of his way as he approached. "What's going on, is she in labor?"

"Not yet. It's just her water, but she's early. Nothing to be alarmed about. It happens a lot with multiple births. Especially with women who don't get their proper bed rest," said Chai glancing at Egypt.

"Egypt, are you feeling fine?" asked Margherita.

"I just have a small pain in my lower back. Where's Carmen?" she asked Donna. Donna went to retrieve her mother.

At the hospital, Egypt's whole appearance changed; the pain was very intense. It had gotten to a point where she screamed like a banshee bitch. Carmen did all she could do to help her through it. Egypt's doctor told her there would be three or four interns who would enjoy the experience of a multiple birth.

"Are you ready to know how many babies you will give birth to?" said the doctor. She replied, "Just surprise me please."

They took her from the labor room and into a large delivery room. The interns came in. One of them was somewhat familiar, but she couldn't concentrate because of the severity of the contractions. She started howling, and one of the male interns took hold of her hand but didn't say anything and just watched the doctor. As Dr. Mati explained it step by step, he told her to sit up as she had each contraction. As each contraction repeated itself with more severity, the doctor told her to bear down and push.

She had done well with the first child; it was a boy with powerful lungs. He came out with no problem. Within eight minutes she pushed out another boy. He was curled up and quiet and barely cried. The nurse cleaned out his mouth and nose, and he joined the choir. But the last one was giving Egypt problems, and she became tired of pushing. Dr. Mati continued to encourage her to try pushing harder. Egypt knew she was tired, but she had to bear down.

Her attention was caught on this one intern because his eyes were so familiar. A female intern put some ice chips in her mouth. Before she knew it, the doctor told her the baby girl was going into fetal distress and he might have to do a C-section. She bore down harder with more strength than she knew she had in her.

"It's a girl," replied an intern.

"Damn, it would be a bitch like her mother," shouted Egypt as she cried in joy. She turned to the male intern. He was fixing his mask since it had fallen below his nose.

She couldn't believe what she had just seen. He looked so much like Baron that she began to call his name. The doctor overheard her cries and tried calming her down. Dr. Mati saw she was getting a bit hysterical and had her sedated.

When Egypt came around, everyone was at the hospital with balloons and flowers. Carmen wanted to know what was happening.

"Mommy, can I ask you something? When Poppie died, did you ever feel like he was still around, or did you see him?"

"I felt like his spirit was near me, but never did I see him. But everyone has their own ways of handling it," replied Carmen.

"Hey, chica couldn't just have twins. Had to have three. They're beautiful. The little girl, where is she?" asked Noel.

"Angel Egypt Gianelli is in the neonatal ward. She was only three-and-a-half pounds. The boys are five pounds each. Dr. Mati was very surprised at their weight. The two look so much alike, don't they?"

"Baby, I have to make it home. I'm gonna let Noel go down so Jose could come up. I'll be back tomorrow," said Carmen and kissed Egypt good-bye.

"Well, chica, it's you and me now. So talk. Momita told me you flipped after you delivered the triplets. So tell me what's up?"

"Noel, who would have ever thought you and I could talk this calmly? I don't understand, but I feel lost and abandoned. Confused and everything. I should be thrilled about the threesome and I am, but I can't help but keep drifting back to Baron. You won't believe this, but that intern looked so much like him. If I could have snatched that mask off, I would have sworn it was him," said Egypt with hope in her voice.

"Chica, gimme your hand. Listen, let's go back to your wedding day? Remember when you saw an image of Poppy there? It wasn't Poppy but only to you."

"Noel, it wasn't the same. I knew that it wasn't Poppy. I'm not totally *loca*. You're the crazy ass in the family. Be serious. Is there something really wrong with me?" asked Egypt while she sipped on her juice. "You're not crazy," Noel said. "You're just a mommy. Don't sweat it. Things will fall into place. You're under so much stress, just relax. Because all hell has begun for you. Three at one time, better you than me. If you need to talk, you have my home phone number and pager. You have all seven digits, so if you need to use them, then do," said Noel. He placed a kiss on her cheek and left.

Egypt couldn't believe she was a mother. Little Baron Jr., Michael Christian, and Angel were the most beautiful children she had ever laid eyes on. Egypt reached over and was looking at the things Angela, Franco, and Francis brought to the hospital earlier. She situated herself in the bed and picked up the stuffed animals her mother came with and danced around them for a moment. She wasn't tired yet, just restless. As she put the things in some sort of order, she came across a box that she hadn't noticed earlier.

She picked it up with curiosity. When she looked at it, she just started to cry. The box contained one blue rose and three white roses lying across it.

She took a deep breath and said, "I know that this can't be a coincidence. Baron, I know you're out there somewhere, and I'm gonna find you come hell or high water. I will."

About the Author

Raven Rose was born in Brooklyn, New York and was raised upstate in Rockland County. As a teenager her family moved to Tampa Florida where she attended Eastbay High. Raven performed with International Thespian Troupe 3020, achieving numerous awards for pantomime and monologues. She also wrote poetry which appeared in the schools' yearbook. Shortly after graduation, she moved back to New York to live on her own. Raven Rose enjoyed spending free time reading the works of Shakespeare, Ibsen and Poe which enticed her to begin writing. So far, Egyptian Labels is her first of several novels she has completed.

Raven is presently living with her family in Queens, New York. When she's not writing , she enjoys spending time with her Dobermans, Callisto and Anubis along with their lovable Pit-Akita Chewie. She is very much involved in her local little league, holding the seat of Vice President for several years. When she's not doing all of that, she can be found near a roaring fire barbecuing alongside her pool.

CPSIA information can be obtained at www.ICGtesting.com
Printed in the USA
BVOW071538060313

314864BV00001B/3/P